A
Straight Forward
Theft

By

George Donald

Wednesday 5 February

The weather was dismal, wet and windy and lousy even by London standards when Patrick McLaughlin got off the tube at Goldhawk Road. A little disorientated, he wasn't familiar with the Shepherds Bush area, but Bahir, his Turkish business contact, had been quite specific about the directions and so McLaughlin turned towards the main Goldhawk Road, hands thrust deeply into his coat pockets and shivering in the chilly blast of the afternoon.

The café, according to Bahir's instructions, was located no more than a couple of hundred yards west of the tube station. McLaughlin hesitated, still wondering if this was a good idea, but then remembered the VAT bill that had arrived a few days previously.

He owed almost forty fucking grand.

He had been shocked when he read the letter and recalled thinking, where the hell am I going to get forty grand?

The traffic passed at a rush as he slowly walked towards the café, his stomach a tight knot and his throat dry.

As he trudged along, in his mind he mulled over again and again what he was about to do, trying to convince himself there was no other alternative. For long and weary he had considered alternatives, but it all arrived at this. It was this or risk losing everything.

It didn't surprise him that Bahir had suggested the meeting.

For almost a year Bahir had been his main supplier of computers and equipment and he had tried to convince himself that it was all legit, but deep down he had known otherwise. No one in the trade and certainly not a legitimate dealer could supply him with all that stock at those prices.

The stuff had to be knocked off.

Yet still it hadn't been enough. His two computer shops in the malls at Silverburn in Pollok and the Braehead Shopping Centre continued to run at a loss; partly due to the influx of foreign competitors and because he couldn't compete with the knockdown prices the chain stores offered their IT goods to the customer.

He stopped briefly at a bus shelter, ignoring the elderly black woman who cast a furtive glance at him; she seeing a man of medium height, his dark, thinning hair wet and plastered against his head and the beige coloured raincoat tightly buttoned to the throat over a navy blue two piece suit. His shoes were highly polished and for some reason she couldn't explain, the old woman guessed he didn't present a threat and sighing, almost immediately turned away to watch for the number twenty-six bus that was *again* overdue. Behind her, McLaughlin fished the scrap of paper from his pocket and again read the name he was to ask for; Fevzi. Was that a forename or a surname, he wondered?

He took a deep breath and left the shelter to continue the last fifty yards to the café and there it was across the busy road, sandwiched between a launderette and a derelict shop. The sign above the window declared it to be 'Edip's Fine Turkish Coffee House.'

He took a deep breath and pushed open the door, activating the bell that was suspended above the door on a spring. The smell of coffee and the heat from within hit him a hammer blow and almost immediately he felt a rivulet of sweat drip down his back, but whether from the heat or his nervousness, he was unsure.

Two dark haired, swarthy men, one aged about thirty and the other about fifty, were playing cards at a table at the rear of the customer side of the cafe. They stared suspiciously at him while a third man, the proprietor he presumed, busied himself behind the high glass counter and ignored the new customer.

McLaughlin swallowed and made his way to the counter. He judged the man behind the counter to be about sixty years of age, short in stature with his body running to fat and was dressed in a soiled white tee shirt and an apron that similarly had a number of undetermined stains, with a three inch scar running down the left side of his jaw. The man stared curiously at him for a few seconds and then, in heavily accented English, he asked, "Can I help you, mister? You want coffee?"

"I'm looking for...I mean, I was told to ask for Fevzi."

The man smiled and staring curiously at McLaughlin, took a few seconds to reply, but then answered, "There no Fevzi here, mister. You got wrong name maybe, eh?"

It must be some kind of test, thought McLaughlin who scrambled in his pocket and took out the paper with the name written by Bahir.

"Here, maybe I didn't pronounce it properly. This is the name. Look," he replied.

The owner ignored the paper held out by McLaughlin, seemingly enjoying his discomfort and again replied, "Me no read English, mister," he shrugged and then added with a shake of his head, "There no *Fevzi* here, mister."

McLaughlin felt stupid, standing there like some kind of numpty holding the paper like an errant schoolboy and eyes blinking rapidly, snapped, "Fine. I must have made a mistake then, eh?"

It was as he turned towards the door the younger of the men sat at the table waved a hand and called out, "Hey mister, why you looking for this man Fevzi?"

He stopped and turned and was about to take a step towards the table when some inner sense of self-preservation caused him to think maybe it was wiser to stay by the door, just in case he had to get out quick. He felt a stream of sweat rushing down his spine. He swallowed again and in a hesitant voice, said, "I have a problem. I was told that Fevzi might be able to help me with the problem."

"What kind of problem you got mister?"

His eyes darted from the two men at the table to the man behind the counter, seeing he had apparently lost interest in the conversation and with his back to McLaughlin, was rearranging glasses on a shelf, but McLaughlin was in no doubt the portly little man was listening intently.

A little bolder now, he replied, "I have a bill to be paid, a large bill. My business, my computer business," he explained, "isn't covering all my bills and I need to…diverse."

"Diverse? What is this diverse? What you mean?"

With growing confidence he said, "I need a new supplier of a different type of product. What I need…"

The man slapped a hand loudly onto the table top and interrupted, "What you need is to…" then placed a finger against his closed lips. That done he then turned the hand towards McLaughlin and with the same forefinger indicated McLaughlin wait. From an inner pocket, the man produced a small notebook and pencil and head bent, wrote briefly in the notebook. Standing, the man walked towards McLaughlin and held the notebook out towards him

McLaughlin took the notebook from the nicotine stained fingers and read '*rite adress*,' but with both words misspelled,

Forcing himself to be calm, he wrote the name of the popular chain hotel in Bank Street, Southwark, then added '*room 229*' and returned the notebook to the man.

The man read the message and smiled, then wrote '*8pm tonite*' and held the page for McLaughlin to read. He nodded and then smiled again and said, "Like he told you mister, no Fevzi here. You go now, yes?"

Almost with relief, McLaughlin nodded and hurried from the café into the welcoming cold outside.

Across the road, the SO15 surveillance officer sitting within the cold of the grey coloured transit van blew hot breath onto his hands to try and keep them warm, but still managed to snap half dozen shots of McLaughlin and record the time, just as he exited the cafe.

Showered, he lay atop the double bed clad in dry, clean trousers and open neck shirt, worried that he had made a mistake, that in some way he had been conned.

On the tube back to Southwark, he had run through his mind a dozen or more times the few minutes he'd spent in the café, wondering what the hell the written messages was all about and finally, to his horror, reasoned that the man must have suspected they were being bugged. He'd almost fainted with shock when he arrived at that conclusion, thinking that the cops had been listening.

But he hadn't done anything to get himself arrested.

At least, his brow furrowed; not yet.

He turned to the digital alarm clock; seven-fifty four. He exhaled and clenching his fists at his stupidity, beat at his brow.

The trip to London had been to simply negotiate with Bahir a delivery of Tablet computers, hoping that Bahir might consider payment on the drip; an HP agreement that McLaughlin promised he would honour when the Tablets sold.

He hadn't been prepared for the flat refusal and even less prepared for Bahir's suggestion that if he wished to consider it, Bahir would provide him the name of an associate he could deal with who could supply him with 'a different product.'

Heroin.

The very name sent a shudder through him and he had been aghast. Well, at first that is. Then Bahir had explained that if he was *for* the deal, the profit to be made was enormous. Profit, Bahir had stressed, that could lift him clear of the financial fucking mess he was in.

"You could save your business," Bahir had tempted him, "and also stave off bankruptcy." He had listened with growing dread, yet it had all seemed so simple at the time, so straightforward. With the profit that he made it would enable him to keep the house as well as the two kids at their private school.

Then there was the club fees, the monthly payment for the cars and all sort of sundry bills.

His thoughts turned to his family and he managed a grin. For all her faults, his wife Gloria was one hell of a woman and still turned men's heads when she walked by. His two sons, precocious nine year old twins were a delight and…

The sudden rap on the door startled him and he almost leapt from the bed.

He took a deep breathy and slicking back his still damp hair, opened the door.

The younger man from the cafe, dressed in a black leather bomber jacket, stood there grinning at him.

Behind the young man stood the café owner who stared blank-faced and in perfect, London accented English, said, "Good evening, Mister McLaughlin. My name is Fevzi. Earlier this afternoon, I spoke with a mutual friend. I understand that you might wish to discuss a business deal?"

It was just over one hour later when the man called Fevzi and the younger man descended the stairs to the hotel reception.

The slightly built Australian student was engrossed in a men's magazine when Fevzi stepped behind the desk and gently ushered the student to one side, away from the computer.

"Hey, you can't…" was as much as the student managed to utter before Fevzi's associate took the student by the elbow and firmly pushed him into a corner, then stood quietly but menacingly, staring at him.

Too terrified to resist, the student could only watch as the older of the two intimidating men concentrated on the computer screen and slowly typed in room 229, whereupon the details of the current occupant flashed onto the screen. The student watched as wordlessly, the man reached out and took a small notebook from the younger man and then glancing at the screen, wrote down an address before returning the notebook to the younger man, who with a smile released his firm grip on the student.

Both men stepped to the public side of the desk and made to leave, but the older man stopped and turning, withdrew a twenty pound note from an inside pocket that he slapped down onto the reception desk.

Staring at the student, he quietly said. "This didn't happen, did it sonny?"

The student, mouth open but stunned into silence, could only shake his head and watching the two men exit the main doors, glanced nervously about him before slipping the note into his trouser pocket.

CHAPTER ONE – Monday 10 February

Michael Thomson was known by several names in the housing estate where he grew up and continued to live.

He had first come to the attention of the local residents of Drumchapel as Big Mick Thomson during his disruptive school days that abruptly concluded when over six feet tall and aged just fourteen years, he head butted and broke the headmaster's nose. A few years later, Big Mick became 'Tomahawk' Thomson when, aged eighteen years and a member of the Young Drummie Fleet gang, he used a small axe during a territorial squabble with a neighbouring gang to sever three fingers from an opponents raised hand, a mutilation that he was widely credited for, but never charged with for the simple reason he threatened to murder his victim's parents.

His mutilated victim believed the threat to be more than viable and so, the assault was never officially reported to the police.

As time passed, Thomson's nickname was abbreviated to 'Tommo', a name he courted along with his reputation as the Drum's hardest man

It was while Thomson was in his early twenties that he was recruited by Charles 'Chic' Fagin, the amenable Band Sergeant of the local Orange flute band, the Drum Loyal True Blues and where he developed a passion for physical fitness. His height and growing stature marked him as the obvious choice to carry the large drum and with pride, Thomson exalted in the position and remained with the band for several years until crossing one year for the annual twelfth of July parade in Belfast aboard the ferry, he attacked and seriously injured a fellow bandsman. However, by now his reputation for violence was widespread and a deal with his band mates was brokered by Chic Fagin. The victim would not involve the police if Thomson stood down from the band.

Now, aged forty-nine and standing at six foot two inches, the shaven headed and bearded Thomson's strong and muscular physique was testament to his daily and rigorous gym sessions. A man, the locals whispered, to be feared and avoided and this attitude was particularly relevant to the women of Drumchapel and the surrounding areas, for it was also widely known that Thomson was not just chauvinistic, but treated women as nothing more than objects with which to satisfy his voracious sexual appetite. More than one woman had discovered to their cost that the initial charm of the man was deceiving, that once they were bedded by him his sadistic streak took over. Failing to sexually perform as he wished, many of them learned their reluctance provoked a quick and violent reaction, for Thomson was not beyond slapping or punching his women to persuade them to conform to his perversions.

He was not legitimately employed, having persuaded the locally overworked, elderly and fearful GP to agree that Thomson's 'bad back' made him unemployable and the timid doctor took the easy course; colluding with him and providing him with a document that conned the social services into agreeing Thomson's alleged bad back merited a regular disability payment.

However, this payment aside he lived a relatively affluent life due to his income derived from his more lucrative businesses; his illegal money-lending, to his less fortunate neighbours at exorbitant interest rates, and the occasional contract from local drug dealers, who wished either a debt immediately settled or alternatively, violence meted out to the errant debtor. This income added to his DSS payments and provided Thomson with some luxuries that included a year old white coloured Nissan Juke, the latest model in the I-phone range and a top of the range laptop that he used primarily to scour the network for porn.

Of course, the police knew much about Michael 'Tommo' Thomson and his activities, but while their file on Thomson expanded through the years, without credible witnesses, they were powerless to act.

Widowed some fourteen years previously, Thomson's young bride had been a local girl, Patricia Meikle; a naïve eighteen year old whom he married when she was pregnant with her only child, a daughter whom Patricia named Grace and who now lived locally with her own nine year old son. His bitter disappointment that his wife produced a girl and thereafter was barren infuriated him, a disappointment that he never forgave and during their marriage daily reminded her, both verbally and with the occasional slapping.

Grace Thomson, now aged twenty-eight, both despised and feared her father; hated and blamed him for her mother's early demise and for sending her off as a young teenager to live with his bullying spinster sister-in-law who had since died, but within whose flat Grace and her son continued to reside.

Feared him because of his veiled threat to involve himself in her son's life if Grace did not, twice each week clean his flat and fetch his shopping, for which he paid her a minimal gratuity.

Though so employed, Grace had no other contact with her father, the agreement being that during the two hours she worked in his flat, he would be out somewhere, for Grace did not trust him and baulked at the thought of ever again being alone with him.

Thomson enjoyed the privacy of the area where he lived, a first floor two bedroom former council flat in Goyle Avenue, where the neighbours were so terrified of him that he knew nothing untoward could occur nearby of which he would not be informed.

It was on this day that he received the phone call.

"Hello?"

"Mister Michael Thomson, please," asked the polite male voice.

"Aye, that's me. Who's this?"

"Mister Thomson, call me John. I have a proposition for you that could earn you a great deal of money. Are you interested?"

"I'll no fucking ask again. Who *is* this?"

"Like I said, call me John. I wish to inform you of a money earner, Mister Thomson. I will phone back in two minutes by which time I expect you to have a paper and pen handy to take a note of an e-mail address. Do you understand?"

Thomson's brow creased and he wondered; was somebody at the fucking windup?

"Look, I don't…" but the line went dead and he stared at the handset. He pressed the one four seven one call back number, but the caller had been too cute; the number was withheld.

On the other end of the line, Patrick McLaughlin breathed a sigh of relief, a little surprised when he saw that his hand holding the phone was shaking. However, it had gone a little better than he had hoped. Seated at the desk in his study at home, he glanced at the wall clock and waited till the two minutes were up, then taking a deep breath, dialled Thomson's number again.

The call was answered almost immediately by an irate Thomson, who said, "What's your game pal? Just who the *fuck* are you?" Realising that his nerve might get the better of him, McLaughlin had wisely written down his script and so carefully read from the sheet of paper.

"Please take a note of this e-mail address and password Mister Thomson. Everything will be explained in the e-mail. If you agree, then that is how we will communicate. We will share the e-mail address and the password. I will forward you an e-mail and you will respond to the same e-mail address. Do you understand?"

"You want me to check out an e-mail? Is that what you're telling me?"

"That's correct, Mister Thomson. If you comply with my requests, we will make a lot of money together. Does that interest you?"

"Okay pal, I'll play along for now," replied Thomson, unconsciously nodding his head to the phone. "What's the address?"

McLaughlin exhaled with relief and slowly read both the address and the password to Thomson, then said, "I won't phone again, Mister Thomson. Our future contact will now be by e-mail. Goodbye."

It took Thomson a few minutes to log onto the laptop and, glancing at what he had scrawled on the paper, a further minute to log into the e-mail address. His eyes narrowed and he shook his head as he read then read again the e-mail from the man who called himself John. A slow smile crossed his face. If this was genuine, he thought, this guy John was offering him the opportunity to make some real money.

Patrick McLaughlin nervously drummed his fingers on the top of his desk and glanced at the computer screen. By his reckoning and if Thomson was for it, then there should be a reply to the e-mail within the next five or so minutes. He abruptly stood up and walked towards the full length window that looked out onto the expansive garden area behind the house. The rain beat a steady tattoo against the window as he stared at the neatly trimmed lawn and the trees beyond, his mind a jumble of 'what if's.' Behind him the computer pinged to alert him of an incoming e-mail.

He tapped at the keyboard and anxiously read the message, then smiled with relief.

Thomson was in.

Force Support Officer Harry McInnes sat behind his desk within the Intelligence Department room located on the first floor of Pitt Street police office. The building, once the headquarters of the former Strathclyde Police, now accommodated a satellite office of the Intelligence Department since the main body of the Department had been relocated to the newly constructed Scottish Crime Campus at Gartcosh.

A retired Detective Sergeant, Harry had been fortunate to be one of the few civilians retained after the merger with the other seven police forces when all eight forces had formed the new Police Scotland and even more fortunate that he remained at Pitt Street with the Intel unit responsible for collating all the intelligence for the greater Glasgow area.

Yes, all in all, Harry liked his job; it was some of the people that he was obliged to work with that got right up his nose.

He risked a glance across the room at Peter Murray, the Detective Inspector in charge of the unit and inwardly scowled. A jumped up wee shite was Harry's private opinion of Murray; a uniformed cop with connections who had graduated into Intelligence because his father played golf with a Chief Super and within five years and no real practical experience, shot through the ranks to DI.

His head bowed over the paper in front of him, Harry rubbed wearily at his forehead and accepted that yes, he was bitter. Thirty years a cop with almost twenty in Intelligence and now here he was at the beck and call of a moron.

Well, he sighed, it's still a pay cheque at the end of the month, so why should I bother.

"Harry," he heard his name called and glanced up. One of the young detectives was grinning at him. "I thought you'd nodded off there, old yin. That's the cleaner coming in, so better close your screen and bring the blind down."

He acknowledged the warning with a nod and switched off the monitor and standing, turned to the wall behind him. The notice board adorned with photographs and intelligence information had a black cloth blind above it that Harry pulled down and clipped closed. Three times on alternative days during the working week, the regular office cleaner Sally Nelson was permitted access to the room to Hoover and dust round the cabinets. It took Sally just fifteen minutes to do her round, but nothing of Intelligence value that could be read or seen was allowed to be on display and during the time she worked gave the staff of eight the opportunity for an impromptu tea-break. The detective who had called out unlocked the security door and Harry watched as Sally pulled her machine through the door, her head down and smiling shyly at the men and women in the office. He thought her to be about five foot four, a good looking woman in her late forties, shapely in stature with shoulder length, natural blonde hair, but then Harry frowned, for just below her left eye was a dull bruise.

"Been in the wars have you Sally," grinned Murray, pointing to her eye.

Harry flinched, watching as Sally's face reddened and she almost instinctively touched at her face.

"Ah, I had an argument with a door, Mister Murray," she softly replied.

"Need to watch they doors, Sally. They've a habit of surprising you," Murray turned to grin at his staff, some sheepishly returning his grin and the others forcing a smile at their bosses humour. But not Harry.

His face turned white at the idiot's crassness and his fists clenched. If Sally wasn't already embarrassed by her bruised face, she certainly was now, he thought.

He didn't even realise he was on his feet and walking towards her, but suddenly there he was, stood between her and Murray and smiling tightly at her as he asked, "Hello, Sally. How was your weekend? Get up to anything nice? Mine was quiet," he sat his backside against a desk, his back to Murray and effectively shutting the DI out from the conversation, his hands folded across his expanding waistline, aware that all eyes were on him, but really not giving a shit what his colleagues thought.

The other team members including Murray, sensing that something was not quite right, self-consciously shuffled over towards the desk that served as the tea bar and began to talk quietly among themselves while they cast the occasional furtive glance towards Harry.

Harry watched as Sally nervously smiled and almost with relief, replied, "Same old, same old, Harry. Well, apart from this," she self-consciously pointed at her eye.

He saw more than just the bruising; he saw sadness in her eyes and felt the same, curious tightness in his chest whenever he looked at Sally.

Did he fancy her? Of course he did, but it was simply an infatuation, he persuaded himself; a longing for a woman that he could never have, for Harry was already married to Rosemary, his wife of almost thirty years.

"Better let Sally get on with her job, eh Harry?" said the quiet voice behind him.

He turned to see the matronly Fiona, the only other civilian employed in the unit, smiling at him as she held his mug of coffee towards him.

At fifty-five years of age, just a year younger than Harry, Fiona was his only soul mate in the unit and with over twenty-five years service working for the police as a civilian, the last ten as an analyst in the Intelligence Department, she was forever threatening to quit.

However, to her delight, she had recently learned that she was now eligible for retirement and had just weeks left to serve.

Harry of course was delighted for Fiona, but his heart had sunk in the knowledge that once she was gone, he would be the remaining civilian working with detectives of whom the nearest to his own age was fifteen years his junior.

"Aye, right enough," grinned Sally at him, her face already lightening at his intervention, "some of us has *real* jobs to attend to." With that Sally turned to pull the Hoover towards her, but head and eyes lowered, softly whispered to him, "Thank you, Harry," and walked towards the desks.

CHAPTER TWO - Thursday 3 July

Ian Fagin had had a poor start to life. The scrawny teenager was small for his age and, as a result of Foetal Alcohol Syndrome and his mother's teenage lifestyle, poorly developed both mentally and physically. It didn't help that his face was so acne pockmarked that two bags of polly-filler would struggle to cope. On the plus side, today he was celebrating his nineteenth birthday, but so far the memory of the event was a bit of a blur because of the cheap wine and spliffs he had drank and smoked throughout the morning.

He grinned, thinking if his Papa could see him now he'd have a fit at the state of his grandson.

Quietly, he stood partially hidden behind the crumbling brick wall watching her and his breathing became a little more rapid. He saw her push the buggy with one hand, the other hand grasping the small wrist of a wailing toddler who trailed behind while a mobile phone was tucked between her left shoulder and her chin.

As he watched, she stopped and with the buggy handle nestling against her midriff, took the phone in her free hand and turning towards the crying toddler, he heard her shout, "Move your arse, ya wee bugger!"

Casey Lennox, her shoulder length dyed blonde hair lying loose on her shoulders and wearing a dark coloured quilted jacket, tight blue jeans and knee high black leather boots was, Ian thought, the most desirable woman he had ever seen.

He saw her half turn towards him and he nervously ducked behind the wall and then, a few seconds later, looked again and saw Casey had met with the shirtless, heavily tattooed Billy Purvis who had exited the close mouth to meet her and now both were kissing in the front path of the close.

Watching them together, Ian's heart sank, but so intent was he observing his hearts desire's betrayal with Purvis that he was unaware of the presence of the woman behind him.

"Watching something interesting, are we Ian?"

Startled, Ian turned to see a tall, slim woman standing behind him, her blonde hair fiercely tied back in a ponytail, arms folded across her chest, wearing a black trouser suit and with a black leather handbag hanging from her left shoulder. Her model looks were slightly detracted by the pale, narrow two inch scar on her lower left jaw, the result of a bottle attack when she had been a probationary cop.

His heart sank. DC Catriona 'Cat' MacDougall, passing by in a CID car, had noticed the lurking teenager behind the wall and not only knew him, but had arrested him more than a couple of times for minor crime and offences. It was enough to rouse her suspicions.

"Hello, Miss," he mumbled. "I was just hanging about, like. I wasn't doing nothing wrong, honest."

Cat glanced over his shoulder, but all she could see was the back of a couple with a pram and a small child walking into a close in Dewar Drive. A thought struck her.

"You weren't thinking about having a wee go at them, the woman maybe, Ian; were you? I mean, trying for her handbag or something?"

"No, Miss, no, honest. No," he vigorously shook his head and continued. "I would never, ever, ever hurt Casey, Miss. I..." he hesitated and then licking at his lips, with a slow grin admitted, "I like her, Miss."

"Casey? Who's Casey, Ian?"

"Casey Lennox, Miss. She lives with him, Billy Purvis I mean. I don't like him, but I like Casey, Miss, you know?" and he grinned, his face reddening and betraying his infatuation.

Cat inwardly smiled at the lad's description and she suspected that he had a teenage crush on Lennox who Cat didn't really know much about. However, she *had* heard that Billy Purvis, a local takeaway delivery driver, was strongly suspected of being one of the local sub-dealers pushing out the cheap heroin that had so recently flooded the Drum and the Glasgow area in general.

Her nose wrinkled, now catching not just Ian's body odour, but the smell of cheap booze and cannabis emanating from him. She fought to repress a smile, knowing from her sixteen years experience as a cop that while the youngster was a bloody nuisance, he wasn't the worse type of ned she usually encountered.

"Had a wee drink and maybe a wee smoke today, Ian, have we?" Almost immediately realising that Cat was not going to haul him off to her car by the scruff of the neck, Ian grinned, displaying the lack of one front tooth that some years previously had lost an argument with a fist. It's my birthday Miss," he continued to grin. "I'm nineteen today, so I am," he proudly boasted.

"Well," she smiled, then with a straight face added, "congratulations wee man. You'll forgive me if I don't give you a birthday kiss, Ian.

I'm not allowed to kiss the public when on duty," she slowly shook her head at him.

"Oh, that's okay Miss. I wouldn't like anybody seeing me kissing the polis anyway," he replied with a nod, accepting the lie as the gospel truth.

"So, the joint you had today, Ian. Where did you get it, wee man?" Not the sharpest tool in the box, it didn't occur to Ian to question how Cat knew he had earlier smoked a spliff.

"Ah," he grinned at her, "you know I'm not a grass Miss. I can't tell you something like that."

"What," she pretended surprise, "not even if I cross my heart and promise not to tell your Papa?"

She watched as his Adams apple bounced in his throat, his mind wrestling with a decision; tell Miss MacDougall who gave him the cannabis and she'd keep her mouth shut or not tell and she would give him up to Papa and that, he worried, would mean his Papa would be upset and the last thing he wanted was to upset Papa.

Ian loved his Papa, wee Chic Fagin; the man who had raised him from a baby when Ian's mother run off with her Catholic boyfriend to England and who had never, ever contacted her son. Papa, himself a widower, had taken care of wee Ian and raised him to be a good Orangeman; taught him to play the flute and always been there for him through his school and numerous hospital visits, stood by him during Ian's court appearances and never raised a hand to him or beaten him like some of Ian's friends had been beaten by their parents.

His shoulders sagged in defeat and he licked at his trembling lip.

"If I tell you, Miss I could get into big trouble."

"Who would give you big trouble, Ian," she asked, her brow knitted in curiosity.

"Tommo, Miss, he would…" he stopped, his mouth open with shock, then he started to grin. "You tricked me there Miss. You're dead smart, you are. Not like me."

He couldn't know nor would he understand that the mention of Michael Thomson's name caused a slight tightening in Cat's stomach. She was well aware that the CID and in particular, the Drumchapel detectives, had for years sought to libel a charge against that bastard that would stick, but so intimidating was he to the local citizen's that everyone was afraid to speak out against him.

Choosing her words carefully, she took a step closer to him and softly smiling, asked, "So Ian, why would Tommo give you into big trouble?"

He knew the very mention of Thomson's name had been wrong, but his mind was too engrossed with his Papa once again being upset when Cat told of Ian's drug taking that his caution went to the wind. "He told me not to tell, Miss, that if I told, he'd hurt Papa."

Guessing correctly, she said, "It was Tommo that gave you the joint, wasn't it Ian?"

She watched him nod his head and then she asked, "Why did he give you the joint Ian? What did you do for him that he gave you the joint?"

It was then that he thought about running off, his head swivelling around as he sought an escape route; anything to get away from answering her questions, but she must guessed what he was thinking for she took yet another step towards him and now he was backed against the wall. Besides, he knew he couldn't outrun the fleet-footed woman; he had tried that once before, that time she had seen him breaking the Paki's shop window and he had run off, but she had caught him then.

"I sometimes do things for him, deliver wee things, Miss."

"What is it you deliver Ian? What things?"

"Wee parcels like. Just wee parcels, Miss," he licked nervously at his lips, for now he was afraid that someone might see him talking to Miss MacDougall and that would be bad.

Bad if Tommo found out; very bad for him, but even worse for his Papa.

"Where do you collect the parcels you have to deliver Ian…" but her questioning was cut short when the mobile phone in her handbag activated.

"Hello," she snapped into the phone.

"Where the hell are you?" demanded her DI, Mark Walters.

It was then that the slow-witted Ian realised what was being asked of him and in fright made the decision that while Miss MacDougall was distracted, he'd take off.

She reached to grab him as he rushed past her, but missed and stumbled, saving herself from falling flat on her face by catching hold of the wall and loudly exclaimed "*Shit!*"

"What did you say?" thundered Walters in her ear.

"Sorry, boss," she weakly grinned at the sight of the short legged teenager running through the back courts, his head turning to ensure she was not pursuing him. "I was speaking with wee Ian Fagin, but the bugger's run off when my phone went there."

"Right, well, deal with that another time. I'm holding a briefing here in the office in half an hour. There's a DI from the surveillance coming in to speak with us, so get your arse back here for then, okay?"

"Right sir, I'll be there," she simply replied and pressed the red off button.

Returning across the uneven ground of the back court to her CID car parked nearby, Cat inhaled and shook her head, angry at both losing Ian Fagin just when he was about to give her something that might be really interesting, but just as angry at Walters terse and rude attitude towards her.

The married and always suavely dressed DI who at forty-four was eight years her senior, had been promoted to the Division just a few months earlier and almost immediately appointed to take charge of the Drumchapel CID office. It wasn't long after that the ruddy faced Walters had begun to make advances towards Cat, suggesting that over dinner some evening he could help her with advice to further her career, then occasionally but deliberately bumping into her and making comments that were just short of lewd. At first she had tried to be tactful, pretending she didn't understand his suggestions or misinterpreted his body sliding against hers, but it had come to a head a few weeks earlier when he called her into his office and closed the door behind her. Alone, he had stood in front of her, close enough to nauseate her with his sweet breath that resulted from his addiction to chewing gum. Pretending to flick a thread from her suit jacket, his hand strayed from her shoulder to her breast and without thinking she instinctively kneed him squarely in the balls.

Shocked by her actions, she watched as he grunted and his ruddy complexion turning to a deep scarlet, slowly crumpled to the carpeted floor.

Gasping, he stared up at her and threatened to have her disciplined for assaulting a senior officer until Cat quickly countered by leaning down towards him and through gritted teeth, threatened to accuse him of sexual assault. The resulting stand-off had seen him hiss that she "*Fuck off!*" out of his office, adding that he would ensure her career was screwed into the ground.

Storming through the door, she had coldly replied, "Aye, very good, but you'll not be screwing *me*, you fucking pervert!"

The next day it had begun with him designating her every little petty inquiry that crossed his desk; every shitty little job he could think of and endeavouring to find fault with her reported cases to the PF.

She had accepted his petulant revenge without complaint, but soon become aware of her colleagues whispered curiosity why Cat, one of their more successful pro-active detectives, was being treated so.

But none dare complain on her behalf, for the simple fact was that Walters held their *own* careers in sway and to go against him might provoke his anger at them.

Such was the way of things.

Driving back towards the recently opened police office located on Drumry Road East, Cat reflected on her career so far. To request a transfer to avoid the spiteful Walters she knew would be like giving in to the bastard and *that* was not in her nature. Of course, she thought, she could apply for one of the squads, but the CID hours suited her personal life and that thought brought a smile to her face.

Her husband of eight years Gus had himself been a cop, but was now retired after a life changing accident almost crippled his left leg.

Though deemed to be unfit for operational duties as a police officer, Gus now run his own small, but successful gardening business.

Besides, Cat enjoyed the CID shifts, the semi-regular hours that permitted her time with Gus and their secret hobby; a hobby that she daren't discuss with her cynical colleagues, for she was an ardent ballroom dancer, a pastime that not only permitted her to enjoy the regular fitness, but the strict regime also kept Gus active and ensured the muscle in his damaged leg remained supple.

Moving to a squad she knew would likely mean undetermined working hours, perhaps even shifts changes and that, she shook her head, just didn't suit her.

Turning into the yard at the office, she saw a tall, heavy set man exiting a dirty and tired looking, dark coloured Ford Focus. The man turned when she got out the drivers seat and with a grin, called out, "Bloody hell, Cat MacDougall. How's it hanging?"

Pumping her hand up and down, the rugby mad Andy Dawson continued to grin and asked, "How long has it been now, hen? What; must be six, seven years maybe?"

"Eight years, Andy," she smilingly replied, leading him towards the front door of the office. "The last time I saw you we were both on the detective's course at Tulliallan…and you were pissed."

"Aye, that would be right enough," he admitted with a grin and held open a first floor door to permit her to enter.

On the other side, standing by the door to the conference room, DI Mark Walters frowned and pointedly glanced at his watch.

"About time, MacDougall," he scowled at her and then staring at the large, scruffy man with her, venomously added, "Who the hell is *he*?"

In that split second, Dawson intuitively realised that there was some friction between the two and, while he knew and at one time fancied the hell out of Cat MacDougall, this weedy looking guy was a stranger to him.

Poker faced, she begun to reply, "Detective Inspector Walters, this…" but was cut short when Dawson, with a steely edge to his voice, interrupted her and towering over the slighter built Walters, said, "*He* is Detective Inspector Andy Dawson of the surveillance unit, here at the request of *your* boss. So, Detective Inspector, perhaps you might care to show me where I set up to deliver my address?"

Casey Lennox, the object of Ian Fagin's desire and imaginative dreams, slowly closed her eyes and screamed at her toddler son, "For *fucks* sake, Brad, shut up and give me a minute's peace, will you! Wee Kylie's trying to sleep!"

However, the three year old wailing child did not fully comprehend her shouted request and nose bubbling with snot, sat on the lounge floor amid his Lego bricks and continued to cry unabated.

"Can you not get him to shut up for five minutes, Casey," demanded her latest paramour Billy Purvis, who at twenty-three years of age, was three years her junior.

Dressed in lime green coloured tracksuit trousers, dark green coloured training shoes and a white vest worn to better display the tattoo sleeves on both arms that united in a fiery dragon's tail on his neck, the shaven headed Purvis dropped himself down onto a stained and faded leather couch and tried to concentrate on his hand held games console, but angry at the noise the toddler was making, threw the machine aside and exclaimed, "I'm out of here."

"What? Where you going to?" asked Casey, frowning at the thought of being left alone in the two bedroom flat with her kids.

"Anywhere that I can't hear that wee shite," he nodded towards the toddler, grabbing the tracksuit jacket from the couch behind him.

"Are you going to see *him*?" she demanded.

He hesitated, not wishing to provoke yet another argument with her about his business dealings with Tommo.

"Look, hen," he rounded on her and pointed a warning forefinger at her. "Get this straight, Casey; me and you are an item, aye, but that's it. If I want to do business with Tommo, then that's what puts the grub on the table and they fancy clothes on your back as well as your weans backs, okay? Because I'm shagging you doesn't mean you own me, right?"

His voice grew louder the angrier he become. "Just remember, Casey, you're not adverse to a wee joint yourself, now and again. Now and again?" he laughed sarcastically. "Every other fucking night, I should say. If I have to get my stuff from Tommo, then *that's* what I'll fucking do, *okay*?" his hand raised and his voice now a scream.

She stepped back, white-faced and fearing that in his rage, he would strike her as so many boyfriends before him had done.

Her son Brad, she realised, had stopped crying and was watching them open-mouthed.

Purvis shook with anger and turned on his heel, leaving her standing there in the lounge wondering if she had blown it, that the three months they had been together was over, that he might not come back other than to collect his things. Her lower lip began to tremble and fists clenched, she fought back the tears. If Billy left like all the others, she thought, it wouldn't be bad; it would be a *disaster*. Right enough, the social paid the rent and the benefits she received just about covered her food bill and other wee things, but his money from the drug-dealing provided her with extra's she couldn't get elsewhere. The clothes for her and the kids and aye, he was right about that too. The nights out, the week's holiday a month ago when the four of them had been down at the Centre Parc place in Cumbria. She could never afford these things without him. Even driving Casey and her weans about in his flashy yellow coloured Mitsubishi Evo, taking her shopping; all these things would be gone if he left her. Weakly, she sat down on the edge of the couch, suddenly aware of the futility that was her life.

Opening her arms to permit the now sobbing wee Brad to climb onto her lap she began to softly cry.

Ian Fagin's grandfather, Charles Fagin had always been known as wee Chic to distinguish him from his own father, big Charlie. Small in stature like his grandson, Chic had led what he believed to be a simple life. In his late twenties, his career as a shipyard welder had been cut short when a gas tank had unaccountably exploded near him and the resulting blast caused him to be thrown across a yard with such force that the sudden impact with the bow of a ship fractured most of his ribs, broke his sternum and collapsed both his lungs. Rushed to the nearby Southern General Hospital, the skilful surgeon quickly operated and was able to prise the shattered bone from Chic's crushed lungs to enable them to be re-inflated. His life saved and discharged some months later, Chic learned he was deemed unfit for manual labour and being too poorly educated for office work, received a pittance of a pension to support his wife Sara, young daughter Agnes and himself and then only because the union had tirelessly fought his case for him. Never a drinker and not a man to complain or whine about injustice, Chic made the best of life as it was and being a naturally exuberant individual, sought a pastime to expend his energy. Shortly thereafter and faithful to his Protestant upbringing, Chic soon learned the local Orange flute band, the Drum Loyal True Blues needed musicians.

Those who knew Chic Fagin would invariably agree that he was a nice wee man, who preferred to do somebody a good turn rather than a bad turn and some even asserted, his allegiance to the Orange order aside, that Chic didn't have a bitter bone in his body.

In time, Chic ascended to the position of Band Sergeant and discovered not only a talent for playing the flute, but also a talent for teaching the playing of the flute.

Financially bereft as they were, Chic and his wife Sara were reasonably happy and though luxuries were few, they strove to do the best by their daughter that they could, even accepting that through her teenage years, Agnes had developed a fondness for alcohol and on weekends, would often arrive home worse the wear for drink.

Being the concerned parents they were, Chic and Sara stood by Agnes and for a time she seemed to be improving, though it did concern them that most weekends, she now stayed out and away from home.

However life with his lovely Sara, Chic thought, could not get much better, but just as he was settling happily into his new position as Band Sergeant, Sara contracted double pneumonia and within days of being diagnosed, died in Gartnavel Hospital.

The devastated Chic had not yet come to terms with his bereavement when his daughter Agnes whom he adored, announced she was pregnant, but flatly refused to name the father. Confounded, Chic did his best to support his daughter through her pregnancy, distressed that once more she turned to drink and most evenings, would leave their council flat to socialise and invariably consume alcohol.

Without the guidance of his beloved Sara, Chic just did not know how to handle the situation.

In time, Agnes was admitted to hospital where she delivered his grandson, Ian. Underweight and undoubtedly a victim of FAS, Chic could not have been more proud and loved his grandson from the start.

Three days later and four hours after he fetched Agnes and Ian home from the maternity ward, Chic popped out to buy milk and upon his return to the flat, discovered Ian crying in his cot and a note on the kitchen worktop from Agnes that informed him she had gone to England with her boyfriend and would not be coming back. Adding insult to injury, the shocked Chic read that Agnes's boyfriend was a Catholic, but still she refused to disclose the name of wee Ian's father.

Tears formed in the old man's eyes when he read Agnes's words on the note that he later burned on the gas stove in the kitchen. She might have abandoned her son, he had thought then, but *he* would not.

From that time his grandson Ian became his life and through the years, through the difficult times of school, the police and the courts, Chic stood by Ian, raising him as best he could; trying to guide the young lad to accept truth and honesty, not deceit and lies. Initiating him into the band as a flutist, he thought this might give young Ian some focus, only to see him abandon his musical lessons and turn away from the band to the drugs and the drink.

Coming to the attention of the police had been the worst of times, he slowly shook his head. Ian wasn't a bad lad, he knew in his heart, just sometimes stupid through his use of the alcohol or soft drugs. The last time Ian was arrested, it was the tall policewoman who had come to the door; the blonde detective with the nice smile who sat with Chic and over a cup of tea, agreed that maybe it might be an idea to move out of the Drum and away from some of the bad characters that influenced the easily led Ian.

Aye, Chic had agreed, though the detective lassie had been kind, moving away from everyone and everything you have ever known isn't that easy, he had told her. It had been fortunate she was dealing with Ian's case for she was able to get him bailed, though Chic recalled with a sigh, he is still paying up the court fine.

Is it me, he often asked himself. Is there some sort of destructive gene I have first passed to my daughter and then onto my grandson, he wondered.

But the answer eluded him and Chic, being the man he was, got on with life and with alacrity, pursued his favourite pastime; continuing as the Band Sergeant of his flute band and his good deeds in his community, though some of these deeds would never be publicly known.

Through the years, the band had achieved some minor successes in competition, mainly due to Chic's strict observance of discipline and the high standard he set in the playing of their music. Of course, there had been hiccups and some band members had been dropped because of their lack of sobriety at events, a lack of musical talent or in the case of Mick Thomson, Chic recalled with distaste, expelled for violence.

Chic was not a man who commonly used the word hate or considered that any individual was beyond redemption; but Michael Thomson?

No, Chic shook his head, Thomson was the exception.

Thomson *was* beyond redemption.

CHAPTER THREE

Within the conference room at Drumchapel police station, DI Andy Dawson stood in front of the assembled group of eight detectives and the dozen or so uniformed officers. Introductions made, he commenced his short speech.

"The plain and simple truth, lads and lassies is that for the last couple of months, regular and multiple supplies of heroin, diamorphine, smack, call it by whatever name you will, is being delivered into the greater Glasgow area. Now, you may ask what's so different about this heroin and, considering that heroin has been on our streets for years, why is it that *this* particular batch is attracting the attention of senior management who instructed me to come out here and speak with you guys?"

He shrugged as if the answer eluded him and then continued. "It might be because the quality of this particular batch of heroin is so pure and so regular, it's driving the street price down and to be honest, it's an indication we're losing the war on drugs."

A murmur went round the room, silenced when Dawson raised a hand.

"What," he slowly smiled, "did you think we were *winning*?" then shook his head.

"No guys, we're not winning; at least not at this time or in my opinion, for the foreseeable future. I stress, that's my opinion, not managements who continue to issue statistics to the general public that, quite frankly, baffles the *fuck* out of me."

His honesty drew a mild guffaw from his audience, with the exception of Walters who sat at the rear of the room and continued to scowl at him.

"Anyway, I digress," Dawson smiled at the officers and spread his hands out wide. "Here's a wee thought for you. The price of heroin drops and that makes the drug more available to the street dealers. Once it's adulterated, they in turn can offer it cheaper to their regular customers and of course, as we all know from our experience as cops, cheap drugs attract more customers. Over time, this flood of new customers or, let's call them what they are, junkies, becomes an outbreak and the public demands more action, because quite apart from the *existing* junkies committing crime to fund their habit, these new junkies have also become hooked on the heroin and in due course, will need more funds to feed *their* habit."

He paused and glanced about the room. "Consequently, minor crime takes a sharp rise and suddenly, Joe Public fears walking down a darkened street in case he or she gets mugged or encounter an aggressive street junkie begging and so on and so on. The upshot is the media demand police act to counter this crisis that in part is *created* by the bloody media. Funds from our already limited budget are diverted to combat this apparent rise in drug abuse and the cuts to fund this police action, guys and gals, are made in other areas such as Traffic, uniforms and equipment, Community Patrols, recruiting and God forbid," he grinned at them, "overtime."

"So, why am I here today? Maybe I'm here to scare you. No, you lot are far too ugly and frightening to be scared by me," he grinned at the jeers then more soberly said, "My purpose here is to ask for your assistance. The analysts and Laboratory geeks have determined from the small street seizures we have made that this new batch of heroin definitely originates in Afghanistan and without boring you rigid, makes its way through northern Pakistan and finally winds up in the London area. Our colleagues in the Metropolitan Police's SO15 have learned that the heroin is being imported from Europe by a gang of Turkish nationals, an Organised Crime Group if you will, who are selling it on to a supplier or suppliers here in the West of Scotland While the Met inform us that they are making inroads to arrest the members of the OCG, we're more interested in the customer or customers in *our* area and who the local supplier or suppliers are and how they transport it up here. Frankly," he slowly shook his head, "we haven't got a Scooby Doo. What we *do* suspect and from the little we've gleaned from touts, is that the main local supplier is located here in Drumchapel; the guy who seems to be organising the collection of the heroin and distributing it to the sub-dealers throughout the West of Scotland, then collecting the payment in cash from these sub-dealers. Where the money goes after that, we're not certain."

"Do you have a name for this supplier, Inspector?" interrupted a portly Detective Sergeant.

Dawson pursed his lips and nodded. "The name Michael Thomson *was* mentioned by a source, but I have to stress we have no clear and firm intelligence to confirm that Thomson is the supplier," then he smiled and cast a glance about the room. "Well, not unless you guys can tell me different?"

"Wouldn't it be simple to use your surveillance team to catch Thomson hands on and lock him up, sir? Wouldn't that solve the problem?" asked a young uniformed constable.

"I'm not going to dismiss that suggestion, son," replied Dawson, "but the plain truth is that locking up the supplier, whether it be Thomson or not, won't solve the problem. What we need to do is find the guy who is orchestrating the deliveries, the middleman between the OCG and the local supplier. If we *do* identify the supplier and arrest him or her and remember," he shrugged and smiled, "the supplier *could* be female, then the middleman will simply find someone else and continue his or her importation of the heroin from the OCG. No, we need to identify the middleman, the top dog as it were and cut the head of this particular route."

"Won't the Turkish importers just find someone else to deal with up here?" asked the portly DS.

"If we can identify and arrest the middleman up here," explained Dawson, "the Met have indicated they have sufficient evidence to proceed against their own targets, but it all hinges on us because the Met have agreed to hold off arresting the members of the OCG till we find our middleman here. Yes," he nodded, "it does put some pressure on us to identify the middleman and back track the evidence to London and that, guys and gals, is basically why I'm here. You are the local polis, out there speaking daily to Joe Public. What I'm asking is for you to keep your eyes and ears open as I'm certain you do, but with a particular emphasis on anything, anything at all that might suggest or identify the middleman. Once he or she is identified, my team can mount an operation against that individual and hopefully it will lead to the supplier who is our number one target."

"Right then," he rubbed both hands together, "any further questions, no? Okay, guys and gals, just one further thing that I must remind you of is that if you *are* running a source here in your division or you recruit a new source, you must inform the Source Handling Unit, okay? All information received from a CHIS…" he stopped when a hand shot up, seeing it to be the same young cop who red-faced asked, "What's a CHIS sir?"

"My mistake son, I should have explained that a CHIS is the acronym for a Covert Human Intelligence Source; just a fancy title for a tout." Then to laughter added, "You *do* know what an acronym is?"

Sitting among her colleagues, MacDougall's eyes narrowed. The short conversation she had with Ian Fagin simply indicated that Mick Thomson was dealing drugs, but whether or not it was heroin she hadn't time with young Fagin to ascertain. Certainly, it seemed to her that Thomson had paid the wee man off with a joint so, she wondered, was it perhaps cannabis that Thomson was dealing and not heroin? She stood as the rest of the room began to crowd out through the door and waited till Dawson was alone.

"So, how's your man Gus these days?" he asked her, then added, "I heard about the accident."

"Oh, he's fine and knows he was very lucky to keep the leg. He's got his own wee gardening business and doing quite well," she proudly grinned.

"That's good," nodded Dawson and then cocked his head to one side. "Was there something else, Cat?"

Nodding, she quickly related her encounter with Ian Fagin and with a grin, included his escape from her grasp. "This suit," she added, plucking at the material on her arm, "cost me over a hundred quid in the January sales and no way was I chasing a wee shite like him across waste ground and risk tearing it or dirtying it by going down on my backside," she grinned at him. Then with a shrug, continued, "The thing is Andy, when you mentioned Mick Thomson, I thought you should be aware of what I learned, not that it's much."

"This lad, Fagin, would it be worth me having a quiet chat with him do you think?"

She shook her head. "He's a bit simple, a birth thing," she replied. "To be honest, I don't think there's much more he would tell you. If he is as he said delivering parcels for Thomson, it's unlikely he'll be aware what's in the parcels. It could be heroin or cannabis, you know what I mean?"

Dawson nodded, a little disappointed that what initially seemed like a lead proved to be nothing. "My problem Cat is all I have on this guy Thomson is local Intel that frankly, is shite. What you've just told me is more or less similar to the CHIS information that I'm getting from the Source Handling Unit, that we *can't* corroborate because you know what touts are like; they'll tell you *anything* to keep you sweet and off their back. By the way," he tapped the side of his nose with his forefinger, "keep my opinion about the CHIS to yourself, if you don't mind. I don't want any hassle from the Source Handling guys because to be honest, they think the sun shines out of their source's arse, but *I'm* a wee bit suspicious of what he's telling them and in turn, what they tell me."

He sighed and with the heel of his hand, rubbed at his brow.

"Another problem is if I go to my boss with what little info I have, he won't authorise a surveillance team for Thomson without something a little more positive." Dawson rubbed his forefinger and thumb together then grinning at her, added, "Everyone's budget and cost-conscious these days, Cat."

However, he was pleased to see Catriona and eyes narrowing, asked, "Your boss DI Walters. What's his story then? Seems like a po-faced arse, if you ask me."

She smiled, a quiet smile and replied, "Arrived a couple of months ago from Ayrshire, but I don't know from what division or anything about him nor do I know enough about him to comment on his ability as a DI, but let's just say his attitude towards women is stuck somewhere in the nineteen sixties," then grimly added, "We're liberated these days and don't take kindly to being manhandled or propositioned."

Dawson's brow furrowed and his face turned pale as the inferred allegation struck home. "If his behaviour is inappropriate Cat, there are channels you can use…"

"Don't worry about it Andy," she raised her hand and interrupted him with a grin, "I dealt with it," but didn't add that Walters was making her work life difficult. She knew Andy Dawson of old. Big and rough he might be and while also suspecting that he once did have a serious crush on her, never had he on any occasion, drunk or sober, acted other than the gentleman he was.

The door knocked and a young civilian bar officer popped her head into the room. "Hi Cat," she smiled warmly at MacDougall and then said, "DI Dawson? Your office was on the phone and requested you give them a call as soon as possible, sir. You can use the phone at the uniform bar if you want."

"Right then," he acknowledged, but before taking his leave of MacDougall, he fished into his rear denim pocket and produced a crumpled police business card upon which he scribbled his personal mobile number and handed it to her. "If you get anything else Cat, give me a call," he grinned.

As he followed the bar officer downstairs, his thoughts were on what MacDougall had said…or hadn't said, he inwardly corrected himself. He remembered Cat as a capable and tenacious young woman, but Walters was a DI and he knew the reality was that Walters was in a position to make life awkward for Cat.

At the front office the bar officer pointed to a phone on a desk, telling Dawson he could use that one and turned away to get on with her paperwork.

Dawson dialled the internal Force number that put him straight through to his office and spoke with his DS then, almost as an afterthought, said, "You worked down in Ayrshire, didn't you?"

"Aye, the Kilmarnock office," replied the DS, "why?"

Standing in the centre of the football field at Abbotsford Primary School, Des Brown blew the whistle and beckoned the fifteen boys to gather round him, watching with a quiet smile as the eager nine and ten year olds all came at a run. Dressed in an assortment of strips and training gear, the boys puffed and panted and stared at their coach, the balding, slightly stooped, slim figured man who similarly dressed in an old, worn black coloured tracksuit, certainly didn't look like the amateur boxer and junior footballer he once had been.

"Right lads," began Des, glancing about him at the upturned shiny faces, "good session there. Plenty of effort and energy today and that's what we need for Saturday's game against the opposition. Right, on my whistle, into the school and get changed out of your training gear and get yourselves away home. But first, any questions?"

He knew it would be wee Steven's hand that would shoot up. Des was aware that the boy idolised him and he worked hard at treating him the same as the other boys, but the wee lad was so keen to be noticed it was sometimes difficult not to favour him.

"Yes, Steven," he pointed at him.

"My mum says that the strips will be washed and ready for Saturday, Mister Brown," he gasped.

"That's great news Steven. Now, any other questions," but before there was a rush of hands, Des blew his whistle and waving, indicated that they all to run towards the school.

Following them at a more sedate pace, he saw the grinning janitor Willie McKee standing leaning on a yard brush, watching as the boys run past him into the school.

"How do you find the time let alone the energy, Des," asked McKee.

"Believe me, Willie. If I could find somebody to replace me, I would and in a heartbeat," he shook his head.

"What's that, five years you've been running the team now Des?"

"Aye, over five years now, Willie," he stood and smiled at the older man. "Ever since my boy Paul was in the team. When he left and went to the secondary, I thought that I was finished here, but the head teacher couldn't get anyone else to run the boys team, so here I still am," he sighed.

"Away, you love it really," McKee grinned.

"Aye, I love curries as well, but too many isn't good for you, Willie," he responded and went into the building to get changed.

Ten minutes later, he was stood at the school gate, waiting patiently and watching as the lad's parents or family members collected their charge, waving each lad away until at last, he stood alone with Steven.

"Does your son play football Mister Brown," Steven stared up at him through the thick lenses of his NHS issue spectacles, the legs tied together round the back of his head with a black shoelace.

"My boy Paul played for the school here, Steven," Des smiled down at him. "In the same position as you do, on the left wing."

"Is that right Mister Brown? Was he good?"

"Aye and he still is good. He plays for the under fifteen's at the High School now."

An old style Nissan Micra pulled up at the kerb and a slim, but visibly harassed young woman with shoulder length auburn curly hair got out of the driver's door.

"I'm so sorry Mister Brown," said Grace Thomson, her eyes betraying her anxiety "I completely misjudged the time."

"Mum," called out Steven and run into her waiting arms.

Watching, Des was in no doubt of the affection that existed between mother and son and smiled. "It's not a problem Missus Thomson. Steven and I were chewing the fat here, weren't we, wee guy?" and to the boy's delight, ruffled his hair.

Grace Thomson visibly relaxed. She couldn't explain why, but on the odd occasion she spoke with Des Brown, she was always nervous; shy even.

"Ah, Steven was saying that you would have the strips washed for Saturday, Missus Thomson. That's very decent of you."

"It's *Miss* Thomson actually," she admitted, unaccountably blushing and then added, "Or Grace, if you would prefer."

"Well, I'd prefer Des," he smiled at her, "eh, me I mean. Not me calling you Des," he blustered and then was pleased to see that she laughed and to his own surprise, thought it a very nice laugh.

A few awkward seconds passed and then as if unwilling to leave, she said, "The football strips. When shall I bring them to the school?"

"They'll need to be ready for Saturday, Mum, we've a big game that day," Steven interrupted to remind her and added, "Isn't that right Mister Brown?"

"Absolutely correct, wee man," he grinned at the boy.

"So, delivered when?" she asked again.

"Ah, what would suit you?"

"Why is it you men can never make a decision?" she pretended annoyance, then continuing to smile, suggested, "Look, you leave on Saturday morning for the game in the school bus from here, don't you? Well, I'm on the PTA committee organising Friday evening's event. I can bring the strips then and leave them in the janny's room if that's okay with you, Des?"

"Fine," he nodded then his brow furrowed when he asked, "What's Friday night's event then?"

"Don't you read the notice board? It's a fundraising dance. A bring your own bottle affair."

"Ah, no, I don't really go into the school that much these days," he replied. "My son Paul's at secondary now."

"Paul's in the secondary school team, Mum; a left winger, just like me," beamed Steven.

Now it was Grace's turn to ruffle her son's hair as she said to Des, "Oh, I thought you still had a son at the school; in the team, I mean."

"Not for a few years now," he grinned and added, "Long story."

"Well, if you and your wife want to pop along on the night, I can reserve two tickets. We're *desperately* trying to flog them and it *is* for a good cause," she tried to cajole him.

"Ah, I sense a wee bit of blackmail there," he grinned at her, "and thanks, but no thanks. I might be working," though felt a wee bit uneasy in telling the lie, particularly knowing that he was actually dayshift that coming Friday, but an explanation why he wouldn't go would take too long. Besides, he reasoned, why would it interest this young woman?

"Well, anyway," she shrugged, "the strips will be there Saturday morning. I promise," and smiling, turned away to open the passenger door to let Steven slip into the rear seat.

Watching as she leaned into the rear of the car, Des could hardly avoid staring at the slender figure and shapely rear of *Miss* Grace Thomson and instinctively, quietly inhaled. Satisfied her son was buckled in, she drew herself back out of the car and waving to Des, called out, "Bye" as she rounded the car and got into the drivers seat. He watched her drive off and with his sports bag slung over one shoulder, made his way over to his old Ford Mondeo and glanced at his watch. Still time, he thought, to nip over to his parent's house and ensure Paul was safely there and maybe grab a cuppa before he had to go on duty at Govan CID office.

Billy Purvis knocked a little hesitatingly on Mick Thomson's door, his mind still reeling from the argument with Casey. Bitch should consider herself lucky I'm taking an interest in her *and* her weans he scowled.

The door was snatched open and surprised, he took a step backwards.

"Well, well, it's my wee pal Billy," Thomson grinned, glancing over Purvis's shoulder to ensure that he was alone. "Come in, come in," he beckoned before turning and walking away into the hallway.

Purvis followed Thomson into the lounge and was waved to the leather couch while the older man sat down in the matching leather swivel chair. "For my bad back," he had once told Purvis who had thought, there was nothing wrong with the big bastard's back when he was lifting the weights at the gym.

"So, Billy, what can I do you for?" he folded his fingers into a pyramid in front of his nose.

"Eh, the stuff Tommo, I was wondering if there is any likelihood I can get a bit more, but to be honest, it would need to be on the drip."

"How long will you need it for son or what I *should* ask is, can you settle your current bill before we discuss more of the…" he hesitated and slowly smiled, "the big H?"

"Oh aye, the money's there Tommo," Purvis nodded and eagerly agreed. "I've got it sitting in the boot of my car. It's there when you want to take it," he added.

"What's there, Billy?"

"Nine grand, Tommo. Well, fifty short of nine grand, I should say." Thomson narrowed his eyes, his mind calculating the debt owed by Purvis. If he was just the fifty pounds short of nine thousand pounds that he claimed he had then he was just one thousand and fifty short of the total bill of ten grand. Well, this month's bill anyway.

"Will I go and get the money now, Tommo?" Purvis interrupted his thoughts.

Thomson stared hard at him and replied, "Are you off your *fucking* head, Billy? Bringing *that* kind of money into my home? What if the polis show up and give the place a turn? Don't be stupid," he scoffed. "Nothing's changed. It will be the same arrangement as before. You use the bank account details I gave you and deposit the money into the three accounts. Remember though," he sat forward and stared at the younger man, "when you're making the deposit Billy, it's a collar and tie and you hide those fucking tattoos so they can't be seen and you make sure you are on your best behaviour in the bank, eh? We don't want the bank staff getting a wee bit suspicious, do we Billy?"

Purvis inwardly sighed. It was a real pain in the arse wearing that business suit and tie and visiting all those bank branches, but he knew that if that was what Tommo wanted, that was what Tommo was getting. Arguing otherwise might mean upsetting the big bastard and *no* way was Billy risking *that*.

"No, Tommo. I'll do as you said."

Thomson sat back again, and again arched his fingers in front of his nose. "Has there been any kind of suspicion at all, Billy? From the banks, I mean?"

Purvis shook his head. "There was one guy about a month ago I think it was, that asked what the money was for, but I told him it was a loan for my car that I was paying off to my uncle. He didn't seem that interested after that."

"What bank was it?"

"The Crow Road branch, Tommo."

Thomson inhaled and though reflecting on Purvis's statement and then shaking his head, said, "Don't use that branch again. At least not for a while, okay? It's not worth taking chances in case some nosey bastard gets suspicious at the money you keep turning up with and lodging in the accounts."

Purvis nodded in understanding. He was desperately keen to know who controlled the accounts and while he had the sort codes and the accounts numbers, but not the account name, he suspected it wasn't Tommo, as he had first thought. But these were thoughts he daren't share with anyone, least of all *this* fucking headcase.

"Right, in other issues Billy," Thomson interrupted his thoughts, "any late payers that I might need to deal with or any problems collecting the smack or getting cash in?"

Purvis shook his head. "No, the regular meetings with the lorry drivers are timed to a T and the customers know that if the payments are late, they're in the shit with you."

Thomson grinned for it was as he had always believed; fear is the best inducement.

"How many customers do you have on your books now, wee man?"

"My tick list is hidden in the car, but from memory, we're talking nearly fifty suppliers, Tommo, but I've no idea how many customers they have themselves. Hundreds, likely," he opined with a grin.

"You'll be a busy man then, my wee friend."

"Aye," he replied, relieved that the weekly report was going better than he thought and there was the likelihood of getting more of the smack to distribute too.

"The bill, the large sum of cash Billy; the thirty-two grand that we need to deliver to the courier. It's all wrapped up and ready to go?" asked Thomson.

"I've only today managed to collect it all in, big man. There was some difficulty with a couple of the dealers getting their cash in, but it's all there now," he nodded and assured Thomson, "Just like you ordered, big man," he continued to vigorously nod. Then, as if hoping to divert Thomson's attention from the issue of the late payers, he said, "It's been the same Paki guy for the handovers. Well, I *think* he's a Paki, but all these bastards look the same to me. Anyway, it's the same guy the last four or five times. Doesn't say anything, doesn't even smile, just takes the parcel and away he goes."

Thomson nodded, but his thoughts were on the monthly lump sum that went south to who knew where.

"The stuff you're putting out, Billy," his eyes narrowed with curiosity, "where are you storing it and are you using the benzo, like I told you?"

Again, Purvis nodded. "I ordered the Benzocaine through the Internet from a pharmaceutical supplier down south and had it delivered to my grannies address. She's a bit dolly-dimple," he waved a forefinger around his head, "and thought it was a home-brew kit I had ordered," he grinned. "Like you told me, the benzo is the only stuff I've been using to cut the smack and I've been *very* careful to make sure that the stuff is going out as pure as possible. The thing is, Tommo," he felt his mouth suddenly dry, uncertain if he should broach the subject, "would it not maximise the profit if you let me cut the smack using more than just the benzo? Something like," he paused and shrugged, "I don't know, something like wheat flour?"

Thomson's mind flashed back to the instructions in the e-mail from the mysterious partner John and shook his head.

"As long as we put the good stuff out we'll get more customers, Billy," he patiently explained, wondering why the wee shite just couldn't do as he was told without questioning everything. "If the customers want to adulterate the smack even more, then that's down to them, but as long as *we* keep it as pure as we can, we'll make the money and ensure the sales and the stuff *won't* be coming back to us because of its impurity; it'll be a one way transaction every time, do you not see that?"

"Whatever you say big man," replied Purvis with his hands up and then added, "As for storing and cutting it, I've got the keys to a flat that was empty, in a shitty close over in Kiniver Drive. Most of the tenants have been decanted by the council before they start renovating the buildings so there's not a lot of people left living there. Just so that there won't be any bother from the council, what I did was make an application for tenancy."

"You applied for tenancy? But in whose name?" asked the genuinely surprised Thomson.

Purvis smiled. "That mad wee dick, Ian Fagin."

"That halfwit, Chic Fagin's grandson, you mean? For fuck's sake, Billy, he's too stupid to be trusted…"

Purvis raised both hands and interrupting Thomson, grinned widely and said, "But that's the beauty of it Tommo, because he doesn't know. All I did was write an application in his name, using his date of birth in the application and a wee story that he was homeless. I wrote that he was squatting there the now and posted it in to the council. If he gets the tenancy, the papers will be posted out to the Kiniver Drive address. I looked up a website about squatters rights and as long as he's made proper application for the flat, the council won't evict him till a decision has been made whether or not to grant him the tenancy and you know how long these things take; it could be months before we hear anything."

Thomson exhaled and quietly said, "You know I've used the halfwit to run some errands for me? Dropping bits and pieces off, like?"

"Aye, but this is a separate thing, Tommo. He lives with his grandpa, old Chic Fagin and doesn't know about the flat so there's no way it can interfere with anything you use him for, see what I mean?"

With some reluctance, Thomson had to agree and a doubt crossed his mind. Billy Purvis was maybe a wee bit too smart of his own good and might be worth the watching, he decided.

"Anything else?" he finally asked.

"Aye," replied Purvis, biting at his lip, "after I collect the smack and adulterate it with the benzo, I use Fagin to test the smack, give him a MoT like, but he doesn't know where I hide the stuff," he raised his hand to forestall Thomson's protest. "What I do is give him a wee taster every other shipment I collect to make sure it's the real deal and to be fair to the idiot," he pursed his lips, "he's not too bad at deciding on whether I've cut it properly or not. In fact, he usually gives me a one to ten result and then I know if I've cut it properly, you see?"

Thomson stared at him, undecided whether Purvis was taking too many chances by involving his old mentor's grandson in the business, but decided on this occasion he would let the criticism pass. "Right," he slapped a hand down onto each knee then stood up, "make sure that you get that money banked today, wee man."

"Eh, the other thing we spoke earlier about Tommo," Purvis rose to his feet, "the extra smack. I've got customers lined up and ready to go, if you're agreeable?"

Tommo cocked his head and stared at Purvis through squinted eyes. "Get the money banked like I said and I'll think about the additional H, wee man. I'll phone you later this evening, because there's a delivery due and you'll need the post code details to collect it, okay?"

"Okay big man," Purvis grinned and made his way to the door.

He was about to leave the flat when Thomson called to him, "One more thing Billy."

He turned to see Thomson staring blank faced at him.

"We've a good deal going on here and it's making us money, wee man. You're proving to be a bright lad and no doubt got ambitions, but I wouldn't take kindly to it if I thought you were considering overstepping the mark." He quietly smiled and added, "Do you know where I'm coming from?"

Purvis swallowed with difficulty and forcing a grin, nodded. "Count on me, big man. I'll not let you down," and turned towards the stairs.

It was as he sat in his car he began to breathe again, relieving the tightness in his chest and knew if Tommo ever discovered he was skimming smack from the collected kilo's, his life would not be just fucked, it would be over.

From behind the curtain in his lounge, Thomson watched Billy Purvis walking to his yellow Mitsubishi, getting in then driving off. The cocky wee bastard must think I'm stupid, he thought. The telephone complaint he had received from the customer in Duntocher that the delivered smack was a few grams underweight had prompted Thomson to contact three other customers, all who had admitted their deliveries were also slightly underweight, but had been too pleased with the quality of the product to make waves and didn't want to risk falling out with Tommo because of the slight discrepancy that they could easily make up by further adulterating the smack.

But the customers' acceptance of the shortage hadn't satisfied Thomson.

In his mind, Billy wasn't ripping off the customers, Billy was ripping *him* off and that, he viciously banged a fist against the windowsill, was fucking unacceptable!

His eyes narrowed as he saw the small, battered Nissan Micra draw up at the close entrance and he glanced at the clock. He sighed and

turning away from the window, sat down in the swivel chair to wait.
A few moments later he heard the sound of a key in the lock and the
front door opening, the sound of his shopping being dumped onto the
kitchen worktop then his daughter Grace, humming quietly to herself
walked in to the lounge.

She visibly startled when she saw him sitting there, annoyed she
hadn't taken any notice to see if his car had been parked outside and,
her face pale, snapped, "We had an agreement. You would be out for
the hour each day that I was in cleaning the place."

"I had a wee bit of business to attend to," he smiled softly at her, a
smile without humour. Then, his hands extended, he added, "I'll just
quietly sit here and let you get on with what I pay you for, eh?"

She hesitated, her mouth suddenly dry and a sudden urge almost
overtook her; an urge to get out of the flat as quickly as possible.

But Grace was made of sterner stuff and tight-lipped, nodded her
agreement and placing her bag down onto the carpeted floor, fetched
from it a tabard apron she pulled over her head.

He watched her and while the apron was for that brief few seconds
covering her head, his eyes slipped to the firm outline of her breasts
thrusting through the thin material of her blouse and he felt himself
become aroused.

"I'll dust here then Hoover, but you've not to get up from your
chair," she told him, but still the feeling of vulnerability persisted
and tensely uncomfortable that she was in such close proximity to
him.

He nodded with a smile and she left the room to fetch the cleaning
materials and the Hoover.

She returned a minute later and he asked, "How's my wee grandson,
wee Stevie boy then?"

She turned sharply towards him, aware he was goading her. He had
never shown any real interest in her son; never even acknowledged
him as a grandchild and only asked after Steven because he knew it
would upset her.

Ignoring the question, she began to dust the furniture, all the while
aware his eyes never left her.

Her skin crawled because she knew what he was thinking, the
memory as vivid today as it was all those years ago; of his hands on
her, furtively touching and ogling her when she was an adolescent
teenager.

Viciously, she dragged the cloth across the wooden surfaces then that done, unravelled the electric cord from the Hoover and plug in hand, bent over towards the low socket. Later, when she thought of it, she knew it had been a mistake to wear the tight jeans, but had not considered he would be in the flat.

She only realised he had risen from his chair and was standing behind her when she turned. She experienced a feeling of dread like she had never before known. In those seconds of terror, she froze with shock while he bent over towards her. She could feel his hot breath on her neck as he quietly whispered, "Things between us could be good, Grace, if you just think about it."

She didn't know where it came from, but her scream startled even her and as suddenly as he had appeared behind her, he stepped away from her and she ran from the room, shivering and shaking and locked herself in the bathroom.

Distressed, she shook with fear and sat on the toilet bowl. She needed to pee, but would not even consider undoing her jeans let alone dropping her knickers.

He was toying with her, she knew; his little revenge for hating him. But she refused to cry, would not let him see that he had won.

Legs still shaking, she unlocked the bathroom door and listened. She could hear him moving about in the lounge. Her handbag was in there on the floor with her car and house keys in the bag. She had to go back in. Steeling herself, she walked back into the room.

He was stood at the window, looking out and without turning, said, "Are you not going to finish the cleaning, hen? I can't be paying you if you don't finish the job, can I?"

Then he turned towards her and in a low voice, said, "Things could be a lot easier if you come to visit me, Grace. We could have some fun, just you and me, just like we used to have." He smirked and continued, "Or maybe you can bring the wee boy with you if you like. I mean, you wouldn't like *me* to come and visit *you*, Grace, would you now? So, I'll expect that you will want to continue to do my cleaning and fetch my shopping, now. You will, won't you Grace?"

Her stomach tightened with fear at the veiled threat he would interfere in Steven's life. Unable to even look at him, she squatted to lift her handbag from the floor and in a shaky voice, replied, "I'll be in with your shopping and do the cleaning next Tuesday. If I see your car outside," she shook her head, "I'll not come in. We go back to the agreement that you're out of the flat when I'm here. Is that clear?"

"Aye, hen, that's clear," he replied and as she turned towards the door, he added, "but you'll think about my offer, Grace, won't you?" On the way out of the flat and down the close stairs, her mind filled with disgust at his suggestion, her hatred and loathing for her father deepened to an all time low. She knew fine well what his offer entailed, but she was trapped; she had no family and no money to get away. A sob burst from her and her body shaking, she just made it to her car and closed the door before with a gasp the tears erupted from her.

CHAPTER FOUR – Friday evening, 4 July

Sally Nelson, a plastic shopping bag gripped tightly in both hands, wearily used her shoulder to push open the heavy door to the tenement close and shuffled through into the dimly lit corridor. She stared at the stairs and though the flat was just one flight up, wondered why she even bothered coming home.

She already knew what awaited her for it was always the same.

One step at a time, she forced herself to walk towards the stairs and prepared her excuse. He never considered her working day; that going to her shift she had a half hour journey by bus to get there, eight hours of back-breaking labour and the same tiring trip home, but with the added burden of collecting the shopping or some chore or other to perform.

He would wait till she was in the door and then it would begin. Where had she been, who had she spoken with, why wasn't she home earlier?

His jealously and possessiveness was slowly driving her insane.

Yes, he had lost his leg, but that had not been her fault. If he hadn't been drinking then the accident might not have occurred, but she daren't say that to him; not if she wanted to keep her teeth, she wryly thought.

She had stood by him all through the surgery and the lengthy recuperative period, then the fitting of the prosthetic limb that he flatly refused to wear, preferring instead to stomp about the flat with the crutch under his arm, banging it down hard on the floor when he had been drinking because he knew it would annoy the elderly Asian neighbours who lived downstairs.

She stopped on the half landing and leaning against the wall, lowered the bags to the stone floor and took a deep breath.

It was his reluctance to do even the most minor of housework tasks that annoyed her more than anything; not even washing a dish or making a bed. Every bloody thing was left at his backside for her to sort out. It wasn't as if he was *that* helpless.

In the early days she had tried to persuade and cajole him into helping himself, if not helping her, but that only earned her a slap in the mouth for her cheek.

But that wasn't unusual; he had been handy with his hands throughout most of their marriage.

Her older sister Elsie, her only confidante, was constantly trying to persuade her to leave him. "He's not worth it Sally," she would say or "You're not a punch bag for his rage and bad moods," and then there was Elsie's favourite, "*Why* in God's name do you stay with the controlling bastard?"

It was just last month, almost on a whim, he ordered her to stop visiting Elsie as well as banning her sister from visiting their flat, all because Elsie had the temerity to suggest he get up off his arse and *do* something about the house.

Her brow furrowed. Why *did* she stay with him, the question she had asked herself a thousand and one times, yet the answer always eluded her. It wasn't for the boys, for the two of them were long gone from the house now and both settled in New Zealand; Tommy with his English wife and her only grandchild and Neil, living with his Maori girlfriend and working in Auckland. Good boys, she softly smiled to herself, and both anxious that she leave their father and join them there. It wasn't by coincidence that they travelled half way round the world to get away from him. She slowly exhaled and wondered again what was stopping her? Was she afraid of being alone, was that it? She wasn't yet fifty, at least not for another four months, but every day she felt the weight of the years on her. Tricia was forever telling her that she had a good figure and her skin was as smooth as a young woman's, but no matter how she looked, she couldn't avoid being married to a heartless and bullying man.

Was it guilt because of Archie's accident that kept her married to him, she asked herself? But that was his fault, something that *he* caused. She was blameless and had not been in the car with him that night.

Sally didn't hear the door open and startled when he called down to her, "For heavens sake, woman, what are you doing standing there? Come on, get up here. I'm waiting on you making the dinner," then he stomped back into the house.

Tiredly, she bent down and lifting the plastic bags, hurriedly made her way up the stairs to the flat.

Standing in front of the mirror, Bethany Williams sighed and finally gave in. No matter what she did with her wiry brown, shoulder length hair, there was always bits sticking out and no amount of gel or hairclips would keep it down. Damn, she thought, for this evening she really *did* want to impress. Tugging at the green coloured, knee length dress, she knew it was too tight at the hips and stretched across her ample buttocks, but we can't all be Kate Moss, she inwardly sighed, wishing for once God would smile kindly on her and give her the strength to say no to doughnuts and chocolate.

The matching colour high heels were a bloody pain to walk in and she'd always considered her calf's to be too heavy, but dammit, she decided the dress *needed* these shoes and to hell with the pinching pain, for that was what Elastoplast was for.

Deeply inhaling, she let her breath out slowly and stared at her reflection as she adjusted her heavy breasts against the tightness of the dress and grimacing at the slight, but obvious bulge her large nipples made in the material. Finally nodding at the result, she exhaled and decided it was the best she could do. Glancing at the digital clock on the bedside cabinet, she realised she was late and grabbing her handbag from the top of the bed and from under the bed, a pair of flat shoes for driving, she pulled open the door and made her way downstairs.

Her father smiled when he saw her coming down the stairs and said, "You look as pretty as a picture, Beth. Hot date or what?" he teased her.

"Could be, Dad," she grinned at him and then added, "After all, it's Friday night and you didn't think I spent all that time putting on the war paint for another evening at the journalism class, did you?"

He opened the front door and stood to one side to permit her to pass. Grabbing her raincoat from the hook on the wall, she winked and said, "Don't be waiting up just in case I get lucky."

"Aye, well if you do, young lady, don't forget to phone me and make sure he's a millionaire, in his late eighties and with a bad heart condition," he loudly called out after her, watching as she slipped into the driving seat of the old Mini . With the door still ajar, she turned and grinned at him and called back, "Love you, Dad," then slammed the door shut and drove out the driveway into Stock Street before turning onto Neilston Road and heading for Paisley town centre.

"Love you too, darling," her father softly said, wincing slightly at her sudden reckless burst of speed. Nodding his head, he closed the front door and blessed the good fortune that presented him with a daughter like Beth, so that he would not be alone in his twilight years.

The stunning young redheaded woman wearing the short, black cocktail dress and sitting alone on the high stool at the bar in the city centre hotel on Argyle Street, glanced idly at her watch. As usual, Beth was late. The woman caught the eye of the young barman and inwardly smiled, for frankly it wasn't difficult; he had hardly took his eyes off her the half hour she had been waiting. With a perfectly manicured nail, she used her forefinger to lightly tap at her glass for a refill of Chardonnay.

At twenty-nine, Cathy Porteous had commanded a lot attention from men through her life, though to her regret, in the recent past few had stayed with her once they discovered her secret; for Cathy was addicted to cocaine, an addiction she financed by prostitution.

She had fallen into the profession more by chance than design, remembering the first time that evening almost two years previously when sat alone in a hotel bar, slightly tipsy after failing the crucial college exam and feeling sorry for herself; wondering where she was going to find the rent for the flea-bitten pad she had then occupied in the city centre. The first one, the courteous older man she recalled with a smile, had bought her a drink and, she soon realised, mistook her for a prostitute. She was about to lambast him when it occurred to her that maybe she should first inquire what she was worth to him and startled when he had offered her fifty pounds. Pushing her luck, she had negotiated eighty quid from him and been shocked by her boldness; but not so shocked she hadn't delighted in the easy money for just over an hour's work, for casual sex, she inwardly admitted, hadn't been something she wasn't unused to.

The cocaine had come later, a stupid attempt to bond with Keith who she mistakenly thought she loved and loved her, but the relationship had later proven to be so disastrously wrong.

After a few short weeks, the self-destructive Keith was gone from her life, but to Cathy's regret, the addiction to the cocaine remained. As time went on, she realised the potential of her new found occupation; that a suave and sophisticated appearance in the numerous hotel bars around the city attracted the wealthier clients and with her non-taxed earnings, was soon able to afford the plush riverside flat she now rented, but maintained the one strict rule of her profession; all her business was conducted at the hotels and she *never* took a client home with her; or at least, not to date anyway.

As the months passed, Cathy came to realise her earning potential permitted her to not just live a decent and relatively affluent life, but to put money aside. The savings she had so far accumulated were now almost thirty thousand pounds, just short of the money she reckoned she would need as a down payment for permitting her to follow her dream of opening her own business; a chic, drop-in café in the city centre of her native Manchester. Of course, if she *had* offered her services through a pimp, those earnings would have undoubtedly increased, but she preferred to work alone and so far, apart from one scary incident, had not encountered any real threat from a client.

The one time early in her new career she had mistakenly agreed to a night with a drunken punter, the man had attempted to tie her wrists to the bed posts. She had first tried to dissuade him and argued that she wasn't prepared to participate in any kind of sexual bondage. He had ignored her protests and become aggressive, so much so that the frightened Cathy had been forced to strike him across the head with an empty wine bottle and fled the room. For months thereafter, she avoided that hotel and worried the police might be looking for her, but later reasoned he was unlikely to complain about having a prostitute in his room who had assaulted him.

Cathy come to realise that working the hotels as she did she had been very fortunate, for she had not yet come to the attention of the police, but was astute enough to know that her professional life, before the police took an interest in her, was limited. Already, she had been identified as a working girl and barred from soliciting in three of the larger city hotels who now held her photograph and her description, but to protect their business reputation, thankfully had not involved the police.

Walking to wait upon her the barman, no more than twenty she guessed, blushed when she smiled at him, revealing her even, white teeth; the result of an expensive course of orthodontic treatment that cost her a week on her back. After pouring the wine, the barman hesitatingly asked if there was anything else he could do for her. She shook her head and glanced at him as he walked to serve a customer at the other end of the bar and decided he *was* kind of cute. She teased herself, thinking she should have considered his offer by asking if he was willing to pay a hundred quid for an hours ride at her or the discounted two hundred quid for a full night of pleasure at the experienced hands of an woman who was willing to do *all* that he desired, but only if he also footed the bill for the room.

No, she slowly shook her head, and inwardly grinned; *that* might be a little awkward and besides, she sighed; she was already avoiding two further city centre hotels where she thought the security suspected she might be soliciting. Glancing about her, Cathy realised she couldn't afford being excluded from this place too, knowing that the advent of the Commonwealth Games would bring with it the large influx of relatively affluent tourists and it would be foolish to limit her options and her working area.

Her thoughts turned to Beth.

Now *there* is a weird relationship, she thought as she idly toyed with her drink, running her finger up and down the chilled glass. Cathy was acutely aware the younger woman, whom she had first met over two years previously on the college journalism course, idolised her. For some time now, she suspected that the naïve and immature Beth probably hadn't yet decided which gender she preferred. Several times in the recent past, she had almost thought Beth was about to kiss her or touch her and curiously wondered; would she object, laugh it off or, she inwardly smiled, permit her to do so?

Since their friendship had commenced at the college, they had maintained a semi- regular contact and even after Cathy dropped out, though she had never disclosed to Beth the reason nor her current occupation, for she had little doubt the prim and proper Beth, who continued to live with her widowed father in their stuffy little semi in Paisley, would be horrified if she learned of Cathy's lifestyle choice. Since arriving friendless in Glasgow from England to enrol in the course and almost immediately meeting Beth in that first week at the college, she had taken an instant liking to the younger woman and they had become close friends; a friendship she had come to value. Beth, for all her faults she quickly realised, was scrupulously honest and loyal and Cathy was not prepared to risk that friendship, so at least for the time being would continue to maintain her secret.

As far as Beth knew, the fictitious PR job that Cathy devised and confided she was not to discuss with anyone, paid for the plush pad on the waterfront at Broomielaw Quay.

Sipping at her wine, she noticed the two suited men who seated a few yards away, were watching her and whispering to each other. She guessed they were seeking an opportunity to speak and sure enough the younger of the two, a tall heavy set man in his early thirties she thought, stood and approached her.

"Buy you a drink, love?" he asked in a nasally, southern English accent. Here on business, she guessed as she sized the man up and probably an overnight guest; the ideal client.

She was about to reply that maybe if he left his room number, she could visit him later that evening, but then a voice called out, "Yoo-hoo, Cathy," and turning her head towards the doorway saw a slightly breathless Beth striding into the bar, her face shiny with perspiration as though she had been running. Cathy saw the younger man turn slightly towards his companion, whose eyes followed the dumpy girl in the tight fitting green smock dress with the hair resembling a burst straw cushion and the vivid slash of bright red lipstick, walking towards the good looking bird in the short dress and lovely, long legs. With the subtlest shake of his head, the seated man conveyed the message to his colleague that if *he* intended nipping the redhead, no way was the seated man being lumbered with the small, fat bird.

"Sorry," the man graciously and diplomatically said to Cathy, "it seems I'm interrupting your appointment," and with a smile returned to the table.

"Who was that," said Beth, planting a noisy, lipstick smacker on her friend's cheek.

Cathy detected the faintest of body odour from Beth and guessed the younger woman, realising she was late, probably *had* run to the hotel to meet with her.

"Just a Hollywood director asking me to star in his next movie," she joked and then asked, "Drink?", but Beth declined and explained, "I've got my car with me, so I'll just have a coke."

She smiled and narrowing her eyes as though appraising Cathy, gushed, "You *could* be a movie star. You are *sooo* gorgeous!" she drawled.

Cathy was used to men flattering her and aware that yes, she *was* beautiful, but unexpectedly blushed at Beth's compliment and could only smile in response.

Sitting together at the bar, Cathy couldn't ignore the curious glances directed at the ill-matched pair from some of the hotel patrons, who were now filling up the tables.

She certainly wasn't ashamed of being seen with Beth; not at all, for Beth was her closest friend, but neither did she want her own face to become too familiar to the staff and in particular, the hotel security.

Being as lovely as she was, Cathy was acutely aware she tended to attract attention and so suggested to Beth, "Look, honey; why don't we grab a couple of bottles of wine and head back to my place? It's still light. We could kick off our shoes and sit in the balcony with a glass of vino, eh? What do you think?"

Along the bar, the young barman raised his mobile phone to his ear as though listening to a call.

Beth's eyes opened wide. She would like nothing more than to visit the flat again and secretly wished she lived there with Cathy, her stomach knotting in the hope that Cathy might even invite her to spend the night. Her heart leaped at the thought that maybe the older woman had the same feelings for Beth as she had for her. Feelings that Beth was slowly coming to understand and accept were more than just sisterly.

"Yes, let's," she enthusiastically agreed and added, "My car's parked just down the road."

"Right then," Cathy grinned, but didn't fail to notice the look of expectation in her friend's eyes and wondered just what the evening together might bring.

She finished her drink then hooked an arm through the smaller Beth's and together, the two women strode towards the door, unaware that the young barman had used his phone to snap a photograph of Cathy; a photograph of the good looking bird for the intention of showing to his mates on his day off and was already anticipating their jealousy when he would boast that the redhead had chatted him up while he was working.

Mick Thomson sat the laptop on the kitchen table and typed in the address for his favourite teenage porn website. The screen burst into life and he slowly scrolled down the page, savouring the coloured photographs of the young semi-clad and nude women displayed in differing poses. He was a paid member of several pornographic websites, favouring those whose films showed women being subjugated or beaten as they were sexually abused. The machine beeped and a small window opened in the corner of the screen to alert Thomson that an e-mail message had arrived.

He opened a new page on the screen and carefully typed in the e-mail address and password that he now knew so well and opened the message.

Thomson read that John, or whatever the fucker's name really was he thought, confirmed the money had been paid into the three accounts.

"Just as well," Thomson growled to himself, for if it had not then wee Billy Purvis would be getting a knock on his door and his balls booted.

He continued to read the e-mail that informed him at about ten o'clock on Sunday evening, a lorry described in the message would be parking up for the night in a lay-by over in Kelvin Avenue in the Hillington Industrial Estate. Thomson knew the location, having sent Purvis there twice already in the previous month. The driver, the message continued, would have a delivery for Thomson; four packs of fruit juice that Thomson knew was code for heroin.

He re-read the message again then pressed the 'reply' button and laboriously typed a return message, that he would get the stuff put out and asking when the next shipment would be, already knowing what John's response would be.

Sitting at his desk in his house in Kirkintilloch, Patrick McLaughlin slowly smiled when he read Thomson's reply.

The chancer was at it again.

Quickly he responded, informing Thomson that when the current shipment of fruit juice was sold and when 'John's' payment was in the three accounts, Thomson would receive a further e-mail with details of a new shipment and then pressed the send button. He didn't wait for a response, but concluded the message 'John' and closed the computer down. So far so good, he sighed almost with relief.

Since setting up the operation in late February, the money he was earning from the drugs had not only saved his business, but he was actually able to save a considerable sum in the separate bank accounts; accounts that Gloria his wife would never learn of and therefore could never squander.

He grinned to himself. The deal with the Turks was so far going very nicely; the money that was the profit from the sale of the drug was divided up with his cut being transferred into the three accounts; Thomson taking his own slice and also arranging that the cash payment for the supplied heroin was delivered by one of Thomson's cronies to the Turks courier.

He sat back and smiled at his own cleverness; the beauty of the scheme being that, because he was never hands on with either the heroin or the cash, if the police arrested Thomson and his cronies he could not be identified and would be in the clear.

His only involvement in the scheme was the e-mail address he shared with the Turks that enabled him to receive information regarding the delivery of the product that he in turn shared with Thomson who by return e-mail, told him when he could inform the Turks that their payment was ready to be collected. McLaughlin simply typed in a time and post code that meant nothing to him.

He sighed, thinking it would have been so much simpler if the Turks had agreed to his scheme that the money be forwarded via a bank account, just as he collected his own payments, but their distrust of the banks and their fondness for hard cash cancelled out that idea.

"Pat, are you coming to bed or what?" his wife called from the doorway.

He turned to stare at her. Even in her early forties, Gloria still retained her beauty. He sighed and then nodded, "Be up in ten minutes love. I'm just finishing some business here."

She turned to go then stopped. "Oh, I meant to say, there was a phone call earlier this evening from that policeman, the man at your golf club; something about the Rotary. I said you would give him a call tomorrow, if that's all right?"

"Yes, that's fine," he again nodded and watched as she closed the door.

Superintendent Burns. Alex. He smiled and thought about the younger man.

Alex was proving to be a useful contact, a very useful man indeed.

Across the city, Mick Thomson returned to the website and again peered at the pornographic photographs of the young women, but his thoughts turned to yesterday's visit from Grace and he grinned, remembering grabbing her and how he had considered having some fun with her. He had always wanted her, recalling her slim figure and prominent breasts, wanted to mount her and punish her for ignoring him all these years. He grew angry at her, the way she ignored him; her stuck up attitude towards him. His throat tightened as he imagined what he would do to her, how he would abuse her naked body and he felt himself become aroused.

His brow narrowed and then he remembered the phone call from earlier in the afternoon, the old mate who wanted Tommo to collect an outstanding drug debt of almost three grand from some old bird that lived in Kinfauns Drive, suggesting it would be a quick five hundred quid for Tommo, if he could manage it.

Thomson, his mind still filled with visions of how he would sexually punish Grace, drew a deep breath and gently closed the lid of the laptop and decided now might be a good time to collect the woman's debt.

Grinning evilly, he wondered if the woman looked anything like Grace.

Detective Sergeant Des Brown signed off work just after seven that evening at Govan CID, tiredly got into his trusty old Mondeo saloon, drove out of the back yard at Helen Street police station and headed towards his parent's house in Drumchapel to collect his son Paul.

As always, Des was grateful for the latitude his DI permitted him, both with his single parent status and running the kid's football team. In turn, the tacit agreement was he readily made himself available when some inquiry or other cropped up or a lack of resources required him to make a sudden change of shift. When that happened as it frequently did, his parents Eddie and Agnes and to his eternal gratitude, were always on hand to step in and mind his son Paul, though he secretly believed they loved every minute of it, for fourteen year old Paul was a gentle and lovely young lad.

Just like his father, Agnes would beam.

Driving through the Clyde Tunnel, Des's thoughts turned to yesterday's brief meeting with Grace Thomson and he smiled. He had no right to be even thinking about the young woman, but he sighed with pleasure as he remembered her good looks and slim figure and realised it was hard not to.

Since the break-up four years previously of his marriage to Margo, he had not been in any kind of relationship, had not even been out with a woman though a couple of times, he exhaled, he'd had to field tentative offers of a date from one of the more mature secretaries at Govan who he suspected had a keen interest in him and was, he had heard it whispered, looking for a new daddy for her two weans.

As he drove his thoughts turned again to Grace Thomson and of course, he *knew* who father was. Hell didn't everybody, but he had also heard from some of the parents of Des's football kids that *Miss* Thomson, he inwardly grinned at her admission, had nothing to do with Mick Thomson.

Though Des had never any personal or professional dealings with the man known throughout Drumchapel as Tommo, like his detective colleagues he was privy to the monthly confidential CID bulletins whose local intelligence information suggested Thomson was currently suspected of illegal money-lending as well as being suspected of acting as an enforcer for the local drug dealers and also being involved in the distribution of drugs in the Drumchapel area. Not a nice man at all, inferred the bulletins.

At last he turned into the driveway of his parent's modest former council semi-detached house in Airgold Drive, not far from Paul's High School.

Getting out of the car, Des took a few seconds to admire his father's neat and tidy garden, Eddie's pride and joy since his early retirement from the railways.

The door opened before he got to it and his brow furrowed at his mother's concerned face.

"What's wrong, has something happened to…"

Agnes held a firm hand up to cut him short. "Paul's fine," she said to his relief, "but you'd better come in, son. There's been a wee incident at the school. Well, outside the school actually," she added as she stood to one side to permit Des to pass her by and then closed the door.

She followed him into the lounge where Des saw his son sitting on the couch with Eddie, the dirty dishes evidence of their Friday night treat of fish and chips sitting on the low table in front of them. Eddie reached for the remote control and switched off the television.

The first thing Des saw was the swelling and blackening under Paul's left eye.

Forcing himself not to react, he sat on the comfortable single chair opposite Paul and Eddie and said, "Look's like you've been in the wars there, son. Care to tell your old man what happened?"

Paul turned to stare at Eddie who rose to his feet and beckoning Agnes, said, "We'll get the kettle on hen. Let these two guys have a wee minute together, eh?"

Des's eyes followed his parents to the door and when it closed behind them, he turned towards Paul and with his hands clasped on his lap, softly smiled at his son.

"So, what happened?"

It took a hesitant Paul almost ten minutes to tell his father what had been going on. It had started over two weeks previously with the snide comments, then when he was moving between classrooms, the odd push and shove that today, culminated in the bigger, stronger and year older youth grabbing Paul outside the school and punching him to the face.

Because, the red-faced lad finally admitted, someone had told him that Paul's father was a police officer.

"Who is this guy, Paul?"

Paul hesitated and Des saw his son was clearly embarrassed at having to admit he was unable to fight back against the larger bully.

"Look, there's no shame in this, wee man," he softly continued, "Sometimes we have to step back from a fight that we know we won't win. This guy isn't a hard man; we both know he's a bully. If he was a hard man, he wouldn't be picking on a smaller guy, now would he?"

"You're not going to tell the school are you? I don't want to be called a grass," Paul's face displayed the panic of teenage peer pressure.

"No," Des shook his head and in a calm voice, continued, "but I will have a word with his dad. There's no way round that, son. This has happened and unless I speak with this guy's father, then what happened today to you will continue to happen. Do you not see that?"

Paul, his head lowered, nodded for he was astute enough to realise that his dad was correct, that something had to be done or his life at school would be miserable for as long as he attended there.

Quietly, he replied, "His name's Cole McCormick. He stays with his mum and dad in the last close at Ladyloan Avenue on the corner with Kilcloy Avenue. I don't know the number though."

"Don't you worry about that," said Des, rising to his feet. He stared down at the seated Paul and added with a smile, "Look son, don't be worrying about getting a black eye. I've had more than my fair share in *and* out of the ring," he forced a grin for his son's benefit. "In fact, what happened to you is the *exact* same thing that happened to me and your granddad sorted it out, just as I'm going to sort this out by speaking with Mister McCormack, okay?"

"Honest?" Paul replied, his eyes widening at Des's admission.

"The very same thing," Des nodded, "so switch on the tele and I'll be back in half an hour then we'll head up the road, okay?"

"Okay Dad," grinned a relieved Paul.

In the hallway outside, Des refrained from grinning at his parents who had quite obviously been anxiously listening at the door.

"You heard?" he asked Eddie, who nodded. "If he asks, I went through the same thing with you," said Des and saw his father nod in agreement at his son's white lie.

In the car, Des gritted his teeth with anger at the moron who had bullied his son and starting the engine, softly said under his breath, "Right then, Kilcloy Avenue."

It took Des but a few minutes to drive the short distance to Kilcloy Avenue. Switching off the engine, he took several deeps breaths to calm himself, then exiting the car, glanced up at the close in the tenement building. Head down he walked along the narrow path between the overgrown hedges and pushed open the door where his nostrils were immediately assailed by the smell of fried food, damp and other odours he didn't care to guess at.

The graffiti scarred one door in the ground flat had no name and he couldn't hear any noise from within. He trudged up the stairs and discovered the only flat on the first floor seemed to be occupied, but the name on the door wasn't McCormick.

It was when Des was passing the rusted bicycle and discarded washing machine on the landing between the first and second floors that he heard the muffled shouting.

Again, he took a deep breath, calming his anger and arrived at the door. The cheap, plastic nameplate said 'McCormick', but clearly the bell on the door frame wasn't working, if the electric wiring hanging from it was any indication, so Des hammered with his fist on the door. Still, the shouting from within continued unabated and he hammered a second and third time before he heard a man's voice shout, "That was the door, somebody get it, pronto."

He listened to the sound of something falling over then the door was dragged open.

A sullen faced youth aged about fifteen and a good six inches taller than Des's son, Paul stood staring curiously at him. He guessed this was Cole McCormick.

The youth slurred, "What?" just as a man's voice from inside the house called out, "Who the fuck is it, Cole?"

That settled it then, thought Des. This was the bully-boy from the school and he quietly said, "Cole, ask your father to come to the door please."

"Cole!" demanded the aggressive sounding voice again, "Who's at the door?"

"Who are you mister?"

"I'm Paul Brown's father, so like I said, ask your dad to come to the door, son."

He saw some hesitancy in Cole's face, also perhaps a little fear and watched as the youth turned his head and shouted, "Da, it's somebody for you. It's that guy's Da, the one I battered at school the day."

Des inhaled and kept his cool, resisting the urge to reach in and grab the wee shite and throttle him.

Over Cole's shoulder, he saw a lounge door open and a heavy-set, unshaven, balding man about six foot tall, wearing a stained tee-shirt, black training trousers and shoeless, stride to the door. Without looking at Des, he pulled Cole back by the shoulder and snarled, "You! Get to fuck to your room. I'll deal with this."

McCormick watched as his son walked along the narrow hallway and disappeared through a door that was slammed, then with his face displaying his belligerence, turned to Des and said, "What the *fuck* do you want, coming to my do at this time of the night?"

Des returned McCormick's stare and in an even voice, replied, "Your son Cole has been bullying my boy and…"

"If you can't teach your boy to fight for himself," he snarled, then raising his hand and pointing a forefinger, took an aggressive step towards Des and added, "don't fucking come whining to me, okay?"

"I don't think you understand, Mister McCormick," Des maintained the even voice. "The reason I'm here is that your lad is far too young for me to deal with so every time he looks at my Paul the wrong way," then without any warning, stepped forward inside McCormick's raised hand and with an uppercut punch, connected to the heavier man's jaw. The blow literally took McCormick off his feet and sat him back onto his fat arse. Des, his face white with rage and his fists visibly clenched, took a further step towards the shocked and dazed man and added, "I'll not come to your door for your *son*, you bastard! I'll come to your door for you! Deal with your boy or *I'll* fucking sort *you* out, understand?"

McCormick, open-mouthed with fear in his eyes, could only stare at the wiry Des and slowly nodded.

Des stepped back and this time it was he who pointed the forefinger, telling McCormick, "You're warned, ya bastard!" then turned on his heel and made his way downstairs.

A moment later, sitting in the driving seat of his Mondeo, Des's body began to shake as the adrenalin kicked in. He glanced at the grazed knuckles on his right hand and waited for a further couple of minutes till his body settled down. Then, with a slow grin, he started the engine and drove towards his parent's house to fetch his son and take him home.

CHAPTER FIVE - Saturday 5 July

Catriona MacDougall arrived at Drumchapel office just after eight that morning, a little early for her shift. The DI's campaign of vindictiveness had already begun, changing her from late shift to an early shift that Saturday without prior notice and causing her to cancel a planned lunch with her husband, Gus.

Locking her pride and joy, her Audi car she made her way into the station and smiling at the bar officer, learned the two detectives on night shift duty were still out attending to a call. She nodded in acknowledgement and climbed the stairs to the CID office on the first floor and pushed open the door.

The young black man wearing the navy blue suit sat behind a desk nervously jumped to his feet when she entered the room, startling her.

"Hello," she smiled a little uncertainly at him, "can I help you?"

"Constable Munro, Ma'am," he replied, "I'm here to start my secondment as an acting Detective Constable. I was told yesterday by my Inspector to report here for late shift, Ma'am."

Cat dumped her handbag on her desk and strolled over to the table that served as the tea bar and called over her shoulder to him, "Well, Constable Munro, two things you need to know. The first thing is I'm not Ma'am, I'm Catriona MacDougall, but you can call me Cat, okay?"

Munro smiled and asked, "And the second thing?"

"If you're in before me, get the kettle on, sweetheart. I'm usually gagging for a cuppa when I arrive."

"Yes Ma'am, eh, I mean, Cat."

"Right, do you want a tea or a coffee?"

Now visibly relaxing, he walked over to join her at the table and asked for a black tea, then said, "No pun intended," and grinned at her.

His infectious grin made her smile and the small joke caused her to think he was completely at ease with his colour.

A few minutes later, sat at her desk with Munro sitting nearby, she sipped at her tea and said, "So, what's your story then, Colin? What service you got, what's your background and why exactly are you here, apart from the obvious?"

The next ten minutes was spent with him telling her he was twenty-eight with almost five year's service, most of it served at the Alexandria police station, had an interest in joining the CID, was single and lived with his parents and brother in Dumbarton.

"Dad was a US sailor based at the Holy Loch, met my mum and when his time was up, he stayed and they got married. Apparently it caused a bit of a stooshie at the time, him being a black guy and that. My big sister arrived first, then me and then my wee brother two years later. She's married now and living up in Glasgow and my brother is a fireman in the base at Faslane."

"So your Dad was a nuclear submariner, then?"

"Ah, not really," he grinned, "he was a cook based on shore, but it stood him in good stead because he and my mum now run a café in Dumbarton. If you're ever down that way I'll get you a polis discount," he smiled.

"Have you met or spoken with the DI yet?"

Munro shook his head. "My Inspector phoned him yesterday and all I was told is that I was to report here and neighbour you, Cat."

Well at least I'll have someone to talk to she thought, for she had believed she was working the early shift alone.

"Right," she inhaled, "here's the plan then, Colin. You nip down to the uniform bar and check if there's any crime reports outstanding while I…" but didn't finish because she was interrupted by the desk phone at her elbow ringing.

"Cat," said the female bar officer, her voice hushed as though she didn't wish to be overheard. "There's a guy in here wants to speak with the CID, a George McCormick. He says he wants to make a complaint about a police officer. Oh and Cat, watch yourself with this bastard. He's been through the cells here a couple of times for domestic assault. A right devious swine, so he is."

Cathy Porteous, barefooted and naked beneath a light blue coloured dressing gown wrapped about her, stood on her balcony with a mug of coffee cradled in her hands. Through the open patio doors, she could hear Beth in the kitchen noisily singing along to an ABBA song playing on the radio.

Staring into the River Clyde, Cathy slowly exhaled and worriedly shook her head. How the hell she had let it get out of hand, she would never know. Perhaps it was the wine she thought, that had lessened her inhibitions or maybe even, as she had long suspected, she had an inherent desire for the attention of another woman.

She heard Beth pad through the lounge in her bare feet and come out onto the balcony then stand behind her, but didn't turn round when she wrapped her arms about Cathy. Slipping her hand under the dressing gown, Beth gently took hold and massaged Cathy's left breast, then snuggled into her slim back before reaching up to kiss the nape of her neck.

"Do you want some toast?" she asked, eager to please.

"No, I'm fine thanks," replied Cathy, her eyes closing and preparing herself for what she knew she must do.

Sensing something might be wrong, Beth asked, "Are you all right? Did I do something wrong?"

Cathy balanced the mug on the balcony rail and disengaging herself from Beth's grasp, slowly turned to face her. "No," she smiled, anxious to explain, but uncertain how to do so without hurting her younger friend. "Look, Beth. Last night was…different," she softly said. "Definitely a first for me and you too, I'm sure." She hesitated and continued, "You and me, we're the *best* of friends…"

"With benefits," grinned Beth, then the grin slowly died when she realised that Cathy was no longer smiling. Her eyes narrowed as she stared up at Cathy. "You think, what we did…you think it was a mistake?"

"Yes, Beth. Last night *was* a mistake," then granted the younger woman a warm smile when she added, "a *hugely* enjoyable mistake, but still a mistake."

Beth stood back and folding her arms, her eyes downcast, replied, "Well, I didn't think it was a, mistake. I thought…" she hesitated, unwilling to continue.

"What did you think, Beth? Did you think that because we had sex together," she paused and inhaled, really not wishing to hurt her friend and instead said, "Because we made love, that everything would be great, that you and I would be a couple together? Look, honey," she shook her head, "You know that I value your friendship, I really do, but that's what I want from you; your friendship. You must realise that, Beth?"

The younger woman flinched as though she had been struck, her eyes filling with tears and swallowing now with difficulty. Unable to speak, she turned away and stumbled through the flat, desperate now to collect her clothes and leave as quickly as possible, get away from what was becoming the biggest disappointment of her young life.

"Beth!" Cathy called after her, her stomach churning and realising that she had made a complete fuck-up and that her honest stupidity had probably lost her the one true friend she'd ever had.

In the bedroom, the weeping Beth was struggling to pull her dress up about her waist when Cathy stepped through the door.

"Beth," she stood in the doorway and pleaded with her hands outstretched, but the younger woman ignored her, too intent on running away from her shattered dream.

"Beth!" said Cathy, more insistently and striding towards her, forced her arms around the weeping girl who first struggled, then collapsed sobbing against her.

They stood like that for a few moments, gently swaying together and holding each other close, then Cathy stroked the wiry hair from Beth's face and unable to help herself bent down to kiss away the salty tears. Their breathing became a little laboured as Cathy's lips found Beth's.

The dress slowly slipped from Beth's waist to the floor.

Cathy hesitated and knowing she was about to compound her earlier mistake then almost resignedly shrugged the dressing gown off her shoulders and naked, stepped out from it, sighing when Beth's trembling fingers stroked her breast then slowly closed her eyes and bent her head back as Beth's eager mouth found Cathy's suddenly erect nipple.

Des Brown grinned and loudly applauded when the referee blew his whistle to signal the game taking place in the grounds of St Joseph's primary school was over.

The lads cheered wildly, their arms raised and punching the air, delighted with their six-nil trouncing of the opposition. Hugging and back-slapping each other, they made their way towards their coach. Still clapping loudly, Des cried out, "Well done, good game lads," then turned to shake hands with the other team's coach who he vaguely knew was the janitor of the defeated school.

He was aware of a figure beside him and turned to see Grace Thomson smiling at him. "Thought I'd come and pick Steven up, if that's all right? I'd promised to take him for a McDonalds after the game," she explained.

Her short, auburn hair pinned back for her face with pink coloured clips, a matching coloured scarf tied loosely about her neck, hands stuffed into the pockets of a short, black coloured warm jacket and wearing the same tight jeans and knee length black leather boots, Des could only stare at what he saw as a vision of loveliness.

"Eh, if that's all right with you, Des?" she repeated, her eyes narrowing and wondering why he didn't reply.

"Aye, yes, of course," he finally found his voice, the boys now crowding around him, their faces upturned and seeking the praise they knew must come.

"Ah, let me get these hooligans organised first, Miss Thomson…"

"Grace," she smiled at him as Steven threw his arms about her waist, eager for her attention and crying, "Mum! I scored a goal! Did you see me Mum?"

"Grace," he returned her grin, then almost with relief, busied himself, shaking hands and rubbing heads before sharply ordering, "Right lads, grab your gear and onto the bus with you."

"Mum," Steven pulled at her arm, "can I go on the bus with the guys? Please Mum? Please?" he begged.

Des knew that with the euphoria of winning the match, young Steven would want to be with his teammates on the trip back to the school and celebrate the drubbing they had inflicted on the opposition, to again exalt in the glory of his goal and be praised and back-slapped; to be part of the team, to be one of the lads.

Grace hesitated, but caught Des's eye and clearly, she saw he agreed that Steven travel back on the bus. She couldn't know that when the short fifteen minute journey was completed, it would give Des the opportunity to again be and speak with her, if only for a short time. Nor could *he* know that at the previous evening's fundraiser in the school, Grace had engaged the old janny Willie McKee in conversation and from him learned that no, there wasn't a Missus Brown, that as far as Willie was aware Des Brown, "…good man that he is," added Willie with a nod of his head, had divorced a number of years ago when young Paul was a pupil at the school and that Des was a single parent, "…just like you, Gracie."

She worried that perhaps old Willie had suspected why she was asking about Des and her chest had tightened at that news that the quiet and courteous Des Brown might be…she had hesitated, too embarrassed to even consider the word; available?

Helping out during the evening at the school had passed in a blur, her thoughts filled with 'what if?'

She had hardly slept during the night, wondering was she being foolish or naive even. Besides, she tried to tell herself; how the hell could I even *broach* the subject let alone tell him I have an interest in him and self critically wondered why would I even consider that *he* might have an interest in *me*. Was she simply convincing herself that his smile and courtesy was some sort of curiosity in her, mistaking his curiosity for attraction?

A sudden dreadful thought occurred to her. She knew from Steven that Des was a police officer. Could it be that when he looked at her, he thought of Michael Thomson?

She didn't need another reason to hate her father, but her stomach had lurched that she might be identified as someone not to be associated with because of who she was; Thomson's daughter.

She had finally dozed off and got out of bed with a headache and made her decision. She would deliver Steven to the school for his football match and leave him with his pals without speaking to Des. Later, she would arrive at the game with the pretence of taking Steven from the match for a McDonalds even though she privately disapproved of fast food restaurants, but on this one occasion…

Now, here she was agreeing that she would follow the mini-bus back to the school and collect Steven there. It was as she suspected, Des merely saw her as Steven's mother, a parent whose child he coached in the school football team. Bitterly disappointed she could only nod her agreement, but as she turned away, Des called her back.

"Look," he began, his hands outstretched, "the wee man's dead keen to travel with his mates. You can guess he's on a bit of a high now after he scored his goal. Well," he nodded to the excited boys now boarding the bus and grinned, "they all are. But I was wondering..."

She held her breath, staring at him.

He tensed, preparing himself for the knock-back and inhaling, said again, "I was wondering if you might like to travel back on the bus with us. When I've dropped the kids off and parked the bus up in the school, I have to drive past here anyway to get home and I can drop you and Stevie back at you car, if you like?"

"Yes," she smiled happily at him, a feeling almost of relief sweeping through her, "I'd like that."

Dick Smith, wearing a tight fitting pale blue coloured Levi denim shirt that didn't quite hide his expanding waistline, used a hand to finger comb through his thinning blonde highlighted fair hair and gave the young dark haired barmaid a wide grin. When she turned to fetch a clean wine glass from the shelf behind her, he leaned slightly forward to cast an approving eye over her shapely backside in her short, tight fitting, black skirt. What Dick couldn't see was the teenager watching him in the small mirror beside the till or guess at the shudder of disgust running through her; that an old pervert like him was paying her *that* kind of attention.

"I'll have a pint if you're buying," said the quiet voice behind him. Turning, he continued to grin, but this time at his former police neighbour, Tom Fraser.

"Thought you were travelling in with Harry?" asked Dick, reaching for his glass of red wine from the barmaid and requesting she also pull a pint of Tennents lager for Tom.

Older by two years, Tom had joined the job within a week of Dick and with their new mate, Harry McInnes, been posted to the old Gorbals office as raw probationary cops, coincidentally winding up on the same shift to replace three cops who were suspended and later sacked for theft; caught when they attended a sudden death of a pensioner and later found to be sharing the money they had discovered secreted in the old man's house.

It took all of an hour for them to realise that by posting them together, some comic at personnel must have thought it a great joke, for the three new cops almost immediately came to be referred throughout the station as Tom, Dick and Harry.

Thrown together, the three young bachelors had quickly become friends and though their police careers took them on different paths, continued their friendship through their thirty years service to retirement.

Now here they were, regularly meeting on the first Saturday of each month in the Counting House pub, the popular venue just off George Square in Glasgow, for two or three drinks, a bar meal and to chew the fat for a couple of hours.

Tom shook his head. "Harry phoned me this morning, said he was getting the bus in, that he would be a wee bit late. Said he had something to do at Pitt Street."

Of the three, Harry was the only one who after completing his thirty years service, returned to the police to work as a civilian Force

Support Officer, an FSO, while his former neighbours were now fully retired.

"So, what you been up to this last month?" asked Tom, sipping at his pint as he espied then quickly made his way towards an empty table in the bustle of the pub, getting there seconds before a group of giggling teenage girls.

Dick, with some difficulty, squeezed his wallet into the back pocket of his jeans and sat awkwardly down, his eyes following the pert bums of the young women as they moved towards a nearby table.

Trying to repress a laugh, it seemed to Tom that Dick's jeans were at least two sizes too tight and that if there *was* in any danger of him getting a hard-on, his balls would likely explode.

He smiled and nodding to Dick, said, "Do you not think you should be getting some clothes that fit? You're like a refugee from an Oxfam shop there, Dick. Look at you," he joked. "One, you need a haircut and two, you're dressed like a young thing. You should consider acting your age."

"What are you, my father?" Dick snorted. "Look, pal, you know the old saying. You're only as young…"

"…as the women you feel. Yeah, heard it," smiled Tom, sipping at his pint.

He knew he was wasting his time. Dick treated all women like a challenge and would go to the grave pursuing them. His libido and predilection for women, Tom imagined, would keep a roomful of psychologists in conference for a week. Young or old, tall or small, fat or thin; Dick was irrepressible in his pursuit of the fairer sex and that pursuit had so far cost him two marriages and God knew how many relationships.

The first marriage to Alison, with whom he had his daughter Melanie and from whom he was completely ostracised, folded in a messy divorce when Alison caught him cheating on her with Joan. Then, he suppressed a smile at the memory, the ink on the marriage certificate had hardly dried when the short lived marriage to Joan ended a few weeks after their honeymoon when *she* caught Dick with…now there's a thing, he thought. I can't recall that blonde woman's name, but reasoned it didn't really matter because there had been so *many* bloody women in and out of Dick's life, before, during and after his marriages.

Now, with a goodly portion of his pension and most of his final lump sum awarded to his former wives, Dick lived alone in a rented ground floor, two-bedroom flat in Cowan Street in the west end of Glasgow.

It also didn't escape both Tom and Harry's notice that at this, their monthly get-together, when it came to the drinks order Dick invariably missed a round, but neither man would ever mention it for old pals just didn't comment on things like that.

"How is your wife Sheila these days?" asked Dick, his head swivelling as yet another attractive woman passed by their table.

Tom, watching him, sighed and nodded his head before replying, "She's well, thanks. She's helping out today in Kelvingrove Park at a Yorkhill Children's Charity fun run. You know what she's like, Dick. She *always* needs to get involved in something. If it's not the Yorkhill thing, it's the local cancer research shop or some do-gooder event. It's all to do with not seeing the grandkids," he slowly shook his heads. "Since our lad moved with his wife and two weans down to that new job in England, Sheila's had time on her hands and has to do *something* or it would drive her mad. She's never really been a stay at home housewife and since most of the neighbours round about us in the Crookston area are coffin dodging, she's become a one-woman home help and taken it upon herself to feed half the street *an*d it's costing me a bloody fortune in groceries," he sighed.

He loved his two mates like brothers, but a sudden thought of that time, of Sheila as she was two years ago, still caused a chill to run down his spine and he inwardly regretted not taking them into his confidence.

"Still keeping up with the Jones's too, is she?"

"Oh, aye," smiled Tom. "I thought about hiding her flexible friend, but since she had to give up work because ..." he hesitated as he saw Dick was only half listening and then said, "Well, you can guess the rest. It's just my bloody luck I'm always giving in to her." He shook his head and then continued. "She insisted we get a new car a few weeks ago and she's been looking at the four by four Lexus range. I ask you, what the hell do I need a new car for," he growled and shook his head. "That and I got in the other day from my jog to find a conservatory salesman sitting with her having a cuppa and my dining table covered in travel brochures too."

"At least you've *got* a dining table. I eat my dinner on my lap."

"Sorry, Dick. I know sometimes it must be a struggle for you."

"Sometimes, Tom?" he stared at his friend. "Huh, every bloody *day's* a struggle." He shook his head and exhaled. "What, with the money deducted from my pension to pay the gruesome twosome, it doesn't leave me much to see the month through. I'm so sick of penny pinching. I'll never get another bird on what's left of my pension," he moaned.

"Have you thought about getting a wee job?"

He stared curiously at Tom. "Think about it," he replied. "Who do you know that will hire an ex-cop at my age? Remember, I was CID most of my working days, passed through the Serious Crime Squad, a spell with the Branch, three divisional CID's, but what's *that* worth to an employer? Absolutely fuck all."

"What you moaning about, you irritating git?" said the voice behind him as a hand was slapped down onto Dick's shoulder.

Both he and Tom glanced up to see Harry towering over the table. A formidable figure at a little over six foot one and carrying a stone more than his fighting weight, the cheery face of Harry McInnes was topped by a monk's crown of coal black hair. "So, who's getting me a drink then?" he glanced at both his friends then drew up a chair and sat down.

"Lager?" asked Dick, getting to his feet.

"That's my poison," smiled Harry and turning back towards Tom, continued, "What's going on then? You guy's ordered food yet?"

"No, waited for you," smiled Tom, sipping at his pint. "What was so important to get you to call into Pitt Street on a Saturday then?"

Harry slowly shook his head. "Well, you know where I work," he began in a low voice.

"Yeah, intelligence or something like that you said."

Harry nodded and with a glance about him and a lowered voice, continued, "There's a bit of a flap on in the recent months. Some bugger has been importing good quality smack up from London and flooding the market, so much so that the price has dropped and it's being made available to more than the usual number of junkies. My lot are getting it in the neck from the management because we're not sighted on where the stuff is going to, up here. We know that the source of dispersal is Drumchapel, but..."

"Here you go old pal," said Dick, handing a frosted glass of lager to Harry and sitting down. "I took the liberty of ordering food for us;

three fish and chips all round, if that's all right? It was a meal deal, two for the price of one and we can split the bill three ways, if that's okay with you guys?"

"Fine by me," agreed Tom, though could have done without fish again, but acutely aware that the cheap deal was likely all Dick could afford at the minute.

"And me too," added Harry with the subtlest of glances at Tom.

"So, what's the *craic* then? What we talking about?" asked Dick.

"I was telling Tom here that the city is being flooded with smack and we don't have a bloody clue who is dealing the stuff up here."

"Oh, right. How about your job, Harry?" asked Dick. "Still having problems with your supervisors?"

Harry shrugged. "It's more about me than them, I suppose. I don't mind the job so much, but these young cops today," he wearily shook his head. "They spend a couple of years on the street then they are encouraged to get promoted and find office jobs. I might have the savvy up here," he tapped the side of his head with a stubby finger, "but of course most of the villains I dealt with when I was a DS are either in jail, dead or no longer of real interest to the polis. It's the up and coming young team that my lot are interested in. Kind of brackets me in the old farts division," he smiled.

"Can't buy experience though, Harry," replied Dick with a shake of his head.

"How are you coping with the computers?" asked Tom. "The last time we met here, you said you were having a problem with them."

"Aye, well I'm slowly getting used to the new systems and the programmes Tom, but I have to admit," he shook his head, "I'm not half as fast as the guys I work with. It's one thing *knowing* the neds and their ways, but quite another trying to convince the management that it's *not* computers the Intelligence Department needs; it's somebody out there, turning the neds over and collecting the information. Of course, I'm too old for that kind of business these days and besides, it's a cop's job; not for a civilian like me to go and meet touts in pubs."

"But your mob is still on top of what's going on I suppose?" asked Dick.

"Most of the time," sighed Harry, but then his face turned sombre. "That said, a lot of the stuff that crosses my desk bursts my arse, I can tell you. Bloody drug dealers living in fancy detached, four bedroom houses and driving big cars and never worked a fucking day in their miserable lives; never paid a penny in tax and *they're* the ones rolling in cash."

"Here we go then, three fish and chips gentlemen," said the young waitress, smiling as she balanced the plates on her forearms.

The three men shuffled their drinks round the table to permit her to lay the food down and when with a smile she politely asked if there was anything else, Tom quickly forestalled Dick's cheesy response by thanking her, while Harry merely smiled knowingly at Tom's quick intervention.

"So," Tom turned towards Harry, "you were saying?"

"Oh, it's nothing I haven't said before. I just get so sick of reading intelligence reports about the amount of money that these bastards are making while I'm…" he stopped and then said, "Let's just eat, eh?"

"How is your Rosie doing these days?" asked Dick, wolfing down his food.

"It's Rosemary, you ignorant git. You know fine well she hates being called Rosie," sighed Harry, picking his way through his chips.

"Hates me as well, if I remember correctly," replied Dick.

Aye and hates me too, thought Tom, but kept that comment to himself and instead diplomatically said, "She is doing all right then?" Tom asked.

"Just the usual moans and whines about everything in her miserable life, but mostly complains about me," replied Harry, placing his cutlery down onto the plate and the half eaten meal. "Why have they got that and we haven't," he parodied his wife. "What did I do wrong to deserve a failure like you, was her latest complaint," his eyes narrowed. "Honestly, I just can't seem to do anything right in her eyes."

It was obvious to his friends that Harry was a bit depressed. Tom risked a quick glance at Dick who discreetly nodded that Tom ask what was happening in their friends life.

"Are you telling us there's a problem Harry? With you and Rosemary, I mean?"

Harry took a quick gulp of his pint and replied, "There has been a problem in our marriage for a long time now, Tom and don't you two dare pretend you didn't know."

An awkward silence fell between the three of them as Tom and Dick waited for Harry to explain.

"The truth of the matter is that the marriage died a long time ago." The admission he was about to make wasn't easy, but he trusted these two guys better than brothers. He placed his cutlery down onto the half eaten food and dabbing at his mouth with the paper napkin, said, "When our Robert moved out after he completed his University course, I moved into his room. That's been, oh," he shrugged and rubbed at his chin as though trying to recall, "I'm guessing it must be about three years now. The only thing keeping us together is convenience. That and our debt," he sadly smiled.

"Sorry Harry, but I thought that with your pension as a DS and your job, your current salary I mean, that you'd be all right financially?" asked Dick.

"We were, at least for a short time anyway, but with our Elaine getting married; the fancy wedding, then helping her and her hubby out with a deposit for their bloody house and the payments for Robert's Uni course down in Oxford. I'm not saying I don't love my kids and wouldn't help them if they need it, but hard as it is for me to admit this they *are* a pair of ungrateful bastards. Well, that said, the money just seemed to dribble away. That and with Rosemary's flat refusal to find herself a job, it seems like I might *never* get to retire," he sighed.

Both Dick and Tom chuckled and the conversation turned to what had been happening in the three men's lives during the last month. As they spoke, laughed and enjoyed each others company, Harry's thoughts turned to Sally Nelson, her face flashing before his eyes and he knew that close as he was to these guys, his growing affection for the office cleaner would have to remain his deep and private secret.

CHAPTER SIX

Mick Thomson lay in bed, his head against the headboard and knees propped up to support the laptop that nestled against them, slowly masturbating while his eyes followed the antics of the two naked, slant-eyed teenage girls with fixed smiles, their eyes closed and teeth clenched as they pretended to enjoy the sexual humiliation of each other and themselves for the benefit of the paying public.

An empty glass sat with a half full bottle of whisky on the set of drawers by the bed and the remains of a joint in the overflowing ashtray.

Though he watched the porn, his thoughts were of the previous evening and the things he had made the woman do for him. The address had been easy to find; a scabby flat in a rundown area of the Drum. She had at first denied owing so much money then promised through her tears that she would settle the debt; she knew of his reputation with women and promised she would do anything to avoid what she suspected he had planned for her.

He had ignored her protestations and almost with indifference, ordered her crippled, bespectacled husband to fuck off to the pub or anywhere, just to get out of the flat, that he wanted a private word with the man's wife and pushing the man through the front door, locked it behind him.

The slightly built man, who limped and leaned heavily on a thick, wooden walking stick, not only persuaded himself but chose to believe that was all that Tommo really *did* want, a private word with his wife and head bowed had left the flat, too frightened of the powerfully built man and too fearful to protest, for he also knew of Tommo's violent history.

Alone together in the kitchen of the flat, the woman had thrust the money at him, a handful of notes that fell far short of the three grand she owed the drug-dealer and shaking in terror, her back pressed against the wall, whined that her customers were late with their payments.

He had ignored her and stuffed what money she had into his pocket then grabbed her and pushed the woman in front of him into the shabby lounge of the flat, closed the curtains and switched off the main overhead light in preference of a small table lamp. While she fearfully watched him, he had selected a CD and inserting it into the portable play, turned the music up loud.

Making himself comfortable in the old and worn armchair, he had commanded she stand in the centre of the floor a few feet in front of him and ordered her to strip to the music, grinning that she take her time so that he might enjoy the show.

She had been too embarrassed at first and flatly refused then tried to argue, but he had angrily risen from the chair and holding her by the arm with one hand, delivered a backhanded slap to her mouth.

Persuaded by the threat of further violence, her face beetroot red and lips beginning to swell from his blow, she avoided his eyes as she slowly removed her clothes and at his instruction, threw each article into the corner of the room till she stood naked in front of him, softly weeping and shivering with fright; one trembling arm protectively held across her breasts and the other demurely covering her crotch. He ordered she drop her hands to her side and had sat for several minutes leering and studying her as with his forefinger he directed the shaking woman slowly turn first this way then that way, all the while calling out obscenities to her that promised what he intended to do to her and enjoying the feeling of power he wielded over her. After several minutes, he knew he was as aroused as he was likely to get and rising from the chair, shocked the cowed woman by suddenly taking a handful of her hair and forced her to kneel on the stained carpeted floor in front of him. Her hands instinctively grabbed at his fist to relieve the pressure and pain from her head, but with his free hand he slapped them back down, hissing at the sobbing woman that she was to unzip the fly of his trousers. With trembling hands, she did as she was bid and then with mounting excitement and still holding her by the hair, he slapped her heavily on the head to remind her to comply, preferring to use the flat of his hand rather than a punch with the belief his fist would leave too many bruises and broken bones.

Then her painful humiliation had begun.

Later, much later, when he had finished his violation of her bruised and beaten body, he left her lying curled up semi-conscious on the floor, safe in the knowledge that she wouldn't grass him up, that it would never occur to her to complain to the police; that during the course of the hour he had abused her, what he did to her was so shameful for her to ever repeat and confident that she would never tell.

He had left the flat with the door lying wide open and had casually returned to his car parked in the roadway outside, ignoring the furtive glances from behind curtained windows and the husband who leaned heavily on his wooden stick and watched with sad eyes from the vandalised and graffiti ridden bus shelter across the street.

Before starting the engine, he had phoned the drug-dealer and described in laughing detail how he had dealt with the debtor, unaware that his vivid description of his abuse had shaken even the drug-dealer who inwardly feared that the violent Thomson had this time, gone too far. Thomson regretted that the bad news was after he had taken his wages, there was but three hundred quid left for the drug-dealer.

He knew the man wouldn't complain, that to object would only invoke Thomson's wrath against him and that nobody in their right mind crossed Mick 'Tommo' Thomson. Besides, the drug-dealer knew that word would get about; that he had contracted Thomson to settle a debt and those who were currently outstanding would whisper their opinions about what Thomson would have made the woman do, what indignities she would likely have suffered at his hands and rush to him with their payments, for nobody wanted Mick 'Tommo' Thomson calling at *their* door.

In his bed, he sighed and grinned for last night was a good night for it not only reminded people who he was, but he now had five hundred quid in his pocket for having his pleasure at the woman's pain.

His eyes narrowed for in his mind he had not abused the forty-something woman, for during that hour of sexual pleasure, all he had thought of was Grace.

With a sigh he glanced again at the porn on the laptop screen and decided that tonight he would visit the city, have a few drinks and find himself a real tart.

Colin Munro sat silently in the corner of the interview room cautiously watching the man who sat at the table opposite Catriona MacDougall. George McCormick was angry, so angry that twice already Cat had to tell him to calm down.

"What, tell me to calm down? It's your fucking mate in the polis you should be telling to calm, down! Came to my house and assaulted me, so he did! Bastard!" he spat out.

"Right, Mister McCormick," she replied, "from what you are telling me sir, you allege…"

"Allege fuck all! What I'm telling you is that wee bastard for no good reason punched me on the jaw, ya skinny wee cow!"

Munro rose to his feet, but without looking at him, Cat waved for him to sit back down.

"Insults won't help, Mister McCormick," she smiled humourlessly at him. "Now, as I said, from what you are *saying* is this police officer, this, eh…"

"I don't know his first name, he never said it, but his second name is Brown and his boy's called Paul Brown. He's fourteen, two years below my Cole at the High School," he nodded.

"Right, the police officer is called Brown. So, what you are *saying* is that this man Brown, for no apparent reason…"

"Why are you no recording this then?" he pointed with a stubby finger towards the tape recording machine that was bolted to the table.

"Are you a suspect, Mister McCormick?"

He sat back and stared in surprise at her and replied, "Fuck no, of course I'm not."

"Then that's why I'm not recording it," she sweetly replied then visibly inhaling, started again. "So, this man Brown for no apparent reason turns up at your door and punches you to the jaw?"

"Aye, that's correct," he formally replied, folding his arms in righteous indignation. "Hooked me a dull yin, right on the jaw," he obligingly added with a nod, then further added, "Took my by surprise otherwise I'd have battered the wee bastard."

Cat sat back in her chair and folding her arms, pursed her lips as she stared at McCormick.

"What?" he stared suspiciously back at her.

"I'm a wee bit puzzled, Mister McCormick. You are telling me, that right out of the blue without any previous history between you, this man you think is called Brown…"

"That's what Cole says his Da's called and that's the name he told Cole when he turned up at my door."

"Aye, that's another curious thing. You say there's been no previous contact between you, yet the father of this boy Paul Brown, who is apparently known at school to your son Cole, turns up at your door, punches you and walks away? Is that correct?"

"Aye, that's right."

"Is there any history between your son Cole and this lad, Paul Brown? I mean, are they friends or anything?"

"No, nothing like that," he shook his head.

She sensed that maybe now a little crack was starting to appear in McCormick's tale of woe.

"But the boys know each other, yeah?"

"Aye, I suppose so," he mumbled, glancing away from her and then believing he might distract her line of questioning and take the initiative, nodded with furrowed brow to Munro and said, "Who's the darkie sitting there, then? Why is he here listening to this?"

Cat bristled, but kept her cool and ignoring the tension that had suddenly become apparent in the room, replied, "That man is my colleague, a detective just like me."

To Munro's surprise, Cat was ignoring the racist comment, but angry as he was, decided not to interrupt.

"So the boys, Mister McCormick," she continued, but with an icy edge to her voice, "what's the story between them?"

He sighed and shrugging, replied, "There was a wee bit of hassle there. I think it was a fight or something."

"A fight between your son and this lad Paul Brown, is that what you are telling me?"

"Aye, my son Cole gave the wee guy a bleaching," he admitted with a hint of pride in his voice.

"I believe you said that Paul Brown is two years below Cole at school. Is that your son Cole I saw that was sitting with you downstairs at the waiting area, Mister McCormick?"

"Aye, it is," he replied, slightly suspicious and now wondering where this was going.

"So, quite apart from the difference in age, I presume there is a height and weight difference between these two boys?"

"What does that mean?"

"Is your lad bigger than the other boy?"

"Oh," he grinned, "You saw him, didn't you? My Cole is built like the side of a brick shithouse," he proudly nodded.

"Well, quite apart from that graphic analogy," she patiently continued, "am I right in guessing that the fight between the two boys was pretty unequal, that your Cole giving the other lad a bleaching was because your Cole is bigger, older and stronger?"

"Oh aye," he readily agreed, the pride in his son's achievement shining from him.

"What was the fight about then?"

"Eh, how the fuck am I supposed to know that? All I want to do is charge the bastard that belted me on the jaw and he's one of yours," he pointedly reminded her.

She again sat back in her chair and clasped her fingers behind her head as she stared at him.

"Point one, *we* do the charging if indeed a charge is to be libelled," she quietly said, then added, "Point two, I think this man Brown arrived at your door to remonstrate with you, Mister McCormick because your lad Cole beat Brown's son, but you had an argument with Brown and that led to fisticuffs and you came off worse. This is no more than a minor handbags at dawn scuffle and in your pettiness, you think we the polis will take up your complaint and go hunting a man whose son, in my humble opinion, was battered by your son because your son is bigger. Isn't that the truth of the matter, Mister McCormick?"

His face turned red and his fists clenched.

In the corner, Munro prepared to launch himself at the bigger man, but Cat continued again.

"I'm not accepting your complaint of assault, Mister McCormick. I'll certainly make a note of it in my notebook, but as far as I'm concerned, there does not appear to be any injury here other than to your pride, so my advice is that you go home and forget about the alleged incident."

He snarled at her and banged a fist on the table, causing Munro to rise warily to his feet and hissed, "I want to see somebody else! I demand that I speak to your superior!"

"The only *superior* I have, Mister McCormick" she calmly replied, staring into his eyes, "is the good Lord himself. However, if you mean a *senior* officer, then my colleague and I will be more than happy to take you downstairs to the charge bar," she smiled, "a place I understand you are familiar with if your domestic abuse convictions are any indication and where you can make your complaint to the duty Inspector while I am charging you."

He startled and his face turned pale. "Charge me? What the *fuck* are you on about, charging me?"

"Why Mister McCormick, by discriminately referring to my colleague Acting Detective Constable Munro as, and I quote 'a darkie', you must be aware that by making such a racist comment you contravened the Equality Act of 2010 and as such I have little option other than to report you and," she theatrically took a deep breath, "I believe it is a custodial charge which means that you will be locked up here at the station till you appear before a Sheriff on Monday."

He stared aghast at her, his mouth hanging open. What had seemed like an ideal opportunity to get one back at the fucking polis was now turning into a nightmare.

"You can't be serious" he gasped.

"Oh aye," she nodded, her face as straight as a twelve inch rule, "deadly serious, Mister McCormick."

His jowly throat was working overtime and his planned evening of a Saturday night curry and a few beers in front of the tele watching Strictly Come Dancing was fast disappearing.

"Is there no something I can do here, pal? Can we not come to some kind of an agreement?" he whined at her.

She inhaled and releasing her breath through pursed lips, slowly shook her head. "Mmmm, I'm not certain Mister McCormick. A lot of it would depend on how my colleague here feels about the racist insult you made towards him," then turned towards Munro and with the subtlest of winks, asked him, "what do you think, Mister Munro?"

He pretended to consider her question, then slowly replied, "I suppose it's fortunate that we *didn't* record Mister McCormick's allegation against this man Brown. It also means only you and I know the *dreadful* name he used to describe my skin colour and I suppose," he shrugged as if struggling to come to a decision, "if we were to let Mister McCormick go home without charging him, well, it would need to be by some kind of agreement, Missus MacDougall."

"Aye, I suppose you're right, Mister Munro. Now," she turned towards McCormick, "*if*, and I use the word reservedly, *if* you were to be released without charge, Mister McCormick, what guarantee do I have that your son Cole won't again be involved in a fight with this lad at school? How do I know that you won't be coming back to me to make a complaint of assault for it seems to me that the whole thing hinges on you controlling your boy; I mean, if Cole gets into a fight with this lad Paul Brown, then Brown's father will be back at your door and you'll be getting your jaw punched again, won't you?"

McCormick stared at her, his mind racing through a jumble of thoughts that not only included him worrying about Brown again sticking one on his jaw, but getting locked up just because he called the guy a darkie and eventually concluded he was in this mess because of Cole.

"Hand on heart, detective," he replied, "you'll no see me in here again over this. That boy of mine will be getting it and I'll see he's no more trouble, if you're happy with that?"

Cat loudly exhaled and nodded, then said, "Okay Mister McCormick, it's a deal. In the *meantime*," she stared at him with heavy emphasis on the word meantime, "Mister Munro and I will hang off any racial charges and you keep your lad in order, okay?"

He thrust a meaty paw at her and with relief, shook her hand.

"You're a doll, so you are missus. Stand on me, by the way; I'm a man of my word," he added.

Aye that'll be bloody likely, she thought and watched as Munro opened the door and led McCormick downstairs to his waiting son. She was back in the CID office when a few minutes later, Munro returned, a grin plastered to his face. "Hardly out the door but he was slapping his lad on the back of the head and growling at him," he laughed.

"That was well done, Cat. Handled to perfection, but what about this guy Brown; the guy that McCormick thinks is a cop? Do you know who he is?"

She shook her head and answered, "No, but come Monday morning, I'll need to make a phone call to the admin office at the High School and do a bit of digging."

She cocked her head to one side, a puzzled look on her face. "Do you hear that?" she said.

"No, what was it?"

"Sounded like you putting the kettle on. I'll have tea, thanks," she grinned mischievously at him.

Chic Fagin, wearing a clean kitchen apron to protect his sparkling white dress shirt, used the fish slice to turn the eggs and shouting again, "Ian, come and get it son," shook his head at the lazy bugger's lengthy lie-in.

"Boy needs a job," he mumbled to himself then turned when Ian stumbled through the door wearing what passed for him as pyjamas; a rumpled Rangers football top and football shorts, his hair in disarray and rubbing the sleep from his eyes.

"Oh aye, here's the back shift arrived," Chic grinned. "Get yourself sat down there," he pointed with the fish slice to the chair at the kitchen table, shaking his head at the state of his grandson. "You were on that wacky-baccy again last night, weren't you?"

"No, Pop, honest," Ian vigorously shook his head as he lied, unable to look Chic in the eye.

Chic sighed and shook his head. There was no point in getting into it. No matter how many times he lectured, cajoled and even on occasion, threatened him, Ian just wouldn't listen. The folly of youth, he thought, thinking that they always know best and old codgers like me know nothing.

"You're wearing your band trousers Pop," said Ian, keen to change the subject from him.

"Aye," Chic raised his leg and glanced down at the light blue trousers with the vivid red stripe up the side, the crease as sharp as a fishwife's tongue, then returned to concentrate on the fried egg, "We've a wee practice parade today. Local though, just us and a few supporters walking through the Alexandria area and shouldn't take more than an hour."

"Oh aye, so why don't I come and watch it and support you," grinned Ian.

Chic turned with a half smile and replied, "What, nothing else on have you?"

"Ach, don't be like that, Pop," Ian frowned. "You know I like watching you in charge of the lads."

"Then why don't you come down one night to band practise and *you* can be one of the lads," he snorted.

"I'm no that good with the flute. You said it yourself," Ian mumbled and waving his hands, grinned "Stubby fingers."

"There's other jobs you can do," Chic turned towards him and bending down to fetch a plate warming in the oven, carefully laid the egg alongside the sausages, bacon and tomatoes before laying the plate before Ian then that done, he lifted the teapot from the cooker and sat down at the small table opposite his grandson.

"You not eating Pop?" asked Ian as he wolfed down the breakfast.

Chic poured the tea into two mugs and replied, "Some people get up early and have their breakfast in the morning, not lie in till all times of the day," he pointedly replied and nodding towards Ian's plate, continued, "that's not so much your breakfast as your lunch."

"What jobs?"

Chic's eyes narrowed. "What do you mean?"

"You said there are other jobs I can do in the band. What jobs?"

"Oh, I see. Well," he drawled, "Flag bearer for instance or supporting the band with a bit of stewarding…"

"You mean I can carry one of them batons and wear the white gloves like?" he eagerly asked.

"Aye," Chic cautiously replied, "but it's just a ceremonial duty son. We don't go about bashing people on the head or anything like that."

"What, not even the Catholics?" then seeing the stark disapproval on Chic's face added, "I'm only *joking*, Pop."

Chic wagged a forefinger at him and said, "Some of my friends are Catholic, Ian, and I worked in the yards with a lot of good men who were Catholic. Aye, I admit it," he nodded, "I *do* reject Papism and I am a proud Orangeman and believe in the fundamental principles of the Protestant faith and that's why I attend church each Sunday morning, but I'm *not* a bigot and don't you forget it, young man."

He could see that his explanation wasn't really getting through to Ian and taking a deep breath, he leaned across the table and said, "Look, son, each of us has to find the faith that he believes will lead him to God. Think of it this way. If say, you want to travel from Glasgow to Edinburgh, you can walk, you can run, catch a bus, drive a car, ride a bicycle or ride a horse and even catch a train, isn't that right?"

A little uncertainly, Ian nodded, not sure exactly what his Pop was trying to tell him.

"Well," Chic continued, "think of Edinburgh as being *God* and all these different ways of getting from *Glasgow* to Edinburgh as religions trying *their* different ways to get to God. There are so many options, but they all lead to the same place, do you not see that?"

"Aye, I think so," said Ian, but it was clearly apparent to Chic that the young man was agreeing to appease his grandfather and just didn't comprehend the explanation, so rather than be annoyed, Chic was disappointed for in reality he knew that though it wasn't his fault, Ian would struggle through life trying to understand the most basic things.

But that didn't stop Chic from loving him and gently, he reached across the table and ruffled his grandson's hair.

"Right," he smiled at him, a sudden tightness in his chest as once more he worried what would become of Ian when he passed on. "Get that finished and you've half an hour to get yourself ready then we'll go down to the hall and catch the bus with the lads, eh?"

CHAPTER SEVEN

Des Brown and Grace Thomson smiled together as they watched her son Steven slurp his way through the sundae, unaware that he had a coating of brown chocolate ringing his mouth.

"You do realise of course that with the amount of sugar the wee man's putting away he'll be up to midnight, don't you?"

"Probably," she nodded her agreement with a smile, but as far as she was concerned, her son could stay up all night for she was just so happy that Des had agreed to accompany them to McDonalds and blissfully oblivious that he was just as pleased to be invited.

"Where's your son...Paul isn't it? Where is he today?" she asked, sitting back and sipping at her beaker of Coke.

"Ah, Paul's spending the day with his mother, my ex-wife Margo. I gather they're having a mother and son day out, over in Edinburgh at the Castle. She'll keep him overnight and bring him back tomorrow evening in time for school on Monday morning."

"So, you're divorced then?"

"As if you didn't know, *Miss* Thomson," he teased her.

She blushed and admitted, "Yes, well, I did ask Willie McKee at the fundraiser last night," and shook her head. "I wouldn't have asked you here today Des if I thought you were still married. That's not my style," she cast her eyes to the table.

Not my style, she thought. Bloody hell, he'll be getting the impression I'm some sort of man-eater, she angrily chided herself. Inwardly taking a deep breath, she said, "You okay with that, I mean, him staying with...what am I saying," she hid her mouth behind her hand, she's his mother, for God's sake. "What I mean is..."

"I think what you're really asking is how do I get on with Margo, now that we're divorced," and he smiled. "Actually, since we split up, what," his brow furrowed as he tried to recall, "yeah, just over six years now, divorced for four, we get on all right, in fact probably better now than we did when we were married," he grinned at her. "Besides, she's remarried and before you ask, a really nice guy; John's his name. He brought his own baggage to their marriage,"

Des waved his forefingers in the air. "A boy and a girl slightly older than my Paul and Paul he tells me is that when the kids are together, they get on fine."

"I'm a nosey bugger, aren't I?" her face crinkled then she broke intro a smile

"No, you're not being nosey, just curious, Grace," he replied.

She liked that, him saying her name.

"So *Miss* Thomson, exactly what is your style then?" he lounged back in the chair or as far as the rigid plastic seat would permit him to.

"You're not going to let that go, are you?" she grinned at him, comfortably leaning towards him.

"Mum," interrupted Paul, "can I have another chocolate sundae?"

"You *are* chancing your arm, wee man," grinned Des and turning towards Grace, said, "I think he believes if we stay here any longer there's a real chance he might get another sundae. Maybe we should head off, and besides," he jokingly grimaced, "my backside is aching with sitting here."

She smiled, but her insecurities kicked in and inwardly wondered if Des was subtly suggesting that their short time together was over, that she had completely misread him and that he had only accompanied Steven and her to McDonalds out of politeness.

"Right, I had better get you dropped at your car," and reaching behind her lifted her short jacket from the back of her seat. As he leaned across Grace, the faint scent of her perfume drifted towards him and his throat tightened.

It was now or never, he decided, working up the nerve to ask her out. He held her jacket while she draped her scarf about her neck and turned to slip her arms into the sleeves and was about to speak, when Steven excitedly burst out, "Look Mum, there's Cheryl McGuigan. She's in my class at school," and waved across the restaurant to the girl who was coming through the front door with a man and woman who each held the hand of two younger children.

The girl shyly returned Steven's wave then turned away to speak to her curious parents, both bent over and listening to their daughter explaining why and to whom she was waving.

The couple smiled politely across the room to Des and Grace, who smiled and nodded in return.

"That's it, Grace. Your reputation's ruined. You've been seen with a baldy, older man," he wisecracked. "That couple will think you're having lunch with your father."

Almost immediately, he realised what he had said and though she still had her back to him, he saw her tense.

"Right," she briskly replied, "I think we'd better be going, eh?" and held her hand out to Steven.

The lad took her hand and turning, stared curiously at Des. Something had happened, but he didn't know what and he sensed his Mum was upset.

Des, trailing after them from the restaurant, watched as Grace briskly stepped out across the car park towards his Mondeo, almost dragging Steven with her.

She walked quickly as if trying to put some distance between them and stopped at the passenger door, her head bowed and silently fuming.

She knew that Des must of course have known who she was; she had not expected otherwise, but to bring Michael Thomson into the conversation. It had taken her aback and she had not known how to react.

Infuriated by Des's insensitive comment, tears stung at her eyes as he approached and she realised he was standing silently in front of her. She lifted her head, her face pale and lips trembling and boldly returned his stare. Seeing her so upset tore at him, though curiously, he thought she had never looked lovelier.

Aware that he was now either going to fix this or blow himself right out of the water he took a deep breath and said, "Right, here's how it is, Grace. Yes," he nodded, "I know who your father is and to be frank, I don't really care. I made a stupid comment, but I refuse to always walk on eggshells, wondering if I'm going to say something that might inadvertently upset you. I lived through too many years of marriage doing that and to be honest, I couldn't go through it again." He paused, conscious that the wee man was staring in turn at them both.

"I like you. No," he shrugged a little self-consciously shook his head, "it's more than liking you. I'd like to get to know you better, Grace; see more of you," he corrected himself. "Spend time with you and maybe find out…well," he suddenly discovered he was stuck for words and simply stared at her.

She realised that he was handing her an olive branch and that he was genuinely sorry, but still she hesitated, wondering was he *really* worth taking a chance with?

"I'm sorry, it's just the very mention of him…" she took a deep breath and exhaled slowly, rubbing at both her eyes with the heel of her hands. "It took me by surprise," she admitted.

They stood in silence for a moment, until Steven pulled at his mother's hand and said, "Mum, Mister Brown didn't mean it, did you Mister Brown?" he turned and stared up at Des, willing him to say something so that they would all be friends again. The small boy had no idea what had caused the change, but instinctively reached for Des's hand and taking hold of his fingers thought if Mister Brown was to say sorry *again* to Mum, everything would be okay and back to normal because he really, *really* liked Mister Brown.

Des smiled ruefully and with his free hand, ruffled Steven's hair then glanced again at Grace.

"What can I do to fix this?" he quietly asked.

Her eyes narrowed as she stared at him and then she softly smiled and calm now, an idea struck her.

"Your son's at his mother's tonight, you said?"

"Yes, overnight," he slowly answered, suspecting what he hoped was going through her mind.

"Well, if you've got an *empty*," she wagged her fingers in the air, "why don't Steven and I come over later and bring in some fish and chips?"

Feeling as if a great weight had suddenly lifted from his chest, though maybe just a *little* disappointed that Steven was coming too, he smiled and replied "That sounds like a plan."

Standing beside her and for reasons he was too young to comprehend, Steven sighed with relief that things now seemed to be okay.

Sally Nelson finished dusting the lounge and tiptoed behind her husband Archie's armchair while he watched the racing on the television and bent to pick up the discarded betting slip he had flung to the floor.

"Leave it!" he snarled at her without turning his head, his eyes glued to the screen, willing the five to one horse to pip the leader at the post and then screamed "Shite!" when the horse failed to do so.

Wisely, knowing the mood he was in, Sally made to leave and went to open the lounge door when he snapped at her, "Get me a cup of tea."

She didn't reply, merely closed the door behind her and leaning back against it sighed, but whether from relief or exhaustion, she was never quite sure these days.

She made her way into the narrow galley kitchen and switching on the kettle, glanced at the small, plastic framed mirror that hung on the wall above the gate-leg table. She turned towards the mirror and holding it steady between her hands, hardly recognised the blonde hair woman who stared back, seeing the small crocodile wrinkles now forming at the eyes and the downturned mouth. Staring at her reflection she touched delicately at her cheek, stroking it softly and wondered, when did I become old yet knowing that inside her was a younger woman, her true self crying out to be free.

Be free.

She tried to dismiss the thought but that was exactly how she felt, just like a prisoner. For so long now, so many years she had suffered Archie's abuse. First came the verbal abuse, then later the physical abuse and always, always the mental abuse. His constant whining and 'me, me, me' was more than wearing her down, it was killing her as slowly and as surely as if she had slit her own wrists.

She startled and swallowed hard, her eyes tightly shut and her hands balled into fists. More than once she had considered the ultimate option; ending it and releasing herself from his bullying control of her. Slowly she opened her eyes and again heard her sister Elsie's voice, urging her to leave him, to flee and let him fend for himself. She took a deep breath as the kettle whistled behind her and clicked off. Mechanically she fetched a teabag from the tin and emptying the teapot, re-filled it with the boiled water and set it upon the gas ring to brew. She fetched down a mug from the wall cupboard and then to her surprise, realised she was crying, the tears spilling from her eyes to her cheeks and dripping onto her blouse.

She grabbed a handful of paper towel and dabbed at her red-rimmed eyes as she poured the milk and sugar into the mug, took a deep breath and gritted her teeth while she fought to compose herself. It wouldn't do for Archie to see her upset for it only set him off on one of his rants, how easy she had it while he had to suffer the loss of a leg.

"Sally, what's keeping you, where's my tea?" she heard him call out and taking another deep breath, poured the tea and forcing a smile, carried it through to him in the lounge.

On the trip home to his bungalow in Netherdale Road in the Crookston area of the city, a slightly tipsy Tom Fraser sat on the lower deck of the bus and stared out at the passing tenements of Paisley Road West. Covering his mouth with his hand he loudly burped then with a quick glance about him to ensure he hadn't been heard, grinned like an errant schoolboy and with the same hand wafted the odour of the alcohol from him.

As always, Tom had enjoyed his couple of hours with Harry and Dick, the tales of their exploits during their respective careers a bit like old wine, getting better and raucously maturing as both the stories and the tellers of the fibs aged through the years.

Yes he smiled; it had been good keeping in touch with the guys even though their careers had parted, they had not.

He felt a little sorry for Dick and guessed that his friend was lonely, that it wasn't just Dick's lack of money that so annoyed and upset him, but a lack of real female companionship. Mind, he sighed, Dick really had no-one to blame but himself for his problems, but did he or would he listen, Tom ruefully shook his head; would he hell.

Harry on the other hand worried Tom a little. It was plain to see the big guy was unhappy and again Tom sighed. No secret why though, for Harry's wife Rosie…Rosemary, he corrected himself, was a whining cow with a face that looked like an Alsatian dog chewing a wasp.

He grinned at his own analogy and as he had done several times over the years, wondered why Harry just didn't up and leave the sour faced bitch, then felt a little remorseful that he should think of his good friend's wife like that.

Still, Rosemary had never made it a secret she didn't like Tom or Dick or Tom's wife Sheila or any of Dick's women. She didn't even approve or care for Harry associating with his old mates.

He shook his head for he really suspected that the eternally pessimistic Rosemary was just a deeply unhappy woman who being of the half empty bottle of milk genre, took pleasure in ensuring her husband was also a deeply unhappy man.

He thought of Harry's comment in the pub that the only thing keeping them together was their debt and sadly smiled, for that thought reminded him of Sheila.

Sheila was a class act, he had to admit and even after all these years he still found it hard to believe that of her many suitors, she had chosen him, a young and slightly naïve probationary cop. Their marriage had been the happiest time of his life, the only worry being all those years ago when Sheila had discovered the lump and the months of concern that followed. The resultant mastectomy had severely damaged her morale and, his brow knitted as he thought of that horrible time, perhaps that was why he indulged her spending. Inwardly he sighed, recalling the phone call from his old mate, now the manager of the local bank who some weeks previously called him in for a coffee and a chat to warn Tom that Sheila's spending had to stop, that Tom's pension and savings had recently taken a bashing and while the Fraser's were not poor, he suggested they seriously give consideration to watching the pennies with a keener eye.

The bus halted at a stop near to Paisley Road West's junction with Corkerhill Road to permit an elderly woman carrying a shopping trolley to alight from the bus.

While the driver considerately assisted the old woman from the bus, Tom's eyes idly drifted towards the two middle aged drunks who were arguing and pushing at each other on the pavement, one trying to grab what looked like a five pound note from the other's grasp. He couldn't hear what was being shouted, but watched as the elderly woman who had just stepped from the bus gave both men a wide berth and a scowl.

Tom smiled at the scene, guessing one drunk was trying to rip the other off and surmising if they continued pushing and shoving at each other, they were in danger of getting themselves lifted for a breach of the peace.

Watching the men, his eyes narrowed and he was later to remember it was then that the idea came to him.

CHAPTER EIGHT

Standing at her first floor flat bedroom window, her dressing gown again wrapped round her, Cathy Porteous watched as a happily grinning Beth waved and climbed into the driver's seat of her car. When the car had driven off, she turned and stared at the rumpled bed and the duvet on the floor and shook her head. Her mind was in a flurry of indecision, part of her annoyed with herself for giving into temptation and not ending it last night with the younger woman while part of her recalled with pleasure Beth's first tentative, then searching lips upon her body.

Cathy shook her head, startled at the revelation she had enjoyed the sex with Beth and though much experienced as she was in the ways of men, surprised now to find she had delighted in the sensual exploration of another woman. While Beth had proven to be an eager pupil who willingly and enthusiastically agreed to all that Cathy asked of her, Cathy had been the one who had instigated their probing and exploration of each other, teaching the younger woman where and how to touch her.

"My new found love," Beth had whispered over and over again. The memory of her adulation had made Cathy smile and oddly, feel protective of the younger woman as she had held her close to her. But it could not continue, she knew. Her lifestyle and lifelong ambition would not permit her any long term relationship with Beth who, she frowned, would be aghast to learn that her new her 'new found love' was addicted to cocaine as well as being a prostitute. Her thoughts turned to her addiction and curiously, her eyes narrowed while she swept the sheet from the bed for these last twenty something hours she had not indulged or even given any thought to her addiction.

Gathering the sheet and duvet cover she walked through to the kitchen and dumped them in a pile by the washing machine, but her thoughts were of how she would break the news to Beth and whether she did so when they met for coffee tomorrow, as they had arranged or waited and risk Beth finding out herself; she just could not decide. She sighed and walked through to the bathroom, dropping her dressing gown to the floor and staring at her reflection in the full length mirror that hung behind the door.

Inhaling, she decided that for now, she would defer from her decision for tonight would be busy in the city hotels with punters from the north of Scotland arriving for the football match against the local team, Celtic and, she grinned, a lot of the supporters were oilrig men with money to burn and no doubt intent on having a good time.

Ian Purvis glanced at the incoming caller's name on the screen and closing his eyes, took a deep breath. Forcing himself to sound cheerful, he pressed the green button and said, "Hi Tommo, what can I do for you?"

"Mind you keep yourself available for tomorrow night, wee man," replied the deep voice.

Standing behind Purvis, Casey Lennox stood upright from the wash basket at her feet with a set of child's pyjamas in her hand and as she folded them, silently mouthed the words, "Is that Thomson?"

Purvis nodded to her and said into the phone, "You'll need me then I suppose, big man?"

"Aye, just keep your blower on and I'll text you a PC. You have got a SatNav on your phone, haven't you?"

"Aye, it's the latest gizmo and all I do is type in the post code and…"

"I don't need fucking details, you moron! Like I said, just be ready to collect the parcel and get it tested, okay?"

"Aye, right enough, of course Tommo."

"Anything else you need to know, wee man?"

"No, can't think of anything," then he grinned. "I heard a wee whisper you made a visit last night to that woman up in…"

"Shut your face, you fucking idiot!" snapped Thomson, then added, "Never on the phone, understand?"

Purvis swallowed and meekly replied, "Aye, sorry Tommo," but the line had gone dead.

"Wanker," Purvis muttered under his breath and pressed the red end button, angry that he had been so summarily dismissed by Thomson.

"What did he want?" asked a curious Casey, while she continued to fold the clean clothing.

"Nothing doll; just a wee business conference between a couple of pals," he grinned at her.

"Pals my arse," she retorted, her voice dripping with sarcasm as she added, "he shouts and you go running. What was it this time, Ian and what were you talking about, putting a post code into your phone?"

His face suddenly hardened and he turned on her, gripping her tightly by both shoulders.

"Listen to me, Casey and listen well," he hissed at her, his nose inches from hers. "Don't you ever, *ever* fucking involve yourself in my business? You get your cash in hand when I've got the money, but you do not *ever* ask me how I make it, get it."

Her eyes narrowed and she pulled herself free from his grasp for Casey Lennox was no shrinking violet and no guy, whether he be her boyfriend or not, was going to lay hands on her or dictate to her in *her* house.

"Well, you fucking listen to me, Ian Purvis," she screeched at him, her eyes wide and her teeth bared, "I know what that bastard is like and what he does to women. He's even tried it on with me when you were doing your three month stretch and I went to try and get a loan from him," she beat at her chest with both fists, "pawing and groping me, telling me that if I shagged him he would make it worth my while! You didn't know *that* about your pal, did you? That he tried to *fuck* your girlfriend when you were in the nick at Low Moss! Some pal Tommo is, eh?" she sneered at him.

Stunned, Purvis could only stare at her then to her shock, drew back his right hand and slapped her on the face.

In truth, it wasn't a hard slap and she'd had worse from the weans, but it was the fact he had dared to do that to Casey that so enraged her. She gasped and stepping back, instinctively reached up to hold her cheek then with a growl, launched herself at Purvis who fell backwards onto the carpeted floor with her on top of him and beating at his face with her small fists, all the while screaming "Bastard!" over and over.

He parried her blows with her hands and forearms and grabbing the struggling Casey by the wrists, shouted at her, "For fucks sake, Casey," but she ignored him and continued to struggle until at last, exhausted she rolled off him and pushing herself to her feet, stared angrily down at him as he worked himself into a sitting position.

"Get your things together," she snapped at him, "and get yourself to *fuck* out of my house!"

"You're overreacting," he replied, his hands apart as though beseeching her, "and we both know you like the money I bring in," he reminded her, but wisely thought it best not to grin lest it provoked her to attack him again.

"Not if you're going to slap me about," she hissed at him, her arms folded across her chest and calmer now as her mind raced.

The memory and realisation of the penny-pinching hardship she had endured before he had come to live with her forced her into a decision. She took a deep breath as she stared at him and inwardly admitted that while she had known, but denied to herself the knowledge of his drug-dealing, she had never questioned him about his source of income and chose instead to believe his story of the good wage he received in his part-time job as a food delivery driver. She closed her eyes and shaking her head, slowly opened them and said, "I swear Ian, if you ever, *ever* hit me again, I'll fucking have you? Do you understand?"

He tempted a small grin and nodding, said, "Aye, sorry, babe."

She turned away to continue folding the washing while he sat there, his back against the couch and stared at her, but his mind was occupied by what she had admitted, that while he was in the nick and behind his back, Tommo had tried to screw his bird and that, he inwardly scowled, was unforgiveable.

Big as he was, Tommo was due getting it, but he knew that if that was to happen then he would need to be team-handed or catch the bastard unaware for no way, Casey being fondled or not, was he going up against Mick Thomson alone.

Harry McInnes had also returned home by bus and got off at the stop in Kilmarnock Road, then walked home towards his semi-detached home in the Merrylee area of the city.

He took his time, but not because of his alcohol intake. No, Harry was in no rush to get home for he knew when he stepped though the door his wife Rosemary would be all over him like a bad rash, sullenly reminding him that it was all right for him to go for a bevy with his cronies, that he never took her anywhere and her life was just one shitty day after the next, that she never got to go anywhere; blah, blah, fucking blah.

Head down and hands in his jacket pockets, he slowly trudged unhappily along the quiet street, his thoughts full of her and their failed relationship. Of course, it didn't do any good reminding her that he had given up asking her to accompany him to the pictures or the theatre or for a meal and even for a walk in the park, because Rosemary always had some excuse not to go.

She was a women without friends, recalling the couples they had previously mixed with and who through time had given up associating with them, for while Harry knew he was a reasonably popular man with their friends, the wives detested the rude and spiteful Rosemary and one by one, persuaded their husbands they could no longer tolerate being in her company.

Embarrassed, the husbands had offered their apologies and excuses and through time cried off inviting Harry and Rosemary to their homes or popping by for a visit.

He inhaled and slowly released his breath through pursed lips. The alcohol, he realised had lowered his inhibitions and mouth grimly set, he thought about going home, telling her he had had enough, that he was off for good and she could have the house, the pension and he would live off the salary he was earning.

Yes, that was a plan, but then reality kicked in and he knew he couldn't do it and slowly shook his head, for he knew it was a pipedream.

Turning into Merryton Avenue, he was strolling slowly towards his house when he saw the elderly neighbours who lived across the road arm in arm and who nodded a smiling greeting towards him. For some curious reason, their courtesy provoked thoughts of the office cleaner Sally Nelson and he smiled.

He liked Sally; no, he vigorously shook his head as though to clear any doubt. He *really* liked her and if he was honest with himself, also fancied Sally, but like the idea of leaving Rosemary, these thoughts were also a pipedream for Sally was married and…his eyes narrowed. Apparently not happily married though, he thought, angrily recalling her blackened eye. He stopped and glanced along the road towards his house, seeing the old Volvo estate car parked in the driveway.

So she's in, he thought and half-laughed to himself. Where else would she be for other than grocery shopping, she never went out. He guessed she would be waiting at the window, watching from behind the curtain for him coming along the road, eager to berate him for drinking.

While he couldn't explain his decision, he suddenly took a deep breath and grinned, the old saying about better being hung as a sheep than a lamb coming to mind. Still grinning, he turned on his heel and headed back the way he had come, determined to find a pub on the Kilmarnock Road.

If I'm going to get screamed at for having a couple of pints, he thought to himself, I might as well make it worth my while.

Lying on her back top of her bed in the chill of the darkening room, the curtains tightly closed and still wearing her dress from the night before, Beth Williams was in heaven.

In her wildest dreams she had never really believed that Cathy would have returned her affections. Turning her head slightly, she closed her eyes and sniffed at the expensive scent that still clung to her dress then hugging her old and faithful teddy bear to her, sighed with pleasure, the memory of Cathy's touch and caress imprinted forever in her thoughts. In her twenty-three years, Beth had not known the love or affection of a man, not even the gentleness of a passionate kiss or embrace, but with distaste could recall when attending the occasional night out, the darkened lanes at the rear of city centre pubs or drunken parties held in smelly flats, the lights turned low and furtive hands up her dress trying for her knickers or groping at her ample breasts; being pawed by some half-drunk fellow student, her face burning with shame in the full realisation that her would-be suitor would be some guy who had already been knocked back by another girl and that Beth was always the last option for a fuck.

Her brow furrowed and she slowly exhaled as she thought of her life. She fought against her inner growing suspicion that she was a little different from the other females she had known, simply believed that maybe she just had a low sex drive, that when the right guy came along, she would know. Mixing with her fellow female students at both school and college and listening to their giggling conversations about the guys on the course or their boyfriends or some guy they liked, she had always grinned and agreed and even joined in with their sexual fantasies and ribaldry, because she believed that was expected of her.

In reality, none of the men interested her; well, not in that way. She remembered the first time she thought she was different, her third year at the high school and her crush on the French language teacher; a petite dark haired woman in her late thirties and would often daydream of them together. Not about them *sexually*, because even in her very private thoughts, Beth had been too embarrassed to admit what she would like to have done to the teacher; to touch her and stroke her *there* and been touched by her *there* in return.

Then later when attending college, Cathy had come into her life and she smiled, her eyes still closed and squirmed with pleasure on the bed. She had been enthralled by the tall, slim Cathy whose beauty and confidence was the envy of all her classmates and to her surprise, who had befriended the less than attractive Beth.

Beth had at first been devastated when Cathy had dropped from the course, but could hardly believe it when Cathy insisted they remain friends, that they meet regularly in the city and was overjoyed when Cathy had obtained the PR job that now provided her with such an affluent lifestyle.

Just thinking of her made Beth a little breathless and her eyes still closed tightly, again replayed in her mind the pleasure of the previous evening.

She thought of them arriving last night at the flat, of Cathy's arm protectively about her shoulders and leading her up the stairs to the door, Beth carrying the bag with the wine and Cathy opening the door; both close together as Cathy permitted Beth to squeeze by, then playfully smacking at Beth's bottom.

She smiled as she recalled Cathy pouring the two of them their glasses of wine, then a second and third; then both tipsy and snuggling up together on the couch, their arms about each other.

In her thoughts, Cathy was again nuzzling against her neck, one hand reaching behind Beth's head to bring their lips close together and the other slowly caressing between Beth's opening thighs.

Lying on the bed, Beth softly murmured her new love's name.

The sudden rap on the door startled her as her father called out, "Wake up Beth, dinner on the table in five minutes, darling."

She lay perfectly still, almost too afraid to move and listened with bated breath as he headed down the stairs and with relief, heard the squeak on the second bottom step that assured her he was gone.

Her breath escaped in a self-conscious giggle and she grinned then swung her legs over the side of the bed. Standing upright, she glanced at the wall mirror and frowned. The dress was crumpled, her hair was a mess and her make-up smudged.

But then she smiled

She knew Cathy loved her, so what did any of that matter now?

Des Brown heard the doorbell chime and, raising his eyebrows expectantly at his son Paul, went to open the front door.

Sitting on the couch watching the Saturday evening football results, Paul watched his father hurry from the room and grinned. His Dad was clearly nervous and though he had explained to his son that the woman and her wee boy who were coming to tea was just a visitor, Paul was astute enough and with teenage savvy, to understand that the woman must be a that wee bit special, for as far as he could remember his Dad had never invited a woman to tea before. In fact, Paul was sure his Dad had never even discussed a woman friend with him, let alone had one over for dinner.

At the door, Des took a deep breath and pulling it open, was greeted by Grace Thomson who standing nervously behind her son Steven, was holding a large paper bag in one hand, a plastic carrier bag in the other and a small black leather handbag hanging from her shoulder. He could see her old Nisan Micra parked in the street outside.

"Hello, hope we're not too early," she hesitantly said, only to be interrupted by Steven, who chipped in with, "Hi, Mister Brown, is Paul in? Can I play with him? Is he watching tele?" and strode past Des into the hallway, but stopped dead when his mother snapped warningly at him, "Steven," but without malice in her voice.

Des grinned and said, "No, you're fine. Actually Steven, Paul *is* at home tonight after all. His mum dropped him off." Then, staring at Grace as if by way of explaining, continued, "Apparently one of her husband's kids has gone down with a virus and she didn't want Paul exposed, so he's here now; so come in, come in," and ushered her through the door. As Grace squeezed past Des, her scent caused him to inhale and he inwardly prayed that the evening went well.

He caught his breath at her loveliness and taking the bags from her, he called out, "Paul, come and get the coats, son," and nodding towards a cupboard door in the hallway said, "Paul will hang your jackets in there."

Making his way through the hallway towards the brightly lit kitchen at the rear of the house, he saw Paul coming from the lounge and heard him say, "Hello Miss Thomson, I'm Paul and you wee man," he grinned down at the younger lad, "you must be Steven."

Des lifted the bags onto the kitchen worktop and grinning, almost sighed with relief. Immensely proud as he was of his son, he had worried a little that Paul might have been unhappy at Des inviting a strange woman to dinner, but realised he was being foolish. Paul was a fine young man, well mannered and courteous and Des with pride would boast that Paul took his kind nature after Des's father Eddie, only for Eddie to contradict Des and instead insist that Paul was his *father's* son.

Returning to the hallway, he trailed after them as Paul invited the visitors through to the lounge and where Des got his first good look at Grace.

He guessed she had just washed her hair for even from where he stood he detected the hint of a scented shampoo.

She was dressed in a simple white short sleeved blouse and short, denim skirt that accentuated her slim, but shapely figure, dark tights and calf high, black leather boots that raised her height by two inches. A thin gold chain hung about her neck, but she wore no other jewellery and he saw that with her clear skin, she needed very little make-up.

Enraptured, he thought she could easily have been mistaken for a young glamour model.

"Are you watching the results on the tele, Paul? Did the Rangers win today?" asked an excited Steven, throwing himself onto the couch.

"Steven," she shook her head, but added with a smile, "You should wait to be asked to sit down."

"Oh, he's okay Miss Thomson," replied Paul, sitting beside the younger boy and ruffling his hair.

"Should I call you Mister Brown then?" Grace asked Paul with a hint of mischief in her voice.

Mystified, he glanced at his father and then back at her and eyes narrowing, slowly said, "Eh, no. Paul's fine."

"Well, Paul, why don't you call me Grace, then. Miss Thomson makes me sound like some old fuddy-duddy teacher," she smiled at him.

Watching from the doorway, Des thought that though she probably didn't realise it, Grace Thomson would never be described as fuddy-duddy.

Paul returned her smile and replied, "Okay. Grace it is," then with another glance at his father, returned to watching the sports news with Steven.

Still smiling Grace turned towards Des, who beckoned with a thumb over his shoulder and said, "Fancy giving me a hand in the kitchen and we'll put out the dinner while it's still hot?"

She followed him along the hallway into the kitchen and looking about her said with a nod, "I'm impressed, Des Brown. You have a lovely home."

"Thanks, it's been a bit of a long haul," he explained, "but I've been doing the place up one room at a time. Started with the kitchen here," he waved a hand about him and then reached down to put the dinner plates into the oven to warm. Standing upright, he continued, "Knocked down a couple of cupboards to extend the kitchen, renovated and tiled the upstairs bathroom, decorated the lounge then when that was finished, I decorated the two main bedrooms; Paul's first, and then the hallway."

His eyes narrowed and he screwed up his face as he recalled the order of his renovations. "The downstairs toilet by the door was next, the hallway after that and lastly," he nodded towards the French doors in the kitchen, "had those doors put in when the conservatory was built about a year ago and *that's* where we're dining tonight." He grinned at her surprised face and added, "It's a *big* dining conservatory."

Nodding as though satisfied with his work, he added, "I've still the small room upstairs to start and as you probably noticed when you came through the gate, the front garden's a bit of a riot and the back garden needs attention too."

"Wish I had a garden," she wistfully replied, standing with her arms folded across her breasts, leaning back against the worktop with one leg demurely crossed over the other. "For Steven more than anything, though I have to admit, I quite fancy the idea of getting my hands dirty, growing things; you know, like planning a garden."

Des inwardly shivered at the thoughts that tore across his mind, of getting dirty with Grace and hoped to God she didn't suspect what he was thinking for she would surely slap his face if she did.

"I take it you don't have a garden then?"

"No, we're in a flat in Southdeen Road, two bedrooms. It's the second floor up, so when Steven goes out to play, I'm there with him. It's rented and what I can afford," she said almost defensively. But then her brow furrowed and almost immediately regretting her small outburst, added, "I'm sorry, I didn't mean to be so snappy."

He nodded and a few uncomfortable seconds passed before he quietly said, "You might think that I'm being patronising, Grace, but I know it's not easy raising a child on your own. Remember," he smiled softly at her, "I'm kind of in the same boat, but I also realise that I'm a little luckier than you because I've probably got a better income. But," he pursed his lips, then stared into her eyes, "for what it's worth, no matter what job you do or where you live, your son is a very lucky young man, Grace. Your son has got *you* and in my humble experience, a loving parent is more important than living in a mansion *or* having a fancy job with a huge income."

Grace was not used to a man, any man, being kind to her. She stared at Des, her eyes widening and dared not move and, because of his unexpected kind words, she felt her chest tighten and clenched her jaw against the tears that threatened to spill from her.

She glanced past him through the open French doors to see the dining table already set and candles lit on two low tables.

"Very nice," she nodded, her head turned from him and her eyes rapidly blinking as she took a deep breath and hoped he didn't see how close to tears she was. He could not know how anxious she had been about coming tonight and uncertain why her stomach continued to churn.

Turning back to him, she smiled and he jokingly brushed aside her apology that she had only bought for three with the comment, "How much do you think I eat? Look at me, I'm a skinny wretch!"

Together they divided the bag of food onto the plates then carrying two each, Des called the boys through to the dining table in the conservatory.

"Oh, the wine in the plastic bag," Grace said, starting to rise from her chair. "I brought a bottle just in case…"

"Eh, I'm happy with a cuppa," Des tapped the teapot, "but if you…"

"No, not if I'm driving," she held up her hand and shook her head.

"Well, we can have it another time," Des remarked, but the inference wasn't lost on Grace, who fought to control a smile.

"Steven and I might have a glass then," said Paul with a theatrical wink to the younger boy, who lifted his hand to his mouth and loudly guffawed, thinking how happy he was to be included in the big people's talk and sneaking a glance around him at the big glass room where they were all having their chips.

Grace smiled gratefully to Paul, so very pleased that he was being kind to her son rather than treating Steven as a juvenile interloper to his home. Then, pretending to scold them both, she said, "The only wine *you* guys are getting is the one marked Irn-Bru. I bought a bottle of that too, if you want to grab it from the bag," she told Paul, who obligingly went to fetch the bottle from the kitchen.

Watching the interaction between his son and Grace, Des was just as pleased they were getting on. He hadn't missed Grace being a little upset in the kitchen and wondered if maybe he had been too soppy for her.

As he ate his food, he glanced at her and thought again how lovely she was and curiously, experienced a warm glow that she was here with him.

"And Rangers won too," grinned Steven and that for Des just seemed to be the icing on the cake.

Slowing then stopping to permit a scowling woman in her forties to cross in front of their CID car at the rear gate of Drumchapel station, Colin Munro grinned at Catriona MacDougall, the driver.

"Don't think you made a pal there, Cat," he said.

"I know I didn't," she replied, her face expressionless, but her eyes followed the woman down the street, a puzzled expression on her face.

She couldn't be certain and thought that maybe she had read into something that wasn't there, but had the woman hesitated when she saw Cat?

"Jessie Cochrane's her name. She's a prolific shoplifter and part time dope dealer," she explained, nodding towards the retreating figure, "I turned her house just about two years ago and she got eighteen months plus a reclamation order by the court under the Proceeds of Crime Act on behalf of the hundreds of retailers she had hit over the years. Took her fancy house and car off her and the last I heard was that she and her man were in homeless accommodation, but that was months ago so they could be anywhere now. Must admit though," she shook her head, "I didn't expect her to be back in the Drum. I'm guessing she must only have done," she closed her eyes and mentally calculated the sentence. "Aye, can't have been more than ten months. Wonder what she's up to these days," she murmured half to herself and chewed at her lower lip.

The young man stared with open admiration at his tutor detective. The best sentence he had achieved for a wrongdoer was three months and even that was for driving offences, not crime. Still, he thought, early days yet and Cat seemed like a good neighbour with whom to commence his CID career.

Slightly embarrassed by his attention, Cat added, "Right you, let's get upstairs and sign off. Home time and do you hear that?" she cocked her head to one side.

"Don't tell me you want another cuppa?" he stared curiously at her.

"No," she grinned at him, "That's my hubby getting the dinner on and putting a bottle of my favourite plonk on the table."

It was while he was pulling down the front window shutter of his shop in Silverburn shopping centre that the mobile phone in Patrick McLaughlin's pocket chirruped. He glanced at the screen and seeing the caller's name, took a deep breath before pressing the green button.

"Hello my friend," he forced his voice to sound jovially cheerful for the man he knew as Fevzi. "It is nice to hear from you."

"Cut the crap, *my friend*," the voice dripped with sarcasm, "you are late *again*, but this time with this month's payment; thirty-two big ones. What is the holdup?" was the terse reply.

The hubbub of noise made by the departing shoppers passing by made it difficult for McLaughlin to hear and pressing himself into a corner of the doorway, he held the phone closer to his ear and took a deep breath.

"As I understand it, there was some difficulty with customers managing their accounts," he explained, "and this led to late payments. But don't worry, it's been sorted and the payment will be credited to your account sometime this week."

"What is sometime this week, *my friend*? Is it Monday, Wednesday, Saturday? Fucking *when* sometime this week?" demanded the voice. McLaughlin took a deep breath and arched his back to relieve the sudden tension.

"Wednesday, the money will be credited to you by Wednesday, my friend."

Later, when he thought about it, he couldn't understand why he said, Wednesday rather than Monday, but figured that if there really *had* been a hiccup like Thomson had explained in his e-mail, then the extra two days would give the thug time to sort out the shortfall.

"Then I will expect my accountant to receive the payment by Wednesday and I do not need excuses, I need only for you to fulfil your part of our agreement."

"You have my word. Can I expect as arranged, a further delivery tomorrow?"

He held his breath and waited a few seconds, worrying at the hesitancy and then the voice answered, "I will make the arrangement. However, as agreed the product will be delivered to you on trust. Payment will follow within one month for tomorrow's delivery as per our agreement and any further deliveries will be subject to my account being credited on Wednesday for *last* months delivery, do you understand?"

"Yes, of course and I just want to say…"

But the voice interrupted him and continued, "Do not have me remind you what will happen if you fail to keep up your end of the agreement, *my friend.*"

The phone still pressed to his ear, he heard the flat no-signal tone and realised that Fevzi had abruptly concluded the call.

He looked at his hand holding the phone and saw to his surprise, the hand was shaking. He swallowed hard and for the first time, understood how frightened he really was of these people, recalling with stark clarity the threat that had been made all those months ago in the London hotel room if he fucked them over.

He closed his eyes against the throbbing in his head and felt weak at the knees.

What the *hell* had he been thinking!

It had seemed like a good idea at the time. He pays thirty-two grand monthly for the drugs that he sells for over fifty grand; ten for him and any other profit for the halfwit thug Thomson he used to distribute the stuff. His ten grand paid into three accounts in different banks to avoid any questions while the thirty-two grand was handed directly every month to a courier sent up from London by the Turks. As for the drugs, he didn't care where they went or how many times the dealers cut it or did whatever to it that made it go that little bit further. It wasn't his problem.

McLaughlin had never used drugs; in fact he had never even smoked a cigarette and secretly not only abhorred drugs, but thought that anyone stupid enough to use them deserved everything that happened to them, even if that meant a hideous death.

Of course, he had known that the temptation by Thomson to screw him for the thirty-two grand, to take the money and run must have been overwhelming, but his persuasive first e-mail had convinced

Thomson that to do so would deny him an opportunity to make *annual* income of whatever extra money the heroin brought him and for the preceding months, since their first collaboration in February, their e-mail association had worked a treat.

Or it had until now.

The previous month's payment that resulted in the frightening phone call from the Turk had been late.

According to a recent e-mail from Thomson, the payment was late because of a seizure by the police who turned a dealers house and not only recovered some of that months delivered heroin, but also seized almost five grand the dealer had stashed and was awaiting collection by Thomson or one of his flunkies.

McLaughlin wiped a sweaty hand across his mouth, his mind racing as he remembered what had occurred.

Because of the seizure of the money by the police the knock-on effect was to cause the late payment to the Turks and forcing him to replace the missing five grand with his own money. Added to the twenty-seven already collected by Thomson, it was eventually handed over to the Turks courier several days later.

"Bastard that he is," he unintentionally spat out, his thoughts on the venomous call from Fevzi.

His comment attracted a glare from a passing middle-aged woman pushing a wailing toddler in a buggy. "Sorry," he raised an apologetic hand and grimaced at her, but the woman had walked off. Taking a deep breath, McLaughlin finished locking the store and shoulders bent, headed towards the centre's staff car park.

The private hire taxi dropped Cathy off at the popular Clydeside hotel and when she bent into the cab to pay off the driver, the two young men openly staring as they passed her by thought they had died and gone to heaven and even more so when the gorgeous redhead stood upright and turning, they got a better look at her. Cathy's hair, piled up on top of her head, accentuated her long, slim neck. Wearing a black coloured wrap that hung loosely over her shoulders, her sleeveless narrow-waist top was of shimmering light green coloured silk with a low v-neck that plunged almost to the buckle of the shiny black plastic belt that was almost as wide as the bottle green coloured tight skirt that she wore was short. Her long slim, bare legs were flawless and on her feet she wore her favourite green high heels that, added to her five foot nine inches, increased her height to just under six foot.

"Stunning," one of the men murmured with a grin, then as his head swivelled to continue staring at Cathy, narrowly avoided colliding with a lamppost.

Of course, she was aware of the interest she provoked, but discreetly avoided the men's eyes and strode towards the front door of the hotel.

Already she could hear the raucous noise of football chants and hesitated, her brow furrowed and thinking that maybe this wasn't such a good idea, a woman alone entering the bar among a mob of drunken supporters and particularly dressed as she was. Stood just within the doorway between the spacious and tastefully decorated foyer and the noisy, male dominated bar, she bit at her lower lip and glancing at her watch, sighed with disappointment and considered perhaps she might leave and return a few hours later, when the bar was less crowded and calmed down. No doubt there would be some diehard punters still available, she mused.

The young bartender, in the act of pulling a pint for a loudmouthed customer, looked up to see that the stunning redhead was back, but was distracted when the beer he was pouring spilled over the lip of the tumbler and soaked his hands, earning himself a sarcastic comment from the drunken customer.

Completely unaware of the young bartenders glance, Cathy was about to turn back towards the door when the tall, sturdily built man approached her from behind and in a deep voice said, "Not leaving already are you, darling? I was hoping that we might have a drink together and maybe do a wee bit of business."

Startled, she automatically smiled at the tall, well built man and saw though bearded and bald, he was well groomed and wore an expensively cut three piece suit. Almost immediately she realised that he must have sussed she was on the game. Not security she decided, for there would have been no offer of a drink; no, it would have been a firm hand on her elbow and then ignominiously marched through the front door and thrown out on her ear with a threat not to return.

Her eyes narrowed as she studied him. In his mid to late forties, his beard neatly trimmed, he seemed to her to be a weightlifter or some sort and definitely into some sort physical fitness. Maybe, she thought, the night might not after all be a complete waste.

He flashed a wide grin and with his hand indicating an empty table at the rear of foyer, invitingly said, "Why don't I get the reception to bring us some drinks here? I don't much fancy fighting my way through the crowd in there," he cocked a thumb over his shoulder towards the noisy bar.

"That might be an idea," she smilingly replied and at his invitation, walked with him towards the table where he gallantly pulled out a chair and seated her.

As he turned from her to attract the attention of the foyer porter stood by the reception desk, she glanced at him and mentally worked out what her charms might cost him for the evening.

The conversation was polite, if a little dull she thought, and she hardly glanced at the young waiter who a few moments later delivered their drinks to the table.

Had Cathy paid more attention, she might have recognised the young man as the starry-eyed bar attendant from a few nights ago who now wondered what a right good looking woman like the red-head was doing with an ugly bastard of a thug like that?

They sipped at their drinks and then he turned towards her and asked, "So, what do I call you then?"

At the outset of her career as a prostitute Cathy had decided that she would not use her own name and would simply be known by a forename, adopting a name that she liked.

"Beth," she replied with a devastating smile. "Call me Beth."

"Beth," he slowly said, devouring her with his eyes and leaning forward he placed his hand lightly but proprietarily on her knee and then added, "I like that name, Beth. It suits you."

Then he grinned at her and whispered, "You can call me, Tommo."

CHAPTER NINE

Wee Chic Fagin was pleased by the bands performance at the day's parade in Alexandria and at the musicians' insistence, joined them for a couple of drinks when the bus returned them to Drumchapel and their local Rangers supporter's pub. Though not a drinker, Chic thought it appropriate that as the Band Sergeant, he be seen to occasionally mix socially with the lads and was secretly pleased that though there was a real difference in age between him and most of the band members, they respected him and often sought and would heed his advice.

Well, he inwardly admitted, most of the time anyway.

Nursing a pint of fruit squash, Chic smiled and loudly joined in the Loyalist songs he had learned at his father's knee and that in turn, he had taught to his grandson Ian.

His eyes narrowed as he turned his head back and forth, searching for Ian among the cheerful crowd, but there was no sign of him and with a sinking heart, Chic realised that without as much as a cheerio, Ian had skipped out from the pub and was gone.

He sighed with disappointment, knowing that Ian's participation for the day was over, that the call of the drugs was too strong and head down, Chic placed the pint glass on a nearby table. Then with much back-slapping and hand-shaking, he made his way through the noisy crowd towards the door to walk slowly home.

Detective Constable Cat MacDougall signed off in the time-book lying on the CID clerk's desk and grabbing her coat and handbag, with a grin wished the late shift officers a quiet night.

She found Colin Munro on the first floor landing waiting for her outside the CID office.

"Listen," he started, a little embarrassed, "I just want to say thanks for today, Cat. I know it was my first day and there wasn't really a lot going on, but to be honest I was really nervous. You made it a lot easier than I thought it would be and…"

"Nonsense, Colin. It was nice having some company," she interrupted him with a pat on his arm as they walked down the stairs together. "So, same time tomorrow then?"

"Right you are, boss," he grinned and nodding at her, pushed open the rear door and stepped into the crisp coolness of the evening.

Following behind, Cat walked into the yard towards her car, stroking the driver's door of the gleaming white coloured Audi A3 Sport and with a smile, whispered half to herself, "Let's get home now, my proud beauty."

She loved and prized the car above all her possessions, though her husband Gus would sometimes wonder where *he* came in the pecking order and wisely thought it better not to tempt fate by asking her.

She threw her coat and bag into the rear seat and starting the engine, smiled at the deep-throated roar then selecting her favourite *Eurthymics* CD, drove towards the exit.

Slowing at the gate, Cat checked the road was clear of passing traffic and was about to turn right onto the opposite lane when she saw her standing by a lamppost across the road, staring into the car. As she watched, the woman turned and slowly walked off in the direction that Cat was about to turn, with a fleeting look behind to ensure Cat had seen her.

Cat's curiosity was aroused and eyes narrowed in suspicion, she glanced up and down the road on each side of where the woman walked to ascertain she was alone and then driving the car slowly alongside her, stopped. Lowering the passenger window, she switched off the music and called out, "Hello, Jessie. Were you looking for me?"

Jessie Cochrane, convicted prolific shoplifter and minor drug-dealer, bent her head to peer into the car and a little breathlessly, tersely replied, "I need a word."

Cat could only guess at the effort it must have taken for Jessie to even acknowledge the detective who had not only arrested her and caused her conviction, but was also indirectly responsible for the seizure of her assets. Whatever Jessie wanted with Cat, it must be something extremely important and yet curiously, it didn't occur to Cat that Jessie meant her any harm.

"Get in," she instructed and leaned across to push open the passenger door.

When Jessie was in the car and strapped in, Cat's eyes narrowed as for the first time, she noticed the bruising to Jessie's face, but made no comment and starting the engine, drove off.

They travelled in awkward silence for a few minutes then Cat said, "I know a smashing wee licensed cafe in the west end just off Byres Road, Jessie. It'll take us fifteen minutes to get there and get parked, if that's okay with you?"

Jessie, staring out of the passenger window didn't reply, but simply nodded her head.

Glancing down at Jessie's hands Cat saw she held her handbag in her lap so tightly her knuckles were white.

"Right then," Cat sighed, wondering just what the hell Jessie wanted and added, "The west end it is then."

"Dad," said Paul Brown, "I'm taking Steven up to my room to show him my model car collection. So wee man," he turned with a grin and winked at the young boy, "we'll leave these old codgers on their own, eh?"

Delighted to be part of the joke yet uncertain if he was to be allowed, Steven turned towards his mum who nodded and with a wag of her forefinger warned him to behave himself.

As the two boys scampered through the French doors, Grace rose and began to clear the table, but Des raised a hand to stop her and said, "Leave them the now. That's my job for later."

They sat comfortably finishing their tea and then moved through to occupy the more comfortable chairs in the lounge.

He began by telling her at length of joining the police as a raw teenager and his nineteen years as a cop and made her laugh with a few funny anecdotal stories of his time on the beat. She told him of the drudgery of a life employed as a school cleaner and working for extra income cleaning other people's houses, but didn't tell him of the arrangement she had cleaning Mick Thomson's flat; of her unpaid support work at the school and the pleasure she discovered when volunteering for duty with the PTA, joking it was her only social outings.

He spoke without rancour of his marriage to his former wife Margo, of the years he listened to her without complaint until six years previously when she and her colleague at work decided they were better together than with their marital partners and she left. Of the tears and heartache when she decided to leave little Paul in Des's care, of the difficulties in raising a small child while shift working, of putting his career on hold; of his eternal gratitude to his parents who chipped in when he was feeling overwhelmed with the responsibility of it all.

He told her of the reconciliation between Margo and their son some three years previously and his final acceptance that she had been right to leave, that had it continued, the marriage would have become ugly and it would have been their son who suffered the most.

Sitting in the comfortable armchair, her boots kicked off and her legs tucked beneath her, in a soft voice she told him of the brief relationship with Steven's father, an English student she had thought she loved but whom, unable to accept parenthood at twenty-two years of age, had fled home to England and had never returned. She later came to realise what she thought was love had really been her desire to get away from her mean and loveless aunt with whom she lived; for a new start and she had been prepared to do anything to achieve it. She told him of her devastation at being pregnant at twenty, of the silent unspoken accusation of the spinster aunt and who could never admit to being jealous of Grace because she had lived her own life, unloved and childless.

Her life, her ambitions and her dreams, she continued, suddenly took second place to the bundle of joy that was Steven and to whom she devoted her days.

The unexpected and sudden death of the aunt, when Steven was less than a year old, meant nothing other than Grace no longer had to endure the sneers and accusations of being the mother of a bastard child and for a while, Grace had thought of herself as being as cold and heartless as her aunt. In time, she came to realise she no longer disliked her aunt, but felt sorry for the deeply unhappy woman and regretted never having been able to share with her the joy of Steven's arrival.

Grace sighed and a little self-consciously, sipped at her tea and told him that as for relationships; she stopped and softly laughed and then shaking her head and a little abashed, confessed that since Steven's father there had been no other man in her life.

"So, there's nobody special at the minute, then?" he asked, experiencing a curious tightness in his chest.

"No," she shook her head, averting her eyes and wondered at her nervousness.

He couldn't tell her how pleased he was to hear that.

A little hesitantly, she placed the mug on the low table by her chair and sat back down and he saw she was blushing.

"Sorry, I didn't mean to embarrass you, Grace," he said

"No, it's not you," she replied, biting at her lower lip. She took a deep breath and slowly exhaled. "It's just that, well, what I mean is…"

Sitting in the chair opposite her, he folded his arms and jokingly smiled at her. "Take your time, Miss Thomson. I'm not going anywhere."

"I'm rambling, aren't I?"

"Just a bit," he agreed with a nod.

She took another deep breath and wondered why this was so difficult.

"Look, it's been a long time for me, what I mean is I haven't had an *interest* in a man for such a long time."

He stared at her for a few seconds that to Grace, seemed an interminable time and to her sudden horror, wondered if she had been mistaken; had she misread his signals? Didn't he, as she'd thought, have *any* interest in her?

Des smiled and sat forward in his chair, his arms folded across his knees.

"I'm going on thirty-nine, divorced, subject to hereditary baldness and have absolutely *no* social life. I support a football team that currently couldn't kick their way out of a wet paper bag, have no interest in reality television shows, have no dress sense and drive a car that barely gets me back and forth to work. You, on the other hand, are what, thirty?"

"Twenty-nine, well, almost," she narrowed her eyes and pretended outrage, but could not stop herself from smiling.

"Twenty-eight but *almost* twenty-nine," he repeated and returned her smile. "You're younger than me by just over ten years, extremely good looking. Yes," he held up a hand to forestall any argument. "*Extremely* good looking," he repeated, "and brighter than you probably give yourself credit for. You've a son that you dote on…"

"As have you," she pointedly remarked.

"Agreed, as have I," he repeated and continued, "And of course you drive a top of the range Nissan Micra..."

"Well, it was top of the range ten years ago," she interrupted.

"So, Grace Thomson, why would you have any interest in an old guy like me?"

"That's a bit presumptuous. How do you know I'm talking about you, Desmond Brown?" she pretended surprise.

"Well, I'm rather *hoping* you're talking abut me, Grace Thomson, because I certainly have an interest in *you*," he replied and stared at her.

An awkward silence fell between them, broken when he said, "I was thinking," but then he hesitated and wondered why he was so nervous, "if you've enjoyed this evening as much as I have, if you *might* like to do it again? I mean," he shrugged his shoulders, "without the boys next time. Just me and you, like," his voice quietly tailed off.

"A date you mean?" she replied, trying in vain to keep the growing excitement out of her voice, then more slowly added, "Yes, I'd *like* that," she drawled, "but the only problem is that I don't have any family. No close friends either," she shook her head, "that I could trust to watch Steven when I'm out."

Des screwed his face and replied, "Well, it so happens that I know a couple who I'm sure…no, certain in fact, would love to have the opportunity to watch Steven for a couple of hours one night."

He saw her puzzled expression and rather than tease her, added, "My folks, Eddie and Agnes. They live in the Drum and they're daft on kids. They get to see my Paul regularly, but my brother's kids are in England, so they don't see them that often."

He saw her hesitation and thought that he had overstepped the mark, that she wasn't as interested as he had thought, but before she could respond, the door burst open to admit an excited Steven who ran into the lounge, a foot long model car held in both hands.

"Mum!" he cried out, "Look what Paul gave me!" and thrust the car towards her.

Laughing at her son's excitement, she took the red coloured sports car from Steven's hands as Paul followed the younger boy through the door.

"Is that all right, Grace?" asked Paul, "It's just that he really liked it…"

"Are you sure," she asked, wondering at the tightness in her throat and turned towards Des who standing now, was ruffling the smaller boy's hair and with his head bowed, smiled down at Steven's delight.

"I was just telling your dad," she turned towards Paul, "that I don't get out much these days, what with looking after this scallywag here, so he said that your Gran and Granddad might keep an eye on Steven for me, one of these nights?"

Quick on the uptake, Paul nodded and then replied, "Why don't I stay there with him too? That way the wee man won't feel as if he's been abandoned and it means my dad can get a night out too?"

Turning to stare at Des with his arm round Steven and then at the grinning Paul, Grace suddenly relaxed and biting at her lower lip, wondered at the good fortune that had brought Des Brown and his lovely, kind son into their lives.

Ian Fagin stood smoking in the darkness in the close across the road, peering up at the brightly lit window on the first floor. Through the open curtains he could just make out the figure of Casey Lennox as she strode back and forth the across the room, a child in her arms whose head rested on her shoulder. Ian saw her bobbing up and down as she walked, patting at the child's back and then his eyes narrowed when he saw Billy Purvis in the room who completely unaware of Ian's presence, reached up and pulled the curtains closed. A thought occurred to him and he knew he wasn't supposed to, but the knowledge that Casey was there, so close in her house just across the road, persuaded him. He drew deeply on the joint and nipping the lit end, blew on it to cool it before returning it to his trouser pocket. It took Ian but a minute to get to Casey's door and he frowned when he saw the scrap of paper pinned to the door with the two names scrawled on it; W Purvis and C Lennox. Angry that Purvis should be living there too, he glanced furtively behind him then tore the paper from the pin and crumpling it into a ball, shoved it in the front pocket of his trousers. Taking a deep breath, he nervously knocked on the door and stood back, using his fingers to comb through his lengthy, greasy hair and pulling down on his grey coloured hooded top.

Billy Purvis, wearing black coloured tracksuit bottoms and a bright blue polo shirt, pulled the door open and glowered at him, before asking, "What the fuck you wanting, eedjit-face?"

"Hi Billy," Ian raised a hand in greeting and forced a smile. "I just thought because I was passing by…"

"Then why the fuck did you no just *pass* by?"

Ian was stumped, tongue-tied and wishing he had thought this out a bit better.

"Who's there, Billy" called Casey, walking from the lounge into the hallway behind Purvis with the wailing child in her arms and peering over her shoulder at him.

Seeing it was Ian, she smiled, but couldn't know that her smile melted his heart.

"Hi Casey," he called out to her with a huge grin.

Purvis twitched his nose and turning towards Casey, said, "Get him back to his cot, hen. I'll see to this," and with that, stepped out of the door, drawing it closed behind him. Without warning, he grabbed Ian's hooded top at the front and pushing the slighter built youth backwards, slammed him against the wall.

"You've been smoking a joint, you arse! I can smell it on you!" he hissed in Ian's face, their noses almost touching and spraying Ian with spittle. "You don't come to my door smelling of cannabis you fucking moron!" he venomously added then drawing his fist back, punched Ian in the stomach. It wasn't a hard punch and delivered more in warning than rage, but not a fighter, Ian theatrically crumpled with the blow onto the cold stone surface of the close and gasped. Frightened, tears stung at his eyes.

Purvis considered kicking him when he was on his knees, but instead punched his right fist into the palm of his left hand and bending low over Ian, again said, "Never, ever come to my door when you've had a joint, wee man. Do you understand?"

Ian, too afraid to glance up, stared down at the ground and biting at his lip to stop himself from crying, nodded.

"Right then," Purvis stood back and flicking a thumb at the stairs, said in a calmer voice, "Get to fuck and remember, if I need you I'll phone you. No coming to my door, okay wee man?"

Satisfied that he had done the business with the halfwit and scared him shitless, Purvis turned and re-entered the flat, slamming the door behind him without noticing the missing scrap of paper with the names written on it.

Still knelt on the ground, Ian took a deep breath and with one hand on the wall to steady him, he slowly arose.

Head bowed, he began to walk down the stairs, but stopped on the half landing where he knew he wouldn't be seen and turning, quietly muttered, "Up yours, Purvis," and saluted with the middle digit of his right hand.

Giggling softly to himself, he continued walking down the stairs, knowing that just to see the gorgeous Casey up close had been worth the punch in the gut.

Byres Road was it's usual hectic self that Saturday evening with locals and visitors crowding into the numerous pubs and restaurants that abounded the area. Turning into Cresswell Street, Cat

MacDougall was fortunate to find a parking space on the opposite side of the road from the chic café and parallel parking the Audi, switched off the engine and turned towards Jessie Cochrane.

"There we are," she smiled, but got no reaction and continued, "I know this must be difficult for you Jessie, but you are the one that wants to speak with me. Whatever it is, I'm guessing it's *really* important." Still Jessie said nothing, so Cat took a deep breath and added, "Look, that's the place over there," she pointed past Jessie's head to the brightly lit café.

"It's a nice wee quiet cafe and nobody will know who we are, so why don't we get out of the car and take a wee stroll over, eh?" To her relief, she saw Jessie inhale then slowly nod and reach to open the door.

The café was quieter than Cat expected and together they settled in a corner table, their coats on the chair beside them and their backs to the wall and with a clear view of the door in the unlikely event someone might enter who would recognise either woman.

The dusky young foreign waitress smiled and took their order, coffee for Cat and a glass of red wine for Jessie, who reached for her purse. "No, let me," smiled Cat, but was shocked when Jessie snapped, "I don't need any fucking favours from you!"

Angered and slightly pissed that she was the one doing the favour, Cat quietly hissed back, "Clearly you fucking do, Jessie, else we wouldn't be sitting here now, would we?"

A tense and silent few seconds passed and Cat saw the older woman almost wilt and to her surprise, Jessie's hands began to shake.

It was then Cat realised she was close to tears. She couldn't explain why and later, thinking about it, decided it must have been a reflex reaction, for Cat bent over and wrapped her arms about Jessie's shoulders and pulling her towards her, hugged her while she sobbed uncontrollably.

The waitress, a student Cat guessed, arrived carrying a small tray with the coffee and wine and glanced nervously at the distraught Jessie. Cat caught the girl's eye and grimacing, whispered, "We had a family bereavement today. A death," she added, thinking the word 'bereavement' might not be in the girl's English vocabulary.

"Oh, right, yes, of course," replied the young woman, laying the tray on the table and returning hurriedly to the counter where Cat could see her lift her hand and in turn whisper in the ear of the older woman serving behind the counter, who smiled sympathetically at Cat.

After a few moments, Jessie slowly exhaled and dabbing at her eyes with a handkerchief, stood and walked towards the ladies toilet, returning a few moments later, her face washed and now composed.

"I'm sorry, I thought I was stronger than that," said Jessie.

"Here," Cat pushed the wine glass towards her, "get that down you. Do you need anything to eat?"

"Try not to be kind to me, DC MacDougall," Jessie weakly smiled at her, "I'm a bit fragile as you can see."

"Well, whatever's upsetting you Jessie, if you call me Cat…short for Catriona," she smiled, "then maybe we can talk about it, eh?"

Jessie nodded and then, as if reminding herself that Cat was a police detective, said, "I'm not in the habit of grassing people up, DC…Cat. You know that, don't you?"

Cat nodded and replied, "I understand, Jessie and *you* have to know that whatever you tell me, if it relates to a crime, then I'm duty bound to either report or investigate it."

She saw Jessie's eyes open wide, but before the older woman could respond, Cat raised a hand and added, "Maybe the best thing is if you tell me what's troubling you, Jessie. You never struck me as a woman that could be easily upset and if it's anything that I can help you with, then I'm *equally* duty bound to do that too, okay?"

Jessie stared at her as if trying to decide whether to go ahead or not and then slowly said, "The reason I wanted to speak to you yourself is that you were fair with me. You didn't treat me like shite, not like that other guy you were with."

Cat's eyes narrowed, recalling her neighbour at the time of Jesse's arrest, a chauvinistic bully she was obliged to work with and who she heard recently left the police, it was rumoured, ahead of the posse of rubber heels from the Police Standards Unit who sought to charge him with corrupt practises

"If I tell you something that might get *me* the jail, will you arrest me?" continued Jesse.

Cat had a decision to make and did so almost immediately, making a point of looking about her and replied, "I don't see any other cops here, Jessie. Anything you tell me can easily be denied by you if you need to, can't it?"

Jessie forced a smile and nodded. "Okay, then. Here's what I want to tell you, hen. Things have been a bit difficult recently and my man Gary, you remember him, don't you?"

Cat did, a slightly built man about Jessie's age or perhaps a few years older who following an accident at work, walked with the use of a stick.

"Anyway, the Social cut Gary's money when some bastard grassed him in that he was working, lifting the tumblers in the pub for a few quid at the weekend and emptying the bins and that, just a bit of pocket-money, you know; nothing too strenuous on account of his disability. He's a good guy, my man, but he's no a fighter."

She took a deep breath and another sip of her wine. "This guy I know," then glanced sharply at Cat, "I'm no saying his name, hen."

"That's okay, Jessie. Go on."

"So, this guy I know, he offered me a job; doing a bit of selling like." She took another deep breath, but no wine this time. "Smack, I was selling. Not a lot," she defensively raised her hands, "just personal I was dealing, hen. Honest. It's no as if I was making a lot of money or anything," she wistfully sighed, "but we needed what I did make, me and Gary I mean. It's no as if I'm employable, not with my record anyway and as for my Gary. Well, he's just not fit."

At the mention of the heroin, Cat's stomach clenched, but she made no overt gesture, afraid that if she probed Jessie might clam up.

"Well, when I was selling the smack I got a bit behind in my payments; three grand I owed, though," her eyes narrowed as if mentally counting off in her head, "I had collected about just under a grand."

She stared down to the wooden topped table and her voice dropped to a whisper. Her hand was at her mouth as she chewed on the knuckle of her forefinger, pausing while she again composed herself.

"The guy I owed the money to. He hires Mick Thomson as a debt collector. You'll know that name, hen," she spat out.

Cat nodded, sensing the sudden tension in Jessie's voice and desperate as she was to ask questions, not wishing to interrupt Jessie's narrative.

"He sent Thomson round to collect the debt," she whispered with a quaking voice so low that Cat was now straining to hear. "When he arrived, Tommo I mean, he threw my Gary out of the house and locked the door."

During the following ten minutes, Cat's half-drunk coffee grew cold while Jessie, with graphic detail, faltering voice and shaking hands that held her handkerchief at her tear ridden eyes, described to the shocked young detective how Jessie was made to stand in front of Thomson, who ordered her to strip and who beat her and who sexually abused and humiliated the naked Jessie and laughed as he did so. How he had pulled her about the room by her hair and threatened to kill her if she did not indulge him in his sexual perversion and who visited upon her such degradation that the shame of that horror filled hour would haunt her forever.

"I'm still sore where he…" she paused and gulped, "you know, did they things to me. I thought about going to the doctor," she sighed, "but he would want to know how I got the injuries in…those places and honest, I just couldn't tell him, hen, even if he is a doctor, you know what I mean?" she sniffed and again began to softly weep.

"And that's how you got your sore face, Jessie?"

Jessie nodded.

Across at the counter, Cat noticed the two women were almost at pains to discreetly ignore her and Jessie, though some other customers were now nudging each other, their eyes betraying their curiosity.

Cat couldn't say when it happened, but saw that she was tightly holding Jessie's hand and squeezing it instinctively, she knew that Jessie wasn't lying nor was she exaggerating. Her anger almost overtook her good sense when she said, "I'll go after him Jessie. I'll *get* that bastard," she softly hissed through gritted teeth, "I promise you. I'll *do* for him!"

"No!" Jessie round on her, her eyes wide with alarm as she rapidly shook her head and pleaded, "Oh God, no! That's not what I want hen! The reason I'm telling you this *isn't* because I want to get him arrested! For fuck's sake, no!" she continued to shake her head. "Jesus Christ, hen, I can't go into a court and tell the world what he did to me! I can't even tell my *doctor*, so what use would I be in a witness box?"

"Then what *do* you want me to do, Jessie?"

Jessie turned towards her and still tightly gripping Cat's hand, swallowed hard before she replied, "Get the bastard for the heroin, hen." She vigorously shook her head and added, "I'm not supposed to know this, but it's Thomson that supplies the heroin to the guy I get it off. It's Thomson that's the main smack dealer in Drumchapel. He's the guy that supplies everybody with the *good* stuff!"

Mick Thomson stood at the foot of the bed and stared down expressionlessly at her while he slowly buttoned his shirt. He glanced at his watch and saw that almost two hours had passed, two hours of pleasure at her expense. He had enjoyed riding her and hurting her, making the bitch squeal as his large hands had twisted her tits, bit at her nipples and poked her where she didn't want him to go. He grinned and stepping into his trousers, pulled them up and fastened the belt before pulling up the zip.

It hadn't been difficult persuading her to take him back to her flat, explaining to her that he preferred that to a hotel room and glibly lied that he was well known to his fellow football supporters, that he was sharing a double room with a mate and didn't want to be seen with a woman in case his wife found out.

Her initial flat refusal was easily overcome, recalling how she had first hesitated then her eyes had greedily lit up when he offered her not the two hundred she asked for, but the five hundred in the tightly bound wad of notes he produced from his pocket. His brow creased for it reminded him he had better collect the cash from her purse, before he left.

He yawned, tired now and walking to the window, pulled aside the curtain and looked out, seeing the darkness that enveloped the walkway below. The river shimmered as the tide changed and a thought came to his mind.

There wouldn't be that much to clean up. He hadn't used the other rooms in the flat other than the bedroom and after he'd peed, already wiped down the toilet pan and handle with the bleach wipes he found in the small cupboard under the vanity unit. The sheets and pillow cases he would take with him and dump somewhere.

A low moan caused him to glance down at her.

Cathy Porteous lay naked face down on the bed, her blonde hair untidily spilled across the pillow, her head turned to one side. Her eyes were closed and puffy where he had repeatedly punched her on the face. She moaned again through the tight gag that he had made with the seamed black stocking he had discovered in a drawer and used the matching stocking to bind her wrists behind her. A further pair he used to tie her ankles to the posts at the foot of the bed when after beating and raping her, she had tried to protest his anal violation of her. He saw where the dried blood now adhered to the top of her buttocks and stared with disgust at the blood from her broken nose and burst lips that had splattered onto the pillow case and sheet by her head. Dirty bitch, he sighed and shook his head. He glanced again at his watch and knew it was almost time to go. He heard her moan again and quietly cough, unaware and also uncaring that she was swallowing her own blood among the fragments of her shattered teeth.

He shrugged into his jacket and ensuring the Nissan keys were in his pocket, lifted her handbag from the floor and rifling through it, retrieved the wad of money before throwing the bag into a corner. Her head flopped to one side when without concern he pulled the pillows from the bed and pulling the pillowcases off, threw the pillows into the corner. The top sheet and quilt cover he stuffed with the second pillowcase into the other. The bottom sheet he pulled out from the constraint of the mattress so that it lay loose on either side of the bed and ready for what he planned.

From his trouser pocket he fetched a small, cheap imitation of a Swiss army knife and   sawed through the knot, releasing her feet from the bedposts, but left the cut stockings tied to her ankles and watched as her long legs relaxed from the constrained position she had been subjected to. Returning the knife to his pocket, he carefully got onto the bed, the firm mattress dipping slightly as he knelt astride her, careful that the dried blood didn't stain his trousers at the knees and felt himself again become erect at her naked helplessness. She moaned when she felt the weight of him sit on her lower back, involuntarily struggling against him and trying to turn her head to plead with him not to hurt her again, but the gag was too tight and she panicked because it was so difficult to breathe. He smiled at the memory of how she had fought him and had been surprised at her strength. Slowly he lifted her bound wrists from her back so that her arms were pulled sharply up and backwards and watching her torso contort as he tortured her, he continued to smile when he heard her wincing as her shoulders were forced together.

"Now if you struggle girlie I will *really* hurt you," he whispered to her and let go her wrists, releasing her from the agonising pain. Almost gently with his forefinger, he stroked her spine and wondered, was there time for one last ride at her?

With a sigh he decided there wasn't and besides, he inwardly argued, he'd need to undress again and clean her up a bit.

"Sorry, darling," he whispered almost apologetically, then taking her blonde hair in both his fists, raised her head slightly and turning her face towards the mattress, pushed the panic-stricken Cathy's head hard into the unforgiving material and forcefully suffocated her.

CHAPTER TEN – Sunday 6 July

Patrick McLaughlin was one of the earlier members arriving that crisp morning at the golf club. Closing the boot of his BMW five series, he turned when his name was called out and saw Alex Burns, an associate member, exiting his own vehicle and cheerfully waving at him. McLaughlin sighed in irritation, but forced a smile and returning the wave, saw Burns walking towards him.

"Morning Patrick, it's a fine day for it, eh?"

"Morning, Alex. Aye, right enough," he glanced towards the clear sky. "Who are you matched with today then?"

"Oh, nobody," replied Burns with a shake of his head, "but I thought if perhaps you weren't playing against anyone?"

McLaughlin continued to force his smile. The last thing he wanted was to spend time with the boyish Burns, particularly with him being a copper, but then it occurred to him. It might not do any harm to keep Burns onside, for one thing he had quickly learned about the Superintendent; he was a habitual gossip and forever relating stories about the goings on in his police division. With an inward sigh, McLaughlin said, "Good idea, Alex. Shall we say one hundred quid for the clubs charity and lunch on the loser?"

He watched as Burns hesitated at the sum being waged, but then with a tight smile and nod of his head, the younger man replied, "Why not."

As they walked together towards the clubhouse, McLaughlin inwardly grinned, well aware that Burns was currying favour in the hope McLaughlin would sponsor him for full membership of the both the prestigious club as well as the local Rotarians and favoured him with a wide smile. Besides, he thought, the match might be another opportunity for him to quiz the unsuspecting cop, considering that maybe a round of golf might be just the thing for finding out what was happening over in Drumchapel and in particular, if there was any news about Mick Thomson, a favourite topic of Burns.

He choked back a grin, wryly recalling that it was Burns who boasting about the villains his officers had to deal with, had unconsciously informed McLaughlin about Mick Thomson.

It had all come about just after the clubs post-New Year celebration party held in the members' large lounge, when alcohol had flowed freely, staid inhibitions drunkenly forgotten and the openly light-hearted dalliances between married members of the opposite gender that for months thereafter was the stuff of club gossip.

McLaughlin, realising that he had no contacts in the Glasgow drug scene, had deliberately introduced himself to the naïve Burns and his dull wife and immediately impressed the Superintendent by namedropping some high profile contacts in the Rotary club.

In his eagerness to become a local Rotarian and during several weeks of arranged lunches, Burns quite willingly discussed his job with McLaughlin, boasting of his meteoric rise through the ranks to become the Commander of the Drumchapel sub-division.

It also didn't take much to work out that much of Burns success in his chosen career was mainly due to his being the nephew of a prominent local authority councillor.

Through these light-hearted lunches, McLaughlin would ply Burns with alcohol and good-humouredly quiz the Superintendent about the type of criminal his officers dealt with.

It was during the anecdotal tales that one name seemed to stand out; Michael 'Tommo' Thomson who, according to Burns, was the evilest bastard in his division.

Thereafter, making use of his IT skills, it wasn't too difficult for McLaughlin to obtain Thomson's home phone number and thus, the contact was made.

Acting Detective Constable Colin Munro arrived earlier than his new neighbour Cat MacDougall and relieved the two weary nightshift detectives who almost running out the door, called out that the twenty-four hour summary notes were up to date and that the Drum had been unusually quiet that Saturday night.

Humming softly to himself Munro strode over to the duty roster pinned to the wall and saw that it was just he and Cat who were on duty that morning, though the nightshift guys had said the DI might pop in later. Turning he went to the table in the corner and boiled the kettle then in the midst of preparing two mugs, turned around when the door opened and Cat called out, "Morning, neighbour."

Dumping her bag and coat onto her desk, she asked, "How was your evening?"

"Quiet," he replied and eyes quizzing, stared at her as he held up a mug.

"Oh yes, please," she sighed and flopped down onto her chair.

"Hardly slept a wink all night," she added, brushing her blonde hair back from her face, but reluctant to explain that after last night's meeting with Jessie Cochrane, her mind was still in a whirl. She had already decided it wasn't fair on Colin Munro to share Cochrane's story, that if for any reason it was later learned she had been told but not acted upon the rape allegation, it might cause a more than a little problem for Cat.

"The nightshift said there wasn't anything doing last night," he handed her the mug of tea, "and what they did attend to is all in the boss's notes."

He handed her the notes and sat down in the chair opposite, watching as she placed then read the notes on the desk before her while she used both hands to collect her long hair behind her head. Rolling it tightly, she fetched a black plastic clasp from her bag and clipped it on top of her head. Glancing at her, Munro thought even the lighter coloured small scar on the left side of her chin couldn't detract from her model looks.

She turned and saw him staring at her and brow creased, asked, "What?"

He blushed, lost for words while Cat, with sudden realisation suggested, "Why don't you nip downstairs and check with the uniform bar that there's no crime reports lying there that might have been missed, eh? You can ask them as well if there are any calls outstanding we need to attend."

She watched as he left the room and smiled. Cat had always been aware that throughout her service, her blonde hair, slim figure and good looks had been of interest to men and she had become used to the attention of her fellow male officers. Even, on one embarrassing occasion that caused her smile to turn to a bashful grin, a female colleague who propositioned her on a shift night out and apologised the following day, blaming her intoxication.

However, when she had met her husband Gus, Cat lost interest in other men and those colleagues who knew her well quickly realised she was not a woman who was interested in any kind of frivolous dalliance. No, she thought as she sipped at her tea, Cat MacDougall was a strictly one-man woman.

Still, she smiled and thinking of young Colin's attention, it was nice to know she still had it.

Her thoughts turned to last night's meeting with Jessie and her insistence that Cat did not make it official, that if there was any kind of inquiry Jessie would completely deny that anything had happened between her and Mick Thomson.

The door opened and Munro, slightly breathless, re-entered the CID room to report that no, there was nothing doing for now.

"Right then," she nodded, "if there's nothing doing for the minute we'll finish this tea and," she paused and theatrically cocking her head to one side, her eyes widening, said, "did you hear that?"

Munro stared suspiciously at her and slowly drawled, "No."

She grinned at him and grabbing her coat and handbag, stood and continued, "That was the wee woman at the cafeteria in Sainsbury's shouting that the cooked breakfast you're buying me is almost ready."

Lying in his bed that Sunday morning, his hands behind his head, Des Brown thought of the previous evening's visit by Grace Thomson and her son Steven. He smiled and exhaled, believing the night had gone even better than he had hoped and recalled when they were leaving, Grace hugging his son Paul while her courteous kiss on Des's cheek, with her hands squeezing on his arms, suggested a promise of things to come.

He had earlier explained he would need to check his shift pattern before they set a day for their date, but she didn't mind for it gave him an excuse to contact her again. His parents, he knew wouldn't mind what date they cared for young Steven, for their home was always open to kids.

The youngster was a nice lad too, Des thought and his mother, while doting on her son, didn't let him away with much either and it was obvious she had brought him up to be respectful and polite. Yes, he decided, Grace Thomson was definitely a catch for some man and brow furrowed, wondered if he was that man.

A confident individual in most issues, Des was a more than competent police detective, a good and loving father to his son Paul and a loyal and trusted friend to his colleagues, but his marital experience with Margo had caused him to accept that his self-assurance where women was concerned, was low. The bruising he had suffered throughout the marriage from the acerbic tongued Margo had taken its toll and he worried if Grace might see through his lack of self-belief.

He sighed as doubt crept like a shadow into his thoughts, thinking again of the age gap and Grace's own vulnerability; her openly defensive posture because she was the daughter of one of Drumchapel's most virulent gangsters.

He heard the sound of the toilet flushing in the bathroom, A moment later, the door knocked then opened and Paul, his hair a riot and wearing his pyjamas, stuck his head in and said, "Just popping downstairs, Dad. Shall I stick the kettle on?"

Grinning, Des replied, "Morning, son. Good idea. Give me a minute and I'll be down too and while you're there, shove some toast on as well."

"Are you working today?"

"Yeah, I'm doing a late shift today then an early shift tomorrow, so your Granddad will be round here till about three o'clock and stay with you until I get home and you've to go to their house tomorrow after school. Is that okay?"

He realised his son had little choice in the arrangement, but always tried to explain it as if Paul was making the decision.

"No problem, Dad," Paul replied with a nod of his head and then with a little hesitation, added, "It was a good night last night, wasn't it?"

"Yeah, it was and thanks son; for looking after the wee guy for an hour, I mean."

"Oh, he was fine. I like Steven," he paused, "and Grace too. She's nice Dad. I hope that you two get on well."

Before Des could respond, Paul ducked out of sight and closed the door. He felt a lump in his throat. His son was a bright, perceptive young man and he suspected that Paul realised that even with the company of his own parents and his son, as well as his colleagues at work, his father was a lonely man.

Laying his cutlery down on the empty plate, Tom Fraser seated at the kitchen table hid his burp behind a napkin and smiled at his wife Sheila.

"That was delicious sweetheart. Thanks," and toasted her with his coffee cup.

"What have you planned for today?" she asked as she reached across the table for his plate, her dressing gown slightly open and the swell of her breasts shuddering in the loose fitting nightdress.

His involuntary stare at her cleavage caused her to softly laugh as she stood up, a plate in each hand and stared down at him. "Wasn't last night enough for you, you lecherous old bugger?"

He inhaled deeply and smiled up at her as she turned towards the dishwasher, watching as she bent over to load the plates and cutlery and tongue in cheek replied, "Last night was as good as ever Sheila and if you're up for it, we could have a lie-in this morning?"

She stood upright and turned towards him, a bold grin on her face and her cheeks flushed.

"I can guess what *your* lie-in will involve, Tom Fraser, and you've got the glint of the devil in your eye, so brush your teeth before you come through," she said with a slightly husky voice and coyly shrugged her dressing gown off to land on the kitchen floor. As he watched her walk away, he could see that the fading scarring was now almost indiscernible. With a beckoning forefinger over her shoulder, she walked through towards their bedroom.

It was just about an hour later when Sheila got out of bed, kissed her husband on the cheek and closed the door in the en-suite to shower and ready herself to attend and assist at the church fete.

Tom, lying in bed, yawned lazily and squirmed with pleasure, but then his thoughts turned to the idea that had been fermenting since yesterday when from the bus he had watched the two drunks squabbling over the money. Try as he might, the idea would not go away and persisted and he knew that, no matter what, the craziness would stay with him until he was talked out of it. He listened as Sheila sang loudly, if incredibly off tune in the shower and grinned. Her voice wasn't her best feature, thinking happily of the last hour. His brow narrowed as again the idea hammered at the forefront of his mind and he bit at his lower lip. Risky didn't begin to describe the nonsense he was contemplating and decided that he would discuss it with Harry, but then almost immediately changed his mind. No, Harry McInnes was a close and trusted friend, but to lay something like that on him just wasn't fair, for it would be Harry who was taking the greatest risk.

He would be better first speaking with Dick and the thought caused him to smile. If there was a money to be made, Dick would be all for it, regardless of the risk.

"Penny for them," said Sheila, stepping naked from the en-suite and rubbing vigorously at her wet hair with a towel. The thick cloud of steam from the shower followed her through the door and he sighed. She'd forgotten again to open the small, hopper window and likely the tiles would be crashing from the wall any minute now.

He stared at her still slim figure, her breasts bobbing up and down as arms raised, she rubbed at her hair and a slow grin spread across his face.

"Think you'd be missed if you didn't show at the fete?" he asked. She stopped rubbing at her hair, a wary look on her face and slyly replied, "Bugger off Fraser and that reminds me. I'm changing your diet. You've far too much testosterone for a man your age."

He laughed and knowing that she wouldn't be persuaded back between the sheets, swung his legs from the bed and said, "While you're at the fete, I have to pop out, love. So I'll need the car and I'll drop you off. You know what the buses are like on a Sunday."

"Where are you going?" her face betrayed her curiosity.

"I need to visit Dick Smith for an hour. Something we discussed yesterday," then seeing she was about to ask, he lied, "It's about Harry McInnes. He isn't doing too well these days, you know, with Rosemary."

Tom knew that he was on relatively safe ground about any discussion that included Harry's wife, for Rosemary was intensely disliked by Sheila.

"I'm surprised he's still with that obnoxious woman," she tartly replied and then almost regretfully added, "I really like Harry. He's a nice man and always been very civil towards me, but her," she shuddered. "God forgive me for saying this, but if ever there was a justification for domestic abuse…"

She shook her head and still naked, sat on the bed beside Tom, the towel demurely draped across her lap and her arms folded across her breasts.

He looked at her and felt bad that he was deceiving her, but the truth would shock her and no matter what occurred in his life, Tom Fraser would never willingly or knowingly do anything that might hurt his wife.

The small, red coloured if slightly battered Mini drove speedily into the resident's car park and stopped at a visitors parking bay close to the entrance for the door to Cathy Porteous flat.

Bethany Williams switched off the engine and leaning forward to peer through the windscreen saw that Cathy's curtains were still tightly drawn and smiled. The plastic bag on the passenger seat contained rolls, sausage and bacon, Beth's surprise breakfast for the woman she loved.

She opened the door then still sat in the driver's seat, glancing upwards again at the curtained windows and hesitated as a horrible thought crossed her mind.

Cathy wasn't expecting her to turn up unannounced. What if she was with someone else?

Beth swallowed hard, now uncertain if she should bang on Cathy's door or just leave. Perhaps I should phone first she thought then almost immediately dismissed the idea. Cathy wasn't stupid and besides, now that she was here, she didn't want to be sitting in her car when some stranger hurried out the flat's entrance door.

No, she took a deep breath, if there *was* someone with Cathy, now would be as good a time as any to find out, but her heart beat rapidly in the hope there was no-one with her for she just knew she couldn't *bear* it if there was.

At the entrance door, she hesitated again in the realisation there was no option, she would need to press the buzzer for Cathy's flat for her to operate the lock on the close entrance door. Her shoulders sagged and she was about to turn away when the polite voice said, "Good Morning."

Beth startled, being unaware of the presence of the elderly man who carried a plastic bag in one hand and a rolled up newspaper in the other and who arrived suddenly behind her.

"Lost your key or just visiting?" he cheerfully asked as he produced a key and inserted it into the lock, then pushed open the door.

"Visiting," replied a grateful Beth with a smile and held up her own plastic bag.

"Come to see my friend with the rolls," she added as the old man held the door open to permit her to pass by.

"Well, you enjoy your breakfast with your friend, my dear," he courteously smiled at her and strode down the corridor towards his own flat.

She glanced at the stairwell and again a sense of doubt shadowed her. Should she knock on Cathy's door?

She took another deep breath and climbing the stairs to the first floor, patted at her unruly hair and forcing a smile, knocked on the door.

Almost a minute passed before she knocked again, but a little harder this time. A third knock still produced no response and finally, Beth knelt down onto the horsehair door mat and prised open the stiff letterbox. The hallway was in darkness and she could hear no sound from inside the flat. She thought about calling out Cathy's name, but realised that if Cathy was at home, calling out her name would only make Beth sound desperate.

Disappointed, she accepted with reluctance that either Cathy *wasn't* at home or worst she was there with someone else.

Tears stinging her eyes, Beth slowly walked towards the stairs, glancing back and hoping the flat's door would be snatched open and Cathy would call out her name, but it didn't happen.

Getting into the Mini, she fumbled in her hand bag for her mobile phone and called her father. Learning he hadn't yet had breakfast, she smiled through her unshed tears and told him that she was coming straight home, that she would bring breakfast in with her. With a final glance at the curtained windows, Beth reversed from the parking bay and sped out of the car park.

The two beat cops in the van, a cynical older man with less than two years left to serve before his pension kicked in and his probationer, a young idealistic woman, arrived at the derelict waste ground that was once the busy and industrious King George the Fifth docks near to the Braehead shopping centre. Driving in through the open rusting metal gates, the older cop saw the man wearing the bright fluorescent jacket in the distance running towards the van, arms wildly flailing and guessed it would be the security guard who had made the call.

The male cop was of the genre who believed probationers should only be spoken to when it was necessary and curtly instructed his neighbour to call in that they had arrived at the locus.

The young woman, a honours graduate who believing the recruitment hype, had joined the police a year earlier in the belief that it was the career her degree would help her to make a difference not only to her own life, but the lives of others.

Privately she thought her neighbour was a lazy wanker who should have been shuffled off to a retirement home years ago, however, without comment did as she was told.

Slowly and cautiously the cop bounced the marked police van over the rutted ground towards the running guard, who breathlessly waved for the van to halt.

It didn't help that the guard's excited and distraught state as well as his disjointed English not only frustrated the older cop, but when the guard began to pull at the cops arm, he grabbed the almost hysterical man and with his hand raised, shouted, "For fuck's sake, pal! Calm down! Calm down, will you?" then added almost under his breath, "Fucking immigrants."

The cops angry voice seemed to startle the guard who wide-eyed, almost immediately quietened, staring from one officer to the other until the young woman, her hands raised to attract the guard's attention, with pursed lips said, "Shhh, there, that's better eh? Now," she smiled to soothe the guard and waving her hands slowly up and down, continued, "you phoned, yes?"

"Course he fucking phoned," interjected her bored neighbour, "do you see any other bugger here, eh?"

Ignoring him, she continued to smile at the agitated guard and pretending to make a phone call, pointed her forefinger at the guard who eagerly replied, "Yes, yes," and in turn pointing at her, added almost beseechingly, "You come fast. Please."

With that, the guard turned and quickly retraced his steps, but after a few yards, stopped and glanced back to ensure the two cops were following.

"I'll wait here, you see what the fuck's he's on about," sighed the older cop, leaning back against the front of the van and tipping his hat to the back of his head before reaching into his trouser pocket for his fag packet and lighter.

Teeth gritted with anger at her neighbour's indifference to the mans obvious anxiety, the young woman followed the guard who a few minutes later led her into a derelict shed, their footsteps echoing in the vast space and finally to an open door on the other side. The door led out onto the dockside and warily stepping over rusting railway tracks, she watched as the guard went to the water's edge and with his hands, beckoned her forward and then eagerly pointed downwards.

The young woman's stomach unaccountably lurched as one hand on her cap to prevent it falling from her head she stepped cautiously towards the edge of the crumbling concrete and leaned over the side to see what the man was pointing at.

She took an involuntarily intake of breath and then quietly said, "Oh, I see."

There, in the oily and murky water some ten feet below her, among the flotsam that washed against the side of the dock and wrapped in what looked like a light coloured shroud, floated the distinct shape of a body.

CHAPTER ELEVEN

Grace Thomson, dressed in her warm and comfortable navy blue coloured dressing gown over her bright pink cotton pyjamas, was relaxing in the kitchen at one side of the small foldaway table, elbows on the table and her hands wrapped about her cup and sipping at her tea, while opposite her sat her son. She watched as Steven shovelled away his second bowl of flakes, eager to return to the cartoons. From the lounge she could hear the television and the sound of the children's Sunday morning channel.

Though her eyes were on Steven her thoughts were of Des Brown. She had really enjoyed the previous evening, though from the outset had been unusually nervous and at one point, while driving to Des's neat home in Balvie Avenue, considered a dozen excuses for failing to arrive.

Now, sitting here with Steven, she was so very glad she went.

Grace could not recall the last time she had been on a social evening and particularly, not with a man. She almost smiled. Steven's father had been the last man she had known with any kind of intimacy and, but for her son, *he* was instantly forgettable. In fact, her brow narrowed, having foolishly got rid of all her photographs from that time she could now barely recall what he *had* looked like.

"Mum," Steven interrupted her thoughts and holding up his empty bowl, "can I go and watch the tele now, please?"

"Sure," she smiled at him then almost as an afterthought, called him back from the door and said, "Steven. You had a nice time last night didn't you? At Mister Brown's house I mean?"

The small boy's face broke into a wide grin and he enthusiastically nodded. "It was great and Mister Brown's really funny and playing with Paul…" he suddenly became quiet.

"Did you enjoy playing with Paul?" she coaxed him.

Steven bit at his lip, blushed and nodded again and then almost shyly added, "It was just like having a daddy and a big brother," then run from the kitchen towards the lounge.

Startled, Grace stared at the doorway, almost afraid to breathe and her hands frozen in midair as she nursed her cup, uncertain how to react to her son's simplistic opinion of the evening.

'Like having a daddy,' he had said, unwittingly causing her to wonder, was she too fussy? Did she owe it to her son to find herself a man to give him a father figure in his life?

Slowly, she placed the cup onto the tabletop and sighed. Was she sacrificing Steven's upbringing because *she* couldn't bear to be hurt again?

Her shoulders slumped as the uneasiness of a possible relationship with Des Brown worried her for she wondered, if Des really *was* that interested in her, would she be committing herself and Steven to a relationship with him for the right reasons? The brief evening of happiness had just been dashed as yet another anxiety weighed her down.

Chic Fagin studied himself in the mirror and straightened the knotted tie, then shrugging into his suit jacket with a slight nod satisfied himself that he was worthy to enter God's house and readied himself to attend church.

Making his way to the front door, he stopped and quietly opened his grandson Ian's bedroom door and sighed almost with relief. Even with the curtains tightly closed, in the dim light of the room he could see the lad lying asleep, the quilt having fallen off him as he gently snored, his clothes untidily abandoned on the floor by the bed.

Chic's nose involuntarily twitched at the strong smell in the room of body odour and alcohol, but inwardly accepted it was preferable to the sweet, sickening smell of the cannabis Ian had recently been using.

He closed the door and straightening his shoulders, set off to have a word with God about keeping his grandson safe and hopefully showing the lad the way to redemption through the word and teachings of Jesus Christ, the discipline of the Orange Order and the character building faith of the Church of Scotland.

Detective Inspector Jamie Dalgleish pulled the Vauxhall Zafira into the driveway of his house and watching his family get out of the car, barked at his boisterous sons to be quiet.

Carrying the three plastic shopping bags in his hands, he asked his wife who was carrying their toddler daughter and Dalgleish's mobile phone in her other hand, who had called.

"One of your detectives from the Renfrew CID who said you've to give them a call back," she replied, handing him the phone after setting the bags down onto the kitchen table, then turning to her children, raised her voice to be heard over the din and said, "Okay, coats and shoes off and slippers on." Almost immediately she shouted after them, "No running! You've been told about that."

Dalgleish pressed the call-back button, grinning at the unruly twin boys scampering towards the hallway and his wife's admonition of them. Aye, he thought, like they'll listen.

The call was answered by Helen Meadows, one of his duty detectives and he guessed correctly from the noise in the background that she was in the open air somewhere, probably at a locus he guessed.

Meadows greeted him and said, "Sorry to call you out on your day off boss, but we've a body washed up at the dockside in the water beside the KG Five. A woman it looks like if the shape is anything to go by," she added then continued, "and before you ask, no; I'm not getting a pole and shoving it over to the Partick division's side of the Clyde."

He wondered briefly at Meadows reference to the 'shape', then unconsciously grinned at her morbid humour and asked, "Who's on the scene now?"

"The usual mob," she quickly replied. "Scene of Crime, forensics and I've contacted both the casualty surgeon and duty Fiscal who are also attending. They should be arriving here within the next twenty to thirty minutes. I've also got the uniform sealing off the area and the river polis are on hand to give us a hand to fish the body from the water."

"What, the body's still in the water?" he replied, slightly confused.

"Aye, it's beneath a part of the docks that has a ten to twelve foot drop over the edge, so we're going to need a wee hand to get her up onto the dockside."

"What are we looking at here Helen, a suicide or something a bit more sinister?"

He didn't miss the sharp intake of breath when Meadows replied, "Murder, boss and my first thought is that it's not pretty either. You'll be coming down?"

Dalgleish glanced at his watch and said, "Be with you in say, twenty minutes, Helen." "Good," she replied, then before concluding the call added, "And don't forget to bring your wellies. The ground round here's like a bog. My fucking high heels are a write-off."

He grinned at the obvious annoyance in Meadows voice and then sighed as he stared at his wife in the hallway, the toddler in her arms as she ushered the boys in to watch the television in the lounge. Here comes the hard part, he thought, telling the missus the Sunday brunch was off.

Well, at least for him it was.

In the privacy of her bedroom, curled up on her bed, Beth Williams was undecided whether she should once more call Cathy or trust that the three messages she had left on Cathy's mobile phone answer service would do.

She couldn't understand why Cathy didn't answer the door or why she had not responded to Beth's call for after all, didn't people in love *always* want to be with or hear from each other? She didn't want to believe that just when she had found someone to love and to love her in return, that such happiness might be snatched from her. Since driving away from Broomielaw Quay, she had imagined all sort of scenarios, the worst being that Cathy had realised their night together had been a mistake, that she had found someone else, that she simply saw Beth for what she was; a desperate young woman on whom she had bestowed a night of love and passionate affection. But she knew that wasn't so, she thought, shaking her head. No, she was convinced Cathy *did* love her and if she *was* true to her word and the things she had whispered in Beth's ear were true, where was Cathy now?

Cat MacDougall had come to a decision. Finishing her fry-up, she excused herself from the table, telling Colin Munro with a smile she'd be a few minutes and headed for the ladies toilet at the rear of the cafeteria. Out of sight of the young officer behind a barrier of fake greenery that bordered the toilet area, she fished in her handbag and withdrew the crumpled business card, then dialled the number scribbled on the back.

When the call was answered, she said, "Andy? It's Cat MacDougall. Sorry to call you on your day off, but I need a word with you about that subject of interest we spoke the other day." She glanced about her to ensure she was not overheard and added, "I can't meet you in the office."

She listened as Dawson suggested a meeting time and location and then replied, "Okay, I know where that is. I'm early shift tomorrow, so I'll make some excuse and see you there at midday."

Ending the call, she smiled at a woman and small child as they pushed their way out the door of the ladies toilet and followed them back towards the cafeteria area.

Four teenagers were now sitting across the aisle from Munro, the two girls giggling at the two young lads, one with fair hair that she saw glanced furtively towards her colleague.

Cat sensed that something was amiss, but chose to ignore them and smiling, resumed her seat opposite her neighbour.

That's when she heard the insult from one of the youths speaking with his hand at his mouth, the insult that caused the two giggling girls to erupt into further fits of laughter.

"Like fucking salt and pepper," she had heard him whisper, but a whisper that she realised the youth intended to carry towards their table.

Tight lipped, she stared hard at Munro and realised he too had heard the youth.

"You finished?" she asked him and when he nodded his head, quietly leaned towards him and said, "Follow my lead."

Standing, she slipped a hand into her handbag to retrieve the small black leather wallet then shrugged the bag onto her shoulder.

Folding her arms, with a curious Munro at her back, she turned towards the four teenagers.

Staring down at the fair haired youth, she quietly said, "Fucking salt and pepper. That's what you said, wasn't it?"

The youth first grinned uncertainly at his companions, then half turning in his seat, stared brazenly up at the slim, blonde haired woman and forced a nervous grin.

"What if I did, sweetheart, what the fuck you going to do about it? You and your," the youth paused and glancing for support from his friend, sneered as he added, "darkie pal?"

Cat could almost feel Munro behind her, tense himself while the diners at the nearby tables bowed their heads as they took a serious interest in their food.

She realised with a sure certainty that the show of bravado was to impress the girls at the table and glancing at the four of them, saw the clothes they wore and the girls smudged make-up suggested they had been at an all night party. That and their accents seemed to indicate that none of the group was local to Drumchapel, but from either the affluent Milngavie or the nearby Bearsden and guessed the youths had pulled the two young women at the party.

Cat pretended surprise at the youth's response and eyebrows raised, replied, "My *darkie* pal? Oh, you mean the *Detective Constable* who is with me," while opening her hand and flipping open the small leather wallet that contained both her warrant card and Police Scotland badge.

"So, you ask, what am I going to do about it?"

She smiled at the surprised youth and in a level voice, continued, "Well, right now I'm considering arresting you for a racial breach of the peace. What that means is you will be taken from where you sit, handcuffed, marched out of here to my police vehicle that's parked outside and conveyed to the charge bar at Drumchapel police office where you will be detained till your appearance tomorrow afternoon at the Sheriff Court in Glasgow. As you will probably guess," she continued to smile, "my colleague and I will later be called to give evidence against you and I have no doubt you *will* be found guilty of the charge and thereafter the racist conviction will remain with you for time immemorial. If you don't *understand* what that means, it means that every time you make any application for any kind of employment say or perhaps even the armed forces or anything that requires you to provide a statement regarding previous convictions, the *racist* conviction will need to be declared…by you. As for your pals there sitting with you, *sonny*, I'm thinking about arresting them as art and part for laughing and agreeing with your racial joke. Now, does *that* answer your question?"

The youth, now white faced and jaw almost hitting the table, stared at her in horror while his mate and one of the girls took a sudden interest in their empty coffee cups. The second girl continued to stare at Cat, but now with trembling lips as she fought back tears.

"I'm sorry, miss," the youth mumbled to her.

Aware that the little tableau had attracted a silent audience from the other early morning diners sitting near to the table, Cat leaned down and theatrically cupping a hand to her ear, replied, "Sorry, what was that?"

"I'm sorry," the youth repeated, a little louder.

"Still can't hear you," said Cat.

"I'm sorry!" the youth unintentionally bellowed, attracting an even wider audience.

Cat said nothing, but simply stared down at him, then with one hand on the table to steady herself leaned forward till she was almost nose to nose with the youth and in a low voice, said, "My CID colleague is worth any number of you, you snivelling little shit. I catch you *anywhere* in my division as much as walking fucking weirdly, I'm having you, do you understand?"

The youth, now visibly shaking and afraid to divert his eyes from the maddened woman, nodded furiously.

"Right then," Cat stood upright and smiling brightly, added, "enjoy your coffee, boys and girls," then with a nod to Munro, walked from the restaurant.

It was in the car before he started the engine that Munro turned to Cat and with a grin, told her, "Don't be taking this the wrong way, Cat, but you are one crazy bitch."

"Thanks," she smiled appreciatively, tugging at her seatbelt.

DI Jamie Dalgleish arrived at the King George docks to find a uniformed constable on duty at the gate that unfamiliar with the DI's vehicle, raised a hand to stop the Vauxhall Zafira before seeing it was driven by the Dalgleish.

"Sorry, sir, I didn't recognise you there," apologised the cop.

"No problem," smiled Dalgleish through the open driver's window. "So, where am I going then?"

The cop grimaced and replied, "Can I suggest you park your car over there," he pointed to where four other vehicles sat side by side on a patch of concreted ground, three that he recognised as police vehicles while the fourth, a top of the range BMW was not known to him. "The ground's pretty rough and boggy near to the river sir, so you might not want to drive over there."

"Whose car is that?" he asked the cop, nodding towards the BMW and, getting out of his own vehicle, walked round to the boot to fetch his wellingtons.

"The Procurator Fiscal Depute, sir," the cop replied, then grinning widely he added, "but she didn't bother bringing *her* wellies, so she's not in a very good mood."

Balancing against the car while he changed into the wellingtons, Dalgleish asked the cop, "Has the casualty surgeon not arrived then?"

"Been and gone, sir," replied the cop, flipping open his notebook and relating the times to Dalgleish. "In fact, he's just away a few minutes before you arrived."

Dalgleish stamped down into the wellington's then inhaling said, "Okay, that's me, so point me in the right direction," and being shown where to go, started walking across the derelict dockyard.

Tom Fraser pulled into an empty bay in Bank Street and fetching the rolls and sausage from the rear seat, locked the car and strode towards Dick Smith's ground floor flat in Cowan Street. He pressed the buzzer at the close door and a few seconds later, pushed it open when he heard it click.

Dick, still wearing his dressing gown, was standing at his front door. His eyes lit up when he saw the paper bag Tom held.

"Good lad, breakfast," he grinned and added, "The kettle's on."

While Dick busied himself in the galley style kitchen, Tom made his way into the comfortable lounge and again it didn't escape his notice that the flat, small though it might be, was comfortably furnished and cosy and with an inward grin, recalled that Dick was always boasting how domesticated he was because he never knew when he might be bringing a new conquest back for the night. He never admitted that he suspected Dick's conquests these days were likely few and very far between.

Five minutes later, when the breakfast rolls were laid onto plates and set on the coffee table in the lounge and both men comfortably seated, Dick asked him, "So Tom, what brings you out to my place on a Sunday morning?"

Tom took a deep breath in the absolute certainty that no matter what he said to Dick, it would never be held against him.

"The conversation we had yesterday with Harry. Some of the throwaway comments he made," Tom began to remind him, leaning forward and sitting his mug on top of the glass covered coffee table, an earnestness in his eyes.

"Harry told us about some of the Intelligence reports that crossed his desk; about the amount of money that's getting collected here in Glasgow that the druggies are sending south to their suppliers."

"Yeah, I remember him telling us," replied Dick, the wariness obvious in his narrowing eyes.

Tom took a deep breath and licked at his lips, a gleam in his eye. "What if," he held up both hands in a defensive position, "and let me finish here Dick. What if that money *didn't* go south? What if it was," he struggled for the word then said, "intercepted?"

"By intercepted," Dick slowly repeated, "you mean blagged from the dealers up here like?"

"Exactly," Tom sat back in his seat, "and the money that is being collected here, I'm probably correct in guessing it's all used notes, nothing traceable."

"Yeah, maybe so," replied Dick, still uncertain and feeling a tremor in his stomach for he was guessing where this was going. "But the money is the proceeds of crime, Tom. Are you suggesting that we, me and you I mean, that we *intercept* this money?"

Tom stared at his old friend and slowly nodding his head, added "Yeah, me, you and Harry and let's face it, if we did do this then the druggies are unlikely to go to their local cop shop and make a complaint, are they?"

Dick inhaled and his head drooped slightly as he considered what Tom had just proposed and then replied, "Have you spoken with Harry about this?"

"No, I thought I'd run it past you first, see what you thought."

"Have you considered the consequences of this? If we got caught, it would mean prison and you know what the cons think and do to former cops in prison, don't you?"

"Then we *don't* get caught," Tom replied earnestly. "I'm not talking about a new career here, Dick. Maybe just a couple of turns to earn us enough money to help us get off our arses and let's face it," he sat back and waved a hand about him, "you were saying yesterday how difficult things are for you anyway and I know that from what Harry told us, he's looking for any opportunity to get away from that torn-faced wife of his."

Dick softly smiled. "Torn-faced is the mildest description I'd use for Rosie," he then began to grin. "Tell you what, Tom," he sat forward, his clenched hands in front of him, "we speak to Harry first, ask him what he thinks because after all, he's the guy that has the info. Without him on board, the whole thing is academic anyway. Why don't you set up a meeting between the three of us; here say, tomorrow evening, when Harry finishes work."

Tom took a deep breath and also grinned.

Dick was on for it.

All he had to do now was persuade Harry.

Dalgleish saw a uniformed cop standing by the large, derelict warehouse who cautioning him to watch his step, told him that he was quicker making his way through the warehouse than following the roadway round it and then directed Dalgleish towards the door on the opposite side.

Exiting the gloomy and foul smelling warehouse, his eyes narrowed as they adjusted to the bright sunshine and the first thing he saw was the large square and transparent plastic sheet laid on the ground near to the water's edge that was surrounded by a half dozen police personnel, both uniform and CID. He could just make out the wheelhouse of the police launch that was in the low lying tide and moored against the dock. As he neared he could see a young woman's naked body stretched out on top of a lighter coloured, sodden and crumpled sheet, her blonde hair damp and lying like tendrils about her head and across her bruised and battered face.

"Boss," DC Helen Meadows nodded in acknowledgement of his arrival, then stepping closer to the plastic sheet nodded down towards the dead woman, who lay upon her back, her arms folded beneath her.

The Fiscal Depute, a woman in her mid twenties wearing a smart business suit and heavily mud-stained high heels as well as splashes of mud on the rear of her legs, looked decidedly pale and uneasy. She spoke briefly with Dalgleish to confirm her agreement it was murder and taking her leave of him, began to tip-toe back towards the warehouse.

Watching her leave, Meadow, herself now wearing borrowed wellington boots, couldn't hide her grin at the Depute's discomfort then commenced her report.

"The security guard was the reporter," and pointed with her forefinger towards a middle-aged black man wearing a high visibility jacket who sat on a bollard on the dockside some distance away, his hands folded on his lap and who watched the officers.

"I've noted his statement, but other than seeing the body in the water, there's nothing he can add to it. His English is poor and he's likely working here in the black economy, so he's also probably an illegal."

"If he's an illegal immigrant, how will we contact him later?" asked Dalgleish.

"All I can do is note the address he's provided, boss," she shrugged then asked, "Unless you want me to contact the Immigration people?"

"No," he shook his head, "there's no need for that. The guy did what he thought was right so who are we to punish him by turning him in? Before you go though, impress upon him how grateful we are for his cooperation and give him a contact card. Let him think he's a vital witness and he's to keep in touch with you," then paused and sighed, "which I suppose he is. In fact, if he skips we'll just need to deal with that when it happens. Did he use a mobile to contact the police?"

"Yes boss. I've got the number, but it's probably a pay as you go so I'll check, but I'm guessing it won't be registered," she sighed, then turning towards the body, began.

"Right then, according to the casualty surgeon," she was about to continue, but stopped and turned towards Dalgleish. "Sorry, boss, you just missed him, but he said he'd give you a call later. He'd another shout to attend. Anyway, according to the doc she's been in the water for a matter of hours only and, though the PM will likely confirm it, he formed that opinion because there was no wrinkling of the skin or anything. If he's correct, we're pretty lucky she washed up here as soon as she did. He is also of the opinion she was asphyxiated. Strangled," she added as if in explanation.

He smiled and replied, "I know what asphyxiated means, Helen, even if I have trouble spelling it."

She blushed and continued, "She was wrapped in that sheet underneath her. It was tied at the ends, so we had to unknot it to get her out and confirm it *was* a body. Nothing unusual about the knots that I could see; just straightforward granny type knots, I suppose you would call them. Looks like a bed sheet," she volunteered and pointed down and then, with a slight shudder, added, "and as you can see, she's taken a hell of a bleaching. The doc reckons it was a beating rather than a collision with anything while she was in the water. Whoever did this to her boss probably enjoyed it. Bastard!" she spat out, her venomous opinion of the unknown killer.

"What's that tied to her ankles?"

"I think they're stockings, boss, rather than tights. I also think they've been cut away from whatever they were tied to. Her wrists are tied behind her too, but I thought it best to leave the bindings on till the pathologist gets her onto his table. Besides," she shrugged, "they seem to be pretty tightly tied so I figured we might lose evidence if we remove them here. Not very dignified for the poor soul, but she's past caring now I suspect."

"Yeah, I agree. Good decision," he nodded and then asked, "I suppose I'm farting against thunder wondering if there is anything that might identify her? Tattoos or scars, I mean?"

Meadows pursed her lips and shook her head and though it was daylight, her eyes blinked against the bright flash of the Scene of Crime photographer's camera as the white suited woman took a series of evidential snaps.

"I only got a cursory look at her body, but nothing obviously visible," she replied then turning towards him, sighed and remarked, "I suppose that with her being submerged in the water it's probably contaminated any forensic evidence we might have obtained from the body, boss. What do you think?"

Before he could reply, the portly female Scene of Crime supervisor approached and said, "DI Dalgleish? That's us finished here, sir. I can't think of anything else we can do here," and turning with a sweep of her arm, waved towards the line of a half dozen uniformed cops slowly walking towards them. "I know your DC there instigated the search," she smiled at Meadows, "but with the victim being washed up in the water it's unlikely they'll find anything further that we can help you with. So, with your permission, we'll mosey on back to the ranch and I'll ensure the statements and photos are with you by say, midday tomorrow?"

"That will be fine," he nodded and smiling at the small woman, added "Thanks for coming out so promptly."

"Double time for a Sunday?" she grinned as with her photographer she turned away and added, "Who wouldn't turn out?"

"Right," Dalgleish turned towards Meadows, "phone for the shell to take her to the mortuary at the Southern General, Helen, and then you and your neighbour follow the body there. Once the body is booked in, seize the sheet, but leave bindings on the wrists and feet until the PM that," he screwed his eyes in thought, "I suppose will be tomorrow at the earliest. See what times will be available from the duty clerk and make the appointment. I'll head back to the office and see you when you get back. It's going to be a long day," he inhaled, "so bring some filled rolls in with you, okay?" and with that, made his way back towards his car, thinking that once again in his eighteen year career, he was missing Sunday lunch.

CHAPTER TWELVE

The middle-aged Londoner had been driving heavy goods vehicles long distance throughout the length and breadth of the UK for almost thirty years. Thirty years of sweat blinding graft and weekend working, frequently missing his kid's school concerts and important family events as well as Saturday afternoon's supporting his beloved Fulham.

Every month had been another letter from the bank or the mortgage company, every week another struggle to meet the bills and make ends meet; every penny a prisoner. Overtime money was a necessity, not a luxury for his meagre salary still meant scrimping and scraping to get by, the only respite in the year being his annual two weeks off and a cheap deal holiday to the Costa del Sol with his missus and kids, when they were young.

Until last year.

He had thought long and hard about the offer, worried about the consequences and even the ethics of what had been asked of him, but the lure of the money had been too great and so, with some hesitation, he had said yes.

Once a month, he had been promised. That's all, they had told him; just one delivery a month. There would be no problems, he had been assured. Nobody would ever suspect that his established and prestigious company's lorry would be used for the transport of drugs.

All he had to do was pick up and drop off along with his usual and legitimate deliveries, but most importantly, keep his mouth shut and to persuade him to do that, they had sent him a package through the post.

Nothing fancy, a plain brown envelope addressed to his home that contained the first of his payments and a coloured snapshot of his six year old granddaughter with some school friends, the girls smiling as they walked through the gate of their primary school in North London.

There was no letter with the photograph, for there was no need of a warning.

The message was crystal clear.

Do as you are told and you will be well paid, but do *not* fuck with us.

Now here he was, northbound on the M74 motorway towards Glasgow and the regular drop-off at the factory premises in the industrial estate in Hillington, alongside the parking bay where he would lie-up overnight for the unloading in the morning.

He knew, however, before he kipped down for the night in his cab, his door would be knocked and then he would retrieve the heavy package from beneath the bunk in the rear of the cab and hand it over. No matter the location, whether it was Glasgow, Swansea, Manchester or wherever, it was the same routine; the usual man or woman.

Normally in the other cities or drop-off points, he would receive a lighter package in return, but when he delivered to Glasgow there was no return package and he guessed that other arrangements had been made.

However, he knew better than to question these other arrangements. Not when his granddaughter's life was at risk.

Mick Thomson turned the television down low, but kept it switched to the Adult Channel and half watched while he used the text facility on his I-phone. His stubby fingers laboriously typed out the message that included the post code for the handover.

That done, he pressed the green send button then laid the phone down on the coffee table and lifting the can of lager, settled down to concentrate on the sexual antics of the two men and one women on the screen.

Less than a mile away, Thomson's text message was received almost immediately by Billy Purvis who sitting in his car unconsciously nodded at the message and then glancing at the dashboard clock, realised he had just under two hours to meet the lorry driver.

Grabbing the plastic bag that contained the aromatic food, he stepped from the car and made his way to the front door of the tenement building to deliver the takeaway food and the dozen small sachets of heroin that nestled tightly against his skin under his thick, football socks.

DI Jamie Dalgleish, seated behind his desk in Renfrew CID office, stretched his arms wide and yawned. It had been a long day though he knew better than to go home and complain to his wife who would frown and remind him, "Try entertaining three moaning faced weans for the day; now *that's* what you call a long day."

The door knocked and disturbed his thoughts.

DC Helen Meadows, looking equally tired, popped her head in and asked, "That's the incident room fully set up boss. The HOLMES people are asking if there's anything else they can do or can they call it a night?"

He waved a hand at Meadows and replied, "Nothing more we can do this evening, Helen. Tell them thanks from me and I'll see them all in the morning when we can have our first briefing." Cocking a head at her, he narrowed his eyes and continued, "I suppose there's nothing back yet from fingerprints at Pitt Street?"

"No," she shook her head, "but they did say they were working with a Sunday shift and that's fewer personnel, but hope to have a result, either positive or negative by tomorrow morning. Also, one of the analysts has been through the missing persons report; in fact, she went back a month and used the PNC to include *all* the missing persons throughout the UK, but nothing remotely close to the deceased's description has shown up." Meadows slowly shook her head and then added, "She must have been quite a looker, that poor lassie."

Taking a deep breath as though to stave off her tiredness, she said, "Oh, and another thing, sir, I've booked the PM for ten o'clock tomorrow morning."

"Good, then you keep free for that time. I'll want you to accompany me, okay?"

She nodded then turning, stopped as if remembering and said with a grimace, "Sorry, boss, I meant to say. DCI Mulgrew phoned earlier to speak with you, but you were on the phone with the media people, so I said you you'd call her back. She told me she'd be at home and that you have her number. Sorry, sir," she grimaced.

"It's no problem, Helen," he smiled tightly at her, but almost as quickly realised she had been on duty for almost fifteen hours without a break and waving at her, said, "Go home and get some rest. I'll need you here tomorrow at eight sharp," then as he reached for his desk phone, called her back and added with a nod, "Helen. Good work today, hen."

"Thanks boss," she flashed him a grateful smile and closed the door. He listened as his call rung and then was answered by a woman who said, "Yes?"

"Hi, good evening. It's DI Jamie Dalgleish at Renfrew. Can I speak with Miss Mulgrew please?"

The woman told him to hang on then he heard her call out, "Cathy, it's for you. It's a DI Dalgleish."

A few seconds passed then he heard the rustle as the phone exchanged hands and Mulgrew say, "Thanks, Jo. Couldn't pop the kettle on, could you sweetheart?"

He smiled at his inadvertent intrusion on Mulgrew's conversation with her partner then inhaled as she addressed him and said, "Hello,

Jamie. Thanks for getting back to me. So, what's the story about your murder?"

Sitting back in his chair, Dalgleish rubbed a weary hand at his temple as he recounted the discovery of the woman's body, the actions his officers had taken so far and the setting up of his inquiry.

"So, you have no identification yet?"

"Nothing so far, boss," he replied, "but the fingerprints might have a result for us tomorrow, either positive or negative."

"What about DNA?"

He shook his head at the phone and replied, "I haven't instigated any kind of search at the minute on the DNA database. I decided to wait till the PM tomorrow before we obtained a sample. I'm concerned that any intrusive examination we make now might cause evidential problems in the event we arrest a suspect. To be honest though, I'm not to hopeful," he added, "given that the woman was immersed in the water for at least a number of hours. You'll know yourself boss that the likelihood now of any suspect DNA on the body is slim to none."

There was a slight pause while Mulgrew mulled over this, then she replied, "I agree it's unlikely, but obviously we'll need to try."

There was a slight pause and then Mulgrew said, "You sound tired, Jamie. What time is your briefing in the morning?"

"Eight-thirty here at Renfrew, then I've the PM set for ten at the Southern General Hospital."

"Right then, I'll be there for the briefing, but for now I'm ordering you to get home to the wife and kids. From what you've told me," he heard her sigh, "you'll need to be bright and fresh in the morning for it sounds like you've a real whodunit on your hands."

When he had replaced the handset, Dalgleish stared briefly at the phone then mustering his tired body, rose to grab his coat and head for home.

The lorry driver tiredly watched for junction twenty-six off the west bound M8 and moved to the inside lane. He knew from previous trips there was a late night fast food place just off the motorway and stomach rumbling, promised himself a double cheese burger and the opportunity to refill his flask with coffee. Then, after the handover, he would kip down for the night and breakfast at the delivery factory's works canteen in the morning before returning south.

It took him just ten minutes to grab his food and another three or four minutes to park up in the lay-by adjacent to the factory in Stephenson Street, within the industrial estate in Hillington.

The lorry safely closed down for the night, the driver turned to his food and demolished it with relish while he tuned the small, portable television to the BBC coverage of the days football highlights in the vain hope they had footage of his beloved Fulham's match.

The bright lights of the car flickering in his wing mirror alerted him to the time and as the yellow coloured saloon passed him by, watched it disappear round a corner further up the road. A few minutes later, the same car returned and slowly passed him by in the opposite direction.

He guessed the saloon car driver was being cautious and checking there was no police hiding up somewhere in the vicinity.

The lorry driver thought with a sudden fearful chill if the local plod *was* waiting nearby, they certainly wouldn't be sitting where they could be discovered and fearfully glanced at the package in the foot well of the passenger seat.

The yellow car returned again and this time parked directly in front of the lorry.

In the glare of an overhead halogen street light he watched as the cars lights were switched off and a slim built youth exited the drivers' door and approached the lorry's passenger door and banged on it.

Taking a deep breath, the Londoner reached across and unlocked then shoved the door open.

"You've got something for me mate?" the young guy said, his face pale and apparently anxious.

Wordlessly, the Londoner simply pointed to the parcel in the passenger foot well and watched as the young guy wrestled the package from the floor, then slammed the passenger door closed.

Exhaling with nervous relief, the Londoner watched the guy hurriedly return to his car and throw the package across the driver's seat before driving off.

In the darkness of the cab, the Londoner breathed a sigh of relief and settled back down to watch the football on his portable television.

CHAPTER THIRTEEN – Monday 7 July

After a quick shave and shower in the en suite, Des Brown hurriedly dressed then carrying his shoes in his hand, quietly knocked on the spare bedroom door and pushed it open. His father sleepily opened his eyes as Des whispered, "Morning Dad, That's me grabbing a quick coffee and then I'll be off. Thanks for staying the night. You probably guessed I'd got caught up in something."

"I heard you come in the back of two this morning," his father propped himself up onto one elbow and squinted at Des while he turned and reached for the glasses on the bedside table. "You're okay though?"

"Oh aye," Des nodded. "A domestic assault that ended up in a stabbing," he sighed. "The wife was taking a beating, but then she grabbed a pair of scissors and plunged them into her man's shoulder."

He didn't add that he thought the bastard deserved it, but that would be for a jury to decide at a later date.

"Right, away you go then," his father shooed him off. "I'll see the young 'un gets his breakfast then run him to school." Almost as an afterthought, he asked, "What's this about you having a date then?"

Des grinned and then with a pretend scowl, replied, "You and your grandson been having a wee gossip have you? Well, for the minute it's a need to know thing, so don't be saying anything to mum for now," knowing fine well it was the first thing his father would tell Agnes when he returned home this morning.

"Oh, and you'll not need me this evening I suppose?" his father wanted to confirm.

"No, thanks," Des shook his head, "I should be home for the back of five so I'll pick Paul up at your place."

"Right," his father replied, then with a twinkle in his eye, added, "but if you *are* seeing your lady friend tonight, we'll be happy to hang onto Paul for another couple of hours."

Des didn't bother to reply, just wearily shook his head and softly closed the door.

Across the city, Bethany Williams had not slept well. Her fearful worry that she had mistaken Cathy's affection for love haunted her all night, but by the dawn that worry was slowly replaced by her faith in Cathy's friendship and instead grown into a real concern that something untoward had happened to the woman she adored.

Whether or not she had mistaken Cathy's intentions, she reasoned, Beth was confident that the older woman was not so callous that she would refuse to respond to Beth's calls and text messages; even if just to demand that Beth stop calling her.

She reached under her pillow and groped for her mobile phone, but there were no new messages other than the battery needed topped up. Downstairs she could hear her father, a habitual early riser, rummaging around in the kitchen and guessed he would be preparing her breakfast, excited that this morning his daughter had her first real interview for a position as a trainee journalist with the 'Glasgow News.'

She crawled from bed and using both hands against the side of the wardrobe to prop herself upright, examined her reflection in the full length mirror attached to the door, seeing the teary-eyed young woman she was, her skin blotchy and unlikely to impress any prospective employer with her looking like a failed face-painting model.

She startled when her door knocked and her father called out, "Beth honey? You awake? It's a big day for you today, young lady."

She heard him chuckling to himself as he returned down the stairs to the kitchen, as thrilled for her as she was dismayed at the thought of the interview.

Still staring at her reflection, she exhaled and readied herself to shower and get dressed, but whether she would be ready for the interview later than morning, she just didn't know.

She glanced at her mobile phone, now plugged into the charger at the electric socket and with a shrug decided one more call wouldn't do any harm.

Across the city, Cat MacDougall arrived at the CID office in Drumchapel police station to find Colin Munro already there and glancing through the nightshift notes.

"The DI's not in yet, Cat," he told her. "Should I wait for him before we go out? I mean, will he want to see me for…" he paused, "I don't know, welcome me to the department or anything?"

"Unlikely," she replied with more than a hint of cynicism in her voice, but realised perhaps she was being unfair and shouldn't influence Colin with her opinion of Mark Walters. "Look, you wait in his office and that way he can't miss you," she suggested. "I've to phone the high school anyway about that complaint from Saturday."

"Oh aye, the guy we interviewed; George McCormick?"

"That's him," she nodded. "I want to find out if like he said this man Brown is a cop…"

"If he *is* a cop, will you report him?" Munro interrupted, his brow creased.

"That's not my intention Colin. We'll wait and see first what his reaction is to my warning to him, so for the minute, we keep the interview between us, yeah? There's nothing that the DI needs to know."

"Got you," grinned Munro, then his face betrayed his curiosity.

"What about the school, Cat. When you make the inquiry about one of their pupil's father, won't there be some kind of data protection issue?"

"I suppose there *might* be if I was going through official channel's," she nodded, "but the woman I intend speaking to works as an assistant in the admin office at the school and got her house screwed just over a year ago. I didn't get her property back," she shrugged, "but I did nick the neighbour that turned her over. Added to the other houses in her street that he did, he's now serving eighteen months and she *did* say if ever I needed a favour."

She couldn't know that his respect for her was now just short of adulation and, as far as Colin Munro was concerned, right now Detective Constable Catriona MacDougall could do no wrong.

It did no harm either, he guiltily thought, that she was very pleasant on the eye.

He left the room, nodding to the three detectives who entered and after greeting Cat, the trio made their way to the coffee table, their voices raised as they argued about the football that was played during the weekend.

Cat searched through her file and finding the phone work phone number and extension she needed, made the call from her desk phone.

Explaining she first needed to establish if a Paul Brown was a pupil at the school, the assistant confirmed Paul was a pupil and then inadvertently volunteered the information by asking, "Isn't Paul's father one of your colleagues, DC MacDougall?"

"Oh, is he?" Cat pretended surprise and then truthfully added, "Can't say I know him. What's his name?"

"Oh, wait, I've got Paul's personnel card here," said the assistant. Cat heard the phone being placed down and then the assistant lifted it again and said, "Ah, here it is; it's Desmond Brown and there's two emergency contact numbers for Paul. One number is his grandparents. Nice people," said the assistant, distractedly. "I met them at the school fete this year. Live locally," she added as Cat patiently listened, then with a laugh, the assistant added, "Listen to me, I'm rambling. Now, Paul's father's phone number is…" and rattled off the digits.

After concluding the call, Cat unconsciously nodded, recognising the phone number as that for Govan CID. Taking a deep breath, she dialled. The call was cheerfully answered by the CID clerk who informed her that DS Brown was out on a call, but she would leave a message and get him to phone Cat back.

Colin Munro arrived back at her desk and she thought he seemed a little chastened.

"You okay?"

"Aye," he replied then exhaled and with a glance at the three detectives standing together drinking coffee, continued in a low voice. "I've just met the DI. Told me to keep my eyes and ears open and my mouth shut, that the last thing he needed was to wet nurse a trainee, that if I didn't bother him or cause him any trouble during my six months here he'd ensure I'd get a decent appraisal for my Inspector."

She saw that he was embarrassed and avoiding eye contact and instinctively knew there was something else.

"What?" she demanded.

Munro took a deep breath then staring her in the eye, said, "He also told me that I had to watch out for you and that you were quick to complain against male colleagues and that…" he paused, "well, report back to him if you were out of line in any way and basically, not to fully trust you."

Cat tightly smiled, but was aghast and inwardly fuming.

In his position as the CID office manager, responsible for overseeing the careers of his subordinates, Walters was supposed to encourage his staff, not make them feel like the spare part at a whores wedding and definitely not to try to sign them on as an office tout. To cap it all, the bastard was warning young Colin against *her*?

However, she knew she was in no position to challenge him for that would disclose Colin had confided in her and besides, she thought, she already knew what the DI's opinion was of her. The last thing the young acting detective needed was being discriminated against because of her.

"Right then," she forced herself to sound cheerful, "let's you and I collect our allocated inquiries and get out there, eh?"

"Okay boss," he grinned widely at her, his spirits uplifted that she hadn't gone off on one.

He wasn't to know that by truthfully relating the DI's warning to him, he had already earned Cat's trust.

DI Jamie Dalgleish's briefing to the murder team that comprised his own officers and the half dozen detectives drafted in from the Force's Major Investigation Crime Unit, as well as a handful of civilian analysts and HOLMES personnel, had went as well as it could with the limited information that he had to hand.

In short, he had informed the team there is nothing at this time, no fingerprints or any kind of identification to identify the deceased and admitted it was likely the waters of the River Clyde had washed away all DNA traces of her killer or killers. However, the PM would confirm or negate this particular line of inquiry.

"So, ladies and gentlemen," he had concluded, "the office manager DS Prentice will issue your HOLMES actions for the day.

Obviously, with the little we've got to go on meantime, we're limited in what inquiries we can make so bear with us and if *anyone* has any ideas," he grinned, "I'm all ears."

Walking to his office with Cathy Mulgrew, he called back over his shoulder to Helen Meadows and with a wink, asked if she'd sort out two coffees for him and the DCI.

"No bother boss," she replied then called back, "I'm organising my neighbour to do a roll run. Do you want anything? You and Ma'am, I mean?"

Mulgrew smiled and shook her head.

"No you're all right, thanks," he replied, then closed the office door.

"Did you get any sleep?" asked Mulgrew, settling herself into the chair opposite Dalgleish.

He rubbed a weary hand across his face and sighed. "I might have done, but the wee one is teething and it's not fair on my wife to expect her to be up all night, so I take my turn," he grinned.

"Can't be easy for a baby, teeth bursting through their wee gums I mean."

"Difficult for the parents too," he replied with some feeling.

"So, the dead woman, Jamie; what's your plan?"

"Well, as you know I've the PM at ten this morning. I'm taking a couple of my team, DC Helen Meadows, that you met just there, and her neighbour with me," he added. "She and her neighbour were first on the scene and I'm keen to develop her and add to her experience. Her neighbour's an old hand, so for continuity purpose, I'll instruct him take the pathology samples to the Forensics."

"Is she worth keeping an eye, Meadows I mean?"

"Aye, boss," he pursed his lips and nodded. "Level-headed, calm under pressure and keen as mustard. She's sharp, as well. I know her uniform sergeant and he is a fair judge of character and tells me she's got bottle too. Not afraid to make a decision in a crisis and will stand by that decision."

"Sounds like you're describing yourself there, Jamie," Mulgrew grinned at him.

Dalgleish returned her compliment with his own modest grin and stared at her, inhaling the faintest scent that emanated from her and tickled at his nostrils. Cathy Mulgrew, he thought now in her late thirties, was a cracking looking woman. Taller than average at five foot ten inches, her copper coloured shoulder length hair was French braided and her clear skin was highlighted by her piercing green eyes. Dressed in a figure hugging bottle green two piece trouser suit, she was the stuff that most men dream of.

Dalgleish knew that some years previously Mulgrew had made it clearly known to her colleagues in the job that she was gay and while aware there still remained some homophobia in the police, her gender preference had not in any way interrupted her steady rise in the CID. He had even recently heard a whisper she was soon to be considered for a Superintendent post.

Of her ability, he had no doubt, having on more than one occasion served under Mulgrew who as the Senior Investigating Officer had been tasked with solving some serious and high profile crime.

Sitting in front of her, his thinning fair hair tousled, having poorly shaved that morning with bags under his eyes and wearing his favourite if slightly worn suit, he felt positively dowdy.

"Penny for them," she quietly said, interrupting his thoughts. Dalgleish blushed and Mulgrew inwardly smiled, for the DI wasn't the first man she had caught staring at her and probably wondering at her homosexuality.

"Ahem, yes," he politely coughed to cover his embarrassment at being caught out. "So, boss, the inquiry. The PM will of course determine if she was alive when she was in the water and drowned or was murdered first. Really, I'm going to have to wait for the results, but what we know," he paused, "or should say suspect from what the casualty surgeon said, is that the deceased was badly beaten then suffocated, bound in the sheet and thrown into the Clyde."

He inhaled and continued, "I've a press bulletin that I'd like you to approve and want to have issued for the midday media to catch the radio and television broadcasts this afternoon and, hopefully, the late editions of the local papers this evening."

Her eyes narrowed.

"You're starting with local media then?"

He nodded and sighed, "Yes. I know that because she was found locally and hadn't been in the water too long might be not mean she *is* local, that she could have been murdered elsewhere in the country and her body brought to the river and dumped here, but I need to start somewhere. If the appeal *should* prove negative locally, I can then extend my inquiry with an outward sweep." He raised his hands in a defensive posture and added, "I need to start somewhere, boss."

Mulgrew raised her own hand towards him and explained, "Yes, I agree with you, Jamie. I'm not criticising and I also realise how little evidence you have to begin your inquiry so, the real question is, how can I support you?"

"Can't think of anything at the minute boss," he wiped a weary hand across his face then grinned, "but if something *does* come up, guess who will get my first panic-stricken phone call?"

The door knocked and was pushed open by Meadows who held a plastic tray upon which lay two steaming cups of coffee that she placed on top of the desk.

Reaching for hers, Mulgrew smiled and said, "It's DC Meadows, isn't it? I'm hearing good things here from the DI about you. So," she blew softly onto the mug, "how are you enjoying the CID?" "Really enjoying it, Ma'am," the younger woman blushingly nodded, slightly uncertain whether to remain in the room or leave. "And the DI here," Mulgrew cocked a head towards Dalgleish and turning her head so he couldn't see, winked at Meadows, "treating you fairly, is he?"

Catching on, Meadows bit at her lip and slowly drawled, "Well, for a guy his age Ma'am, he's not *too* bad."

"You'll have other duties to attend to, DC Meadows," Dalgleish pretended to glower at the young woman and watched as with a slow grin, she closed the door behind her.

"I watched you in the briefing, Jamie and I like the rapport you have with your staff. It makes for a good working atmosphere. So," held her mug up towards him and continued, "Here's to a successful conclusion to the inquiry."

Sat at his desk nursing a mug of tea, Harry McInnes stared down at the written reports scattered across his desk in front of him, but didn't see them for his thoughts were elsewhere, his mind turning over the previous night's phone call from Tom Fraser who had asked that Harry meet Tom and Dick at Dick's flat in the west end of the city. Tom hadn't disclosed why he wanted Harry to meet there, but simply said he would explain on Monday evening.

"Harry. Harry?"

He turned to see the matronly Fiona pointing towards the office security door and adding, "That's Sally coming in to sweep the room, Harry. Better close up your computer and put that paperwork away."

"Oh, aye," he replied and opening his desk, watched as the door was pulled open by one of the younger detectives and Sally Nelson, her hair tied back and wearing the light blue smock of the cleaning company and faded blue jeans, came through the door, awkwardly carrying in the small electric Hoover. The detective didn't try to help her, but stood to one side to permit her entry. The rest of the office rose from their desks and graduated towards the tea table to benefit from the impromptu ten minute break while Sally worked around their desks.

Without realising it, Harry found himself walking towards the blonde-haired woman and greeting her.

"How was your weekend then Sally?" he asked while inwardly wondering was that the *only* bloody thing he could think of to say? Sally stopped and bent to switch the Hoover off.

"No different to every other weekend, Harry," she shyly smiled.

"What about you? Out partying, I suppose."

"No, nothing like that unfortunately," he shrugged, his arms folded across his chest. "Saturday breakfast with a couple of old guys like me, chewing the fat and telling uproarious lies about how good we used to be when we were cops and like old wine, the stories get better with age."

She didn't know why she did it and couldn't help herself. Raising her hand, she held it against flatly against his chest and quietly replied, "And I bet you *were* a good police officer, Harry."

He stared down at her, a sudden tightness in his chest and was about to reply, when beside him, Fiona said, "Sally, you couldn't sweep that Hoover under my desk, could you sweetheart? I had a roll this morning and I've spilt crumbs all over the place."

"Aye, of course Fiona," Sally turned towards the older woman. The moment had passed and as he saw her turn away, Harry exhaled almost with relief, afraid that he had been almost about to say something stupid and make a fool of himself. He turned towards the group now chattering at the tea table, relieved to see that none had apparently taken any interest in what had just occurred.

None except Fiona who catching his eye, raised her eyebrows and with the most discreet of nods indicated he join her in the corridor outside the office.

As Sally worked her way Hoovering round the office, Harry followed Fiona through the security door and closed it behind him.

"What?"

"What?" she repeated with a frown and taking him by the arm, ushered the bemused Harry further down the empty corridor and away from the security door.

"Do you think I'm blind, Harry? Do you think *everyone* in that office is blind? My God, I'm surprised you don't give Sally a bloody *hug* every time she walks through the door! Look, Harry, its plain to see you have an interest in Sally and it's just as plain to see she likes you, but whether that's because you're kind and a gentle man in the true sense of the word, I don't know. But what I *will* say is you need to watch yourself. You're a married man, for God's sake and *she's* a married woman."

Fiona took a deep breath and placing both her hands on his arms, stared up at him and said, "Harry, you know how fond of you I am and yes," she nodded, "I know that things at home aren't too good. But that doesn't mean you put your job at risk. If that twisted bugger Pete Murray suspects that you, a married man might have…" she searched for the word and then continued, "some kind of feeling for Sally, he'll use it to revoke your security vetting and she'll be sent to work elsewhere in the building, if not fired. We both know that the bastard will do anything if he thinks it will bring himself to the attention of the bosses and earn him some kind of kudos."

She paused for breath and then quietly added, "If you do decide to… I don't know, see Sally outside of work, just be careful, Harry. Like I said, she's a married woman and even if I don't know what her personal circumstances are," she shook her head, recalling with inward anger a number of occasions when Sally turned up at work sporting some kind of facial bruising, "though I can guess they aren't too good, just *don't* get caught."

She released her hands from his arms and stood back and glowering up at the tall man, added, "There, I've said my piece, okay?"

He returned her stare and then slowly grinned. "I'm going to miss you when you retire, you know," then bending down, took Fiona into his arms and gave her a bear hug.

Along the corridor, the security door opened and Sally Nelson, carrying the Hoover in both arms, stepped into the corridor and saw them entwined. Her stomach lurched and head down, she turned and walked soundlessly the other way.

CHAPTER FOURTEEN

Acting Detective Constable Colin Munro turned the CID car from Garscadden Road into the rough patch of ground that served as the sports pavilion's car park and switched off the engine.

"That must be the complainer there," said Cat MacDougall, squinting against the bright sunlight as she peered through the windscreen at the figure standing by the side door of the pavilion. Getting out of the car, she smiled at the elderly man who walked towards her and who, when he saw Cat, returned her smiled with his hand extended.

"I didn't know it was yourself, Mister Fagin," she reached and shook his hand, then introduced Munro to him.

"Mister Fagin and I have met before," she explained.

"Aye, Miss MacDougall has always been very helpful to me with my grandson," nodded Chic as followed by the detectives with Cat gingerly picking her way in her heels across the broken ground, he turned towards the doorway. "My Ian isn't the brightest of lads and he's had his wee brushes with the law on occasion." Turning towards Cat, he added, "but he's trying to keep out of bother now after you had that word with him."

Cat dutifully smiled and didn't think it necessary to tell the old man of her recent encounter with his grandson.

"So, we got a report of a break-in, Mister Fagin?"

Chic pushed open the door and pointed to the broken lock. "Looks like it was kicked in," and held the door while Cat and Munro passed through. "The pavilion committee permit the band to practise here on Tuesday and Thursday nights and to store our instruments in that cupboard there under the stage," he pointed across the dimly lit hall.

"Your band?" asked Munro, thinking Fagin looked a little old to be a rock star.

"Aye, the Drum Loyal True Blues," he replied with a hint of pride, "and that's why I've got a key to the place.'

Their footsteps reverberated across the scuffed wooden floor as he led them to the cupboard.

"They tried to force the lock here as well," he pointed to a sturdy padlock, "but they didn't get in."

The relief in his voice was evident. "There's a lot of valuable equipment stored here you know."

"You've informed the pavilion committee about the break-in?" asked Cat.

"Aye, they said to report it to you and I've to get a crime report number from you, so they can arrange for the council send a joiner out to fix the door."

While Munro stood with Chic Fagin and noted the details for the crime report, Cat wandered a few yards away to answer a call on her mobile phone.

"Hello, DC Cat MacDougall? It's Des Brown at Govan CID. I understand you were looking for me?"

"Ah, Sergeant Brown I was wondering…" but he interrupted her and simply said, "Des, please."

"Des," she smiled tightly at the phone. "I was wondering if you might be in a position to call by my office sometime today. It's about a complaint that was made by a George McCormick."

She couldn't fail to hear the sharp intake of breath and then Des asked, "Who are you really, Cat; the Professional Standards Unit?"

"No," she sharply replied, more sharply than she intended and added, "I'm with Drumchapel CID and the complaint was made to me. Look, I'd rather not speak on the phone so if it suits you…"

He interrupted again and with a sigh said, "I finish here the back of four this afternoon. Will you still be on duty then?"

"Yes," she replied and added, "Shall we say four-thirtyish then?"

"That'll suit me," he abruptly agreed and concluded the call.

Returning to the two men, she smiled at Munro and said, "All done?"

Munro thought she looked a little irate and guessed her phone call hadn't gone well, but nodded and closing his notebook, returned it to his inside jacket pocket.

"Unless my neighbour thinks otherwise," he turned to Cat, who shook her head, "there's nothing here that's worthy of a scene of crime visit, Mister Fagin. I take it you'll be staying till the joiner arrives then?"

"Aye, I'll hang on," agreed Chic.

Munro nodded and said, "Okay then, I'll give you a phone within the next ten minutes with the crime report number Mister Fagin," then his eyes narrowed. "You said you're the band sergeant for the Drum Loyal True Blues?"

"Aye, son, that's right."

"Why are you not called the *Drumchapel* Loyal True Blues or is that your full title, the Drumchapel Loyal True Blues?"

Chic exhaled and then with a quiet grin, replied, "Because son, we can't have the word *chapel* in our name, can we? That would infer some sort of connection with the Roman Catholic faith and *that* just wouldn't do."

Munro turned towards Cat with a bemused glance, but before he could respond, he saw her turn with a smile to Chic and explain,

"His Da's an American, Mister Fagin," as if the comment excused Munro from understanding the tribal rivalries in the West of Scotland, but more importantly to avoid further sectarian discussion. Taking their leave of Chic, the two officers returned to the CID car and with a final wave to the old man, drove off.

He opened the fridge and yawning, scratched at his arse with the other hand, angry that he had forgotten to buy milk. The wall clock showed it was almost eleven o'clock and eyes narrowing, he frowned. That little shit Purvis had not yet phoned and confirmed collecting the package last night from the lorry driver.

Slamming the fridge door shut Mick Thomson, wearing a faded Scotland rugby jersey and black coloured tracksuit trousers, stomped barefooted towards the lounge and grabbed his mobile phone from the top of the television set. Settling himself back into his favourite armchair, he scrolled down the directory until he came to Purvis's number and pressed the green button.

The phone was answered almost immediately and he could hear a crying child in the background.

"You were to call me," he rebuked Purvis with a growl.

"Sorry big man. I got tied up with something, but the package was delivered and I've got it up in that flat I told you about," replied Purvis, though Thomson had a curious instinct there was a slight edge to the younger man's voice.

Suspicious, he asked, "Is everything all right?"

"Oh, aye, everything's fine. Brand new, in fact," Purvis hastily replied. "I'm just heading to that flat within the next few minutes…" Thomson grinned as he heard Purvis shout, "Listen hen, will you get him to shut the fuck *up*!" then returning to the phone, said, "Sorry about that, big man, but that wean never stops greeting."

"You were saying?"

"Eh, oh, aye, I'm going up to that flat and meeting…" he paused, remembering Thomson's warning against using names on the phone, "the simple guy there. He's going to do a wee tester for me, just to make sure it's the same quality of stuff, yeah?"

"Right, well phone me when you get a result," Thomson ordered then added, "You haven't forgotten about tomorrow night, have you?"

"The collection you mean, big man? No, I'm on course for that. I was told that the documents are ready for me, just over thirty-two big ones in the package. Once I have them, I'll eh," he paused, then grinning, said, "I'll deliver the documents to the guy like I usually do."

"See that you do. I don't want any fucking surprises, okay?" Thomson replied and abruptly ended the call.

He sat for a moment, reflecting on the conversation, but the suspicion he wasn't being told the whole story still niggled at him. He wondered, was there something in Purvis voice, some hesitation that caused the suspicion.

Slowly exhaling, he threw the phone onto the low coffee table by his knee and reaching down for the remote control, switched on the television and scrolled along the menu bar to the Adult Channel.

Billy Purvis sighed with relief that Thomson had not questioned him further. He glanced again at the phone and chewing at the inside of his mouth, selected the number he sought and pressed the green button.

"Hi Billy, it's me, Ian," was the response he got. Purvis raised his eyes to heaven and sighing, replied, "Of course it's you, you fucking idiot. It was me that phoned you."

Ian Fagin laughed in his ear, the animosity after Purvis beat him now forgotten.

"Do you still want to see me, Billy?"

Purvis ground his teeth and forcing himself to be calm, said, "Yeah, I do wee man. Listen, have you got your kit with you? I've a wee job for you, a MoT test. Are you up for it?"

The few seconds of silence that followed grated on Purvis nerves as Ian Fagin slowly came to realise what was being asked of him, then replied, "Oh, a wee sniff you mean? Aye, I've got my kit and it's no bother Billy," then he grinned at the phone and said, "And you'll give me a lift in your car, Billy, the nice, shiny yellow one? When will you…?"

"Where are you the now?"

"Eh, I'm down at the Co-op in Dunkenny Road getting some sweeties, Billy. My Papa thinks…"

"Yeah, yeah," the impatient Purvis again butted in. "Right, stay there and I'll pick you up in five minutes," he instructed and pressed the red button to end the call.

The old janitor Willie McKee poured the boiled water into the old, but gleaming silver teapot and milked five mugs, leaving his own without milk and grinned, for he would jokingly tell the cleaners he liked his tea like his women; strong, sweet and black.

The door pushed open and the gaggle of cleaners in their council tabards burst in, desperate for their morning brew that four of the women would grab and then, in observance of the strict no smoking ban on council property, head to the school gate to drink in the roadway outside where they enjoyed their fags.

The exception was Grace Thomson who, as a non-smoker, would sit and idle away her fifteen minute morning break with McKee.

The old janitor liked Grace and enjoyed her company and through time and their exchanged confidences, they had become firm friends.

"Busy weekend then, hen?" he asked.

"Not too bad, Willie," she replied, her mug cupped in her hands and blowing softly on the hot liquid.

"So," he pressed, "what did you and wee Steven get up to then?"

"Well, Steven had the game on Saturday morning then we went for a burger after the game," she shrugged, uncertain just how much she could or should reveal to the old man. She could not know that at the Friday night school fundraiser when she had asked McKee about Des Brown's marital circumstances, she had inadvertently caused him to wonder if Grace had an interest in Des Brown.

McKee prided himself that not much went on in his school that he didn't know about and sitting back in his old patched swivel chair, nursed his tea. He knew he was teasing her, that she couldn't know an excited Steven earlier that morning had told the old janitor all about Steven's new model car, a gift from Des Brown's son Paul.

Straight-faced, he asked, "Anything else happen over the weekend?"

Unaccountably, she felt the heat rising from her neck and she blushed. "Well, Steven and I had dinner on Saturday night with a friend."

"Anyone I know," eyebrows raised, he fought not to smile.

She theatrically banged her mug down onto his chipped and stained desk and pouting, stared at him with narrowed eyes.

"You old bugger. How did you find out?"

"What, you mean about your date with Des Brown?" he slowly swivelled in the chair and pretended innocence. "I have my sources," he quietly replied, pretending to be mysterious.

"Yeah, and I can bet your source is nine years old and wears glasses," she slowly replied and exhaled. "What am I going to do, Willie? He's such a nice man. I just…" she talked off, uncertain how to explain the feelings that overwhelmed her, the feelings that she dare not admit to. Feelings that were alien to her and, she inwardly admitted, a little daunting.

"Are you asking me as your friend or as a father figure, Grace?"

"Both," she simply replied.

He took a sip of his tea and blew through pursed lips.

"I've known Des Brown since his son Paul was at the school. A nice lad Paul," he nodded. "I have to admit though that I *don't* know Des socially, I did hear on the grapevine at the time that when his marriage broke up that it wasn't pleasant, though you wouldn't have known how it affected Des for he was always a nice man with time to stop and have a wee chat with you. I think it's the mark of the man that he puts himself out for others. I mean, when young Paul left for the secondary, Des could have walked away from running the football team here, but he didn't. He stayed so that the young lads wouldn't be disappointed. He took responsibility for other parents sons, some of whom couldn't bother their arse what their wean gets up to when they're out the house," he added with a touch of bitterness to his voice, but then he sighed. "Des, in my humble opinion, is one of life's good guys. He's a good man and a good father to young Paul. I know he works shifts and sometimes he can be working all the hours that God sends, but he fits his working life in about his son and helping out here. I'm guessing he doesn't have much of a personal life and though, as I said I don't know him socially, I suspect that he has a strong interest in you, young Grace," he nodded to her.

She blushed again as he continued, "I also think you are one of life's good guys as well, Grace and as you've asked me what you think you should do? For what it's worth, hen, speaking as a sixty-two year old husband, a father and a grandfather and," he grinned at her, "I regret that unfortunately these days while I'm no longer a threat to women's chastity, I do have a modicum of experience in relationships." He took a deep breath and with a smile, continued, "I'll give you the advice that I would give to one of my daughters. I think you should grab Des Brown with open arms before some other lucky woman gets there first."

The door opened and the supervisor cleaner popped in holding the four empty mugs in both hands. "Ready to get back, hen?" she smiled down at Grace and then watched with surprise when the younger woman stood and placing both hands on McKee's shoulders, bent down to kiss the old janitor on the forehead.

DC Helen Meadows drove the CID car from the Pathology bay towards the Govan Road exit of the Southern General Hospital with DI Jamie Dalgleish in the passenger seat.

"You sure you're okay to drive?" he asked her again.

"Fine boss, honest," she replied, but her pale face still worried him.

"It's not an easy thing to witness," he quietly sighed. "You won't be the first detective to have thrown up," he added.

"I feel *such* an idiot!" she fumed. "I didn't really think that…" and shook her head to rid her mind of the images she had witnessed.

"Don't knock yourself, Helen. What you saw there is a lot more than what the public perceive a post mortem is. They watch the police or forensic programs on tele and think that it's cold and clinical, that it's like standing in queue in the local supermarket waiting on the butcher chopping up a piece of meat for your dinner. But it's not like that at all," he continued with some feeling. "The TV doesn't adequately present the true circumstances of a PM, like the overpowering smell of formaldehyde to kill the odours a body produces, the sight of organs being exposed or more importantly, the realisation that the body on the table was once a living, breathing human being who loved and likely, was also loved. If you forget *these* things, Helen, then it's time to chuck this job."

He half turned in his seat to stare at her and continued, "One last thing though, our compassion for the victims must *never* overwhelm our determination to get the bastard who killed them."

She drove in silence, no longer nauseous, but contemplating what Dalgleish had said, her stomach now settled, but mouth still raw and wishing she had some chewing-gum in her bag to take away the taste of the bile.

"The…things…that the pathologist took from her body that my neighbour is taking to the laboratory; what will they be tested for?"

"The samples you mean, from the liver, stomach, kidney and the blood? Well, the laboratory will conduct several tests, but primarily to determine that the victim wasn't suffering from some fatal disease that in fact resulted in her death, to confirm that she was or wasn't pregnant and also to establish if there was any illicit drug in her system that she was either addicted to or been induced to take prior to her demise."

"You mean like rohypnol or something like that?"

"Yeah, that and sadly," he shook his head, "it includes alcohol that is probably the worst type of commonly used drug for lowering a young woman's moral defence."

"The binding on her wrists from the stockings and the tearing of both…" Meadows paused and blushed, "you know. It would seem to indicate she was violently raped rather than a sex game gone wrong."

"I agree. What goes on consensually between a man and a woman behind closed doors is their business Helen, but the damage that young woman suffered was no game. When you were, ah," he grinned, "otherwise indisposed…"

"You mean chucking up in the loo," she returned his grin, but eyes still on the road in front of the car.

"Aye, saying hello again to your breakfast. Anyway, while you were gone even the pathologist commented that it was the worst type of beating he had come across on a woman. What she underwent. The pain that poor lassie suffered…" he gave an inward shudder and a few seconds of silence fell between them, before through gritted teeth he repeated, "The pain that wee lassie suffered; well, let's just do our level best to *get* the bastard, eh hen?"

Harry McInnes watched as the DCI who was in charge of the Covert Human Intelligence Source unit, the CHIS guys as they were more commonly referred to, was admitted to the office by Fiona who with a smile pointed him towards the glass enclosed cubicle in the corner that was used as an office by DI Peter Murray.

Harry turned his attention again to the reports in front of him and with a bored sigh, stamped the paperwork as Confidential, wondering why the antics of a looney extreme left wing fringe couple of Vegans should be of interest to Crime Intelligence. Still, he sighed again, when you're marching, you're not fighting, as his old neighbour used to say and redirected the report towards the Counter Terrorist Intelligence Unit.

He heard his name called and looking up saw Murray standing at his open door with a sheet of paper in his hand and beckoning Harry towards him.

As Harry approached the small, square office, he saw the DCI sitting behind Murray's desk, the phone clamped to his ear and heard him say, "No, not this time. We'll let it run on this occasion and trust the source to report back and we'll consider evidencing any *further* transactions, Norrie, okay?" and then return the phone to the cradle.

"Here, Harry, stamp this Secret and file for now," instructed Murray, handing Harry the sheet of paper and turning away, effectively dismissed the older man as he closed the office door.

And not a fucking thank you, Harry inwardly exhaled and turned back towards his desk.

He sat heavily down at the desk, idly wondering how much longer he could stand to work in the place and reaching for the Secret stamp, glanced at the sheet of paper. His eyebrows knitted together as he quickly read the CHIS report that was documented on the official form. As his eyes danced over the report, Harry read the information that indicated the time and place where a sum of money, the proceeds from the local sale of heroin and estimated to be in excess of thirty thousand pounds, was being delivered by a drug sub-dealer to a courier acting for the drug supplier.

Bastards, was his first thought and wondered at the DCI's phone call that nothing was being done to take the money from the druggies. 'Norrie', he had heard the DCI say and that, thought Harry, must be Norrie Campbell, one of the DI's in charge of a surveillance team who was probably being instructed on this occasion to ignore the handover.

Harry slowly shook his head at the negativity of the decision, for in his opinion, the loss of the money might cause some confusion among the druggies. He had always advocated a war of attrition against the drug-dealers; keep hitting them in the pocket, he had argued, but management had their own agenda and to his increasing anger, paid no attention to an experienced Intelligence Officer who, Harry assumed, they probably thought was past it.

Angrily, he stamped the sheet of paper and with it in his hand, made his way to the secure CHIS cabinet to file it among the other reports that lingered there.

Billy Purvis parked the Mitsubishi a tenement block away from Kiniver Drive and, with Ian Fagin carrying a small plastic bag and tripping at his heels, cut through the back courts towards the rear close where he already knew the security door hung uselessly from its hinges. Leading Fagin into the dark and graffiti ridden close, his nostrils wrinkled at the nauseating smell of urine and faeces that lay just inside the rear of the close where someone had decided to loosen their bowels. Tiptoeing carefully past the undetermined mess, he grimaced when he heard Fagin whisper, "Oh shit, I've stood in it," and waited impatiently for a few minutes while the younger man scrambled about the debris in the close for some waste paper, to wipe clean the underside of his training shoe. At last, the two men started to climb the stairs to the top floor where on the landing Purvis fumbled with the keys in the stiff lock of the door of the flat and at last, got it open.

Ian Fagin, still scraping his shoe on the concrete steps, stumbled through the door after him as Purvis closed and locked the door behind them and then bent to lift the letter and advertising pamphlets that were piled behind the door.

When he saw the brown envelope that was addressed to 'Mister Ian Fagin' at the flat's address, he quickly stuffed the letter into the pocket of his tracksuit trousers.

"Right wee man, through here," he instructed with a nod of his head and led Fagin to the larger of the two bedrooms. In the room, he closed the paper thin curtains that hung crookedly from a plastic rail, but enough sunlight still penetrated without the necessity of him switching on the overhead bulb.

From his pocket, Purvis produced a small, narrow bladed electrician's screwdriver and kneeling in a corner on the floor, first pulled back the cheap carpet and then prised up two floorboards. Staring over his shoulder, Fagin was surprised at the depth that was revealed and then saw Purvis retrieve a heavy package from within the space.

"Take this through to the lounge, wee man," instructed Purvis, who replaced the floorboards and carpet, then stood upright and rubbed the dust from both hands.

He followed Fagin to the lounge where a couch and two single chairs, forlornly abandoned by the previous tenant, sat around a low, Formica topped coffee table.

Purvis strode to the window and pulled closed the dusty and stained curtains, but again enough sunlight penetrated through the thin material to enable them to see without the necessity of electric lighting.

"Is this where you live, Billy?" asked Fagin, his eyes wide and displaying his surprise at the squalor about him and then pinching his nose between a finger and his thumb, added, "It smells pretty rank, you know."

"What? Are you mad? Me live here, in this fucking dump? No, ya bampot, I live with Casey and her weans. You saw me there the other night, didn't you?" and shook his head at the younger man's stupidity.

"Is that the coke, Billy?" Fagin pointed to the package, eager to change the subject and keen to forget that the lovely Casey Lennox was shacked up with someone like Billy Purvis.

"It's not coke this time, wee man. This is the dog's bollocks, the big H. Pure as the driven, so they say," he replied, playfully slapping Fagin on the shoulder in the pretence of establishing some sort of camaraderie with the younger man, the easier to persuade him to sample the stuff with the new adulterant that Purvis had procured at the cut-down price from the Paki supplier, a former cell-mate he knew from his time in the nick in Low Moss.

As he watched, Fagin carefully opened the package and removing a kilo bag, set about unwrapping the tightly wrapped plastic packaging. Purvis licked his lips, aware that if as he planned he was able to skim some of the heroin and adulterate it with his own stuff, then he could sell it on without Thomson being any the wiser.

"You all right there wee man, about testing it I mean?" he asked Fagin who opened the plastic shopping bag he carried to reveal a small tobacco tin and an NHS syringe, still enclosed in its vacuum sealed wrapper.

"Oh aye, Billy," replied Fagin, grinning inanely at Purvis. "I've done this before you know," he said with a hint of boastful pride and then staring curiously at the exposed heroin asked, "Where's the mixer Billy?"

Purvis made his way to a cheaply made, self-assembled television unit that minus the weight of a TV, sat drunkenly in one corner from which he collected an innocuous lemonade bottle filled with a clear, yellow tinged, liquid.

"What's this stuff, Billy?" Fagin, now kneeling by the coffee table, stared curiously at the bottle.

"It's a new mixer wee man. All the rage down south in London, according to my source," he glibly lied.

"Oh aye, is it?" Fagin smiled trustingly at him.

Purvis watched as Fagin with deft fingers adulterated the heroin with the liquid and after drawing and adding some of his blood, heated the mixture on a tablespoon with a plastic disposal lighter. When he was satisfied the mixture was now fully liquefied, he carefully poured it into the syringe and tapped the syringe to dispose of any air bubbles.

Using his free hand and his teeth to tie a length of rubber tubing tightly around his upper left arm, Fagin used two fingers to tap at the muscle of his arm, searching for a vein.

Holding his breath, Purvis continued to watch as Fagin, now seated upon the couch, inserted the needle into a vein and with an audible sigh, slowly depressed the plunger on the syringe, his eyes fluttering closed and moth opening as the mixture entered his bloodstream.

He sat back in the couch, his eyes still fluttering as the sudden impact of the heroin and the adulterant worked their magic and he smiled, a slow smile of pleasure as the room about him dimmed and his thoughts turned to a white painted house with a picket-fence garden and an open gate that led to a flower bordered pathway and neatly trimmed lawn. Casey Lennox stood in the doorway of the house, her smile as broad as her welcoming arms that were extended to greet him, home from a hard days work.

"Casey," he softly murmured in a voice so low that Purvis didn't quite catch what he said.

But then quite suddenly, his throat was dry, his chest felt awfully tight and he couldn't breathe.

"What's wrong, wee man?" Purvis bent uneasily over the stricken Fagin, his face now anxious and worried. "Is it a bad reaction you're having, wee man?"

The younger man's eyes shot open, his face beetroot red and his hands, claw like now grasping at the face above him as his body experienced a series of spasms.

Purvis jerked back in shock and horrified, saw a vein in Ian Fagin's eyes pop like an acne zit on a teenager's face.

"Jesus fuck!" he loudly exclaimed, his fists held against the side of his head as he danced back, watching the spasmodic seizures as the poisonous concoction raced through Fagin's veins. Almost as if with a will of their own, Purvis reached his hands nervously forward in an unwilling bid to help the unfortunate Fagin, but he quickly drew back with disgust at the sight of the drool that escaped Fagin's mouth; drool that now shone crimson red as the tortured young man bit through his tongue.

With a mild shriek, Ian Fagin's body convulsed once more then with a soft whimper, his heart stopped beating, his head slid forward and eyes wide open, he died.

Purvis, his eyes wide with in disbelief and hands clamped over his mouth to stop himself from crying out, backed away from the body and fell over the coffee table, scattering the powder from the opened kilo of heroin to the floor and spilling the liquid from the bottle onto the table. Seeing the liquid run across the Formica top and tip dripping over the side and onto the stained carpet below, he panicked.

"Fuck!" he screamed, the recently dead Ian Fagin for the time being forgotten as he dropped to his knees and used his hands to try and prevent the liquid from mixing with and contaminating the spilt heroin.

Breathlessly, he scooped the powder back into the packaging and dragged it away from the spread of the liquid, muttering incoherently as he did so.

Later, he could not tell if it was five minutes or ten minutes or twenty minutes that had passed, he found himself sitting cross legged on the stained carpet, weeping softly as he stared at Fagin's body and miserably wondering at the mess he had got himself into. He made to wipe his tears away but stopped, staring wide-eyed in fear at his heroin encrusted fingers. He clambered to his feet, careful to avoid the potent drug from touching or entering any part of his body or clothes and made towards the sink in the kitchen. Using his elbows he nudged the tap on and with relief, plunged his hands into the cold water and washed away the powder adhering to his fingers. Satisfied that his hands were now clean of the heroin, he wiped them on his tracksuit trousers and returned to the lounge and the nightmare that was there.

He glanced about him, knowing there was no-one he could call to help. Almost too fearful to even look at the body, he realised he couldn't leave Fagin sitting there, that he would need to get him out of the flat and dumped somewhere.

He realised with an anxious shudder he would need to tell Mick Thomson that Fagin was dead, but the most important thing was that Thomson did not find out that Ian Fagin had died trying out a different adulterant, one that Purvis had provided, because then it wouldn't take a genius to work out that Purvis had been trying to rip Thomson off.

CHAPTER FIFTEEN

Cat MacDougall glanced at her watch, conscious that her midday meeting with Andy Dawson was due in fifteen minutes. She turned to Munro, who was driving, and said, "Colin, I've to meet somebody at twelve in the café that's beside the shops just off Broomhill Drive. Think you could amuse yourself for half an hour while I'm there?"

He turned briefly to stare at her and eyes narrowing, replied, "I'll not ask, because I'm guessing it's personal and you don't want me to know about it?"

"Yeah, something like that," she smiled.

"Okay, you're the boss," he sighed and turned the car towards the west end of the city.

It took him just ten minutes to drop Cat off and leaning across the passenger seat as she got out the car, told her, "I'll pop into Partick office along the road there and phone in the crime report for the pavilion, then I'll call Mister Fagin with the crime number, Cat. When you're ready to be uplifted, call me on the mobile."

She nodded and was about to close the door when he pointed to the car radio and added, "What if somebody's looking for you? What will I tell them?"

"Be inventive and tell them I'm in the loo and take a message," she grinned, then closed the car door.

She watched him drive off then turned and walked towards the café, seeing Andy Dawson through the plate glass window already seated at a table.

"I've ordered a pot of tea and some low calorie buns," he greeted her with a grin, slapping at his expanding waistline in the full knowledge the café was widely renowned for its awesome selection of delicious pastries and cakes.

Cat pulled out her chair and acknowledged the smiling waitress who delivered the order almost as soon as she sat down.

"So, hen, what's so important that you don't want to meet me in your office, not that I'm complaining like," he hastily added and while helping himself to a cream cake that oozed strawberry jam, nodded that she go ahead and pour the tea.

"I had an approach from a woman the other night," she slowly began, "somebody that I helped put away a couple of years ago. She told me a story and also confirmed that the man who is flooding the Drum with heroin is your suspect, Mick Thomson."

He stopped biting at the cake and stared at Cat. "How credible is the information this woman gave you?"

"I'll let you decide for yourself after I tell you what Thomson did to her," she slowly replied, then in the same low voice, related a summarised version of Jessie Cochrane's tale of abuse, describing how Jessie was made to stand in front of Thomson, who made her strip naked, how Thomson beat her and not only sexually abused, but humiliated her; how he threatened to kill her and how she was made to satisfy Thomson's sexual perversions.

"My God," he was genuinely shocked. "Cat, you've enough evidence there to arrest him. Why haven't you?"

She shook her head and shrugging her shoulders, replied, "My informant was so traumatised that she knows if what Thomson did to her ever became public knowledge, she would never live it down. She would always be the woman that suffered these indignities at his hands. You know what people are like, Andy; they'd never let her forget what happened to her. Anywhere she went, there would be whispers, fingers pointed, that sort of thing. No," she vigorously shook her head, "even if I went ahead and reported the circumstances to the Fiscal, she would never attend court let alone give evidence. I know what she's like, Andy; she'd simply clam up and might possibly even disappear from the area."

He sat back and rubbed at his chin with his meaty hand. "You're not daft, Cat, and you've a good head on your shoulders. I suppose there's no doubt she's telling the truth? Nothing to suggest she's feeding you a line?"

"No, I believe her. I can't imagine what it must have taken for her to approach me, the detective that locked her up."

"Aye, well revenge is probably one of the most powerful incentives we know for somebody coming forward with information about another criminal."

He inhaled deeply and pushing the half eaten cake from him, sipped at his tea before continuing. "Right, though I can't know if the woman is telling the truth or feeding us a line, I believe that *you* believe her Cat and that's good enough for me." He returned the china cup to the saucer and pushing it to one side, leant his forearms on the table and leaned towards her. "What I'm about to divulge stays here at the table, savvy?"

She nodded, her eyes betraying her curiosity.

"What you just told me corroborates other information we have, information from a CHIS."

"So, you already were aware of Thomson's …"

He raised a hand to interrupt her and replied, "Yes, but it was information only. What you have just told me backs up the CHIS info so now that two sources have fired in the same suspect, according to the Intel boys that will make it solid intelligence," then with a shrug, added, "at least I hope it does."

"Your CHIS…" she started to say, but stopped when he again held his hand up.

"Don't ask, Cat. You know the rules. Whoever the CHIS is the unit are holding him or her tight to their chest. Even though I'm the SIO in this inquiry, *I'm* not privy to that information."

Dawson sat back in his chair, satisfied that the meeting with Cat MacDougall had been well worth it. At least now he had some leverage with which to persuade his boss that Thomson was worth a surveillance operation. But first, there was only one problem.

"Cat, when I get back to the office I'll be instructing my guys to formulate an operational surveillance plan to target this guy Thomson. First though, I'll need to run it past my boss for authorisation. I don't know if you are aware, but these days there's a bit of legislation called the Regulation of Investigatory Powers Act of 2000 that I need to comply with and basically, what it means is that I have to be able to justify why I'm seeking the authority for the operation."

"You mean that you will have to disclose where you got the information about Thomson?"

"Yeah, that's about it. The days of targeting a criminal because of a backcourt whisper are long gone, I'm afraid. Today," he sighed, "it's all about accountability."

"I'm sorry, Andy, I gave the woman my word. I can't go back on that," she tightly replied, now inwardly wondering if she had done the right thing in bringing it to Dawson's attention.

"Look, its plain from what you've said the woman isn't logged as a source with the CHIS unit and unlikely she would consider signing on either, so the best I can hope for is that my boss persuades the senior management that what you've said is enough to crave a surveillance warrant…"

"But you're not certain?" she interrupted.

He slowly shook his head and replied, "No, I'm not certain. It's the same old story you've known all your polis life, hen; knowing the bad guy *is* a bad guy isn't evidence and as I said earlier, these days it's all about accountability."

She slowly exhaled and hands flat on the table, shook her own head and said, "That's the best I can do for you, Andy. I could say that I would speak again to her, but I already know her answer. There's no way she will come forward. Christ, I can't even get her to complain about what happened to *her* so there is no chance she'll grass Thomson up for the heroin."

"Okay then, we'll leave it at that. I'll do my best with my boss and regardless of what he decides I'll get back to you as soon as I have an answer, okay?"

"Okay," she smiled, aware that Dawson *would* do his best and grateful that at least he didn't dismiss Jessie Cochrane's horrific experience out of hand, that he would at least attempt to persuade his boss to act on Jessie's information, albeit the information would be anonymous.

She glanced at her watch and while Dawson settled the bill with the waitress, phoned Colin Munro and requested he uplift her on the roadway near to the café.

She had taken her leave of Dawson who was walking to his car, but then he stopped and gesticulating that she wait he turned and walked back towards her.

"I knew there was something else I had to tell you," he grimaced. "Your boss, DI Walters; one of my guys knew him when Walters was a DS working down in Kilmarnock."

"Okay," she slowly drawled, "You've obviously learned something?"

"Aye, it seems that your man Walters has more faces than a Rubik Cube and the word is he was promoted out of Kilmarnock ahead of a posse from the rubber heels. According to my guy, Walters was a guns, bombs and bullets detective."

He saw the curiosity on Cat's face and with a slow grin explained, "He didn't take to investigating break-in to cars or run of the mill stuff; you know, wee woman in a council house getting her tele stolen. No, Walters apparently thought himself above that. He was continuously trying to impress the bosses and forever sexing up his reports and not above making up intelligence that this guy or that guy," Dawson held up both hands, with his forefingers pretending to be quotation marks, "has a shotgun or is planning a robbery or has terrorist associates or is a major drug-dealer and drivel like that. Nothing that was ever corroborated or could be proven he was telling a downright lie. Anyway, his colleagues and the bosses all thought he was a right wanker and as a detective, couldn't catch his fingers in a door. It also seems he was a failed applicant for the Special Branch, Serious Crime mob and thankfully, my lot. In short, nobody wanted the dickhead."

"Didn't stop him getting promoted though, did it?" Cat pointedly remarked.

"No, hen," Dawson shrugged, "it didn't, but you know the routine in the polis. Sometimes the way to get rid of someone who is incompetent is to promote him and then he's someone else's problem. Anyway, that's not all my guy told me. Apparently there were a number of complaints about Walters from some female officers about his inappropriate behaviour, but it seems that he's heavily connected somewhere, though my guy doesn't know to whom. I'm guessing that his connections might also be responsible for his promotions too. So, my advice is just watch yourself, hen, but if you can't, make sure you give me a wee phone and I'll come and boot him in the balls for you," he clapped her on her arm with his large hand and walking off, waved at her as he returned to his car. Cat, standing with her arms folded, returned his grin and wondered what Dawson would think if he knew she had already kneed Walters in the balls.

The small café located in the precinct on the corner of Buchanan Street and Sauchiehall Street was emptying after the lunch-break rush, the office staff from the shops and businesses nearby having impatiently grabbed their lattes and croissants from the overworked staff and returned to their places of work.

Sitting alone in a corner booth, Beth Williams miserably reflected on the disaster that earlier had been her job interview at the 'Glasgow News'.

The middle-aged woman from the newspaper's recruiting agency, who had conducted the interview for the post of junior correspondent, had initially been polite and courteous. It didn't take long for the hesitant and stuttering Beth to frustrate the woman who abruptly stopped the interview and curtly suggested that perhaps Beth consider another career, explaining that clearly she had not prepped sufficiently for a post that required the successful candidate to be, as she stressed, "…self-confident, assertive and frankly, pushy."

Close to tears, Beth had fled the small interview room and stumbled from the building to find a dark corner in which to compose herself. Now, here she was sitting staring at an empty mug and a half-eaten roll and sausage her mind a riot of thoughts as to where Cathy Porteous might be.

Swallowing hard, she took a deep breath and determinedly made her decision. Wiping at her eyes with a small, lace hankie, she stood and fetched a five pound note from her purse and paid the bill to the curious waitress at the counter, who wondered at the problem that was bothering the tear-stained young woman.

Stepping out the café door, Beth took a deep breath and strode purposefully west on Sauchiehall Street for like it or not, Beth was going back to Cathy's flat and had decided this time if there was again no reply, the fucking door was getting kicked in.

The incident room was hushed as DI Jamie Dalgleish delivered his report following the post mortem of the unidentified female found in the waters of the River Clyde at the King George the Fifth docks. "Murdered, but also savagely beaten prior to her death," he informed the inquiry team and then nodded to the raised hand of the stick-thin DS Phil Prentice, the office manager.

Dalgleish watched as Prentice first laid his mobile phone onto his desk and shaking his head, then said, "More bad news, boss. That was the lab on the blower there. The samples obtained from the deceased indicate her own DNA is not logged on their database and neither was there any trace of a foreign DNA on the deceased's body nor on the sheet wrapped about her body. The lab surmises if there *had* been a foreign DNA, the water dissipated any opportunity to recover that DNA. The stockings…" he paused and said, "they were definitely stockings, not tights that were tied about her wrists and ankles were presumably her own and their best suggestion is we endeavour to obtain a manufacturers make in the off chance they are a special brand unique to the deceased. The knots binding the deceased were simple granny knots. Her fingerprints have also been checked with a negative result. In short, we don't have a fuc…" he paused and smiled apologetically at the assembled group before continuing, "I regret, the woman remains unidentified at this time." Dalgleish took a deep breath and then slowly exhaling, turned towards Helen Meadows.

"Get on to the media office, Helen and find out where we are regarding the press release. If they're dawdling, tell them to get their arse in gear because right now, we don't have a Scooby who this woman is and if we can't identify her, we can't progress the inquiry. Quick as you like, hen," he added a little more sharply than he intended.

Turning back towards his team, he shook his head and told them, "Phil Prentice will allocate you the few inquiry actions we have, so in the meantime guys and gals, find something to occupy yourselves and if anyone has *any* idea how to ID the deceased, come and knock on my door."

Standing near to the janitor's room in the basement garage at Pitt Street, Sally Nelson stood with her back against the brick wall while her workmates had a fag break in the street outside. Reaching into her pocket, she withdrew her mobile phone to discover a text message from her husband Archie demanding she come straight home after work, that he needed money for the bookies and a couple of pints. She sighed at the curtness of the message, his nasally voice echoing in her mind as she read it for a second time.

It wasn't beyond him to go to the ATM located in the Cooperative supermarket round the corner and draw the cash himself, but the lazy sod would rather sit on his backside and wait for her to come home. She thrust the phone angrily back into the pocket of her jeans and took a deep breath, aware that her anger wasn't all about her lazy husband, but more about her disappointment at seeing Harry McInnes cuddling Fiona in the corridor outside the Intelligence office.

She had been a fool to hope that Harry had any kind of interest in her; an idiot who daydreamed of a life that would never be, she inwardly fumed.

Besides, she had seen the wedding ring and knew that Harry was married and kind and decent man that he was, likely to a wife that adored him.

But then her brow furrowed. If Harry was married, why was he giving Fiona a cuddle? She involuntarily shook her head, unable to understand why a nice man like Harry and Fiona, who she knew as one of the few women who worked within Pitt Street and who had the time of day for the cleaning staff, would risk their marriages if they *were* both happy?

"Sally," called the janitor's voice from his office, "do me a favour, hen, and tell them lazy buggers to wind up that smoke break and finish up before they leave for the day, eh?"

"Sure," she smiled at the janitor and walked towards the car entrance that exited onto West Regent Street. The half dozen women stood smoking in a huddle within a small windbreak near to the pedestrian entrance to the building and as she walked towards them, saw Fiona Kilbride walk out through the glass doors and turn towards her. Fiona nodded to the assembled cleaners then seeing Sally, greeted her with a wide smile.

"Just nipping home early," she slowed and stopping beside Sally, chuckled.

"It's my anniversary today and my hubby and I are off for a pre-theatre and then the pictures," she beamed conversationally.

"That's nice," replied Sally, "how many years is that then?"

"Twenty-eight years and all happy," replied a happy Fiona, but whose face then froze as she suddenly remembered that Sally was maybe not as fortunate with her own home life.

"So," Fiona continued, deciding to both ignore marital issues and mindful that Sally was not apparently as happily married as she was. Trying to lighten the moment, she asked, "I know the weekend's quite a few days away, but got anything planned?"

"The same as every other weekend, Fiona," Sally sighed. "I spend five days cleaning at work then catch up with the housework during the weekend."

"Oh, I'm sorry Sally, I forgot. Your husband's disabled, isn't he?"

"Yes, when he *wants* to be," she bitterly replied. "His disability doesn't stop him though when he wants to get down to the pub or the bloody bookies. But ask him to stick the kettle on to make me a cup of tea," she fumed and then suddenly stopped, seeing the confusion and embarrassment on Fiona's face. "Sorry, I didn't mean to go on about it. It's just that…"

She bit at her lower lip to stop the tears that threatened to spill over and took a deep breath. "Look, I'd better get on. I've to tell the girls to get back to work," she nodded to the laughter thirty yards away.

With sisterly compassion, Fiona instinctively reached across and stroked at Sally's arm and made her second decision within a couple of minutes. "What time do you finish work tomorrow?"

"Finish work? Oh, eh, the usual time, four o'clock."

"Right, well, I don't care *what* excuse you give your man, but I'll meet you here at four and then you and me, my girl," she winked theatrically, "we're going for a wee drink."

Billy Purvis, still in a state of disbelief that Ian Fagin had gone and died on him, had driven manically home and was relieved that Casey and her weans were out when he arrived back at the flat.

The first thing he did was strip off the clothing he wore and stepping into the electric shower, vigorously scrubbed at his body as though determined to wipe away the sight and smell of the flat and Fagin, whose slight body he had lugged down the three flights of stairs and abandoned under an old carpet in the debris strewn backcourt at the rear of the flats. Satisfied that he was as clean as he could get and dabbing at himself with a bath towel, he wrapped his clothing into the towel he'd used and stuffed the lot into the washing machine in the kitchen before pouring a liberal amount of powder in and setting the machine for a hot wash.

He had been lucky that nobody had seen him; almost unbelievably lucky and had decided that to carry Fagin any further in the back court than a couple of closes would have certainly risked someone in the flats peeking out from a window and seeing him. He shook his head as though to rid himself of the memory and knew that anyone at a window could not fail to wonder at him carrying a body and that, he knew with almost certainty, would have definitely meant an anonymous nine-nine-nine call to the cops.

A sudden panic overtook him and still naked, he sat down on the cold linoleum in the kitchen, knees drawn up under him, his back to the kitchen cupboard and his head in his hands.

What if someone *had* seen him? What if the cops were there in the backcourt right now, tearing the old carpet away and finding Fagin underneath it?

He rubbed with the heels of his hands at his eyes and began to weep at his predicament.

It was the not knowing that was bothering and worrying him.

He sniffed and rubbed some mucous from his nose and then startled. He'd went straight to his car after he had dumped Fagin and left the package of smack and the bottle of that shitty green stuff lying in the front room.

He began to beat at his head with his fists, calling out over and over, "Shit, shit, shit…"

He stopped and stared at the wishing machine drum as it revolved. There was nothing else for it. He would need to return to the flat and grab the gear. His brow furrowed and he wrapped his arms around his knees.

It wasn't likely the cops would know about the flat. There was nothing on Fagin's body to connect him to it, but if someone did break in…

He could only imagine how angry Mick Thomson would be if he lost the smack.

Angry? The bastard would murder him!

His mind whirled with a confusion of thoughts.

He took a deep breath and slowly exhaled.

First, he'd get dressed and then he would sneak back to the flat when it was dark, grab the gear and then phone Thomson; tell him that Fagin had fucked up, that it wasn't the gear that had killed Fagin, that the wee man had simply overdosed.

For the first time in hours, he had a glimmer of hope.

Yes, he unconsciously nodded at the idea, that's how he'd handle it. Blame the fuck-up on Fagin.

Beth Williams hadn't bothered driving for that morning's interview, having decided that trying to find a parking space in the rush hour traffic in Glasgow just wasn't worth the hassle and so without her car, had decided to walk from Sauchiehall Street to Cathy's flat in Broomielaw Quay.

During the meandering walk, she considered that Cathy might not be at home, but might be working and had hesitated and almost made the decision to cancel visiting the flat and again just try to phone her. She stood uncertainly at the junction with Douglas Street, ignoring then hissing angrily at the sallow skinned man who tried to press a Big Issue into her hands. As she walked she wondered; was she prepared to go to the flat and wait till Cathy returned home, she asked herself and then assuming that Cathy *did* return home. But she already knew the answer. She had to know if Cathy *did* truly love her and she would wait for as long as it took.

Walking south on Douglas Street, her arms folded and head down, she practised in her mind what she would say to Cathy if she were at home, wondering apprehensively how she would react if Cathy's response was rejection.

Please God, no, Beth inwardly pleaded with a deity she had long ago given up on.

Walking slowly, she guessed her route to Cathy's flat would mean she'd arrive there just after four that afternoon, figuring that if Cathy worked local as she had said, she would arrive home anytime between four and five.

Turning from the street into the private car park, she saw that Cathy's curtains were still closed, but that wasn't unusual and guessed Cathy had left early without enough time to pull them open. At the secure entrance to the flats, she pressed the call button but failed to get any response and didn't even bother trying to phone again, deciding instead to wait till Cathy got home.

Standing by the close door, she shivered in the shadow of the building and it occurred to her if Cathy were to be driven home by someone, how would she handle it? Would she challenge Cathy or simply turn away because she would be unable to bear it to see her with someone else. She glanced about her, but there was nowhere nearby she could stand without being seen. As she pondered her decision, fortune favoured her for right then at that moment the door opened and a young woman leading a toddler by the hand smiled as she stood aside and held the door open for Beth.

Returning the smile, Beth slipped past the woman and in the sudden cloying warmth of the flats entrance, climbed the stairs to Cathy's front door.

The corridor was empty, so she bent down on one knee and opened the letterbox, but the hallway was in darkness and she couldn't see inside.

There seemed little point in calling out again, so standing upright she leaned against the wall to wait.

CHAPTER SIXTEEN

Des Brown signed a little off early and waving cheerio to the late shift officers, headed downstairs from the CID office to his car parked in the rear yard.

He wasn't given to sneaking away, but the phone call with DC MacDougall had worried him. He had guessed correctly that George McCormick wouldn't take a punch to the jaw and forget about it. Likely the bullying bastard would be delighted at the opportunity to make a complaint against the police and sadly, he shrugged in admittance, his complaint on this occasion was genuine.

He was surprised and more than a little curious to receive the call from MacDougall, a DC. He thought it more likely and half expected that a DCI or DI would be tapping his shoulder and leading him into an interview room.

Since taking a poke at McCormick, he had come to realise how stupid his action was, but driving through the gate at Helen Street office, he slowly grinned.

No matter what the polis did to him, his son Paul came first.

If he ended up busted down to beat cop for his admittedly stupid act, but it kept that bullying bastard of a son of McCormick off Paul's back, then it was worth it.

The trip to Drumchapel police station took almost twenty-five minutes as he fought the commuter traffic. Finally arriving he parked in the roadway outside the station and presented his warrant card to the bar office who directed him upstairs to the CID general office.

A young blonde haired woman sat at a desk reading a report while a young black man sat on the opposite desk, facing towards her. Both glanced up when he rapped on the door and asked, "DC MacDougall?"

He watched her rise from her seat and smiling, extend her hand in greeting and reply, "You must be DS Brown." Turning, she nodded towards the young guy and introduced him as, "Acting DC Colin Munro."

He shook first her hand and then Munro's, telling him, "It's Des, son."

"Do you want a tea or coffee, Des?" interrupted Cat.

"No, you're fine, thanks," he held up his palm towards her and dragging a chair out from beneath a desk, sat down. "So, Cat, how much trouble am I in then?"

Cat resumed her seat and hands clasped on her desk formally replied, "As I told you on the phone, George McCormick arrived here on Saturday morning to make a complaint that you assaulted him. Is that correct?"

"Oh, aye," stony-faced, he readily agreed with a nod, yet curious that she hadn't first cautioned him. "And for what it's worth, I enjoyed hooking him on the jaw, too."

Cat forced herself to refrain from smiling, yet inwardly amazed that not only was Des Brown not offering any excuse for his assault, but that the slightly built detective had dropped the much taller and heavier McCormick on his arse.

"Is it your intention to charge me, Cat?" he continued, his eyes narrowing.

"Ah, well, now there's a wee problem, Des," brow furrowed, she shook her head and sat back as she folded her arms. "You see, I didn't call in my DI like protocol requires I should have done, but took it upon myself to deal with Mister McCormick and did the initial interview myself."

She nodded towards Munro, and added, "Colin here neighboured me for that interview, didn't you, son?"

Munro, a tad peeved at again being called 'son', resignedly sighed and nodded in agreement.

"During the interview, Mister McCormick made a serious allegation against you, Des. As I said, the allegation was of assault and to be frank, one I couldn't really ignore."

Des stared keenly at her, sensing that the slim and rather attractive detective was toying with him, but wisely refrained from interrupting.

"To cut a long story boring," she continued, "during the interview, Mister McCormick made a shocking racist comment to my neighbour here that I *also* couldn't ignore. So, in short, let's just say that the three of us, Colin, McCormick and I came to what you might call a wee agreement. Isn't that right, Colin?"

Again, Munro nodded and this time it was he who stifled a grin.

"What sort of agreement would that be, Cat?" Brown slowly asked.

"Well," she drawled, "the agreement is that Mister McCormick refrains from continuing the complaint against you and we refrain from charging him with a racial breach of the peace.

Des stared from one to the other and astounded, replied, "You're kidding."

Cat shook her head and solemnly said, "You *do* understand that if the bugger sits down and thinks about how we conned him, you and I are both for the chop," then turning towards Munro quickly added, "Not you Colin, You were simply doing what I instructed."

"That's not how I see it, Cat," the young man shook his head. "I was your neighbour during the interview, so whatever decision you took was made by us both, okay?"

She inhaled and smiled at Munro and still smiling, turned back to Brown and said, "So there you have it Detective Sergeant Brown. If you go down, the three of us go down so for heaven's sake, no more punching George McCormick; no matter how provoked you feel."

He swallowed hard, aware that MacDougall and the young lad Munro had taken one hell of a risk on his behalf; he being a man that neither of them had previously known.

The relief he felt was overwhelming, for they had not just saved his job and his career, they had saved him from probably being charged by the rubber heels and the subsequent ignominy of a trial.

He shook his head and quietly said, "There's nothing I can say or do and no explanation of my behaviour that night that will adequately repay your kindness, guys." He took a deep breath and slowly exhaled, then stared at each in turn. "All I can do I offer you my grateful thanks and promise you that if there is anything I can do to repay the favour, you know where to find me."

Cat arose from her seat, her hand extended and grinning, said, "I'm guessing your boy Paul doesn't know?"

Des shook his head and then her hand and returning her grin, realised that all along the perceptive MacDougall had known why he punched McCormick. "It didn't seem right to tell him, but I don't think Paul will be having any more trouble at the high school now; at least, not from McCormick's son."

"Well, if he *does* have some more trouble from Cole McCormick or anyone else's son, can I suggest that you consider letting the school deal with it?"

He grinned again and waving to them both, turned and left the CID general office.

In the corridor outside, he was about to walk towards the stairs when he heard a voice call out, "Des Brown. What are *you* doing here?"

Turning, his good humour faded when he saw Mark Walters standing at an open doorway, jacketless and arms belligerently folded as he stared curiously with narrowed eyes along the corridor towards Des.

Des stepped back towards him and scowling, replied, "A long time no see, Mark. How are you these days? Still harassing women?"

Walters face turned red and he snapped back, "Its Detective Inspector to you, sergeant."

Des let the rebuke pass over him and he slowly smiled, then to Walter's surprise, stared him hard in the eye and leaning forward so that their noses almost touched, poked a forefinger hard into Walter's chest.

"*Detective* Sergeant Brown to you, you wanker," he hissed. "*I'm* a detective. You, you're nothing but a predatory shit that should have been locked up in Kilmarnock, so don't give me any of that Inspector crap."

Turning, he retraced his steps towards the stairs, hearing Walters office door slam behind him. As he passed by the CID general office, he saw it was open and a pale-faced Cat MacDougall stood just inside the doorway, surprise registered plainly on her face.

"Bit of history there, Des?" she softly asked.

"Aye," he paused and as he walked on, then slowed his step and over his shoulder softly called out to her, "Watch out for that bastard, Cat."

Harry McInnes took a deep lungful of fresh air and, as the late afternoon weather was warm and cloudless, decided to walk to the west end for the meeting with Tom Fraser and Dick Smith at Dick's Cowan Street flat.

He had no idea what was so important and, curious at Tom's evasiveness on the phone, might have cancelled but for Tom's insistence he attend.

His explanation to Rosemary the previous evening that he might be a little late home from work had at first been treated with indifference, but then a few minutes later given in to her demand to know where he was going and with whom. When he told her it was to meet with Tom and Dick, she had vilified both his friends calling them every rude and crass name she knew until in anger, he had walked from the lounge rather than engage in yet another verbal battle.

Her sneers had followed him upstairs where for the remainder of the evening, he had sat in his own bedroom, listening as downstairs in anger she had banged and battered everything she touched to remind him she was still in the house.

As if she ever fucking left the house, he moodily thought as hands deep in his trouser pockets, he strode west on Sauchiehall Street towards Kelvin Way.

Billy Purvis had convinced himself the best idea was to face up to Mick Thomson, visit the big guy at his flat and play the innocent; tell him about Ian Fagin's fuck-up, but reassure Thomson the smack was all right and that he would get it out and delivered as usual.

He also needed to tell Thomson that the money handover for the following night was still on and hoped that his eagerness would distract Thomson from battering him.

It was with deep trepidation that Purvis parked his Mitsubishi in the roadway one street away from Thomson's flat, but before leaving the vehicle, decided to ensure the bag with the money was still safely locked in the boot.

With a quick glance about to ensure he wasn't being watched, he unlocked the boot and lifted the lid then pretended to be looking for something while checking the plastic bag was still under the boot carpet inside the rim of the spare wheel.

Satisfied, he banged the boot lid closed and with another glance about him, strode towards the corner and Mick Thomson's street.

He was at Thomson's door within a few minutes and licking at his dry lips, thumped his fist on the door.

A few seconds later the door was pulled open by Thomson who with a can of lager in one fist, nodded that Purvis follow him into the flat. He led the younger man through to the lounge and nodding towards the couch, instructed Purvis to sit.

As he did so, Purvis saw the television was loudly tuned to an Adult Channel and watched open mouthed as a young black woman dressed as a slave girl, moaned with practised pleasure as she tended to the sexual needs of two men.

"Did you come to see me or watch the tele?" Thomson's voice rasped from the armchair.

"Sorry, big man. Eh, wee hiccup I'm afraid."

Thomson muted the sound and turned towards Purvis. "Explain wee hiccup?" he growled.

Purvis took a deep breath and related the story he had spent an hour rehearsing, how Ian Fagin had either stupidly or inadvertently shot too much smack into the needle and as a result, had died. How Purvis had gallantly saved the heroin that he now intended to distribute to the sub-dealers when making his rounds as a takeaway delivery man and hoping to impress Thomson, reminded the older man that Purvis had the money, over thirty-two grand, counted and ready to be handed the next night to the English courier.

Thomson didn't take his eyes off Purvis as arising from the armchair he gesticulated that the smaller man to do likewise then with uncommon speed, wrapped his free hand round Purvis's throat.

In panic, Purvis grabbed with his two hands at Thomson's fingers, trying to the prise them from his windpipe as choking, he began to splutter.

"So where the *fuck* did you dump the body?" hissed Thomson, his face so close he covered Purvis in spittle.

Purvis, his eyes wide with terror and unable to breathe, tried to speak, but could only whimper such was the tightness of Thomson's hold on his throat.

As if then realising that his grasp was preventing Purvis from speaking, Thomson loosened his hold then threw the smaller man backwards onto the couch, but continued to stand menacingly over him.

"Where?" he asked again

His breath came in spurts and massaging his neck, Purvis replied, "Round the back of the flats under some rubbish. I couldn't leave him in the place…" he croaked, staring with fear at Thomson.

"Did anybody see you?"

"No, nobody saw me. Honest to Christ, Mick, nobody saw me. Please," he begged, one hand still massaging his throat and the other palm forward as if trying to ward off the expected attack from Thomson.

To his surprise, Thomson backed off, but with loathing continued to stare down at him.

At last, his voice oozing he venomously said, "If any of this gets back to me, wee man, if the polis come knocking on my door, you're dead, understand, fucking *dead*!"

Wide-eyed, Purvis vigorously nodded and slid along the couch out of Thomson's reach then watched as the big man resumed his seat and lifting the remote control, turned up the volume on the television.

In vivid and colourful detail, the cameraman on the Adult Channel programme captured the slave girl now being overdramatically raped by one man as the other held her down, but Purvis saw none of this for he dared not take his eyes off Thomson, who staring at the screen, almost with disdain cast a thumb over his shoulder and calmly said, "Fuck off."

Sally Nelson got off the bus in Duke Street and headed into the Cooperative to collect some shopping for the evening meal, but her thoughts were a confused jumble.

She had seen Harry McInnes and Fiona Kilbride hugging in the corridor, yet when Fiona had spoken later with Sally she had given the impression that she was happily married and about to celebrate her anniversary.

Why then, Sally wondered, would Fiona be flirting with or be in some sort of dalliance with Harry?

She shook her head as though to clear it and at the shop door, idly picked up a plastic shopping basket then almost mechanically made her way into the freezer aisle to collect some oven fish and chips.

In the few years she had worked at the police station, Sally was in no doubt that Fiona had guessed she was unhappily married and probably also guessed that Archie was hitting her. God, it's not as if the occasional black eye and swollen mouth wasn't enough of a clue, she inwardly sighed.

She wasn't certain why Fiona had asked her to go tomorrow evening for a drink, but sort of suspected that the older woman felt sorry for Sally and even more, had surprised herself that she had not refused.

She reached into the large fridge and bending over to lift the packet of frozen fish, grimaced. Her lower back still ached even though it had been several weeks since he had punched her in the kidneys. Another wound to her body and her pride that would never be disclosed.

"How's it going, hen?" said the cheery voice at her back and turning, saw the young Asian shop assistant dragging a trolley loaded with boxes, but a nice wee girl who never missed the opportunity to say hello.

She smiled gratefully in return, pleased that at least one person today had a kind word for her and made her way to the check-out to pay for the fish and the chips.

It was when she was halfway home when her stomach churned as with a sigh she remembered; she had forgotten to collect money from the ATM for Archie.

Three empty cans sat atop the coffee table as the three friends each held their second lager.

Harry stared first at Tom then at Dick and shook his head.

"You two are off your bloody heads," he slowly said. "How the *hell* did you come up with this idea?"

"Actually, it was you that planted the seed, Harry," replied Tom, "when you told us about the intelligence reports that crossed your desk. You remember? When you mentioned the reports about the money that was being handed over in the city between the drug dealers and their suppliers? You said that…"

"I *know* what the fuck I said," Harry snapped back, immediately regretting his outburst. Calmer now, he continued, "It just didn't occur to me that you pair would dream up an idiotic plan like this. You guys have to understand, if you got caught, it wouldn't be a slap on the wrist. You're talking about serious time in the jail for this. That and losing your pension rights because even as retired cops, we are still subject to the Discipline Code and don't think for one minute that the management wouldn't do all they could to fuck us over. You, Tom," he pointed an angry finger at Fraser. "Your missus, how long would she survive without your income from your pension? And you, Dick," he turned sharply towards him. "If I recall correctly, you're renting this place, aren't you because you haven't got a bean to your name. If you *ever* got out of the nick alive, this place would be gone and you'd be homeless. Have you two idiots thought about *that*?"

A pregnant pause settled on the trio and then Dick with a grin said, "Yeah, but think about what we could get if we *didn't* get caught? Have you considered that, Harry? I mean, we're not talking about becoming career criminals here. What Tom and I thought was maybe two or three lifts at the most. Take what money they're passing across to pay for the drugs and then divvy it up between us. Don't tell me that the money wouldn't be useful to you too, Harry. As far as I'm concerned, I know that it would definitely get me out of a hole. Christ," he waved his hand about, "I'm living hand to mouth here. Okay," he raised both hands as if in surrender, "I know from what you have told us that things aren't great between you and Rosie…" he smiled apologetically and continued, "I mean Rosemary, so just think what you could do if you had some cash behind you; cash that the taxman and your missus doesn't need to know about." He paused and then in a softer voice, said, "There must something that you would want to do with that amount of money. Look," he leaned forward, one hand holding his can of lager and the other open towards Harry, "If we even manage five or ten grand each, I know it's not a fortune, but it could maybe turn the corner for us, yeah?"

Harry turned towards Tom Fraser and shaking his head, asked, "You, Tom. You've a nice house and an Inspector's pension. Why would you even *consider* risking that for such a hare-brained scheme?"

Tom took a deep breath and replied, "Yes, I do have a nice house, but the house isn't paid off, Harry. Like Dick pays his rent, I have a mortgage too." He sighed and decided there was no real reason why he shouldn't tell them for after all, it was all history now.

"The house was paid off when I first retired," he began, "but then I had to take out a big loan, a remortgage if you like, two years ago. I'm sorry I didn't tell you guys at the time. To be honest, it was Sheila insisting that we kept it private."

The two former cops stared at their long-time friend, wondering what he was about to disclose, when Tom said, "You both know how heavily involved Sheila is with the Yorkhill Children's Charity and the Cancer charity shop," and saw them nod. "Well, to be frank, Sheila was not always so altruistic; at least, not until she herself was diagnosed." He took a deep breath as the horror of that time came back to his mind at a rush. "Breast cancer it was. The NHS consultant was very helpful, but there was a waiting list. I got so worried that I thought, to hell with it; my wife deserves more than waiting in line for an operation and besides, we were both sick with worry. Like I said, she didn't want anyone knowing in case our lad found out…" he held up his hand to stymie their protests. "I know, I know, I should have said at the time, but you know what she's like," he shrugged and smiled at them. "Anyway, I took out this massive loan against the house and we went private. The whole thing, the mastectomy and the reconstruction was done a good deal faster than was possible on the NHS. Don't get me wrong, I don't regret it, paying for the op I mean; not one little bit. No amount of money can buy the peace of mind in knowing that my wife isn't going to die, lads." He stared at Harry and continuing, said, "And that's why I'm game to take the money off these bastards. A sort of recompense for the money we spent to save Sheila."

Harry, staring down at his second can of lager he held in his hand, shook his head.

The atmosphere had changed to that old familiar camaraderie that they all felt for each other and he felt an overwhelming urge to tell these guys, his best pals, about the feelings he had for an office cleaner, but still he hesitated though not because he thought they might ridicule him. No, it was nothing like that. Harry hesitated because he still believed in the sanctity of marriage and like it or lump it, he was bound to Rosemary. Besides, he argued with himself, what would Sally think if he suddenly blurted out he had feelings for her, a woman who like him, was married?

"Harry?" Dick cautiously interrupted his thoughts, "So, what do you think?"

"I think you two bozo's are off your heads," but then he sighed. "Even if you knew the time and location of a money handover, the chapter and verse so to speak, just how in the hell do you think you'd persuade a couple of neds to part with the cash? Let's face it guys, you're not exactly the young things that you once were…or even *think* you might still be. Look at you Dick," he pointed towards him with the hand holding the can of lager, "You're carrying at least an extra couple of stone there and you, Tom. What makes you think you'd still be able to handle yourself against a young, fit guy who'll likely be as hard as fuck?"

Tom turned to stare at Dick and then shrugged at Harry. "We thought we'd represent ourselves as cops. Well, what I mean is we know the routine, the language and that. Just thought we'd chance our arm, see how we get on. After all, even if we didn't get the money and the neds legged it, we'd be no worse off, would we?"

Harry shook his head and blew through pursed lips before he replied, "No, if you're going to do it, it will need to be done right."

"So you're in then?" Dick asked with a hesitant eagerness in his voice.

Harry slowly grinned at him, but in his mind he was thinking of a CHIS report that had crossed his desk that morning; the report that indicated a time and location of a large cash handover that was due to occur tomorrow night and which the police management had decided to let run, that no action would be taken; meaning the police would not go anywhere near the handover.

"Aye," he nodded, "I'm in."

"You'll be Miss Porteous' friend?" said the polite voice behind Beth Williams, startling her.

She turned to see walking towards her, an old, white-bearded gentleman wearing a long beige coloured raincoat, a Fedora neatly perched on his head and brightly polished black shoes and who stared curiously at her.

"Ah, yes," she smiled a little uncertainly, wondering who the man was.

"I'm Mister McConnachie, I live in the flat along the corridor, at number thirty-two," he indicated with his hand along the way he had just come.

"Is she not in then?"

"Eh, no," replied Beth, "I was just waiting to see if she arrived home from work. I'll give it another ten minutes and then head off," she added with a tight smile.

"What about phoning her, my dear?" he smiled courteously at her. As if I hadn't bloody tried of *that*, she ungraciously thought, but with a fixed smile replied, "No answer, I'm afraid."

"Dearie me, that is a curious state of affairs," the old man's brow furrowed as he glanced at his wristwatch, "for I'm almost certain that Miss Porteous is usually at home by this time of the day. That's when I pop out for my evening newspaper and I can usually hear her music as I pass by her door," he added is if by way of explanation. Then staring intently at Beth, continued, "You *are* a close friend I assume?"

"Probably her closest friend in the world," sighed Beth and then, as if in confidence, blurted out, "I haven't been able to contact her now for a couple of days and I'm so worried and concerned that something might have happened to her…" she stopped suddenly, afraid that to continue might provoke a tearful outburst and took a deep breath.

It occurred to her that she might ask the old man to pass Cathy a message, but to her surprise, he held up a hand to interrupt. Staring hard at her and is if suddenly coming to a decision he shrugged and said, "Wait here, my dear, if you will."

She watched curiously as he slowly returned to his own flat then a few moments later, rejoined Beth.

"I'm not too sure I should be doing this, but as I *have* seen you in Miss Porteous company and you *do* seem to be a nice young lady, let's just satisfy ourselves that nothing untoward has happened to the young lady," and produced a key from his pocket.

"Miss Porteous entrusts me with this spare key in the event that she should find herself locked out. You must understand that I cannot permit you to remain within the flat alone, not without Miss Porteous permission, but to ease both your mind and my own," he reiterated, "let us just check that nothing is amiss and that will be the end of it, yes?"

Beth nodded, but for some inexplicable reason her stomach began to anxiously contract.

The old man inserted the key and turning it, pushed open the door that revealed the darkened hallway.

"Miss Porteous?" he called out loudly, first reaching to switch on the hall light before leading Beth into the flat.

"Miss Porteous?" he called out again and stepped into the darkened, but clearly empty lounge.

"Apparently not at home after all," he said with an almost relieved sigh.

Beth's nose twitched at the familiar smell, realising it was bleach and reached towards the bedroom door handle.

"Now I don't think…" Mister McConnachie started to protest, but too late, for the door was now opened wide.

Even with the curtains pulled closed, the light from the hallway was sufficient for her to see that the room was in a state of disarray and not as Beth remembered it.

The bed linen was missing and a drawer in the sideboard pulled out and left hanging ajar, but what took her attention were the dark, almost copper coloured stains on the mattress and pillows, staining that to Beth's shocked eyes she immediately thought to be blood.

A black coloured material was tightly knotted to the two posts at the foot of the bed; nylons or tights her confused mind screamed.

Behind her, she heard the old man in a shaky voice tell her, "Oh dearie me. I really believe something bad has occurred here. I think, my dear," he placed a cautionary hand on Beth's elbow to gently pull her back towards the hallway and the front door, "we really should consider calling for the police."

CHAPTER SEVENTEEN

The couple whose home had been broken into stood at the door of their flat on top of the splinters of wood from the shattered door lock, the woman silently quietly weeping and the man agitated and angry at the loss of his wife's jewellery and their laptop. Cat MacDougall promised she would do what she could and reminded them not to touch the items that she had left aside and adding that the next morning a Scene of Crime officer would be calling to examine the items for any evidence of fingerprints or DNA.

Leaving her calling card with the man, Cat walked down the stairs towards the car to join Colin Munro, who she had sent to knock on neighbour's doors seeking a witness to the break-in.

Cat MacDougall climbed into the passenger seat and conscious that Colin Munro seemed agitated, asked "What?"

"There was a radio message a couple minutes ago, Cat. All Drumchapel CID are to return immediately to the office and report to the DI. I answered the message and said we were on our way."

"Nothing in the message about why?" she asked, pulling her seat belt across her chest and clipping it into the socket while Munro sped through the quiet Drumchapel streets.

He shook his head and risking a glance at her, said with more curiosity than concern, "Everything okay with you, Cat?"

With an inward smile, she guessed he was referring to her earlier meeting with Dawson and simply replied, "Aye, a wee clandestine rendezvous with a hot, Latin and very wealthy man who's desperate for me to run off with him," she theatrically sighed and added, "but I told him that he would need to wait for a few months because I've a nosey wee acting Detective Constable to train before I can leave the polis and run away to a life of unadulterated luxury."

"So, keep my eyes on the road and my nose out of your business you mean," he grinned at her.

She playfully slapped at the back of his head and replied, "Suffice to say I'm a happily married woman and the meeting was work related, but I'm not involving you in case it goes pear shaped, Colin. Okay?"

"Got it, boss," he continued to grin and manoeuvred skilfully round a slowing bus.

Arriving at the office, they saw DI Walters about to climb into the passenger seat of a CID car, but he stopped and walked over to the driver's door, indicating Munro wind down the window.

"Uniform reported the discovery of a body underneath some rubbish in the back courts at Moraine Drive. Meet me there," he gruffly instructed then turned away to return to his own vehicle.

"Aye, and hello to you to," Cat shook her head.

The short journey took them just under five minutes and upon their arrival Cat saw a uniform van drawn up outside a close with one officer waving at them.

The young dark haired policewoman grinned in recognition when she saw Cat and leaning into the passenger window, said, "The body's a young guy. It was reported by a wee woman out walking her dog, Cat. I've got her sitting in the back of my van at the minute," the young cop jerked a thumb over her shoulder and then added, "unless you want me to take her down to the station. My neighbour is old Tam. He's round there the now, standing by the locus. Looks like a junkie, if the needle stuck in his arm and the rubber band wrapped round it is anything to go by. I've informed the control room about the body and they're contacting the casualty surgeon and the Scene of Crime. Is that okay?"

"Well done, Morag. We'll hang on here till the DI arrives," Cat replied, getting out of the car. "He's en route…"

"Aye, here he is," Morag abruptly interrupted and then frowned. Standing upright, the young cop adjusted her utility belt on her waist as she walked away from Cat to deliver her report to Walters.

Cat stared after her and wondered at the younger woman's sudden change of attitude and it briefly occurred to her that perhaps Morag had some reason to also be wary of Walters. She had heard rumours of course, but nothing specific.

"Bit of a looker, isn't she," commented Colin Munro, standing at her back.

She turned to see the young acting detective staring admiringly at Morag Stewart as she spoke with the DI.

Cat smiled tightly, but ignoring Munro's interest in Stewart, instead said, "Right, let's find out what the story is."

The old and seasoned Detective Sergeant who had accompanied Walters to Moraine Drive cast a warning glance behind Walters back towards Cat, a glance that told her no matter what, don't interfere.

Following the directions of the young cop, the four detectives walked through the nearby close into the rubbish strewn rear court where they saw Tam, the uniformed officer standing thirty yards distant beside a pile of rubble and household debris.

The DS nodded to the large and weary-faced cop who solemnly related the discovery of the body by the woman walking her dog and bending down as he did so, pulled aside a corner of a sodden carpet to reveal the body of a young man, his eyes open and his face contorted in the agony of his death.

Cat took a sharp intake of breath and almost in a hushed whisper, said, "Ian Fagin."

Walters turned sharply towards her. "You know this guy?"

"Yes, sir," she nodded. "His name is Ian Fagin. He's nineteen and lives with his grandfather over in Hecla Place. Number sixty-five, I think it is."

"He *was* nineteen," Walters chuckled, "but it seems he won't see twenty and another junkie bites the dust, eh?"

He glanced at the other detectives with a grin in the belief his gallows humour would raise a laugh, but the three stared impassively at him.

Not so Tam, the old cop, who angrily took a step towards Walters and teeth gritted, stood almost nose to nose with Walters and said in a quiet and threatening voice, "I knew this laddie, sir. He was a bit simple and easily led, but he didn't do anybody any harm and I *do not* think your pathetic attempt at humour over his death is appropriate, s*ir*!"

Walters, ashen faced, blustered, "It was just a joke and don't forget who you're speaking to Constable."

"I'm speaking to a man who should know better, *sir*," the cop angrily retorted while leaning even closer and menacingly towards Walters, "and if you continue to use such language about a deceased individual, *sir*, then let me assure you that you will find your conduct reported to the sub-divisional commander, *sir*!"

The ashen faced Walters took a step back from the big cop. The DS, hands raised and palms towards angry man, stepped between them to placate Tam and quietly suggested he return to the van, that the DS would call him if anything else required his attention.

With a final scowl at the shaken DI, Tam turned and walked away.

Walters, his face still pale and trying to maintain his dignity, snapped at the DS, "This seems to be a straight forward overdose, so there doesn't seem to be anything here for us. The uniform inquiry desk can handle this."

"Then who put him here, sir?" interjected Cat, her eyes narrowing as she glanced about her. "Who brought the body here and hid it under a carpet? You can't believe he did it himself?"

"Well," Walters hesitatingly sought an explanation, realising he had been far too quick to dismiss Fagin's death. "Have the Scene of Crime conduct a full search of the area," he blustered at the DS, "and they've to deliver their report to me." He stopped and stared at Cat. "No, the report instead can be delivered to DC MacDougall. I'm still convinced it's a case of a junkie overdosing, so you can do the follow-up, MacDougall," he pointed a forefinger at her, "understand?"

"Of course sir," she tightly replied.

The DS, glancing between Walters and MacDougall, found his voice and calmly said, "Can I have a quiet word sir?" and without waiting for a response, walked past Walters out of earshot of Cat and Munro. Walters, his face like thunder, was obliged to follow to catch up with the DS.

Though she couldn't hear their conversation, it seemed to Cat the DS was remonstrating with Walters who suddenly stormed off, leaving the DS shaking his head.

The DS returned to Cat and Munro, still shaking his head, and with a sigh, told her, "The bugger's got a bee in his bonnet Cat and insists you've to conduct the inquiry. He's convinced himself there's nothing suspicious about it, that it's a straight forward overdose and whoever the wee guy has been shooting up with dumped the body here out of fear of being implicated. For what it's worth, I'll be overseeing your inquiry and," tapping with a stubby finger at the side of his nose, he added, "I'll be having a quiet word with somebody about this. It's not right; he should be dealing with this. Do what you can hen. You and young Colin here concentrate on this and I'll see that your other inquiries are divvied up between the rest of the team."

Cat was about to reply when from a close nearby, she saw the casualty surgeon arrive, closely followed by two white-suited members of the Scene of Crime unit.

"Right, I'll get on with it," she nodded and watched as the DS returned her nod and turned back towards the close where they could see Walters briskly walking away.

Greeting the doctor, Cat and Munro then stepped some distance back to permit both he and the Scene of Crime personnel to conduct their initial inquiry.

"I'm guessing that it's not commonplace then, Cat, for a DC to conduct this type of inquiry?" asked Munro.

Standing with her arms folded, watching the doctor examine Ian Fagin's body, she shook her head. "The usual practise is when a body is discovered and the death is in anyway suspicious, whether by violence or like this, a drug overdose, a DI or senior officer will investigate until such time it is determined that no crime has been committed. Then it's usually handed over to the inquiry department who report the circumstances to the Procurator Fiscal. Of course, other departments like the Drug squad will also be informed to record the death, what type of drug and…" she stopped and glanced curiously at him. "You've probably been involved in some previous cases like this, yeah?"

Munro sighed as he nodded. "I've been to a couple of incidents of drug overdoses. Unfortunately, it's not that uncommon these days."

"Regretfully, too true," she replied and nodding towards the figures working round the body, she continued. "This has the characteristics of a straight forward overdose, but if you want my humble opinion…"

"Always welcome," he grinned at her.

"Then my opinion is that the DI should be taking this on and if it turns out to be anything other than what it seems," she slowly shook her head, her lips puckered as she added, "this will come back and bite him hard, really hard, on the arse."

Grace Thomson drove the old Nissan Micra slowly into Goyle Avenue and was relieved when she saw that the Juke vehicle wasn't parked outside the close. A thought struck her and ever suspicious of her father, she decided to drive round the nearby streets to ensure that he hadn't parked the car elsewhere and was sitting in the flat, waiting on her.

A few minutes later, satisfied or as best she could be that the Juke wasn't hidden nearby, she stopped the Micra outside the close and narrowed her eyes as she scrutinised the window, but if he *was* watching her, she couldn't see him. Grabbing her cleaning materials in the plastic carrier tray and the bag of shopping in the other hand, she took a deep breath and exiting her car, made her way to the close entrance.

Her heart was in her mouth as she went up the stairs and stood nervously at his front door, but she couldn't hear any sound from inside. Nevertheless, she still wasn't taking any chance and when she opened the door, she wedged it open with the plastic carrier tray and legs shaking, checked each room in turn, dumping the shopping onto the kitchen worktop and preparing herself to dart back towards the door if he *was* in the flat.

Returning to the front door, she closed and locked it, ensuring her key remained in the lock to prevent him from entering with his own key, for she had already decided nothing would make her remain alone in the flat with Mick Thomson.

As quickly as was possible, she went about her cleaning duties and in record time, finished with a sigh of relief.

Grace collected her cleaning materials and snatched at the white envelope, checked first to see that the payment was within before thrusting it into the pocket of her tabard and then hurrying to the front door.

Before she unlocked it, she listened and peeked through the spy-hole drilled into the door, but the landing outside seemed to be empty. Cautiously, she opened the door and biting at her lower lip, pulled it open, half afraid that he would be standing there, waiting for her.

But he wasn't.

She hadn't realised how tense she had been and pulling the door closed behind her, quickly made her way downstairs.

It was only when she was safely locked inside her car that she saw her hands were shaking.

No more, she shook her head.

No matter what he would threaten, she would never return to his flat. It just wasn't worth the risk.

She'd phone him this evening and if he *did* threaten her, she smiled and closing her eyes, leaned back against the headrest, then she would tell him to bugger off; for now she had someone to turn to, someone to support her.

Des.

The uniformed officers who arrived at Broomielaw Quay in response to Mister McConnachie's urgent phone call quickly realised that the old man was correct in calling the police, that it did seem something untoward had occurred within the flat occupied by the absent tenant, a Miss Cathy Porteous.

However, what seemed even more curious to the extremely shaken Mister McConnachie was that Miss Porteous friend, the busty young lady with the hair that billowed uncontrollably from her head, had become distraught and without any explanation rushed off without as much as a by your leave, a fact he soon confided to the constables. Worse, he ruefully shook his head; he had not even asked her name.

That morning and without her husband's knowledge, Sally Nelson brought a blouse and denim skirt to work in her bag, surprising herself at how keen she was to meet Fiona Kilbride for the promised drink after work. She had told Archie that she might be getting kept on at work and ignored his grumbling complaint about his evening meal by baking a mince pie and leaving it to cool on the worktop with a short, written instruction on how to operate the cooker.

He really was a helpless sod, she inwardly grimaced, but aware that his helplessness was more laziness than incompetence.

The day passed quickly for Sally, whose cleaning routine was changed to accommodate a colleague off with flu and who found herself on the west side of the large building, temporarily cleaning the conference rooms and staff offices. As she worked, she listened to the chatter of the clerical staff who either completely ignored her or cast a courtesy smile.

Curiously, she noted, none of the clerical staff bothered to ask where the regular cleaning woman was or why Sally was filling in for her colleague.

Head down, she worked away, but her thoughts were on the meeting with Fiona and with a quiet smile, realised she was excited at the opportunity to socialise with another woman. Perhaps, she smiled again, but this time a little self-consciously, it might even provide her with the opportunity to find out if there really *was* anything going on between Fiona and Harry McInnes.

The three of them sat sombrely in the neat and tidy lounge of the two bedroom flat; the two police officers side by side on the two-seater couch while Chic Fagin slumped in the armchair, his fists clenched on his knees as he stared with disbelief into space.

Through the open window, the noise of cheering could be heard from a crowd of primary aged children playing football in the street outside.

Colin Munro rose to his feet and with a brief glance at Cat MacDougall, quietly said, "I'll stick the kettle on Mister Fagin."

Then as the old man glanced up at him, Munro raised a hand to stop him rising from the chair as he added with a slow smile, "Don't you worry, sir; I know my way about a kitchen."

"Is there anybody I can phone for you Mister Fagin? Some family that you might want to be here with you right now?" asked Cat.

He shook his head and audibly sighed. "No hen, there was just me and…"

A sob escaped him and he buried his face in his hands, his shoulders heaving while he softly wept.

It occurred to her that she might comfort him, but decided instead to give him a minute to himself and joined Munro in the kitchen, her eyes narrowing as they took in the neat and orderly array of kitchen implements hanging from a wall hook and the sparkling surfaces of the worktops and stainless steel cooker top.

"It's never easy, is it Cat, delivering this kind of message I mean," Munro broke into her thoughts.

"No, you're right there, Colin," she agreed, arms folded and her back against the cupboard door while she watched him fill the kettle and milk the white, enamel mugs that sat upon a plastic tray.

"So, you know your way about a kitchen, you said?"

"Aye," he grinned at her. "Ever since I was tall enough to reach the fridge door handle, my folks have had me working in the café, cleaning and serving at the weekends and after school. Then when I was up at the police college, my dad taught me at the weekends how to cook. Nothing fancy like he dishes up I mean," he hastened to add, "just simple fare. Enough for me to get by when I get my own place, or so they tell me," he grinned again.

The kettle clicked off and he poured the boiling water into the teapot and set it on a low gas on the cooker to brew.

"But you still live at home the now?"

"Oh aye," he nodded. "Where clsc would I get my meals cooked, my washing done and my room cleaned for the paltry sum I hand over for my keep? I'm no daft, Cat. At the minute, I'm on a good thing so what I save from my wages is going into a mortgage fund. Didn't stop them buying me a set of cook books for my Christmas though," he grinned at her.

"Well, you'll need to leave the nest sometime, young man," she pulled a face.

"Find me a buxom woman that's got a good job and lives over a pub and I'm out of there," he quipped.

"Sorry about that, hen," said the soft voice from the doorway.

She turned to see Chic Fagin, his eyes red.

She drew a deep breath and with a glance at Munro, followed the older man as he returned towards the lounge.

Courteously, he waited for Cat to sit first before resuming his own seat. "So, what you told me is as much as you know then? That he was found round the back of a tenement after he had been taking drugs?"

"It certainly seems like that Mister Fagin. There will need to be a post mortem, of course, but I'm almost certain that the result will be an overdose. I'm so very sorry for your loss."

Munro entered the room carrying the tray, first handing a mug to Fagin and then Cat before laying the tray on the floor at the side of the couch as he carefully sat back down on the couch with his own tea.

They sipped at their tea in silence, broken when Fagin asked, "Will it be you hen, that deals with this? Are you the detective that will try to find out who gave my Ian the drugs?"

She nodded and replied, "I've been given the inquiry Mister Fagin, so you have my word that I will do my very best and I will keep you informed of anything that I find out."

"I know you will, hen," he returned her nods. "You've always been very fair with me and Ian. But you haven't answered my question, Missus MacDougall. Will you get the person who gave my Ian the drugs?"

She hesitated, not wishing to commit herself to a false promise and simply answered, "I'll do my best."

"Well, I don't suppose I can ask for anymore than that, can I?"

He sipped again at his tea and said, "When can I see him?"

"For the minute, Ian's been taken to the mortuary at the Govan hospital, Mister Fagin. There will need to be a formal identification…"

"But you told me you recognised him," his eyes narrowed.

"And so I did," she agreed, "but the formal identification must be by a family member or close friend, so I'll make an arrangement to have you taken there."

"Can you not take me, hen?"

"I'll do my very best to ensure that I'm the officer that takes you there," she smiled softly at him, but then recalling that Walters had designated the inquiry to her, decided, dammit. "No, I *will* take you there myself Mister Fagin."

She half turned toward Munro and added, "Me and Colin I mean. Leave me to organise it, okay?"

He slowly nodded and mumbled, "Thank you, hen."

She instinctively knew she had made the correct decision, that this old man needed her support; someone's support during what was probably the worst day of his life.

Twenty minutes later, having taken their leave of Chic Fagin and as Munro drove the CID vehicle back to the office, he asked, "When you said we'll be taking Mister Fagin to the mortuary, Cat. That'll be me as well?"

"Aye, Colin," she turned and stared curiously at him. "I'm guessing you haven't attended a post mortem before then?"

"No," he shook his head, his eyes narrowed as he concentrated on keeping his distance from the small Hyundai salon car in front whose driver he could see wore a bunnet and was cautiously ambling along at just over twenty miles an hour. He decided the driver was likely a pensioner and took a sharp intake of breath at the same time as Cat quickly raised her hands towards the dashboard when they saw the Hyundai without indicating, turn sharply right into a side street and across the front of a black hackney cab, whose driver angrily flash his lights and sounded the taxi's horn.

"Jesus!" he heard Cat gasp. "That was close."

"My dad taught me that when I was learning to drive," he grinned, "stay far away from and never trust a driver wearing a bunnet."

"As for attending a post mortem," he continued, "you're right. I haven't been to one yet, but I suppose if I'm accepted for the CID then it's likely that will be something I will have to get used to."

"No, Colin, it's something you have to attend, but trust me," she replied with some feeling and a slight shudder, "it's not something you will get used to."

Wearing her clean change of clothes and her hair loose about her shoulders, Sally Nelson found Fiona Kilbride waiting for her by the commissionaire's desk at the West Regent Street entrance.

"There you are," Fiona greeted her with a wide smile. "You look fabulous, hen."

Then with a conspiratorial wink at the commissionaire, wrapped her arm around Sally's shoulder and added to the grinning man, "Two dolly birds going out on the town, John, so alert the polis and phone the pubs to have the bevy ready and on the bar."

A little light-headed, Sally giggled at Fiona's cheek, yet excited that here she was, stepping out with her new friend for a girls night out and wondering when the last time was that she had felt so carefree.

"Right, where to first?" Fiona broke into her thoughts.

"Eh…"

"Are you happy to leave it up to me, hen?"

Sally took a deep breath and unable to stop herself from grinning, nodded.

Fiona grinned and then arm in arm with Sally, began walking towards Sauchiehall Street and leaning close to her, said with a sly grin, "I know the very place to start."

Outside the school gates, Grace Thomson wrapped her arms about her son's shoulders as he hugged her to him. It still amazed yet pleased her immensely that even though he was now nine years of age, Steven didn't care that the boys in his class thought it sissy to hug their mums, her son ignored the curious glances while she suspected that the watching mothers were a little envious at Steven's open display of affection for his mum.

It was as she opened the driver's door, her mobile phone alerted her to an incoming text message from Des Brown.

Opening the message, she first smiled, but then frowned.

"What's wrong mum?" asked Steven.

"Oh, eh, nothing's wrong sweetheart," she sighed, her pleasure mixed with a little hesitancy, "but it seems we might have two visitors for a wee while tonight." Then with a resigned grin, she added, "But only if you help me get the house ready and *you* can start by tidying your room."

Archie Nelson stomped into the kitchen, already in a foul mood because the *fucking* nag that was supposed to be an absolute certainty at eleven to two didn't even finish the *fucking* race. Still irate, he balanced himself against the worktop and stared down at Sally's handwritten instructions that lay atop of the clean, dishtowel covering the homemade pie. His hand shaking with rage at her selfishness that she had left him to cook the *fucking* thing himself, he crumpled and threw the note onto the floor then lifting the pie in its Pyrex dish, violently threw it against the wall, watching as the meat and pastry splattered about the kitchen while the dish fell unbroken to the floor. The bitch can clean that when she gets in, he inwardly snarled.

He turned sharply and overbalancing, fell heavily, enraging him even further.

He lay there for a few minutes, gasping and then groping for a handhold, pulled himself upwards to stand shakily on his leg and fists clenched, leaned against the worktop.

"*SHITE*!" he angrily screamed and staring at the mess he had made, decided that if his cow of a wife was out *fucking* enjoying herself and leaving him helpless at home, then there was nothing else for it, but to get himself out to the pub and grab something there to eat. That was it, he decided with a nod; some grub and a couple of pints.

The word was soon round the Drum, that the police activity in Moraine Drive and the uniformed officers conducting a door to door inquiry was because a junkie had been discovered dead in the backcourts there.

The more salacious gossip had the deceased variously discovered hanging by the neck or thrown from a top floor window or wandering zombie like about the area, prior to his demise.

The more pragmatic locals opined the deceased was yet another unfortunate individual whose addiction had overtaken him and who had died a sad, lonely and terrible death.

It didn't help that the tight-lipped polis who were knocking on the locals doors with their clipboards in hand, gave nothing away.

What was not initially disclosed was the deceased's identity and so for a while, a number of parents and family members waited anxiously, fearing that knock on their door to inform them that the dead man was their son, brother or friend; afraid to admit that their fervent hope was some other family would get the knock and grieve, rather than them.

This time, anyway.

It wasn't long before a loose-lipped polis, having a fly smoke and cuppa in the back storeroom of the local all-day grocers and keen to demonstrate to his receptive shop assistant audience that the cop had his finger on the pulse, disclosed the dead man was young Ian Fagin, grandson of Chic Fagin, the well known Band Sergeant of the Drum Loyal True Blues.

Literally within minutes, the word was out and faster than the Internet, the areas jungle drums beat out the news the dead junkie was the wee daft guy, Ian Fagin.

Those who heard and who knew wee Chic as a nice man, regardless of their religious persuasion, shook their heads in sadness and grieved for him while the more belligerent republican supporters in the community sneered and celebrated that another Orange Hun had bitten the dust.

However, within a very short time, Chic Fagin's flat was besieged by his neighbours who flitted in and out, offering not only their condolences, but offers of assistance that included food, small sums of cash and a dozen other forms of assistance.

As he sat in his armchair, overwhelmed by the kindness bestowed upon him at this difficult time, the old man could not appreciate that his thoughtfulness and consideration throughout the years to his neighbours and community was at last, being repaid.

As a mark of their respect for Chic, a number of his bandsmen arrived in band uniform to quietly offer their sympathy and as they and his male neighbours stood around the old man, in true Glasgow tradition his female neighbours busied themselves in his kitchen making tea, heating up pots of soup and preparing sandwiches for the long evening ahead.

All at once, a silence fell over the room as the men's eyes turned towards the lounge door.

To their amazement, a small, slightly built nun stood hesitantly in the doorway, her hands clasped in front of her and dressed in a brown coloured habit and sparkling white Guimpe that framed her surprisingly smooth-skinned, but pale face, her clear blue eyes shining behind wire framed spectacles and a soft smile on her thin face.

A little over five feet tall, Sister Margaret of the Franciscan Order belied her almost eighty years. As she stepped almost shyly into the crowded room, the men parted before the saintly woman, staring first at her then towards Chic, who similarly surprised at seeing the nun, rose to his feet and with a sob, approached and embraced her, lowering his head onto her shoulder as she gently patted at his back.

Embarrassed, dumbfounded and completely confused, the men shuffled from the room and crowded into the hallway, but not before they heard the nun in a broad Irish accent, say to Chic, "My poor, poor Charlie, as soon as I heard the news, I had to come."

The senior bandsman of those present and the last to leave the lounge closed the door softly behind him and stared with open curiosity at the crowd of men who now packed the narrow hallway. One of the younger bandsmen, wide-eyed and as a bewildered as his friends, indicated with a thumb towards the kitchen where the women stood around a second nun, a younger woman, but similarly attired as was the old Irish nun.

The senior bandsmen cleared his throat and deciding to act as spokesmen for all, glanced at the other men before asking, "Eh, Sister, we're a wee bit surprised to see a couple of you people here. What's the story then?"

The nun, a pretty young woman in her mid-twenties accepted a cup of tea from one of the women with a grateful nod, then smiled and in a broad Glasgow accent, shrugged and replied, "I'm as surprised as you guys, pal. Sister Margaret," she nodded towards the closed lounge door, "got a telephone call from the parish priest at St Benedict's here. The next thing I know is I'm told to drive her over here. She's nearly eighty, you know. I mean, would *you* trust her on the road at her age?" she grinned at the bandsman.

"So, you're not from round here then?"

"No, we're from St Francis Nursing and Care home in Govan. Do you know it? It's in Merryland Street, just off the Copland Road area. Just down the road from Ibrox. You *do* know Ibrox. It's where the 'Gers play," she said with a gleam in her eye.

The bandsman grinned, realising he was being teased.

"So you're a Rangers fan then?"

"I'm from Govan myself," she replied, "so who else would I support then?"

"And the, eh," the bandsman cocked a head towards the lounge door, "connection between Chic and the old nun. You got any idea what that is all about, hen?"

"No idea at all," she slowly shook her head, "and when I asked Sister Margaret on the way over here, she wouldn't say. Very tight-lipped, she was."

"Seriously? She wouldn't tell you?"

"Seriously," again she shook her head and added, "Look at how I'm dressed. I'm a nun, pal. I'm not allowed to tell lies, even to Protestants," she grinned again at him.

"Well, this is a bit of a turn-up I must say. I mean, you know Chic and the rest of us here," he waved a hand towards the bandsmen, "we're all in the Orange band, hen. The Drum Loyal True Blues," he added with a hint of pride. "Wee Chic's our Band Sergeant so we're just a bit surprised that he has a…" he hesitated, "I don't know what you'd call it, some kind of relationship with a nun; a representative of the Catholic Church."

"Are you a Christian?" asked the nun.

"Aye, of course I am."

"Well, pal, maybe you and I have got more in common than you think, eh?" she winked at him as she sipped at her tea.

The women in the kitchen slightly relieved that the possibility of confrontation between the Orangemen and the nun that they had feared would not now occur, started to hand out sandwiches and mugs of tea and soup.

As hushed conversation broke out among the crowd, the bandsman shuffled closer to the young nun and with quiet word and solemn intent, told her of the bands respect for Chic Fagin, of Chic's history in the community helping others less fortunate, but in the end being unable to help the one person who mattered most to him; his grandson Ian.

As she listened, the young nun in turn related a brief history of the older nun, Sister Margaret, who as a young novice had arrived in the mid fifties at the convent that was both a maternity and retirement home; how through the years Sister Margaret had been posted to convents elsewhere on at least three occasions, but always found her way back to Govan.

"So," the bandsman asked with open curiosity, "what you're saying is that there is weans born there in your convent and you take the old ones in as well?"

"Oh, aye," the nun grinned at him and again winked at him. "We bring them in and then we see them out."

He laughed at her description, unable to believe that here he was, a committed Orangeman and hater of all things Catholic, sharing a joke with a nun.

His wife would never believe it.

The lounge door opened and Sister Margaret, escorted by Chic Fagin, stepped into the hallway. A respectful silence fell among those crowded into the hallway and the kitchen.

Her eyes danced brightly among the crowd and settled upon the younger nun.

"Are you ready there, Sister?" she called out in a surprisingly strong and firm voice.

With a grateful smile, the young nun handed her cup to one of the women and then in a whisper, cheekily said to the bandsman, "So, will I reserve a room for you at the retirement wing in the convent?"

"Don't kid yourself, hen," he replied with a grin, "but if you want to take up the flute, give me a phone."

With a friendly, tactile squeeze on the bandsman's arm, the young nun made her way towards Sister Margaret and followed her to the door where the older nun stopped, turned back towards the crowd and with a smile, said, "May the Lord's peace be upon you all and I thank you, for being our Charlie's good friends. I'm so very pleased he has you all with him at this very trying time."

With that, the nuns stepped out into the landing and the door was closed behind them.

Chic stared round at the eyes that settled upon him and with a gentle smile, said, "What's the chance of a cuppa then?"

Turning into Southdeen Road, Des Brown slowed up and drawing to a halt, parked behind Grace Thomson's Nissan Micra. Stepping with his son Paul from the car, he glanced up at the tenement building and grinned when he saw young Steven excitedly waving at him from the window.

"Here, dad," Paul nudged him with a tolerant smile, "maybe it would be better if you carried these up there, eh?" and handed him the brightly coloured bunch of flowers.

"Oh, aye, of course," he replied, turning towards his son who carried his own plastic bag. "What have you got there?"

"It's one of the model cars, the red Ferrari. I thought the wee guy might like it."

"I'm sure he will," Des agreed, wondering for the umpteenth time what lottery he must have unconsciously won to have such a thoughtful and caring son.

Steven opened the door to admit them and to Des and Paul's surprise, hugged them each in turn.

"Mum's got some food ready and then," he turned to Paul, "we can maybe play in my room?"

Des bit at his lip as Paul tactfully replied, "Sounds like a plan wee man. Maybe even play with this if you like," and handed the small boy the plastic bag.

"Hi," Grace stepped smilingly from the kitchen, her hair bundled up into a roll on top of her head and wearing a white blouse and short, black skirt under a bottle green kitchen apron that tied round her waist, only served to accentuate how slim she was. Des grinned and nodded at the fluffy, gaudy pink slippers on her feet.

"Love the outfit," he joked.

"Steven's Christmas present, weren't they sweetheart," she smiled at her son and then added, "I wouldn't dream of wearing anything else around the house."

"They cost me four pounds ninety-nine pence at the Drumchapel market, Mister Brown," the small boy proudly announced, "and I saved up all the money by myself."

"What have you got there, flowers for me?" her face brightened as she reached for them.

"There's no fooling you, is there Grace Thomson," Des grinned as he handed them to her.

"Mum said I've to ask to take your jackets," Steven interrupted, but then quickly turned to Grace and holding up the plastic bag, said, "Paul gave me this Mum. Can I open it now, please? Please!"

She could see there was no holding back her son's enthusiasm and with a grin and a nod, watched as he literally tore open the bag to reveal the brightly coloured red Ferrari.

Steven's eyes widen and his mouth fell open as he held the sleek model in both hands, the bag now discarded at his feet.

Paul bent to pick it up, but as he stood upright to his surprise, Grace leaned forward and gave the teenager a hug.

"Thanks, Paul," she smiled at him, her eyes moist.

Paul shuffled his feet to cover his embarrassment, then handed the plastic bag to his father and said, "Right wee man, where's your room? Let's find somewhere to display it, eh?"

Des and Grace watched as the small boy led his big pal to the bedroom, then Grace turned towards Des and said, "Shall we stand here in the hallway or would you like to sit down?"

In the small front room, he unconsciously nodded at the simple layout of the room, the freshly painted walls and furniture that though not modern, was clean and in good repair and the laminate flooring that was recently scrubbed. An old style television sat upon a chest of drawers in one corner while prominently placed in the centre of the mantelpiece was a wooden framed photograph of Steven's first day at primary school, his mothers hands upon his shoulders as she stood proudly behind him.

Grace cast an anxious glance at Des. He couldn't know how important to her it was that he approved of her flat.

"Well?" she asked.

"Well what?"

"This place," she cast a hand about her. "I know that it's not as big or as fancy as your home, but…"

The last thing she expected was him seizing her gently by the arms and pulling her forward to kiss her.

So close together, he thought the faint scent of her perfume intoxicating.

"I've wanted to do that for a wee while now," he quietly told her and smiled, a little uncertain if maybe he had been too hasty, fearful that he had ruined any chance he might have had with her.

She didn't reply, but her eyes still registering her surprise, she gently held his face in both her hands and returned his kiss, but this time their lips were pressed together a little longer.

He swallowed hard and with his forefingers, brushed a loose strand of hair from her eyes.

Then he smiled.

"Mum," said Steven impatiently from the doorway, "when can we eat because me and Paul, we're *starving*."

The persistently ringing phone annoyed her and stomping from the dinner table, she snatched at it and tersely said, "Hello."

"Missus Dalgleish, its Cathy Mulgrew. I'm sorry to bother you at home, but I couldn't raise your Jamie on his mobile. Is he there with you?"

"Oh, it's yourself? Of course Miss Mulgrew," she replied, her eyes to heaven, "hang on and I'll shout him. He's upstairs, playing with the twins."

On the other end of the line, Mulgrew winced as she heard Dalgleish's wife shout loudly, "Jamie! It's your boss. She's been trying to get you. You've probably left your bloody phone in the car again."

She heard the sound of heavy footsteps, presumably coming down stairs and then a breathless Dalgleish said, "Hello?"

"Jamie, Cathy Mulgrew. I had a call earlier on this afternoon from the Stewart Street CID. Can you get yourself together and meet me? I'm at the new built flats over in Broomielaw Quay. If you come to the car park entrance at the Broomielaw, I'll have a cop wait for you there to direct you to the flat."

He heard her softly exhale as she continued, "I believe we've identified your murder victim."

CHAPTER EIGHTEEN

It had been a good night and not being a woman who was particularly tolerant of alcohol, a giggly and extremely happy Sally Nelson was feeling the effect of the four large glasses of white wine. "Now, are you sure about this?" Fiona Kilbride worriedly called out as she watched Sally get onto the bus. "I can sub you for a taxi if your short, hen," she added a little louder, uncertain if Sally heard her as the doors hissed closed and the driver impatiently moved off. "No, I'm fine, honestly," a grinning Sally inanely called back to the now closed doors and waved through the window to Fiona as a little unsteadily, she made her way along the narrow corridor of the swaying bus, trying with some difficulty to retain her balance as the bus negotiated its way round George Square and headed east along George Street.

With a sigh, she plumped down onto an aisle seat, a smile on her face at the memory of the marvellous time she and Fiona had shared and of the stories they had told, ignoring the frumpy woman next to her who tight lipped, grasped her handbag a little firmer and turned away to stare through the window.

It had been some time since she had felt this lightheaded she thought and conscious that neither she nor Fiona had eaten any supper, the alcohol was having an adverse effect on her empty stomach.

To hell with it, she inwardly grinned. Tonight, I don't really care, for tonight, her tongue loosened by the wine and in the spirit of sisterly confidence, Fiona had told Sally of a secret, a secret that had made her want to shout out loud.

Tonight, Sally had learned that Fiona had no romantic interest in Harry McInnes.

Indeed, Fiona had confided that Harry was deeply, unhappily married and for some reason that she couldn't explain this confidence gave Sally hope.

The bus driver pressed the accelerator a little harder and catching the traffic lights before they turned to amber, the bus continued onwards to Duke Street.

Sally, still smiling, exhaled and watching for her stop on Duke Street, began to rise and make her way to the front of the bus.

"Ooops!" she giggled as a young woman with a fixed smile on her face reached out to steady her and turned to thank her.

The bus came to a smooth halt, the driver in his plastic cabin staring fixedly ahead as the doors opened with a gentle sigh.

Carefully Sally negotiated the step to the pavement and took a deep breath.

The fresh air brought clarity to her mind and her mouth turned down, the pleasure of the evening dissipating as she glanced up at the darkened windows of the first floor flat. Her eyes narrowed as she wondered why the lights were out then a sudden foreboding overtook her.

She glanced along the road towards the pub.

He had been angry when she told him she was going out with a friend for a drink and now was likely getting drunk with some of his cronies and that, she worried, would mean he would be in a mean temper when he got home.

Maybe it was the alcohol or maybe it was the good time she had with Fiona Kilbride or even perhaps the news that Fiona had no romantic interest in Harry McInnes.

Whatever the reason, a sudden madness overtook Sally and a determination set in that tonight she was not prepared for his verbal abuse or to feel the back of his hand.

The light-headedness had gone and replaced with a firm resolve as she quickly made her way towards the close entrance.

Mick Thomson parked the Juke outside the tenement close and exiting the vehicle, ignored the curious stares of the locals who were departing and who stood aside in the narrow pathway for the well known hard man. A few graced him with a nervous smile, keen to be recognised by him, but Thomson, dressed casually in jeans and a black sweater, continued to stare straight ahead as he strode towards the close door.

His loud knock on Chic Fagin's door was answered by an elderly female neighbour who unaware of his notoriety, greeted him with a smile and politely stood to one side to permit him entry.

"Where's the wee man, where's Chic?" his booming voice asked her as he stepped into the flat.

"In the front room there, son," she indicated and continued, "Would you like a cup of tea, son?"

He didn't reply, but walked through the visitors who stood aside in deference of his reputation.

Chic Fagin looked up as he entered and eyes narrowing suspiciously, stood with his hand extended and hesitantly thanked him for coming.

"I know that we've had out differences, Chic," began Thomson, "but I'd like you to know how sorry I am for the loss of your grandson. Ian, wasn't it?"

"Aye, Mick. His name was Ian," Chic sadly replied, but still inwardly wondering at Thomson's presence and conscious that nothing Thomson did was out of kindness or gratitude or without benefit to the large and frightening bully.

"Well, I'm only here for a few minutes," the bigger man gesticulated about him, "I can see that you're busy with family and friends, but I just want you to know that I'll be standing a round of drinks at the purvey."

Chic's eyes opened with surprise. "That's very gracious of you, Mick, but…"

Thomson raised a hand to forestall any protest.

"No argument, Chic my man. You were good to me when I was a young man and I'll not forget it, so that's the end of it. Right," he took a deep breath, "I'll hear when the funeral will be, but for now

I'll let you get on with it," and again shaking Chic's hand, turned and left the room.

As he walked through the admiring crowd, Thomson worked hard at keeping his face straight.

The cost of a round of drinks at the purvey for the hanger's-on after the wee halfwit's funeral service was nothing compared to the kudos he would earn from what people would undoubtedly later speak of as his generosity. The visit to wee Chic Fagin and his offer would soon be whispered throughout the area and that would do him no harm, not if rumours started to circulate that he was in some way connected to Chic's grandson's death.

As he stepped down the stairway towards the close front door, it occurred to him that maybe he had better have another word with young Billy Purvis.

It wouldn't do to have the wee bastard opening his mouth if the cops decided to have a word with him.

He smirked as he dragged open the close door, a smile of malicious pleasure as it also occurred to him how to issue the warning to Purvis.

The uniformed policewoman wearing the brightly coloured yellow fluorescent jacket, who was standing steadfastly at the entrance to the flats car park, raised a hand to stop the Zafira people carrier.

DI Jamie Dalgleish wound down the window and flashing his warrant card, discovered that true to her word, Mulgrew had made the arrangement and he was directed by the young cop towards the entrance to the flats where he could see a marked police vehicle and the anonymous white coloured Scene of Crime van.

Cathy Mulgrew was stood within the foyer of the flats as Dalgleish gave his name to another unformed cop who noted both his name and time of arrival on a clipboard he held.

"Sorry, I got here as quickly as I could boss, but the traffic was murder."

"No problem, Jamie," she held up her hand and continued, "the SOCO guys are up there the now, but it seems more than likely the flat was occupied by our murder victim." She glanced at her notebook, "A Catherine Victoria Porteous, according to a bank statement that was found in a cabinet drawer in the lounge. There's also a passport with her full details and no doubt fingerprints from the victim will be discovered in the flat to confirm her identity. As well as the passport, there's a good quality headshot photograph in a frame that you might want to consider passing to the media department and asking them to consider getting it onto the local news and the papers. See if it will drum up some interest and maybe a witness or two."

"So what do you reckon, boss, the flat's the scene of the murder?"

"Looks that way," she sighed as she nodded. "I had a quick glance in before the examination commenced and I could see what looks to be black tights or stockings had been tied to the bedposts and probably cut away. The bedding wasn't on the bed…"

"…so could be the sheet she was discovered bundled up into," he finished for her.

"Exactly," she concurred.

"Is there anything to indicate if she lived alone or shared the flat with a husband or partner?"

"Now, there's the curious thing," Mulgrew frowned. "The neighbour that called us, a Mister McConnachie, informed us that a female friend had alerted him to the possibility that the occupant of the flat had not been seen for a few days and as it turned out, he had a key that the tenant requested he keep for her in the event she lost her own. He and the woman then opened the door and when they saw the state of the bedroom, he turned around and the woman had gone. McConnachie then phones the polis and that's where we're at now."

"Any suggestion he might be fibbing?"

Mulgrew quietly smiled. "When you meet him, I think you'll agree that the old guy is as straight as a die. A bit embarrassed that he didn't get the woman's name and his description of her is a bit hazy. He described her hair as like a burst straw mattress gone wrong."

Dalgleish shook his head. "She shouldn't be hard to find then," he sighed, "if we put a lookout for a runaway scarecrow."

"So, we're assuming at this time that the deceased lived alone?"

"Certainly seems that way from the brief look I had, though I hadn't been through her wardrobe or bedroom drawers, so I can't say for certain at this time. Curious though," her brow knitted, "I don't recall seeing any personal photographs on the walls or in the lounge, either."

They both turned as a white suited figure strolled down the stairs towards them and who first nodded to Mulgrew and then smiled at Dalgleish.

"Hello, Jamie, long time no see," quipped the Scene of Crime officer.

He recognised her as the middle-aged female supervisor who was in attendance when the deceased's body had been removed from the River Clyde.

"Right," the supervisor briskly started, "we've obtained fingerprint and DNA samples from the areas likely to indicate the usual places that you would expect the tenant of the flat to leave their imprint; the kitchen and lounge and bedroom areas, as well as a number of other areas, but *not* the bathroom as I will later explain. At this time, as you will appreciate, it's only when we get back to the office we will be able to differentiate and compare the samples to those seized from your deceased for elimination purposes. Any samples that are *not* those of the deceased will then be checked against prints and DNA that is currently held on our database."

She grimaced and turning towards Mulgrew, added, "When you were in the flat ma'am, did you poke your head into the bathroom?"

Mulgrew nodded and said, "You mean the smell of bleach? The door was closed tightly, so I closed it back over again."

"Yes, you did the correct thing. The closed door and window also being tightly shut meant the smell was retained in the small bathroom," agreed the supervisor. "I think a packet of bleach wipes were used to wipe down the toilet and sink area that would indicate to me the culprit worried about leaving prints and that's why we didn't find anything, not even the flats tenant's. That said we *did* find an empty packet of bleach wipes in the toilet bin, so the culprit wasn't *that* bloody clever. I've bagged the packet and I'll check the packet for prints when I get back to the office." She smiled at them, but a grim smile and added, "Nobody ever leaves a locus one hundred per cent spotlessly clean. There's always something of the culprit left behind. The trick is finding it."

"So," Dalgleish interrupted, "you're of the mind that the flat is the probably the locus of the murder?"

The supervisor nodded. "The bedding has been removed from the bed and it's not in the flat, so I can only assume at this time it's been taken away by the culprit to avoid me and my team examining it for semen and other body fluids. The mattress shows signs of blood staining, but my guess is the blood is seepage that passed through the sheet or sheets and will likely belong to the deceased. Nevertheless, I'm arranging for the mattress to be seized for further examination back at the lab. I've also removed the remains of the nylon material that was tied to the bedposts and my guess is that it will match the material that was used to bind the deceased's wrists and ankles."

The supervisor gave an involuntarily shudder and shook her head as she added, "Sorry. I've been to all sorts of crime scenes in my day, but I can't imagine what that young woman must have suffered before she died."

"Any indication she lived with or shared the flat with anyone else?" asked Mulgrew.

"Not that I could see, ma'am," the supervisor again shook her head, "but we're almost finished there now, so you're welcome to conduct your own search if you'll give me and my neighbour a couple of minutes to wind up and collect our equipment."

"Right, give us a nod when you're leaving and thanks," smiled Mulgrew, who with Dalgleish watched the supervisor turn and climb back up the stairs. She turned to Dalgleish and continued, "I'll stay with you for now, Jamie, but no doubt you'll want to contact some of your team and get them here to collect anything of evidential value from the flat."

"It's already done, boss. I phoned young Helen Meadows, so she should be arriving anytime, if you want to head off."

Before Mulgrew could reply, the main door opened to admit Meadows breathing heavily, who hurried into the foyer area, her hair tousled and casually dressed in jeans, an old worn anorak and walking boots.

"Sorry I'm a bit late, ma'am," she breathlessly said and turned to nod towards Dalgleish. "I was out walking the dog when I got your call, sir."

"Well, Jamie," Mulgrew fought back a grin as she stared at the dishevelled Meadows, "if young Helen is here now, I'll head into Pitt Street and leave an update for Mister Johnson's twenty-four hour briefing note for the Chief. I'll be there for no more than an hour, so if anything else crops up before then, give me a bell."

She turned to leave, but stopped and turning back towards him, asked, "What time do you propose to have your briefing tomorrow morning?"

"I'll be in the office early, boss, but by the time I get things here sorted out and the team organised, I reckon about nine?"

"Okay," she nodded to him and smiled at Meadows, "I'll try to get over to you by that time, but if I don't, give me a phone after the briefing to let me know how things are."

Once Mulgrew had left, Dalgleish turned towards Meadows and grinned. "Right, Helen, it's me and you now, hen, so grab some gloves and," he grinned down at her heavy boots, "some extra large sized plastic overshoes from the Scene of Crime team. We've a flat to search."

Across the city, Sally Nelson's sister Elsie answered the knock at the door of her modern, detached home and shouted that her husband turn the bloody television down. Bending down, she scrambled on the tiled entrance floor for the catalogue in its wee cellophane bag and thought the Avon lady was a bit early for that weeks order.

The last thing she expected to see was Sally standing there, pale faced and with a suitcase at her feet telling her, "I've left him, Elsie. Can I stay with you for a wee while?"

They met that evening at Dick Smith's flat and the three of them with mugs of coffee before them, sat around the low coffee table to discuss the plan again.

Harry smiled softly at Tom Fraser, dressed in the NATO style pullover, dark uniform trousers of a police constable and black Doc Marten boots and said, "I remember when that uniform was a little less tight on you, Tom."

Tom grinned and then his face becoming serious, replied, "You don't think they'll suss that the uniforms out of date, that the cops these days are wearing polo shirts and cargo pants, as well as stab-proof vests?"

"They'll be too shit scared to notice anything like that, Tom," interjected Dick Smith and pointed to the hat on the floor beside Tom's chair. "All they'll see in the dark is your dice police cap and us shouting 'Police!' as we're running at them. They're not going to stop and ask why you're wearing an out of date uniform," he shook his head.

Like Harry McInnes, Dick was similarly dressed in jeans and a dark coloured pullover with their anoraks lying on the couch next to Harry.

"So, again," said Tom, "we see them arrive and when they're handing the bag over, that's when we make our move?"

"Yeah," nodded Dick, the only experienced surveillance officer among the three. "When I get out of the car, I light the place up and what we need is for you to get into our cars headlights Tom, so there's no doubt they think we're the polis. That's when Harry and I will run in the darkness at the bagman. In my experience, when they're out of their vehicles, the last thing they will do is get back into their wheels. They'll panic and all they'll think about is running away."

"What if they want to fight back, Dick," sighed Harry, "and don't be thinking that I'm fit for boxing these days because frankly, I'll be shitting myself as much as these guys will be. It's been a long time since I've rolled about the ground with a ned."

"It's been a long time since *any* of us has rolled about the ground," grumbled Tom.

"Look," Dick stared in frustration from one to the other, "just *think* about it, eh? According to Harry's information, there will be two guys arriving at the Maryhill shopping centre car park at the same time. They'll drive to a corner of the car park that is the darkest and least used," he used a ballpoint pen to point an A4 sheet of paper laid out on the table on which he had hand sketched rough map. "I've visited the handover locus. There's nine car parking bays that are the furthest from the Tesco Express that's located there with the bays overlooked by the backcourts of a row of tenement buildings and don't forget, there's a ten foot wall separating the back court from the car park as well. Me and you, Harry, we'll be standing in the shadow of the corner of the building's wall that is here," he pointed again to a spot on Garrioch Road. "You, Tom, will be parked with your head down here," he pointed to a trolley shelter thirty yards away. "As soon as they arrive and are parked up and out of their cars, you start the engine and race towards them with your full headlight beams on. Come to a stop just short of them and get out of the car and run into your car headlights so they can clearly see you're the polis and you start screaming 'Stop' or 'Police' or whatever. The important thing is you let them see your uniform and there is no doubt in their minds you're a cop. While you're doing that, Harry and I will be running towards them shouting 'Police', so they will have no choice but to run off in this direction," he again pointed to the map.

"And you're certain they'll drop the money bag?" asked Tom, the uncertainty showing on his face.

Dick sighed and replied, "They'll be on a high and even though they won't be expecting any bother, they'll still be thinking if the worst comes to the worst, the first thing that will go through their heads is that they don't want to get caught exchanging a bag of drug money. They'll do a runner when they hear us shout we're the polis, thinking it's a set-up and all they'll want to do is to get away. Will they run away carrying a bag of money that will earn them a stretch inside? I promise you," he shook his head, "not bloody likely."

"And you're confident that they'll get out of their vehicles, Dick? They won't exchange the bag through the window of the vehicles?"

"In my experience," sighed Dick, "the bag will be in the boot. The bagman won't risk carrying the bag inside the car in case he gets a pull from the traffic or some nosey beat officer. The bag will definitely be hidden against a cursory check of the vehicle, so yes, I *am* confident they two guys will get out of their respective vehicles."

"But if they do resist…" Harry tried again, clearly worried about the thought of violence.

"They won't, trust me," Dick slowly replied then, as if the idea just came to him, said, "If you feel that you guys need for one of us to carry something, I've still got my old, wooden police baton that I was issued with when I joined through in the bedroom cupboard. Do you want me to bring it with me?"

Harry glanced sharply at Tom, who shaking his head, replied for them both. "If we get caught for this Dick, I don't want a couple of years added on because we broke open some guy's skull. I'm not in favour of carrying weapons. If it doesn't work, then so be it. No violence. This is a con, Dick and I can't speak for Harry, but as far as *I'm* concerned, it's a straight forward theft. We pretend to be the police and steal the money and that's it, okay?"

Harry nodded and staring at Dick slowly said, "I agree with Tom. No violence."

"Then it's unanimous, because guys, we're in this together. The baton stays at home."

"And you bought a car?" asked Harry.

"I went to the car market on the M8 earlier this morning and picked up a scrapper for three hundred quid, an old four door Ford Escort. I gave a false name and address and parked it on the Great Western Road. It'll do a turn or two," he grinned, "and because it's not registered to me, we can abandon or torch it as we choose."

"Where did you get three hundred quid?" Tom smiled curiously at him.

"My life's savings," replied Dick, his hand theatrically over his heart, "and by the way, I'll want the money back out of what we get tonight before we divvy it three ways, agreed?"

"Right then," he acknowledged their nods and taking a deep breath, rubbed his hands together and said, "Let's go over it one more time."

The last thing that Billy Purvis expected to see at his door was Mick Thomson who without waiting to be invited, strolled past the startled younger man.

Casey Lennox, her young son balanced on her hip, walked into the hallway from the lounge, curious to know who had knocked at her door.

Her blood froze when she recognised the visitor and it was unfortunate that her choice of clothing that evening included a low-cut top that exposed most of her fulsome, milky white breasts.

Ignoring Thomson who leered at her, she called out, "Billy, I don't want him in my house. Get him out of here."

"Now don't be like that, hen," sneered Thomson as he walked slowly towards her, "Be nice, Casey, I've only come for a wee quiet word with your man, so chill out, eh?"

Behind him, Purvis's face had turned pale, anxious not to upset Casey but afraid that if he tried to eject Thomson, the big bastard might batter him.

"Its okay, Casey," he pushed past Thomson and smiled anxiously at her, "Mick is only here to discuss a wee bit of business, aren't you big man?" he half turned to Thomson.

"That's right, Casey. A wee bit of business," he repeated and then his eyes settled on her breasts. "Looking good, Casey," he said and winked. "If you ever want to earn some extra cash, come and see me."

She glared at him, the inferred offer of his cash in return for sex hanging in the air between them.

Their eyes locked and she spat out, "What the *fuck* do you mean by that!"

He raised his hands defensively and slowly replied, "Nothing hen. Just needing some wee cleaning jobs done round the house and that. Why," he leered again at her, "what did you *think* I meant?"

Between them, Purvis swallowed hard, worried that the tension in the hallway could explode into violence that might result in him being used as Thomson's punch bag and tactfully said, "Casey, can you take the wean into the lounge to watch the tele, hen. I'll speak with Tommo in the kitchen."

Nervously, he nodded for the bigger man to follow him into the kitchen, but his stomach was churning while he tried to maintain some form of manly dignity.

He wasn't prepared for the door being banged closed and as he turned, Thomson's large hand swiftly wrapped around his throat as almost bodily he felt himself being lifted from the floor and slammed against a cupboard door.

"Two questions for you, wee pal and you'd better get the answers right," Thomson quietly hissed at him, his face a mere inch from Purvis's nose.

He knew better than to resist and stared wide-eyed at the large man. "Have you got the cash ready for tonight's handover?"

He couldn't speak, such was the pressure on his windpipe and could barely nod assent.

"Good," Thomson nodded, his eyes boring into the frightened face. "Second question, wee man and you had better get this right as well. Have the polis been speaking to you or have you told anybody…*anybody*," he hissed again, spraying spittle into Purvis face, "about the wee dead halfwit working for you?"

He was struggling now and gasping for air, he rapidly shook his head.

"Good, good," Thomson nodded once more, then whispered, "because if you do and the polis come to speak to me, wee man, no matter what happens to me I'll find you and I'll not just rape your Casey and rape her weans as well," he grinned evilly and then terrified Purvis even more when he added, "I'll fucking rape *you* too."

With that, he suddenly released his grip as Purvis slid to the floor, choking and rubbing at his throat.

The door banged open and Casey stood there, her face red with anger when she saw Thomson standing over Purvis.

"What did you do to him?" she screamed at Thomson.

"Nothing hen," he grinned, "nothing at all. The wee man just slipped, didn't you Billy boy," and reaching down, offered a hand and easily pulled the much lighter Purvis to his feet.

"Get out of my house!" she snarled, trying to avoid the fear that threatened to overwhelm her voice and stood back in the hall to allow Thomson to walk past her.

Hands raised defensively and grinning, his eyes again settled again on her breasts as he walked slowly past the young woman and made towards the door, but then stopped and turning, stared directly at Purvis and said, "Don't forget the wee job tonight Billy boy and about that other thing, just remember my promise. Casey first, then her weans and then you."

He didn't bother closing the door behind him as she rushed forward and slammed it shut and then with trembling hands, turned the key in the lock.

She rested her head against the wooden door and took a deep breath, a wave of nausea rising within her throat and afraid that if she didn't relax her body she would throw up.

Gulping in a lungful of air, she slowly turned and stared at Purvis who stood white-faced, his right hand massaging his reddening throat.

Her voice shaking, she asked him, "What the *fuck* have you got us into, Billy?"

The crowd had left Chic Fagin's flat and he sat alone in the quiet of the lounge, for even the usual noise of the local children playing outside had become muted.

He didn't know how long he had been sitting there in the darkness. He didn't feel hungry or cold nor any emotion at all, which he thought strange.

All he could think of was the last time he had seen and spoken with his Ian.

A sob broke from him and leaning forward, he lowered his head into his hands.

The sudden knock at the door startled him and wearily, he got to his feet, rubbing his eyes on the sleeve of his shirt and slowly shuffled his way along the dark hallway.

He wasn't prepared to see her standing there; it was almost scary, she looked so like her mother.

"Mister Fagin, I'm sorry to call at this time of night," she said, "and you don't really know me, but…"

"You're Tricia Meikle's wee lassie. Grace, isn't it?"

"Aye, that's right," she smiled a little hesitantly at him and wondered how he knew her and replied, "but maybe not so wee these days. How did you know?"

"You're the image of your mother, hen," he returned her smile.

He could see she was nervous and then remembering his manners, said, "Come away in, Grace. Please," and stood to one side to let her pass as he reached up for the switch and turned on the overhead hall light.

Aware of the solemnity of her visit, she had decided to dress simply and wore a short black jacket over a white coloured blouse and knee length black skirt. Her hair was tied back into a tight ponytail and she clutched a small handbag to her.

"The reason I called was I heard about your grandson, Ian," she started to say, but he interrupted her by putting up his hand and quietly replied, "Aye," then beckoned her to follow him towards the lounge, switching on the light as he entered the room and moving towards the window to draw the curtains closed.

"It'll be all over Drumchapel by now, I expect," he sighed.

He turned to see her standing uncertainly in the doorway and waved towards the couch, telling her, "Sit down, Grace, sit down," while he himself returned to the armchair.

"Are you a married lady, Grace?"

"Eh, no Mister Fagin, I'm a single parent. I've a wee boy, Steven. He's nine. He's visiting a neighbour right now," she smiled and then added, "a good neighbour."

She didn't bother to explain the elderly woman in the ground flat in the close was happy to keep an eye on Steven for a few hours in gratitude for the occasional shopping Grace did for her. "Besides," she was always telling Grace, "the wee lad's good company for me."

"How did you know Ian then?"

"To be honest Mister Fagin, I didn't know Ian," she admitted and then added, "and I don't think I've ever spoken with you either." She started to fumble in her handbag and withdrew an envelope that he could see had already been opened.

But then she stopped and stared at him, her curiosity written on her pretty face.

He knew before she told him why she was there, but before he could ask her, she continued, "You said I was Tricia's daughter." Her brow furrowed and she felt a sudden tightness in her throat as, eyes narrowed she asked him, "Did you know my mother, Mister Fagin?"

He smiled at that and took a deep breath, for he was now thinking that it was time for him to reveal a secret that he had kept for a very long time, a secret that this young woman who was the living image of Patricia, needed to know.

"The letter you're holding. Am I right in thinking it is from your mother?"

She slowly nodded and told him that when she had been given by her father Mick Thomson to the care of her maiden aunt, she had been unaware of the letter until after the aunt died. It was when she went through an old, battered brown suitcase that belonged to the aunt she had come across the letter and saw it was addressed to Grace.

"I remember your auntie," he grimaced and shook his head. "I don't want to be offending you, hen, but she was the very worst epitome of spinsterhood, that woman. I can't imagine that living with her was easy."

"She could be difficult," Grace agreed, but still unwilling to speak ill of the dead even though her aunt had been an insufferable old cow.

"The letter, Mister Fagin," she persisted, then stood and bent over to hand it to him. "It's just the one page, but it says that you had been very good to my mum, that if I ever needed a friend, somebody to confide in I was to find you and speak with you; that you were somebody my mother said I could trust."

She took a deep breath and stared down at him as he withdrew the letter from the envelope.

"I've had the letter for some time now, but to be honest, I really didn't want to be disturbing you and the reason I'm here Mister

Fagin, is that I don't really need a friend right now, but when I heard about your loss, I thought that maybe *you* might need a friend."

She stood still, her hands folded in front of her as he fetched a pair of reading glasses from his shirt pocket and quickly glanced over the page of neat handwriting and then sighed.

"She was a rare beauty, your mother," he said as he waved her to sit down again, still slightly bewildered at the likeness of Grace to her mother. "Tricia couldn't walk along the road to the shops but there was some young guy always trying to chat her up," he shook his head at the memory. "But she was a fussy bugger so she was," he added, but with a smile.

"I don't remember that much about her," Grace also shook her head, then joined him with her own smile when she said, "I remember though that she liked to laugh. Well, when my father wasn't around that is."

Chic's face grew sombre.

"How well did you know her?" she interrupted his thoughts.

"Very well, I would say," he slowly began, his eyes narrowing as the memories flooded back, "and of course I was a married man when she was still growing up, so Sara and I were like…what do you call it when it's not your own mum and dad?"

"You mean, like surrogate parents?"

"Aye, that's it," he nodded as he sat back, the memories suddenly flooding though his mind, "surrogate parents. Tricia had been at school with my daughter Agnes, Ian's mother. Your mum lived then with your aunt, who was a bit older than Tricia, but Tricia didn't get on with her sister and she was always round here visiting Agnes and my wife Sara and me. The girls would spend time together in Agnes's room, playing music, talking about boys, the sort of thing that young women did then and I suppose still do."

"Oh, I didn't know that. Is Agnes living locally Mister Fagin?"

"No," he sadly shook his head, "Agnes left shortly after Ian was born. The last I heard from her she was in England somewhere. I haven't heard from my daughter since that time," he added, the hurt of her sudden departure still causing an ache in his chest.

"I suppose it was round about then that my mother met my father?" She thought he seemed a little uncomfortable and prepared herself to say that perhaps she should leave and she would call back another time.

He slowly shook his head and his eyes narrowed as if he was trying to remember and replied, "Well, I'm not sure about the dates, Grace, but there is something you should know, so I want you to prepare yourself for a bit of a shock."

She stared at him, surprised. It had not been her intention to call and ask him to disclose long forgotten secrets. In truth, all she had meant for the visit was to express her condolence at his loss, to thank him for being kind to Patricia and ask if there was anything she could do for him, but now her visit had taken a very strange twist and her stomach churned at the secret that he might tell.

"Are you certain this is the right time, Mister Fagin? I didn't mean to come here and upset you because I can leave, if you want and…"

He raised a hand to hush her and said, "I could never abide secrets or deceit, Grace and this secret has been held too long. Far too long," he added in a quiet, wistful voice.

He swallowed hard and stared with watery eyes at her.

"It's time you were told the truth."

In her room, Beth could hear the sound of her father fumbling around downstairs.

Lying on top of her bed, she hugged the pillow to her.

He had been concerned when she arrived home in an obvious distraught state, but did not have the energy or the courage to confide in him.

She had gone straight to her room in the certainty that her father would not follow her up the stairs, but wait till she was ready to open up to him.

In her heart she knew that something awful had happened to Cathy, something dreadful. Why she had run from the flat, she didn't know and eyes tightly closed, tore at the pillow in her frustration.

Was it the fear of being found out that she was different, that she loved another woman?

She felt she had betrayed Cathy and closing her eyes, hugged the pillow even more tightly, but was still unable to prevent the tears from rolling down her cheeks.

As she cried she tried to remember; had she given the old man her name? Was there anything in Cathy's flat that would identify her? Would the police come looking for her?

She continued to weep, but the fear did not go away.

The clock on the dashboard indicated it was a few minutes to ten o'clock. Billy Purvis turned slowly into the almost deserted car park on the Maryhill Shopping Centre and switching the headlights off, kept the side lights of the Mitsubishi switched on. The few cars that were parked there occupied the bays closest to the Shopping Centres rear doors and, he thought, probably belonged to staff who worked in the twenty-four hour Tesco store. He coasted the car at just over five miles an hour, passing by but ignoring the old dark coloured Ford Escort that was parked next to the trolley stand. He gave the car a cursory glance, but it looked empty and from the state of it, decided it was probably abandoned.

His left foot tapped gently at the brake and pushing the gear lever to neutral, manoeuvred the Mitsubishi into the middle of the nine empty bays and switched off the side lights before turning off the engine. He glanced about him, but other than the occasional car passing by on Garrioch Road some twenty yards in front of the car, there didn't seem to be anyone about.

Purvis involuntarily shivered. He hated meeting in these quiet spots and feared getting a pull from some nosey, passing cop. How he would explain the thick plastic carrier bag full of money he had no idea, but again was inwardly thankful that if the worst came to the *very* worst and he found himself dubbed up the cops, at least he still had an ace up his sleeve.

The time and darkness made the car park the ideal location for a meeting; no CCTV cameras, easily accessed from the main Maryhill Road and easy for the courier he was meeting with to locate by simply punching in the post code to his SatNav. Not that he'd need the SatNav, sighed Purvis, for by now their meetings were getting to be pretty regular.

The lamps situated in the car park were either broken or needing new bulbs and the only light was from a roadside halogen street lamp located on the pavement in Garrioch Road that towered above the car park, casting the shadow of the nearby tenement across the front of his car.

The lights of a car entering through the narrow roadway attracted his attention, but the car pulled into a bay near to the Tesco Express. He watched as a young woman got out the drivers door and hurried into the store. He sighed with relief, unaware of how tense he had been.

A second car negotiated the roundabout and entered the roadway leading to the car park, but as it entered the car park, this time the car drove slowly towards him. He glanced in his side mirror as the car pulled up alongside his passenger door and he saw it was the same swarthy skinned driver he had previously dealt with and was relieved that once more the guy was alone. He didn't like the idea of meeting more than one guy. He didn't know the drivers name, but thought he was probably a Paki.

Taking a deep breath, Purvis opened the driver's door and getting out, made his way to the boot of his car, aware that the other driver was joining him there.

"All right there, pal," he forced himself to sound chirpy and inserted the key in the boot lock.

The guy, dressed in dark coloured jerkin and jeans, just stared with dead eyes and then, almost with reluctance, nodded.

He had just brought the bag out of the boot and was opening it to show the Paki the money when he heard the deep throated roar of an engine starting. Startled, he turned to see the old Ford Escort that was parked no more than forty yards away, switch on its headlights and with its engine revving, race towards the two parked cars.

"What the *fuck*!" he heard himself scream while the Paki guy also shouted something, but Purvis didn't understand the language. Like the Paki guy, he instinctively raised his arm to shield his eyes from the glare of the Escorts full beam.

The Escort came to a shuddering halt just yards from them, catching them both in the full glare of its headlights. Almost as it stopped, Purvis and the guy saw a uniformed copper jump from the driver's door and shout, "Police! Stop where you are!"

The Paki guy turned towards his drivers door, but as Purvis also turned towards his own vehicle, he saw two dark clothed figures running from the corner of the tenement building, waving their arms and screaming, "Police!" and "Stop!"

The swarthy guy took off running and in panic and without any thought other than his own safety, Purvis instinctively took off after him, dropping the plastic bag on the roadway as he did. His first thought was no way was he getting arrested holding that amount of dough.

He ran as fast as he could, believing he must be getting pursued and not daring to look behind when he saw the Paki who was slightly ahead of him, veer off towards the main Maryhill Road and turn westwards.

It occurred to Purvis that the Paki was actually running towards Maryhill Police station and he almost shouted out a warning, but he didn't and quickly reasoned that the pursuing coppers might see the guy as a better opportunity for capture, than was Purvis.

Dodging the traffic, he crossed Maryhill Road and turned into Ruchill Street, then into Shuna Street and with a quick glance behind to ensure he wasn't seen, ducked into a close. Wheezing, his lungs were bursting and his legs shaking as he made his way to the rear of the close and listened for the sound of pursuit.

My car, he screwed his face, tightly closing his eyes and clenching his fists, snarled "Fuck!"

My *fucking* car!

The cops didn't need to chase him. They had his motor and with the car registered to him, he knew then that they would come knocking on his door. That and his dabs and probably his DNA too, were all over the plastic bag of money.

Still shaking, he tried to grin, but the grin turned into a coughing fit and he forced himself to calm down.

His head down and bent over with his hand on his thighs, he blew through his mouth to relax his body and breathe normally. He wondered why the cops had jumped him and the other guy without warning. It just didn't make sense and he couldn't understand why they hadn't told him anything about it and shaking his head, wondered what the fuck they thought they were playing at. If he had at least some warning, he could have prepared his excuse for that big bastard Tommo, but now he had to think on his feet.

He briefly wondered where the Paki guy had run to, but didn't give him much thought. It was up to him to get himself away.

Exhaling, he stood upright and hands still shaking from the violent burst of adrenalin that had coursed through his body, he reached into his pocket for his mobile phone and prepared to make the call that was the ace up his sleeve.

With a grimace, he realised that the story he would tell also needed to stand up to scrutiny.

CHAPTER NINETEEN

Des Brown stared curiously at the late night call on his mobile phone and smiled a little curiously at the time when he saw who was phoning him.

"Hi there, Grace, what you up to?"

His eyes narrowed at her hesitation. He was about to glance at the phone to ensure the call was still live when she replied, "What time do you finish work, Des?"

"I'm late shift and clearing up some paperwork, so I should be out of here by the back of eleven," he glanced about him, then thought bugger it. Grace wouldn't call him at this time of night unless something was wrong. "Never mind that, I can go anytime," he told her.

"It's just that…" she hesitated again. "I need someone to talk to. I've just come home and…"

An awkward silence fell between them, but he didn't want to press her for details on the phone and instead told her, "Look, let me phone my dad. He's at my place with Paul. I'm certain he won't mind staying over, so what do you say to me popping by your flat. You can tell me then what's worrying you."

She answered almost immediately. "Yes, please. I'll have some supper ready for you."

He blew softly through his lips and concluded the call, then pressed the preset number for his father.

The three of them walked hurriedly along Great Western Road from Rupert Street where they had parked the Ford Escort in a lane off the side street. Tom Fraser was for taking the car to a deserted spot and torching it, but Dick Smith had argued against the idea, explaining for one they would then need to call a taxi to get them back to his flat in the west end and two, the car might be useful again, he had grinned at his accomplices.

Harry McInnes had reluctantly agreed with Dick, not because he envisioned using the Escort for another turn, but didn't think hailing a taxi at that time of night was a good idea. He pointedly reminded the other two that if word got back to the police about a three man team heisting a drug dealer's money handover, the taxi driver fraternity would be one port of call made by the inquiring CID whereas three middle-aged guys stumbling along a main road that was full of pubs was less likely to attract attention.

"I'm bursting for a pee," Tom shook his head, still amazed that they had got clean away.

"It's your age," Dick had chided Tom and then added, "Nearly there," and grinned as they passed by Kelvinbridge underground. In one hand he carried a holdall with the plastic bag of money and police cap stuffed inside and with his free hand, clapped Tom on the shoulder.

Walking a few feet behind, Harry's mind was turning over the con, searching for anything that might identify them to the two men who had run off. Anything that they could have did better, but try as he might, nothing had gone wrong and with more confidence, he began to smile.

Moving between Tom and Dick, he wrapped his arms about their shoulders and said, "I'm starving. You guys go onto the flat and I'll nip by the chippy and get us some suppers, okay?"

Before either man could respond, he added with a grin, "And as I've just come into some money, it'll be my treat."

The DCI in charge of the Covert Human Intelligence Source unit was in the bathroom brushing his teeth prior to going to bed when he heard his work mobile phone activate. Inwardly cursing, he spat a mouthful of toothpaste into the sink and hurried through to the bedroom. His wife, already in bed, handed him the phone from the bedside table and returned to reading her magazine. Glancing at the screen, he saw the call was from one of his DC's who handled a paid informant, a tout who was recorded as a highly placed source in an Organised Crime Group that was of interest to the police Criminal Intelligence Department.

Pressing the green button on the phone, he slowly made his way back into the en-suite and listened as the detective related a priority call from the tout. He closed his eyes in frustration and slowly shaking his head, asked, "Is your tout at risk? Is there any likelihood he'll be suspected of ripping off the money and be under any kind of threat?"

"Hard to say boss," was the reply. "All he could tell me was that the cops came out of nowhere. He fucked off one way and the other guy, a Paki he thinks the guy is, fucked off the other way."

"These cops, how many were there?"

"He said he thought about half a dozen, maybe more and at least one, maybe two unmarked cars. According to him, one car that he saw was definitely a dark coloured saloon. Told me he was lucky to escape, that they chased him, but he was too fast for them."

"So, could it be they were some kind of local divisional crime team who were unaware of the significance of the operation we're running? I mean, it won't be any of our surveillance teams, will it? You made certain your tout is flagged up on the computer as a 'hands off', didn't you?"

"He's flagged all right boss, so no, it won't be one of the surveillance teams. I called the local division, but they don't have any of their plain-clothes cowboy teams out the now and frankly, I can't see any of the surveillance teams carrying out a hit without first running it past the Crime Intelligence boys and if they *did* propose an operation, they would be warned off because we're protecting our tout. No, I'm more than certain, boss, that the guys who hit the handover were *not* the polis."

"Well, whoever they were they knew about the handover, didn't they and *that's* the bloody worrying thing," snapped the DCI. He rubbed furiously with his free hand at his brow. "Could your man have organised this thing himself? Is it likely at all he's conning his own people as well as us?"

He listened to the sharp intake of breath before the detective replied, "Can't say with any certainty he's *not* conning us, boss. You might recall that Purvis has got form and he's only working for us because I persuaded him that the last time he was caught, he was looking at serious time unless he signed on to provide us with information."

"Yeah, I know that," the DCI irritably responded. "So what you're saying is we can't rule out that your man Purvis set this up?"

"No boss, I can't."

The DCI wheezed through the phone then eyes narrowed, asked, "One other thing we can't rule out either."

"What's that boss?"

He took a deep breathe and with his gut wrenching at the possibility, quietly said, "We might have a leak in our own organisation."

Chic Fagin dressed in his pyjamas and prepared for bed, yet knew that tired though he was, he wouldn't sleep that night. No, he wouldn't sleep for many nights to come or at least, not till his grandson Ian was safely returned to the arms of his loving grandmother, Chic's wife Sara.

He flushed the toilet and pulled the cord to put out the bathroom light and made his way into the kitchen, seeing with a soft smile that his neighbours had left the place spotless; spick and span, as he liked it. When he opened the fridge to fetch out the milk he drunk nightly to wash down the medicine prescribed for his blood pressure, he saw with a lump in his throat that there was little room left in the compartments, for the kindness of his neighbours included bowls of soup, sandwiches and cold meats, all wrapped in tinfoil, cling film or packed into clear plastic bags.

With a sigh, he poured the milk into a tumbler and sat heavily down at the kitchen table, popped the tablet from its blister pack and swallowed it before sipping at the milk.

Dabbing with a paper tissue at his mouth, his thoughts turned to the visit earlier that evening of Patricia Meikle's daughter, Grace. A stunning looking young woman and the image of her mammy, he had thought.

His mouth tightened and again he questioned the wisdom of disclosing to Grace the secret that he had held of these years, yet inwardly argued that the lassie had a right to know; a right to learn that…he shook his head.

It was done now, he thought, so no need for him to go over old ground.

He saw she had been upset at what he had told her, yet surprised that she had hugged him to her and unconsciously, his hand strayed to his face where she had kissed his cheek while thanking him over and over.

She had stayed almost an hour with him and promised that she would bring her son…he bit at his lip in thought. Steven, he recalled now. That was the lad's name. That she would bring Steven to visit him some time.

When it was all over, he had said to her.

It was as she had left, her tearstained face turned towards him, she had surprised and pleased him when she said, "I almost feel like you're my family, Mister Fagin."

He glanced at the clock and wearily pulling himself to his feet, switched off the kitchen light and went through to his bed.

He paused at Ian's bedroom door and slowly pushing it open, stared into the darkness of the room.

He closed Ian's door and later, in the privacy of his own room, permitted himself to weep for his dead grandson.

Des Brown locked the old Ford Mondeo and glancing up at Grace's flat, saw the dim glow of a light in the lounge and thought it must be from a table lamp. Making his way upstairs, he breathed onto his hand and sniffed, regretting he hadn't stopped to buy some mints.

But that wasn't why Grace wanted to see him, he realised.

Something was wrong, something that had caused her to phone him and he stopped on the half landing as it occurred to him that, yes; it was him that she had turned to, him that she needed.

He continued up the stairs and at the flat door, knocked softly, fearing that he might awaken Steven.

The door was pulled open almost immediately. He could not know that returning home she had changed from the formal attire she wore when visiting Chic Fagin and was now dressed in a dark coloured polo shirt and tight jeans, her hair still pulled tightly back into a ponytail, her face scrubbed and now free of make-up.

But the wash could not hide her tearful eyes and trembling lips.

His first thought was how young and vulnerable she seemed.

He could see she had been crying and stepping through the door, turned and quietly closed it behind him.

She moved quickly towards him and wrapped her arms about his waist before burying her head into his shoulder.

He pulled her to him and held her tightly, her body shuddering as she wept.

They stood like that for several minutes before he whispered to her, "Let me get my coat off then we'll have a cuppa and you can tell me all about it, eh?"

She raised her head and staring at him, nodded, not trusting herself yet to speak.

"Here," he grinned down at her and with a lopsided grin, held out a handkerchief towards her, "You're all snottery. I can't be kissing a snottery woman now, can I?"

She softly laughed through her tears and noisily blew her nose and he watched her shoulders heave as she exhaled.

"Sorry," she said.

"Nothing to be sorry about Grace," he replied, surprised at the lump in his throat as he stared at her. "I'm just so very pleased that you called me. Makes me kind of think I'm special to you."

She returned his stare and said, "You are special to me. Maybe even more than you think."

He pulled her again towards him and one arm enfolded about her, brushed with his free hand at her hair.

"There's nobody else I needed tonight. Nobody but you," she whispered to him.

He closed his eyes and inhaled the scent of her shampoo and wondered at his good fortune.

Then both hands resting lightly on her shoulders, he stepped back and said, "Right, what's this all about?"

Tom Fraser drove carefully over the Kingston Bridge, his eyes frequently darting at the rear-view mirror as if expecting to find blue lights flashing there.

In the passenger seat beside him, Harry McInnes grinned.

"Relax Tom," he said, "we're in the clear. Over ten grand each for a couple of hours work. What's there to worry about?"

"Yeah, you're right I suppose," Tom nodded. "It's just…well, you know what I'm like, Harry. I can't get it out of my head that we've stepped over the line; that we've turned to the dark side."

"Look," Harry patted at Tom's shoulder, "There's only the three of us know about it. As long as we keep it to ourselves, who's to find out what we did?"

"Are you certain though, absolutely certain I mean," he risked a worried glance at Harry, "that there won't be any comeback to you at your office?"

"Well, let's think about it, so first things first," he sighed, yet keen to ease Tom's concern. "You must agree that it's unlikely the neds will come forward to the polis to make a complaint that some bad people who *they* believe to be the cops, stole the ill-gotten proceeds of their drug-dealing activities. Secondly, if word gets back to the CHIS unit from their source about the theft, which we must assume is likely, it's pretty certain the cops are bound to suspect it's a fall-out among the neds and the rip-off is by another gang. If the CHIS unit source tells the cops it was *polis* who committed the theft, they will first check no police unit is involved then assume whoever *committed* the theft simply *pretended* to be cops. Finally, if in the *worst* case scenario, the CHIS unit suspect there *is* an internal leak," he shrugged, "I'm not in the loop about what the CHIS unit is up to Tom. It's above my pay grade, so there's no reason to even look at me."

"Yeah, I suppose you're right," Tom admitted.

"Course I'm right. So, what do you intend doing with the money?"

"I've been thinking about that. Paying it as a lump sum into my bank account might raise some suspicion, so what I'll do is use it instead of drawing pension money, piece by piece. Pay for some bills in cash and let the money from my pension lie in the account until it starts to add up. Might take me months," he shrugged, "but I believe it will be safer that way. Start spending it might cause a few eyebrows," then with a grin he added, "The important thing though is keep it a secret and away from Sheila. That'll be the hardest thing. It's safe for the minute at Dick's place, so I'll let it lie there until such times I can think of somewhere in the house or the garage that Sheila won't stumble across it."

Turning the car onto the slip road for the M77, he risked another glance at Harry.

"What about you? What plans have you got for your money?"

In the darkness of the car, Harry turned his face towards the side window and smiled.

"Like you, I'll leave it for now with Dick. *Nowhere* in my house is safe from Rosemary's prying fingers."

Tom sensed some hesitation in Harry's voice and asked, "What?"

After a few seconds, Harry replied, "For now, this is strictly between you and me, Tom."

Harry wasn't by nature a secretive man and Tom instinctively realised that his friend was about to divulge something, a confidence that was obviously very important to him. Not daring to speak or interrupt Harry's thoughts, he stared ahead through the windscreen and turned from the motorway through a green light onto Dumbreck Road.

"I'm thinking of leaving Rosemary. I've had enough. I spoke with an old pal, an ex-cop that did a law degree and who now works for a law firm. He's told me that I can offer her a deal. She keeps the car and the house and a third of my monthly pension. That will be more than ample to support her."

"But you've your salary as a civilian working for the police, too. Will that be an acceptable deal for Rosemary? How does she see it? Is the house worth *that* much that she would ignore your salary and the rest of your pension income and as I recall, she's not got a job has she?"

"No and hasn't been employed since we married and she can't use that old chestnut about being a full-time housewife. I do as much in the house as she does; more sometimes," he bitterly added. "Neither is she ill or housebound or anything like that so there's nothing to stop her getting off her arse and going and finding a job. I think I've kept her long enough," he angrily responded, but then almost immediately added, "Sorry. You're not the bad guy here, Tom."

He took a deep breath and continued, "The problem is that though I've already made the inquiry with my mate and worked out a deal, I've still to broach the subject with Rosemary."

"For fuck's sake, Harry," Tom hissed, slowing the car and stopping at a lay-by on Dumbreck Road, he turned to face him and asked, "When do you intend telling her then?"

"I wanted to get through tonight, see how it went and if possible, if we get one more successful turn and grab some more cash, then that will set us…" he hesitated, "me I mean; that will set me up with a deposit for a flat somewhere."

Tom wasn't fooled and eyes narrowing, quietly asked, "Who's us?"

Harry slowly smiled and softly exhaling, replied, "There's a woman at work, one of the cleaners. Somebody I've an interest in. Like me, she's in a bad marriage. I was thinking of asking her out. Then maybe see how things go, for the future, I mean."

"Life's not fucking Mills and Boon, Harry. You can't just leave your wife at your age," Tom waved the forefingers of both hands in the air, "and find true love. My God, what are you thinking?"

"For once in my life, I'm thinking of me," Harry forcefully banged a fist against his chest. "You have *no idea* what it's like living with that crabbit faced cow. We barely speak or even acknowledge each other, though we're in the same house. We have separate bedrooms and even cook our meals separately."

Again, he turned his face towards the side window.

"All I want in my life, Tom, is someone to be with. You have Sheila. Me? I'm lonely in my marriage. All I'm asking for is a little happiness. Is that too much to ask?"

They sat in silence as the traffic rushed past, then Tom switched on the engine and patting at his friend's arm, said, "No matter what you decide, I'll support you and," lightening the atmosphere in the car, softly grinned and said, "if you need somewhere in the meantime before you set up your love nest, then come and stay with me and Sheila, okay?"

Not trusting himself to reply, Harry nodded while Tom carefully pulled out into the traffic to drive him home.

In the office of his palatial home in Kirkintilloch, Patrick McLaughlin read and re-read with mounting disbelief the e-mail that had just arrived from Mick Thomson. Wrapped in his silk dressing gown, he felt an unexpected queasiness in his stomach and absently rubbed at his midriff.

He had expected confirmation that the money, the thirty odd grand, was delivered to the Turks courier as usual, not the short, chilling e-mail that informed 'John' that Thomson's courier had contacted him to relate the police had intercepted the money. According to the e-mail, neither the Turks courier nor Thomson's courier had been arrested, but the bad news was Thomson's courier had been forced to flee on foot and his car was left behind.

"*Shit!*" he sat bolt upright, his teeth gritted and his hands clenched into fists.

The loss of the money was worrying and the courier's car would identify him but that, he reasoned, was Thomson's problem.

What concerned McLaughlin was how the Turks would perceive the non-payment of the heroin that was already distributed. He wasn't forgetful of the veiled threat Fevzi made at the previous late payment and decided there was nothing else for it. He would need to plunder one of his accounts and send the payment south as quickly as possible.

He had no doubt that if, as Thomson had e-mailed, Fevzi's courier was not arrested, the Turk would already be aware of the seizure and a cold chill swept through McLaughlin.

What if the Fevzi thought he was being scammed? How would he react?

With nervous fingers, he reached for the keyboard and prepared to send an explanatory e-mail with the fervent hope it would be believed.

Across the city, Mick Thomson sat drumming his fingers on the armchair in front of the television, for once switched off as he concentrated his thoughts on what Billy Purvis had told him on the phone.

How the fuck had the cops got wind of the handover?

He was suspicious of the fact that Purvis wasn't banged up and wondered at his story of running off and escaping. It wasn't unknown for the police to allow their informant to escape and that way avoid any unpleasantness at court, with the informant's defence lawyer howling blue murder that his client had been set up by an uncaring police.

Then of course, Thomson recalled that the little shit was already up to his neck in dealing drugs and had the death of that retard Ian Fagin hanging over him, so reasoned it was unlikely he *was* a police tout. But Thomson's suspicious nature again kicked in and he played yet another scenario over in his mind.

What if Purvis really *was* touting to the cops? Obviously, he wouldn't tell them about his involvement in Fagin's death for after all, they wouldn't dare condone what he had done to contribute to the death and not only did Purvis fail to inform anyone of the death, but actually hid the wee halfwit's body. He had no proof that Purvis *was* a tout but then again, he shook his head as he chewed over the problem, he couldn't rule it out either.

No, he exhaled, there was only one sure way that he could be certain that the police wouldn't come after him and grinning evilly, reached for the television control.

Wearing a pink coloured dressing gown, DC Cat MacDougall sat at her dressing table, combing through her long, blonde hair while from their bed her husband Gus, a book lying open on his lap and his back against the headboard, watched her.

"Okay," he finally sighed, "what is it? What's bothering you?"

She stopped and swivelled her body to face him.

"What do you mean?"

He smiled and shook his head. "You think after all these years we've been together I can't tell that there's something troubling you? Come on Cat, spill it. There's something upsetting you. Is it me, something I've done or *not* done?"

"No, of course not," she replied with a soft smile and still facing toward him, laid the brush down onto the dressing table.

"Then if it's not me, it must be a work related thing. Am I getting hot?"

"As far as I'm concerned, you've *always* been hot," she pulled a face and grinned, but then slowly exhaled as she shrugged. "Yes, you're right. It's a work related thing."

"Want to talk about it?"

She stood and walked towards him and sat on the bed by his side then reached out to take his hand.

"A woman I know, not the nicest person in the world, but that's beside the point. She was raped. Violently assaulted and humiliated and forced to do things that even I'm almost too embarrassed to relate."

Nevertheless, Cat felt the need to unburden herself with what she had been told and there was no-one in the world she trusted more than her Gus.

When she had finished, she could see that he was visibly shocked and then he asked, "It's a case then."

She shook her head and sadly replied, "That's the problem, love. She insists that I don't report it. She's not just terrified that the evil sod who did it to her will come after her, but if *what* he did to her becomes public knowledge, it will destroy her."

"So, I guess you know who this man is?"

"Oh aye, I know who he is," she vigorously nodded. "He believes himself to be untouchable and has the reputation of being the hardest, meanest bastard in the Drum."

"Is there any way that you can get him by applying the law?"

She shook her head. "He has the locals too frightened of him for anyone to come forward. I don't for one minute think I could find a witness to his crimes in the Drumchapel area, so to answer your question, there's no fair and legal way I can think of to bring him before a court and certainly not for what he did to the woman. Besides," she shrugged, "I can sympathise with her on one thing. If her ordeal *was* to become public, she would never live it down and definitely not in the Glasgow area. She would forever be known as…anyway," she softly smiled and tightly squeezed his hand, "it's a work related thing so let's not bring it into our home."

"Maybe not," he replied, "but if it affects you then it affects me. That's what being your husband is, Cat." His eyes narrowed and carefully choosing his words, he continued, "Just one last thing to say about it. Since I've been retired and through the business, I've met and mixed with some interesting individuals, some of whom owe me a couple of favours." He hesitated, but decided there was no easy way to explain it and said, "There's always the *not* so legal way to deal with this type of character, the ways and means act, as it were."

She stared into his eyes and saw something of her husband that scared her just a little, a ruthlessness provoked by his disgust at the actions of a member of his own gender.

"No," she firmly shook her head and raised a hand, "on no account do I want you involved. This man will go down and if it's not by me and not tomorrow, then someday he *will* get what he deserves. Am I absolutely clear in that?"

He smiled as he nodded.

"Crystal," he replied and then reached for her, but as she happily snuggled her head against his shoulder, she could not see the thoughtful look in his eyes.

Billy Purvis, mouth dry and palms sweating, cursed Mick Thomson and his instruction that he return to the car park to see what was going on. For the last thirty minutes, he had carefully scouted the area about the car park, almost shitting himself when a patrol car routinely returning to Maryhill office passed him by.

Nervously, he kept to the shadows as he approached the car park. He knew that because he couldn't see the polis didn't mean they weren't there and if they *were* there, they probably wouldn't know about his touting to the cops and would likely be set to give him a right good kicking if they caught him.

The phone call to his handler had been a waste of time for the bastard was worse than useless, instructing that he keep his head down and that he stay away from Thomson.

Aye right, like that was going to fucking happen. If he hadn't phoned the big man and told him what had occurred in the car park, not only would he have had to go into hiding, but he would have to drag Casey and the weans with him as well for he was in no doubt that if

Thomson couldn't get to him, he would certainly carry out his threat against her and her kids.

He shivered at the memory of Thomson's threat and taking a deep breath, stared hard at his car that still sat closely parked beside the car Paki guy's car. His eyes narrowed and he wondered why the cops hadn't taken both cars away. Surely, he thought, their forensic people would have been all over the two vehicles?

It was as he hid in the shadowy darkness of the nearby tenement building that it hit him like a blinding flash.

Fuck!

Maybe they guys that jumped him and the Paki weren't the cops. Maybe they....

He inwardly startled and his eyes narrowed as he remembered the brief phone conversation with the detective. His handler had sounded surprised when breathlessly, Billy had told the bastard what had happened. It didn't occur to him then, but now he realised why.

The handler hadn't known about any plan for him and the Paki being jumped by cops. There was no plan to take out the money. The guys that jumped him and the Paki… they were *not* the cops!

Holy Shit!

They sat not together, but facing each other across the sturdy, highly polished wooden coffee table, a prize Grace had rescued cheaply from a Dumbarton Road charity shop. The bowl and plate in front of Des now lay empty and both were sat back in the old, worn armchairs with a mug of tea grasped in their hands, the room lit by two table lamps and speaking softly to avoid wakening Steven.

He had patiently listened, spooning the home made soup and devouring the crusty bread as Grace repeated the story told to her by Mister Fagin

Though his natural instinct and detective training had wanted to stop her and elicit more detail, he had fought the urge and let her continue her narrative as he ate.

But now that she had finished, he wanted more details and began by asking, "This man Fagin. Do you believe he's telling you the truth?"

"Yes, I do," she replied, staring at Des yet still unable to fully take in what she had been told.

"From what you've said, Mister Fagin sounds to have been a good friend to your mother."

"Not just my mother, by his account. It seems that back then pregnancy out of wedlock was still unacceptable on both sides of the religious barrier and he helped a few young women. Him and his wife Sara, he told me."

"Let's go through it again, eh? Right, your mum first," said Des. "I know from working in Govan that the Franciscan nuns in Merryland Street run a home there for unmarried mothers and you're telling me that your mum was taken there when she was pregnant with you, by this man Fagin?"

She nodded as she sipped at her tea.

"So, if your mother was unmarried, then...."

"Mick Thomson is *not* my father," she finished for him, but couldn't hide the edge in her voice.

"Not your father," he repeated with a shake of his head and eyes narrowing, asked, "but Fagin was unable to tell you who your real father is?"

"All he could tell me is that my mother had a..." she paused, grasping for the correct word, then continued, "a relationship with a local guy. When my mum's boyfriend, my father I suppose he must be, took off, my mum was apparently distraught and confided in Mister Fagin and his wife about being pregnant. Through the Minister of the church they attended, they made arrangements with a nun that the minster knew to take my mother over to Govan and the nuns there took her in to help her through the pregnancy. According to Mister Fagin, the nuns don't help just the Catholics, but any young woman who finds herself pregnant and has nowhere to turn to. Most of the nuns are apparently trained either as nurses or midwives and encourage these unmarried mothers to keep the children rather than having the babies adopted. If the mothers *do* decide to keep their babies, the nuns, with the support of voluntary donations and other charitable organisations, help and support the new mothers with baby equipment and find them a place to live."

"So, when did Thomson come into the story? I mean, how did he come to be your father or more correctly, your step-father?"

She smiled at the memory of the old man telling Grace just how like her mother she was and a little self-consciously, with a shrug replied, "Mister Fagin said my mother was a real beauty and a lot of the young men in Drumchapel were after her. It seems that Thomson was starting to become known, more for his violence than anything and she agreed to marry him if he pretended the baby, me I mean, was his daughter."

Almost wistfully, she added, "I don't suppose she even guessed what kind of a man he really was and didn't think what kind of life he would give her, other than supposing that because he had money to spend, she wouldn't have to struggle with a new baby."

"Don't be offended by this Grace, but you're suggesting your mum was some sort of trophy wife for Thomson?"

Vigorously shaking her head she replied, "That's *exactly* what I'm suggesting."

He could see she had a fiery gleam in her eye and guessed she was unable to decide if her mother had been so desperate or was deluded by the life Thomson had promised she would have by marrying him.

As if seeing the curiosity in Des's face, she shook her head and volunteered to his unasked question, "What I *don't* know is whether she agreed to marry him for my sake or for the better life she thought he could provide for her. Maybe even she wanted to save face rather than have people know she had a bastard child," she spat out.

He was taken aback by the vehemence in her voice, but realised that what she had learned from Mister Fagin must have been a terrible shock, a complete revelation about everything she had previously known of her mother.

They sat in awkward silence for a minute, Des sensing that perhaps Grace needed the time to calm down.

He suspected that Grace was probably more in a state of shock about the question of her real father and quite likely relieved that it wasn't Mick Thomson and reasoned she likely couldn't decide whether she felt sympathy for or anger at her mother for bringing Thomson into Grace's young life.

She took a deep breath and staring at him, quietly said, "There's more."

He listened with mounting anger as Grace recounted what it was like to grow up and live in the same flat as Mick Thomson,

Pale faced, she told him of the terror her mother had come to know, of Thomson's quiet voiced abuse and her mother's unexplained bruises, the sound of slapping and weeping behind closed doors. He saw her hands twist and turn together as the awful memories described by her were disclosed, of how Grace had learned to walk on eggshells and then, when puberty arrived, the casual strokes and fondling of her maturing body as she passed him by; the man she had thought of as her father. Of the veiled innuendo of sexual assault that continued until the day arrived when her mother died.

On that day, at the age of fourteen, she had been plucked from Thomson's home by her aunt, a stern and emotionless woman and as the years passed, Grace had come to realise whether consciously or not, her aunt had saved her from the predatory Thomson.

It didn't make living with her aunt any easier and it was difficult being grateful to a woman who treated her niece more as a hindrance than family. Then becoming pregnant at twenty increased the living problems even further until quite suddenly, the aunt died, leaving Grace the single mother the flat where she now resided.

Unaware until earlier this evening that Thomson was not her real father, she told Des that with no family or real friends to turn to, she had succumbed to his threats and of her twice weekly servitude to him, cleaning his flat and collecting his shopping; of the menacing threat that if she did not do as he asked, little Steven would suffer. Worse, she had believed him capable of those threats and finally, admitted she still did.

Her voice now faltering, she told him of Thomson's suggestion that she and Steven move to Thomson's flat, of his continued attempts to seduce her and her terror of him.

It was almost with relief that the shame she had known during his lust after her was not after all incestuous, that he was in no way related to her but more importantly, she added, neither was he related to her son, Steven.

She saw the knuckles on Des's hands turn white as he gripped the armchair and his face pale, but wanted him to know if they were to be together, he should know everything.

With her head held high, but her heart pounding, she suggested that Des might wish to reconsider their relationship.

To her tremendous relief, he softly smiled and shaking his head, replied, "What, now that I've found you, give you and the wee guy up? Yeah, like *that's* going to happen."

"The thing is, Des," she twisted her hands in her lap, "if I don't turn up to clean his flat or collect his shopping, he might come after me here, at the flat."

Des, his mouth dry and chest tight, had already made his decision.

"Until we get this sorted out, Grace, there's no question of what needs to be done. First thing tomorrow morning, you and the wee guy are packing and coming to live with Paul and me."

She took a sharp intake of breath and said, "Are you certain Des? Is that what you want?"

He glanced about him and then his eyes came to rest on hers and he smiled. Rising from the couch, he stepped round the coffee table and knelt before her, resting his hands on her knees. He knew that what he said now was critical, that it might determine how or even if their relationship continued and so chose his reply carefully.

"Maybe this is happening a little faster than I anticipated, but yes, that's what I want."

She leaned across and threw her arms about his neck and held him so tightly he thought he might choke. He could feel her tears falling onto his neck and her body shaking as she sobbed. He lifted his hands from her knees and hugged her close to him, but the anger he felt was still there.

Somehow, some way, he was determined that Mick Thomson was getting done.

CHAPTER TWENTY - Wednesday 9 July.

For some of Glasgow's citizenry, the day dawned clear and bright and begun earlier than most of the working population. Detective Constable Helen Meadows rolled over to switch off the alarm before it awakened her sleeping partner, who groaned slightly as the mattress sprung back into shape when Meadows slid from the bed. Turning over, he stared through the darkness at her shape and sleepily asked, "What's up?"

"Go back to sleep," she grinned at him and watched as he rolled over and almost instantly returned to the land of nod.

Showering and dressing in the bathroom, she glanced at her wristwatch and saw it was almost six o'clock.

Thirty-five minutes later, found her driving into the rear yard of Renfrew police office and exiting her car, made her way into the building where she nodded to the departing uniformed nightshift officers and climbed the stairs to the incident room.

The weary-eyed detective on duty, tie undone and feet up on a chair, was finishing his final coffee of the shift and smiled his relief as she bid him good morning and boiled the kettle.

"Interesting development came in through the night," he told her and related a phone call from a young man who, having seen the deceased's photograph on the evening news, called in to report that the dead woman used to frequent the city hotel where he tended the bar.

"He was working last night and didn't finish till about midnight," related the detective, "but saw the item on the television in the bar on the late night news. He sounded credible and a bit excited. Said he had a photo of the dead woman with a female pal, on his phone. He also said he saw her with a guy in the hotel foyer, a couple of nights ago on the Saturday."

"Did you call the boss about this?"

The detective shrugged and shook his head. "The call came in late last night so without a positive identification, I didn't think it worth disturbing him. Time enough today to get the young guy's information checked out, I figured."

He handed Meadows a scrap of paper. "Here's his name, home address and contact phone number. Asked if the dayshift…you that will be," he added with a mirthless grin. "When you call him, make it sometime after nine to let him get some shut-eye."

Meadows took the paper from his hand, but her thoughts were that the DI would go ballistic when Dalgleish learned he had not been immediately informed of what was sounding to be the best lead they had so far.

"Did the caller describe the deceased's friend, this pal or the guy she had been seen with?"

"No, I didn't get that much," yawned the detective. "Besides," he grinned, "you guys have got all today to firm up on what's he's reporting, haven't you?"

Meadows suspected the lazy bastard hadn't asked the potential witness the right questions, but in deference to his seniority in the CID, didn't think it was her place to chin him about it. She watched as the detective eased himself out of his chair and shrugging into his overcoat, waved goodbye over his shoulder as he headed out of the room.

She glanced again at the scrap of paper and unconsciously nodded as she softly exhaled through pursed lips.

The electric kettle whistled and she decided she might as well have a brew while she waited for the shit storm that was about to arrive when she passed the nightshift detectives information on to DI Dalgleish.

Sally Nelson awoke and was at first a little disorientated, confused by the slash of light that pierced the curtains and shone on the football posters before realising she was sleeping in the single bed in her nephew's room.

She rubbed wearily at her eyes and listened for the sound of her sister and family, but couldn't hear anything.

Quietly, she slipped from the bed and wrapping her sisters borrowed dressing gown about her, eased open the bedroom door and made her way to the toilet on the half landing.

A few minutes later, her toilet completed, she stepped back into the landing and turned when she heard her sister quietly call her name from the hallway downstairs.

"I've just stuck the kettle on, hen, so come down for a coffee, eh?" she whispered to Sally.

Joining Elsie in the kitchen, the two women sat nursing their mugs while Sally, suffering a slight headache from the wine and still not quite believing the momentous step she had taken, confirmed her intention not to return to her husband Archie.

"Aye, and long overdue if you ask me," muttered Elsie, who reaching across the kitchen table for Sally's hand, squeezed it and added, "and you have a room here for as long as you need, hen."

She didn't trust herself to reply, so clenched her jaw and willed herself not to cry and could only nod her grateful thanks.

"You know he'll phone here looking for you, hen. He'll not visit because he knows he's not welcome."

Elsie sipped at the steaming mug, and asked, "So, what do I do? Do I tell him you're here or just tell him to fuck off?"

Sally's shoulders heaved as she sniggered at Elsie's crassness, but knew that inevitably, she would need to speak with Archie, tell him that she wasn't coming home again; ever.

She sighed and said, "Maybe it would be best if I went to see him. Told him the truth and that I've left him. He'll be worried sick, wondering what's happened to me. I wouldn't be surprised if he's phoned the polis to report me missing."

"Aye, like that's going to happen. Listen, hen, you don't need me to remind you that your husband is one selfish bastard. All he'll worry about is who's going to make his meals and clean up after him. My God, Sally, have you not run after him for long enough? He treats you worse than a bloody slave and *don't* think I don't know he lifts his hand to you as well!"

Elsie folded her arms and stared at her sister. "All I'll say is if you even consider going back to him, you're worse than a fool. So there."

"Hi, auntie Sally," said the voice behind her. Turning in her seat she saw Elsie's eighteen year old, tall and gangly son, his long hair in disarray and dressed in his pyjamas, walk barefoot into the kitchen. "Thanks for the use of your room, son," she smiled at the lanky teenager.

"No problem. I heard you've left uncle Archie. Good for you," he nodded and then placing his hand on her shoulder, softly added, "We were all worried sick about you living with him and how he treats you. It'll be nice knowing now that you're safe. The man's an arse."

"Language," Elsie snapped at her son, who merely grinned and winked at Sally.

Later, when Sally thought about it, nothing she did nor anything Elsie could say would be as meaningful or as convincing as those few heartfelt words spoken to her by her nephew.

You're safe.

The SO15 officer hidden in the rear of the van had watched the Turkish target codenamed Primary One arrive early to open the small café and perfunctorily snapped a couple of photos. Bored, he sighed. For almost a full year now the photographs he and other members of his team snapped had been compiled into a bloody, wasteful album of Primary One's arriving and departing the cafe. Day in, day out, the surveillance operation mounted against Fevzi had recorded and documented most if not all his associates and for the umpteenth time, the officer wondered when the management would finally make a decision and arrest the wily bugger. After all, he inwardly fumed, it wasn't as if they didn't have enough evidence by now and while it was commonly accepted Fevzi would never be hands on with either the drugs he dealt or the money he made, the police were confident that arresting the top players in his organisation would undoubtedly bring about his downfall. It was argued that the middlemen Fevzi used, when faced with lengthy prison sentences, would probably cause a number of these individuals to roll over on him and turn Queens Evidence.

At least, that's what the management assessed, he cynically thought. The officer shook his head; in his experience it was *always* the way with these bastards, looking out for number one and bugger that 'honour among thieves' crap.

Inside the dimly lit cafe, Fevzi cast a wry glance through the window at the innocuous looking van and then with a soft throaty chuckle, locked the front door behind him. Switching on the brighter, interior lights, he reached across the counter and stretching, turned on the water heaters for the coffee machine.

Blowing on his hands to ward off the chill in the air, he sat at one of the tables and fetched the newly purchased 'pay as you go' mobile phone from one jacket pocket and a slip of paper from the other.

Lastly, he fetched a pair of reading glasses from his shirt breast pocket and glancing at the slip of paper, mouthed the digits as with a stubby finger, he pressed them onto the phone keypad.

The call was answered almost immediately.

In fluent Albanian, Fevzi spoke with his contact he knew to be a former member of 'Batalioni i Operacioneve Speciale', more commonly known as BOS, the elite special forces of the Albanian military.

The call to the Albanian was prompted after one of Fevzi's London based accomplices, in the early hours of that morning, received a phone call from the courier, an illegal immigrant Iraqi Kurd.

According to Fevzi's accomplice, the Iraqi had been panic-stricken and related that the previous evening he had been ambushed at the money handover by police officers and forced to abandon his car, was now wandering the streets of Glasgow.

Earlier that morning before coming to the cafe, Fevzi checked his I-pad and discovered the explanatory e-mail from the Scotsman, McLaughlin.

In response to McLaughlin's e-mail, Fevzi was now setting in motion his own response for he did not for one minute believe McLaughlin's version of events.

During the call that lasted no more than four minutes, Fevzi issued his instructions and from the same slip of paper, slowly read out the home address of Patrick McLaughlin; the address that Fevzi's associate had obtained from the guests register when earlier in the year, both had visited McLaughlin at the London hotel.

It wasn't the first time Fevzi had utilised the services of the Albanian and, he sighed, likely would not be the last either.

But costly though it might be it was worth it for he had learned the hard way it was bad business to permit his customers to take advantage of him, no matter what excuse they might offer.

No, Mister McLaughlin had to be made an example of for if he allowed one dealer to rip him off, the word would get out and others would also try.

His reputation was at stake and in this business, reputation was everything.

The warning had to be clear and concise and violently so. Once the issue had been dealt with, he would ensure that the deed was whispered to his many other customers.

He pushed himself up from the table and walking to the rear of the serving counter, lifted a box of matches and burned the scrap of paper in the sink. Turning on the tap, he watched the burnt paper swirl down the plughole.

Next, he removed the SIM card from the mobile phone and with strong fingers snapped it in half, then carefully wrapped the phone in a soiled dishcloth.

From beneath the counter, he lifted a carpenter's hammer and laying the phone on the counter, smashed the hammer against it several times.

The broken pieces of phone he placed with the snapped SIM card into his trouser pocket, to be disposed of later.

That done he went to the front door to unlock it and with a further glance at the van across the street, awaited his first customers of the day.

On Kilmarnock Road, Harry McInnes stood with his hands in his coat pocket among the queue at the bus stop, still fuming from his early morning confrontation with his wife, Rosemary.

The argument had continued from the previous evening when she had sat in the darkness of their lounge and ambushed him when he arrived home, demanding to know where he had been, with whom and why.

Ignoring her abuse, he had gone upstairs to his own room, shaking with fury at her malevolent attitude towards him.

Jesus, he thought; the names she called him and at one point had seriously thought she was about to attack him.

He'd hardly slept, going over in his mind again and again last nights take down of the cash, trying to recall if by chance he or Tom or Dick had fouled up, left some sort of clue as to their identity.

Coming down stairs that morning, she had been waiting by the front door, lambasting him with verbal abuse that followed him out into the street.

He must have been a full fifty yards away from the house and still she screamed at him before he heard the door slam closed.

No wonder the bloody neighbours think she's a crackpot, he shook his head.

He thought again of the heist and was convinced that they had not messed up, that it was his conscience that bothered him; the transition in a few short moments when the three of them had gone over to what Tom had described as the dark side.

He and the others had become the very people they had always fought and railed against, for they had become the criminals.

He hardly noticed getting onto the bus, absent-mindedly handing the driver his pass then sitting down, so absorbed was he in his own thoughts.

Inevitably, he began to think of Sally Nelson and wondered as he had done so many times what reaction he might get if he were to ask her out for a drink.

He had run so many different scenarios through his mind; how he would speak to her, what he would say and persuade her that he meant no harm, but was seriously considering asking her to leave her husband and join him…

Jesus, he shook his head and wiped his hand across his face. I'm like a bloody love-struck teenager.

His mobile phone activated with a text message and scrolling down, Harry saw it was from his lawyer friend intimating that if he were serious about leaving Rosemary, suggesting that that he meet in his friend's office later that afternoon to discuss the issue and to phone for an appointment time.

He tapped out a response and indicated he would be there by four-thirty.

The acknowledgement arrived almost immediately and for the first time in a while, Harry felt a little upbeat.

DC Helen Meadows was on the phone, the other hand holding a pen while she bent over a desk, scribbling furiously on a pad in front of her when DI Jamie Dalgleish arrived at the incident room.

She saw he was about to head out of the room towards his office along the corridor and raised a warning hand to stop him.

Dalgleish stopped and watched as nodding, she ended the call and returned the phone to its cradle.

Tearing the top sheet from the pad, she said, "Morning boss, two things for you, if you're ready?"

"Shoot," he replied, sensing it was important and folding his arms as he settled his backside against a desktop.

She glanced at the sheet of paper and in a breathless rush, said, "That was the bar officer at Stewart Street police office. He says that a young woman, a Bethany Williams with a Paisley address walked in off the street this morning and said she's the friend of the woman that was discovered murdered in Broomielaw Quay. Also says she was there with an old guy, the neighbour who used the deceased's spare key to get into the flat."

"Is she still there?"

"Yes boss, she's sitting in the foyer. The bar officer said she seems to be very upset."

Dalgleish quickly stood upright and snapping his fingers, replied, "Get back onto the bar officer and tell him to ensure she's to remain there, that we'll get someone over to Stewart Street as quickly as possible to interview her. If she tries to leave, she is to be detained pending our people arriving, okay?"

"Got that," Meadows nodded, lifting the phone from its cradle.

"And what's the second thing?"

Meadows took a deep breath and still with the phone in her hand, related the information that had been passed on by the nightshift detective.

As she correctly expected, Dalgleish exploded.

The arriving detectives and civilian personnel, guessing something was amiss, wisely steered clear of the irate DI.

"That lazy *bastard*!" ranted the DI, angrily using a number of other expletives that concluded with Dalgleish promising if it was the last thing he did, the nightshift detective would be returned to uniform duties.

"Right," he shook his head in frustration, "when you've made that call, grab your coat Helen because regardless of the promise of a nine o'clock call, you and me are going to pay this young bartender a visit, so give me a minute to organise a couple of guys for Stewart Street then we're on our way."

It had just gone eight o'clock and Des Brown was helping a tired young Steven pack his clothes neatly into a large suitcase that Des had brought with him. Then leaving the little guy to select some toys, he went into the adjoining bedroom where Grace was similarly packing a suitcase.

"I feel like a coward, like I'm running away," she turned towards him, her brow furrowed and a worried look on her face.

He folded his arms around her and smiled. "*I* don't see it like that. The way you have coped with life, Grace, makes me think you have more bottle than Coca Cola."

She grinned and kissed the tip of his nose.

"I'm so very grateful that you are doing this for us, Des. I can't think where else I might turn to."

He was about to reply that he was being selfish, that he wanted her in *his* life when the door was knocked and saw the startled, almost frightened look in her eyes.

"Wait here," he firmly said and made his way into the hallway where he cautiously peered through the spy hole in the front door and then smiled.

Pulling open the door, he saw his father standing there with a large suitcase in one hand.

"Here we go," said his dad, stepping into the hallway and holding out the empty suitcase towards Des.

Grace, her eyes filled with curiosity, walked from the bedroom and was introduced to Eddie Brown.

"I can see why my lad's besotted with you, hen," he smiled at her blush. "You're a beauty, right enough."

Behind her, Steven shyly stood behind his mother.

"You'll be the man of the house then?" asked Eddie, moving past Des and Grace and holding out his hand to the young lad. "I'm Paul's granddad and I hear you are one terrific footballer. Is that right enough then?"

It was the perfect introduction to Steven who insisted that Eddie come through to the lad's bedroom where Steven wanted to show off his wall posters.

In Grace's bedroom, Des explained, "I phoned and asked my dad to come along and bring another suitcase, just in case you wanted to take more clothes with you."

"So," she beamed at him, "you must be expecting us to stay with you for some time."

"As long as you want," he grinned at her.

"Sorry to interrupt," said Eddie from the doorway, with Steven standing beside him and one hand on the lads shoulder, "but I was thinking. If you guys want to take the cases to your place, Des and if it's okay with you Grace; Stevie boy and I will nip back to my house for breakfast. Agnes…" he leant down towards Steven and with a smile explained, "That's Paul's granny," and then turning back towards Grace continued. "Agnes is dying to meet him and we'll get him to school from there."

Slightly bemused at his goodwill gesture, she glanced from Eddie to Des and back to Eddie. "Sure, that's okay, if you don't mind?"

"What, me mind?" he pretended surprise. "We'll be talking football all the way. Why would I mind?" he grinned at Steven.

"That's settled then, dad," interrupted Des. "So, let's get this show on the road."

Sitting in Des's car, Grace watched Eddie drive off with Steven in the rear seat, both laughing as they passed by.

"They seem to be getting on," she remarked and then quietly added, "I like your dad."

"Yeah, my dad's like that, good with kids I mean and I'm like him, so what's there not to like?"

Des started the engine and as he pulled the car away from the kerb, she glanced up at the flat windows and wondered when she would be back, but sneaking a glance at him she felt a tightness in her chest as it happily occurred to her that maybe she and Steven *wouldn't* be returning to the flat.

Billy Purvis dragged the grey coloured sweat top over his head and called out, "Casey hen, I'm away to the gym for a workout. I'll be back about half nine to run you to the shops and take the weans to the playgroup."

"Aye, well see that you are here. I'm not dragging them wee buggers and a pram and a bag of shopping onto a bus," was the bad-tempered response from the kitchen.

Purvis shook his head and sighing thought it prudent not to get into an argument with Casey, his first thought common to his gender was thinking her bad mood was likely because she was pre-menstrual, but uncertain what women truly experience at this delicate time of the month.

Wisely deciding not to provoke any further comment, he quietly packed a holdall bag with a clean tracksuit and a towel and tiptoed along the hallway, opening then gently closing the door behind him. With a grin, he slung the bag across his shoulder and softly whistling, made his way down the stairs.

Quietly or not, Casey heard the front door close and still angry at Billy, pushed the loose strand of hair from her eyes and picked up the plastic laundry basket from the hallway cupboard, carried it through to the kitchen and then banged open the door with her hip as she swung the laden basket. She dumped the clothes onto the floor beside the washing machine and kneeling, began to separate the colours and whites from the darks.

It was as when she was stuffing the clothes into the machine she felt something in Billy's tracksuit trousers pocket and pulled out a creased and folded brown envelope. Puzzled, she saw that the business envelope had not been opened and even more curious saw the typed name and address in the little plastic window was for 'Mister Ian Fagin' with a flat number and address in Kiniver Drive. The senders address printed on the top of the envelope was the Council Housing Department.

Brow furrowed, she wondered why Billy would have the envelope when with a shock the name occurred to her. It was the name of the dopey guy who had the mad crush on her.

Jesus, she grabbed at her throat, her eyes now wide with shock.

Ian Fagin, the dead guy from the drug overdose that everybody at the shopping precinct was talking about.

Reaching up to slap the letter down onto the kitchen worktop and shaking almost with disbelief, the laundry forgotten for the moment, she leaned her head against the cool metal of the machine and wondered not for the first time what the stupid bastard had now got involved in.

It was when he turned the corner from the stairs onto the hall landing that Purvis almost collided with Mick Thomson, who was similarly dressed in a dark coloured tracksuit, but curiously, also wearing a pair of bright yellow rubber kitchen gloves.
"Hello, Billy," said Thomson and then without warning grabbed Purvis round the throat with both his powerful hands and forced the slighter man back against the graffiti ridden wall of the close
Dropping the bag, Purvis first reaction was to tear Thomson's hands from his throat, but try as he might, he couldn't pry Thomson's fingers loose.
Seconds became a minute and fighting to breathe, he felt his feet rise from the stone floor of the landing and being bodily lifted.
His eyes began to bulge as the Thomson squeezed even harder.
Both men, their faces just inches apart, stared into each others eyes; Purvis unable to speak and silently pleading for Thomson to stop while the larger and heavier man, his teeth bared and gritted, seemed to delight in the agony and pain he was causing.
His kicks at Thomson's legs were so ineffectual they were ignored and as the seconds passed, he felt himself become weaker.
He grasped at Thomson's arms, but his hands slid uselessly on the nylon material and he could find no purchase to break the hold.
He felt his bladder loosen and a wet trickle of urine run down his legs, adding shame to his terror.
By now past caring, some small veins in his eyes popped and when he stopped breathing, the darkness came quickly and his arms fell uselessly to his side.
Thomson saw the light in Purvis eyes dim and giving one final, strong squeeze at his throat, allowed the body to slide down the wall to the ground.
He cocked his head to one side. From upstairs, he could hear a child crying in one of the flats and grinning, thought of Casey Lennox.
She would need somebody to look after her and her kids now, he thought and who would be the perfect choice, but him.

He hadn't realised that he was breathing heavily and taking a final deep breath, rubbed his gloved hands together as if to cleanse them of Billy Purvis.

Then, almost with a smirk on his face at a problem now solved, he quickly made his way downstairs to the rear of the close.

CHAPTER TWENTY-ONE.

The young bartender, according to the nightshift detective's scribbled note, lived with his parents in Hollybush Road in the Penilee area of the city.

Stopping the CID car outside a mid-terraced former council property, Meadows and Dalgleish pushed through the gate and walked along the path through the neatly tended garden to the front door, but as Dalgleish was about to ring the bell it was pulled open by a tousled haired youth wearing a shabby dressing-gown.

The youth introduced himself as Neil Kerr and invited them to follow him into the lounge.

While the detectives settled into two armchairs, Kerr explained his parents were at work and from the kitchen, fetched through a pot of tea on a tray with three mugs, a bowl of sugar and a milk jug and placed the tray onto a small glass covered table. Meadows thought the tray had been prepared beforehand and that he had been expecting the early visit.

"I thought you might have phoned first and that I'd better get up and wait for you arriving," he explained.

"I understand you're a barman at a city hotel?" asked Dalgleish, watching as the younger man poured the tea.

Keenly staring at him, Meadows formed the opinion that Kerr was a confident young man and enjoying the attention of the CID and likely perceived he was important to the inquiry which, she wryly thought, he was.

"Aye, I was working on the late shift last night," grinned the youth, who settled himself comfortably onto the couch with a mug, his legs crossed over and bare beneath the dressing-gown, "so I'm not usually so ill-kept. The boss likes us to be smartly turned out."

"No doubt," smiled Dalgleish. "So tell me Neil, you recognised the woman whose face featured in the news as a patron of your bar?"

"Aye, she was in last Friday night…"

"That was what, July the fourth?" interrupted Dalgleish.

"Wait, hang on," said Kerr and rising, left the room to return less than a minute later holding his mobile phone in his hand. The detectives watched as he quickly skimmed through the phone directory then held the screen towards Dalgleish.

"That's right, the fourth of July. That's the photograph I took and it's timed and dated. See?"

Dalgleish took the phone from Kerr's hand and impressed by the clear and sharp picture, could see it showed two smiling women who were arm in arm and seemingly oblivious to their photograph being taken.

The redhead he recognised as the deceased while the other was a dark haired, younger woman. Staring at the screen, he recalled DCI Cathy Mulgrew's comment when at the murder locus she related the elderly neighbour's statement that the young woman who had fled from the deceased's flat had 'hair like a burst straw mattress.'

He could see it aptly fitted the description of the woman in the photograph that was with the deceased.

Turning to show the photograph to Meadows, Dalgleish placed the phone onto the table in front of him and then asked Kerr, "This other woman. Is this the woman you reported that you thought was the red haired woman's pal?"

"Aye, that's her. Not nearly as good looking as the redhead and definitely not *my* type," he shrugged, with a coy grin.

Aye and you're God's gift to women, thought Meadows.

"Tell me about the man you saw her with?" Dalgleish suddenly asked.

"Oh, that was the next night, on the Saturday," Kerr resumed his seat. "The bar was mobbed and she was in the foyer having a drink with the guy. A big guy he was," Kerr extended his hands to demonstrate the width of the man, "like a wrestler or a boxer. Looked like a right thug," he added with a sniff.

"It was definitely the next night?"

"Aye," Kerr nodded. "We had a big football crowd in; mostly Aberdeen supporters. The bar did well and I was kept quite busy, but halfway through my shift I was sent through to deliver drinks to a couple in the foyer and it was her," he pointed a fore finger to the phone screen, "and a big guy she was sitting with."

"Why are you so certain it was the woman that featured on the news?" interrupted Meadows.

Kerr blushed and again shrugged. "She isn't the sort of woman that I could ignore. I mean," he added hastily, "she was really good looking and well, her accent. She was English, wasn't she?"

Dalgleish glanced quickly at Meadows. "So, you have spoken with her at some time?"

"Aye," Kerr raised his eyebrows as though the question was stupid, "she ordered drinks from me on the first night, didn't she?"

"On both nights?"

"No," he slowly responded and shook his head, "just on the Friday night, because the drinks I delivered to the foyer had been pre-ordered at the reception desk in the foyer and phoned through from there."

"Phoned through by whom?"

"I don't know. The tab, by that I mean the note," he explained, "was lying there on the bar and the head barman, he said I was to make up the drinks. I did that and like I said took them through. It gave me a chance to get away from the bar for a couple of minutes and I after I delivered the drinks, I took a minute outside the back door for a quick draw at a fag."

Dalgleish felt a slight hope rise in his chest and asked, "The reception area. Do you know if it's covered by CCTV cameras, Neil?"

"Ah," the younger man grimaced. "I know it usually is, but I heard that the management have changed the contract for the servicing for the cameras and the emergency alarm system, so I don't know..."

He stopped and shook his head. "No, I'm certain the new system hasn't been hooked up yet. My boss was moaning about it last week and complaining to the security manager that without the cameras the bar staff was at risk if something kicked off in the bar. You know, with a drunk or something like that. Sorry."

Disappointed, Dalgleish asked, "Who paid for the drinks?"

"The guy paid. He slapped a twenty down onto the tray and told me to keep the change. Fair took my by surprise, I can tell you."

"What accent did he have?"

"I can't remember. Sorry."

"If *he* had been English or foreign, might that have taken your attention?" asked Meadows.

"I *suppose* so. I never thought about his accent, so I suppose he was probably local. Glasgow I mean."

"But you did say there was a lot of Aberdonians in that night?"

"Oh, he wasn't from Aberdeen," Kerr quickly shook his head.

"Why are you so certain?" asked Dalgleish.

"Well," he grinned, "because those bastards are not only hard to understand and especially when they've got a drink in them, but they're also a tight shower and don't throw their cash about, unless it's for their bevy." He shrugged and added, "Tips were hard to come by that night. We even have this trick about giving them their change in coin rather than notes and most punters, when they see it's a load of coins usually just tell us to keep the change, but not the Aberdeen crowd. The miserable gits *always* pocket every penny."

Dalgleish risked another glance at Meadows.

She realised he was about to ask the critical question.

"Would you know the guy again if you saw him, Neil?"

The younger man hesitated before answering and then asked, "Is the guy that was with her, is he the guy that killed her?"

"We can't be certain at this time, but we really will need to trace him, if nothing else, for elimination purposes. It's possible the man you saw the deceased with is possibly the last person to see her alive. Other than her killer," he added with a soft, but mirthless smile, yet the inference was there; the man who Neil Kerr served and saw drinking Cathy Porteous was her murderer.

"Aye, I'll know him again," he finally said, but with a lack of confidence and Dalgleish couldn't decide if the younger man was uncertain or just apprehensive.

Before taking their leave of Kerr, Helen Meadows took more notes and it was agreed that if it was required, Kerr would make himself available for an identification parade.

He was showing the detectives to the front door when Meadows stopped and turning, asked him, "Why *did* you take the photo of the deceased and her friend, Neil?"

The young man blushed and almost with a stammer, admitted he was so attracted to the redhead that he secretly took the photo and later boasted to his pals that she had come onto him.

"Right," Meadows slowly drawled and with a tight smile, walked with the DI to their car as Kerr closed the door behind them.

"He's just a young lad, Helen," said Dalgleish over the top of the vehicle, "and admittedly, Catherine Porteous *was* a real looker, so I can't say I blame him."

"Well, regardless of his intention, boss, he's provided us with an eye witness to the man she was with on the last night of her life. What do you think? Could the guy she was drinking with have been her killer?"

"That, my dear, is the one thousand dollar question, as our American cousins would say. All *we* have to do now is track the bugger down and ask him."

Meadows had just switched on the engine when Dalgleish's mobile phone activated.

As she drove away from Kerr's house, she listened to the one sided conversation and couldn't help but notice the DI become progressively excited until at last he slapped a hand on the dashboard and cried out, "Yes!"

He was returning the phone to his pocket when she asked him, "What?"

He was nodding his head when he answered her. "That was the Scene of Crime supervisor. Do you recall her telling us about a used packet of bleach wipes she found in the toilet bin in Porteous flat?"

"Aye, she commented that the *culprit*, she called him, wasn't that clever."

"Well," grinned Dalgleish, "her *culprit* left a partial print on the wee tab that he tore away to open the packet."

"Did she say if there is enough of a print for a comparison?"

"She's running the check as we speak, so we should know hopefully some time today. All we have to do is hope that the sod is on fingerprint file and if he's not..."

He didn't finish the sentence.

He turned and continuing to grin, added, "Right Helen, let's head towards Stewart Street and see how the guys are getting on with the female pal. We'll be optimistic and hope that with a bit of luck, we might get three in a row, hen."

It was a young Somali woman, a recently arrived asylum seeker leading her child by the hand down the stairs, who a few moments after Mick Thomson departed the close, discovered the slumped body of Billy Purvis.

At first she hesitated, thinking it was a drunken man lying there on the half landing and fearfully drew her three year old to her.

She was uncertain whether to pass the prone man when she saw that his eyes were wide open and realised that he was not drunk, but that he was dead.

Her shrill scream echoed throughout the close and startled Casey Lennox who flung open her door with the intention of telling whoever was screaming to shut the fuck up, but instead saw the brightly clad woman sitting on the lower steps at the landing, in distress and hugging her child to her.

The dark skinned woman turned her head and stared with wide, dark eyes upwards towards Casey, who slowly and with some trepidation walked down the stairs.

When she too saw the dead Billy Purvis, her scream was every bit as loud as that of her neighbour.

Beth Williams sat forlornly in the interview room, a cup of tea cooling on the desk in front of her.

The young, uniformed policewoman sitting in the corner shifted uncomfortably on the wooden chair and calmly studied her nails, seemingly oblivious to Beth's presence.

"I have to go to the toilet," whispered Beth.

"Give it a minute, hen. The sergeant said that a Detective Inspector is on his way to have a wee word with you, okay?"

"No, you don't understand, I need to pee now," she insisted.

The policewoman exhaled with exaggeration and standing up, snapped, "Right! I'll ask if you can go to the loo."

At that, the door opened to admit DI Dalgleish and one of the detectives the DI had sent to interview Beth.

"Eh, she wants to go for a pee," said the policewoman, then pointedly added, "I'm supposed to be on my break, sir."

"Well then, I'll see you get your break later, Constable, but right now, if you don't mind?" smiled the DI.

Tight-lipped, the policewoman nodded and beckoned that Beth follow her.

While the detective stood with his back to the wall, Dalgleish sat on one of the chairs at the desk and asked, "You've spent the last hour and a half with her so, what's the story then?"

"Claims she is or I should say was the victims' best pal, boss," replied the portly detective. "Says that they attended college together here in the city, but the victim gave the course up and was apparently working as a PR for some company here in the city, but doesn't know which one. Admits to having frequented the victims flat and, eh…"

Dalgleish's eyes narrowed at the hesitation and he said, "Spit it out."

"Well, she alleges they were having a sexual relationship and said that she loved the victim."

"Does she sound to be credible? I mean, is there any likelihood in your mind that she might be involved in the murder?"

"Hard to say, boss, but if you want my tuppence worth…"

"Always welcome," smiled Dalgleish.

"I'm of the opinion that Williams is a naïve young woman. Obviously I can't with any certainty say she is or she's *not* gay nor can I confirm that she and the victim did or didn't have a sexual relationship. What does seem obvious to me is that she is suffering real grief here. In the absence of any information to the contrary, I think it might be worth considering Williams as a witness rather than as a suspect, boss."

"Witness to what?"

The detective shrugged and continued, "Background information I suppose, because I think I'm correct in saying we don't have anyone else come forward or any profile information about the deceased?"

"No," sighed Dalgleish, "we don't."

"Well, in the meantime, if what Williams is telling us is correct and there *was* a relationship, it would suggest the deceased was gay and if that is correct and she *was* gay, what was she doing having drinks with a guy on the night she was murdered then?"

Dalgleish's eyes narrowed as a sudden flash of inspiration struck him. "Tell me this, do Stewart Street still run a wee squad monitoring the hookers who work in the city centre and in particular, the hotels?"

"Eh, aye, I think so, boss."

"Right, you and your neighbour get in there and start making inquiry about our victim. She was renting a pretty expensive flat and according to what Helen Meadows said when we searched the place, she had what I'm told was a wardrobe full of designer clothes.

We've no information as to how she funded her lifestyle, so I'm wondering…"

"If she was on the game," the detective finished for him with a grin.

"Got you boss. I'm on my way."

Pulling open the door, he saw Beth and the policewoman about to enter the room and stood aside to permit them to pass by.

When the detective left the room, Dalgleish nodded that the sullen faced policewoman resume her seat in the corner and smiled across the desk.

"Please take a seat Miss Williams," said Dalgleish, who introduced himself.

"Can I call you Beth?"

Biting at her lower lip in an effort to stop herself from crying, she nodded.

He could see she was close to tears and softly said, "I realise that you have already spoken to one of my officers and given a statement, but there is just a few more questions that I would like to ask you. Will that be okay with you, Beth?"

She nodded and twisted at the handkerchief in her hands.

He asked again about her relationship with Catherine Porteous.

She interrupted and reminded him that Catherine preferred to be called Cathy.

He smiled and suggested that Beth was very fond of Cathy.

"I loved her," she replied in a low voice.

From the corner of his eye, he could see the policewoman screwing her face as if in disapproval of the admission.

"Can you think of anyone who would want to hurt her?" he asked.

Her throat felt tight and she shook her head, afraid if she spoke her voice would break.

He inwardly took a deep breath and asked if Beth was aware of any men friends Cathy might have had a sexual relationship with?

She shook her head.

"Cathy's job; you told my officer that she worked as a PR with a city company. That's correct, yes?"

This time she nodded.

"Yet when I searched her flat, Beth, I could not find anything at all, no reference to a job or a company. No salary receipts, no tax returns, no employment contract, nothing and yet Cathy's lifestyle was quite affluent with no apparent means to support that lifestyle. I find that a little strange, don't you?"

Head down as she stared at the desktop, she shrugged, uncertain what he was getting at.

"I don't want you to get further upset, Beth, but I have to ask you. Was Cathy working as an escort?"

Her head shot up and she stared at him with fiery eyes.

He could see she was completely shocked by his question and realised if indeed it was as he suspected, then Beth Williams had no knowledge of Cathy Porteous secret life.

"You mean, you think she was a prostitute, don't you?" she snapped at him.

The door knocked and he nodded to the huffy policewoman to open it.

The portly detective stood there with a sheet of paper grasped in his hand and said, "If you please, can I have a moment, sir?"

He left the room and in the corridor outside learned that the Divisional Vice Squad, a small number of officers tasked to record and police the prostitutes that worked in the square mile of the city centre, had on file some sketchy details of an English speaking redheaded woman who was barred from at least two city centre hotels.

"They don't have any photographs in their office, but the sergeant in charge tells me it's likely the hotel security will have CCTV footage. Apparently, that's how they normally deal with these issues. The security record the prossie soliciting for business in the hotel, then take her to the security room and show her what they have recorded. Then they issue a formal warning and bar the women from frequenting the premises with the threat that if the woman returns to the hotel on any further occasion, the polis will get called. The sergeant also said that there might be more hotels, but not all the hotels inform the police of the women they bar because the hotel security teams don't like involving the police as its bad for business. The reason they have the information from these two hotels," he held up the sheet of paper, "is the security boss in each hotel is ex-job, so there's a good liaison with the local cops."

Dalgleish felt a warm glow in his chest and sensed that he was on the right track. "Right," he said, "you and your neighbour visit both these hotels with a photograph of the deceased. Try and firm up if she was on the game. If we can confirm that, then it's highly likely that the guy we're looking for is probably a punter."

Having sent the detective on his way, Dalgleish returned to the interview room.

"Miss Williams," he smiled at Beth, "I think we have detained you long enough. We have your phone number and home address, so if there is anything else, we will be in touch."

Her face drawn and wane, she stood and asked him, "Was Cathy a....was she, like you said; was she a prostitute?"

He took a deep breath and in a sympathetic voice, replied, "We don't know yet, Beth, but she *was* your friend. Maybe that's how you should remember her, eh?"

Turning to the policewoman he said, "Please escort Miss Williams to the front door, constable," then almost as an afterthought, coldly added, "Then you can take your break."

The policewoman conducted Beth to the glass enclosed foyer of Stewart Street police office and wordlessly, pointed to the front door before turning and walking quickly away.

In the cold of the morning, Beth walked across the road to the bay where she had parked her car and squeezed into the driver's seat. Locking the door, she sat for a moment perfectly still and stared through the windscreen. Then placing both hands on the steering wheel, she slowly allowed her head to sink forward onto her forearms and began to softly weep.

Now returned to his flat, Mick Thomson stood in the kitchen while the kettle boiled and shook his head at what he had done.

Christ, he thought, as he slowly grinned, that was a lot fucking easier than I had thought it might be.

The click of the boiled kettle startled him and he began to grin.

He stared down at his hands, the hands that had squeezed the life from the little shit Billy Purvis.

It had been so, so fucking *easy*!

He was certain no-one had seen him, particularly as he had taken the precaution of dressing in dark coloured trousers and a long, dark coat and wore a dark coloured skip hat. Leaving the close at the rear he had literally hugged the tenement wall, stepping over the dividing fence lines that were mostly broken down and separated the closes until he ducked into the back door of a close and left through the front that exited onto Linkwood Drive. A few minutes later a brisk walk led him to where he had parked his car on the busy Kinfauns Drive.

Easy peasy, he continued to grin.

Pouring the boiled water into a mug of coffee, again he considered if he *had* been seen by anyone, it was a brave bastard that would identify him to the cops and particularly if anyone thought they could be a witness and continue to live in the Drum.

No, people round here were too terrified of him and what he was capable of to speak out against him.

Of that he was more than certain.

He was fireproof, he smirked.

Grace Thomson sat in the lounge with a mug of tea on her hand, smiling at Des Brown who sat in the opposite armchair.

"When are you back on duty?" she asked.

"Well, on *that* point I phoned in to the office earlier this morning and told them that I'm taking a couple of days off. Time in lieu that I have lying," he replied as he smiled at her. "I thought I'd spend the next few days helping you and the wee guy to get settled in."

She nodded to the door that led to the hallway and where the suitcases had been abandoned and taking a deep breath, said, "I think we've been skirting round this Des. Where *exactly* are you going to put Steven and me?"

He nervously chewed at his lower lip and swallowing hard, replied, "Well, I was thinking of clearing my stuff out of the big room because it's got the en-suite and moving into the small room. It's a big comfortable bed for you and I have a blow-up mattress for Steven that will easily fit into the large bedroom. You and the wee guy can maybe share or else, if Paul's agreeable and I don't see him complaining, the wee guy can move in with him. For now I mean."

"Mmmm," she stared at him and leaning forward to place her mug down onto the coffee table, felt an anxious flutter in her stomach when she said, "How about instead Paul has *his* room to himself and Steven moves into the small room?"

"Eh, that would mean that...."

"That you and I would share," she interrupted him and rising from her seat, moved over towards him and to his surprise, slowly sat down on his lap. Circling his neck with her arms, her face a mere inch from his, she said in a soft voice, "Do you think Paul would mind me sharing with you?"

With Grace nestled on his lap, he felt himself become aroused and wrapping his arms round her waist, his breathing a little faster, he stared into her eyes and replied, "Grace, right now, at this minute, I don't give a damn if Paul minds or not."

She could never have imagined herself being so forward with any man, but with Des it seemed to be so right. Her face a blushing red and her breathing laboured, she bent her head forward and in a voice that was soft and seductive, whispered in his ear, "With the boys at school, Des, it's just you and me here. Why don't we go upstairs and have a look at the room and you can show me just how comfortable the bed is?"

The first officers who attended the call within the close at Dewar Drive discovered the weeping and hysterical Casey Lennox shaking the dead body and screaming uncontrollably as well as a dazed woman and small child sitting a few feet away on the cold, stone stairs.

By good fortune, when the officers radioed for CID assistance their call was responded to by DC Cat MacDougall who with her neighbour Colin Munro, was travelling close by and were with the uniformed officers within minutes.

A seasoned professional, MacDougall immediately took charge when she realised the death was suspicious and called for further assistance from not just her Drumchapel CID colleagues, but also back-up from the Scene of Crime personnel stationed at Pitt Street. No stranger to serious crime, MacDougall was well versed in the protocol of murder and also requested the attendance of the duty casualty surgeon and Depute Procurator Fiscal.

To add to the good fortune and to the unspoken relief of his subordinates, it was a stroke of luck that the Drumchapel DI Mark Walters was off that day, though nobody had been told why and so MacDougall was informed by radio message that the dayshift Detective Inspector from the nearby Maryhill office was being tasked to attend the scene.

While she awaited her detective colleagues and uniformed reinforcements to cordon off the area, MacDougall ensured the scene was secured and learned that the distraught woman found beside the body had been ushered upstairs to her flat while the second woman and her child had also been sent to their flat.

"The one that was greeting, says she's the dead guy's girlfriend, Cat," the uniformed officer informed her, a young probationary cop who Cat barely knew and who was standing self-importantly by the body. "My neighbour's up there the now with her. She kicked off when we arrived and was refusing to leave him. Turns out that there's a couple of greeting faced kids in the flat, so we nearly had to drag her up upstairs to see to the weans," he added with a shake of his head. "Screaming blue murder, she was," and then in a voice laden with sarcasm, quipped, "nearly had to do her for a breach of the peace."

"*She'll* be Casey Lennox then," replied Cat in a flat voice.

The officer's eyes narrowed and he was clearly puzzled, yet impressed by the detectives knowledge and couldn't help but ask, "How did you know that?"

"Because he," Cat nodded down to the body, "is Billy Purvis, local drug-dealer of this parish, a ned that you should have recognised from his picture that's prominently posted on the collators office wall."

It wasn't her style to chastise her colleagues, but Cat thought the young cop could use a lesson in decorum for even if Purvis had been a ned he was still someone's son. "If you keep abreast of your local intelligence bulletins, the last one indicated he was living with Lennox. Pays to read and learn, laddie," she stared stone-faced at the ashen faced young cop.

Sending Colin Munro upstairs to seek out and interview the woman who had first discovered the body, Cat satisfied herself that there was no more she could do until the arrival of the casualty surgeon and the Scene of Crime personnel. Instructing the young cop to continue to stand by the body she made her way to Lennox's flat. The front door was ajar and from inside she could hear wailing and a small child sobbing.

In the lounge, a policewoman with a notebook in her hand was patiently standing over Casey Lennox, who was rocking back and forth on the couch while hugging two toddlers to her, one of who was bawling while the other, a forefinger firmly wedged up his nose, stared curiously at the matronly cop.

The cop nodded a greeting to Cat and then an almost imperceptible shake of her head was enough to inform Cat the cop had so far got nothing out of Lennox.

"Casey," said Cat, bending down and ignoring the toddlers, placed her hand on Lennox's knee.

Then, a little more forcibly, Cat said again, "Casey!"

The younger woman, her eyes streaming tears, startled and turned to stare at Cat who apologetically nodded to the policewoman.

With a knowing sigh, the cop offered her hands to the two children, but while the small boy happily took the cops hand, the younger child clung to her mother.

Cat watched as the cop led the boy out of the room and seating herself on the couch opposite the distraught woman, said, "Look hen, I know it's been a terrible shock, but I need to ask you some questions, okay?"

"It was that bastard Tommo," hissed Lennox, the venom in her voice matching the hate in her tearstained eyes.

"Tommo?" Cat's eyes narrowed and she asked, "Do you mean Mick Thomson?"

"Aye, that fucker! He was here the other night, threatening my Billy..." her voice broke into a sob and again she began to weep.

"Did you see him this morning, Casey? Look at me, hen," Cat pressed her. "Did you see Thomson here this morning with Billy? Did you see him murder Billy or see them together?"

Lennox shook her head, unable to answer because of her sobs.

"Cat?" said Colin Munro from the doorway and beckoned her to him.

Standing in the doorway, he told her the casualty surgeon was on the landing examining the body and the rest of the CID office were now arriving and spreading out to conduct local interviews in the adjoining closes while the Scene of Crime personnel were examining the downstairs close area and working their way up towards the body.

"How did you get on upstairs?" she asked him.

He shook his head.

"The poor woman lives there with her wee one. She hardly speaks any English, but I think I got enough to be going on with meantime. She was obviously terrified of me because I'm the polis," he replied with a shrug. "I think she thought I was there to take her away.

Anyway, she couldn't tell me anything other than coming down the stairs this morning she saw the body and screamed. That's when the blonde woman that lives here…"

"Casey Lennox," interrupted Cat.

"Aye, likely that'll be her, then. She doesn't know the woman's name and is a little bit frightened of her. Says the blonde woman usually ignores her. She says when she screamed the blonde haired woman came out of this flat and screamed too. Fair scared her shitless, by all account. Anyway, she panicked and rushed upstairs to her flat and she's got one of these panic alarm things her social worker got for her and she activated it. She gave me her social worker's phone number and I made a call to the number and they confirmed it was them that sent the cops here. The social work thought the woman upstairs was being attacked and that's why the cops quickly responded. They didn't know they were coming to a murder and basically, that's how we were informed. Of the murder, I mean."

"Good work, Colin," she patted him on the arm and could see he was pleased.

The front door opened and they both turned to see a stocky built, world weary man wearing a worn, beige coloured raincoat who needed a haircut and sported a scar on his cheek.

"Can I help you, sir?" asked Cat, moving towards him.

"You'll be Cat MacDougall," he smiled at her and extended his hand to her. "I'm Charlie Miller. I hear your DI's off today, so I'm down from Maryhill to see if I can assist you in any way."

Cat didn't know Miller other than by reputation, but had heard good things about the Detective Inspector from a pal who worked in Maryhill CID.

"Pleased to meet you, sir," she replied and introduced Munro.

"How you doing, Colin," smiled Miller, shaking the younger man's hand then turned towards Cat and flicking a thumb over his shoulder, said, "The casualty surgeon's pronouncing life extinct as we speak and the SOCO people are about to start their examination of the body. The doc suspects that from marks on the neck, the deceased was strangled. In the meantime, can you bring me up to speed, hen?"

Cat suggested that Munro go through and stay with Lennox and seeing the policewoman keeping the toddler amused in one of the bedrooms, she nodded for Miller to follow her into the kitchen.

Cat placed her shoulder bag onto the worktop and then with her arms folded and leaning back against the worktop, in short, terse sentences, apprised him of the discovery of the body of William Purvis, who was known to be a local, minor drug dealer and an associate of Michael 'Tommo' Thomson, who in turn was not only suspected to be a major player in the Glasgow drug scene, but also known locally as a moneylender and a violent headcase.

She didn't think it prudent to inform Miller of her own knowledge of Thomson's brutal and sadistic rape of Jesse Cochrane. That, she inwardly decided, had to wait till such times she could persuade Cochrane to give evidence against Thomson.

"The problem is, sir…"

"Charlie," he smiled at her, a soft smile that immediately put her at her ease.

She acknowledged his courtesy with her own smile and continued.

"The problem is, Charlie that while we all know Thomson is into drugs and other criminality, it's the same old story."

"Aye, proving it," he finished for her with a sigh and nodding towards the lounge, added with narrowed eyes, "The lassie through there, Cat; the deceased's girlfriend. You said she *knows* Thomson murdered her boyfriend?"

"Well, she seems pretty convinced, but to be honest, it's only her opinion. However, she did also say that Thomson was up here the other night, threatening Purvis, but she can't say with any *certainty* that Thomson killed Purvis. The thing is, Thomson is a hated figure locally and he's an awful blight on this community. I've little doubt that Purvis and maybe Lennox has probably had a run in with him at some time or other so, much as I hate to admit it, he's usually the first individual to be credited with any wrongdoing, though to be honest it's not beyond him to commit murder in broad daylight. He's got this community so terrified that trying to find a witness to speak against him is nigh on impossible."

"But evidentially," Miller stared keenly at her, "other than the girlfriend's suspicions and her uncorroborated statement about Thomson threatening Purvis, there is nothing at this time to justify bringing Thomson in for interview for the murder?"

"No, boss, nothing at this time," she sighed as she shook her head.

"Right then, we'll work on what we've got so far and when the girlfriend is calmed down, we'll get a proper statement regarding the threat thing against Purvis. If it's sufficient, we can bring Thomson in for interview and take it from there."

He saw the hesitation in her eyes and asked, "What?"

"If we bring Thomson in because of Lennox's statement that Thomson threatened Purvis, he will know that it was her who grassed him up. I believe that unless we then place her under twenty-four hour protection, Thomson will get at her or her weans and there is a *real* possibility he will hurt not just her, but her kids to. That's the mark of the man, Charlie. He is one vicious, vindictive bastard."

He rubbed thoughtfully at his chin and said, "Obviously, I can't justify taking Lennox and her children into protective custody simply because we *think* Thomson might harm them. So, what do you suggest then?"

"I'm of the opinion that we *don't* bring him in just now that instead we work around him. Let's first find out what the SOCO team dig up from the body and the close. Keep Lennox's statement on the back burner for now as circumstantial evidence to corroborate anything else that we might produce. We both know that if we do bring him in and question him regarding her allegation that he threatened the deceased, he'll simply deny it and there isn't sufficient evidence to charge him with anything, not even menaces, because it will be her word against his. The down side is if we show our hand and disclose we know he threatened Purvis, he *might* get at her and her kids. Right now, we gain nothing by interviewing him, but have a lot to lose."

Miller stared thoughtfully at her and nodded, then said, "Right, that makes sense Cat, so if you finish up here with the girlfriend, I'll go and see how the Scene of Crime people are doing."

It was as he was turning away that she reached behind her for her shoulder bag and drawing it towards her, knocked a brown envelope onto the kitchen floor. Stooping to lift it, her brow furrowed with curiosity and then she startled. The name in the little opaque window clearly said, 'Ian Fagin.'

"Boss?" she called out to Miller and held the envelope for him to see.

"What have you got there?" he turned from the doorway to ask her.

"This letter, it's addressed to a young guy that was discovered dead, a couple of days ago from a drug overdose. But," she shook her head, "the address on the envelope isn't where he lived."

It didn't taken long for Cat and Munro to confirm that Casey Lennox had no knowledge of the unopened Housing Department tenancy letter that was addressed to the dead Ian Fagin, other than it had fallen from the pocket of a pair of tracksuit trousers worn by Billy Purvis nor did she know why Purvis had possession of the letter. Opening the letter Cat had discovered it to be simply an offer to Ian Fagin of temporary occupancy for the flat premises located at the address.

Now, at Charlie Miller's instruction to pursue the inquiry regarding the address, she and Colin Munro were parked outside the tenement building in Kiniver Drive.

Glancing up at the building Cat realised that it was one in a long list of tenements in the area that the council were, finance permitting, slowly renovating while decanting the residents to temporary accommodation. However in the interim, she was aware from local crime reports, that due to the shortage in appropriate accommodation, homeless persons including some asylum seekers were being temporarily housed prior to the renovation commencing.

"What do you think we'll find here, Cat?" asked Munro as he exited the CID car.

"Well, I can tell you for a fact we *won't* find Ian Fagin," she grimaced, "but other than that, it's anybody's guess."

The letter indicated the flat was located on the top floor, but the door had no name attached.

Outside the door, Cat pressed an ear to it and listened, but could not hear any noise from within.

The other door on the landing had a nameplate attached, but the elderly and frightened male resident who opened his door a mere few inches, either had no knowledge of who was using the flat opposite or more likely, Cat assumed, didn't want to get involved.

"Will I radio for a council joiner to come and get the door opened?" asked Munro.

"Bugger that," she shook her head and added, "We're on a murder inquiry, Colin. Use the spare key in your boot."

With a grin, Munro took a step back and kicked at the door that, after his third attempt, flew open.

They both donned thin, forensic gloves and stepped into the hallway. The daylight that filtered through the open doors from the bedrooms, kitchen and bathroom brightened the hallway and dust mites danced in the air.

Each taking a bedroom and after a negative search, they met at the lounge door.

Stepping warily though into the lounge, they saw the abandoned items of furniture, but it was the curious staining on the worn and dirty carpet and one patch in particular that attracted Cat's attention. Her nose wrinkled in disgust and she almost gagged, for it was a sweet, sickly smell that she immediately recognised.

"Colin," she softly said, as she put a restraining hand on his arm to prevent him from stepping further and contaminating the room. "Get on your phone to DI Miller and request that he send a Scene of Crime team here, too. I *think* we've just discovered where Ian Fagin really died."

CHAPTER TWENTY-TWO

After a restless, sleepless night that forced his wife Sheila to bad-temperedly grab her pillows and storm through to the spare room, Tom Fraser was having a leisurely morning sitting in his sunroom reading his morning edition of the Glasgow News and sipping at his coffee. He yawned, but his mind was still working overtime as again he went over the events of the previous evening.

How the *hell* they managed to get away with it, he still wondered.

He had half expected an early morning visit from the police calling to arrest him, but knew that the two neds wouldn't go to the cops and unless either Dick or Harry's conscience got the better of them and one or the other burst and confessed, the three of them were high and dry.

Almost ten grand each, he smiled then wondered; could it likely that the guys might consider doing it again, just one more time?

He knew that the money would go some way to alleviate his dodgy financial situation, but also realised that the short burst of adrenaline he had experienced during the few minutes it took to rip off the drug dealers was the most exciting time he had experienced for a number of years.

The noise of the sunroom door sliding open caused him to turn his head.

Sheila, her hair falling across her face and wearing in a light almost see-through nightdress so fine he could see the outline of her breasts, stood leaning on the doorframe smiling at him.

"You kept me awake half the night, you *bad* man," she pretended to scold him, then crooking a finger, added, "You had better come with me and make up for it, hadn't you?"

Well, he inwardly corrected himself, *almost* the most exciting time he had in years as now, aroused at the sight of her, he stood to take her hand and be led by her though to their bedroom.

Harry McInnes was still reeling from his confrontation with Rosemary both the night before and earlier that morning. He decided that a walk in the fresh air might cool him down and without any explanation, locked his computer, donned his overcoat and headed for the lift to the ground floor.

He exited the lift and was about to exit the Pitt Street building through the West Regent Street door when he saw Sally Nelson carrying a mop and bucket through the foyer area. Dressed as she was wearing her company tabard, jeans, no make-up and her hair piled untidily upon her head, to Harry she still looked like a vision of loveliness, though he did notice she looked tired and strained.

"Hi," he stopped in front of the commissionaire's reception desk and hands in his coat pockets, greeted her and stood smiling as she walked towards him.

"Hi yourself," she shyly responded, dumping her mop and bucket at her feet.

An awkwardness fell between them, but broken when he said, "So, what's up?" and at the same time, mentally kicked himself.

'*What's up*,' he thought. Some fucking chat-up line that!

"Same old, same old," she smiled in reply.

Neither noticed that John Stow, the popular commissionaire, walked away out of earshot to busy himself with some paperwork.

As Harry stared at Sally, he couldn't explain it, had no idea why and certainly had not planned it and later thought that some form of madness must have overtaken him, for quite suddenly, he nervously asked her, "Sally, would you meet me after work today?"

Her eyes and mouth opened wide with surprise and she felt her heart beat a little faster.

That few seconds' hesitation unnerved him and he was about to apologise, tell her that no, it was a foolish question and ask her to forget it when she quietly replied, "Yes. I'd like that, Harry."

Taken aback that she agreed, he began to stutter but then found his voice and said, "Yeah? Great, I know you finish about three o'clock, so I'll knock-off then too, if that's okay with you and meet you at the wine bar on Sauchiehall Street, across the road from Holland Street?"

"I know where that is. Yes, Harry, I'll meet you there," and picking up her mop and bucket, she smiled happily at him before heading towards the lifts.

Stepping through the glass doors into West Regent Street, anyone seeing Harry McInnes who didn't know him would have wondered at the middle-aged man with the inane grin plastered on his face.

In his ground floor flat in Cowan Street, Dick Smith sat in the armchair of his lounge in an old, faded tee shirt, holed football shorts, bare feet resting on the coffee table and nursing a cigarette and a mug of coffee. Once again, he fingered the white envelope with its foreign stamp and stared down at the pile of notes lying on the coffee table.

Taking the money off those two druggies had been far easier than he imagined.

Thirty-two grand, less the cost of the old Ford Escort meant when the money was divvied three ways that was over ten grand each.

He stared again at the envelope and removing the two page letter it contained, read it for the fifth, maybe sixth time; he just wasn't sure. He sat back and brow furrowed, inhaled deeply at his fag and with a relaxed sigh, made his decision.

Almost exactly at midday, the British Airways flight from the Albanian capital of Tirana landed smoothly at Heathrow's Terminal Four. Upon disembarkation, the passengers made their way towards the United Kingdom Immigration Services desk and stood patiently, waiting in turn to be called forward.

The tall, dark haired man wearing the dark blue suit, white shirt and matching blue tie, looked every inch the businessman he pretended to be and carried just one, brown leather overnight bag. When called forward, he produced his legitimately issued Albanian passport and in heavy accented English politely explained to the immigration officer he was staying in London for one night only, that his business with his parent company would be concluded by tomorrow afternoon.

As proof of his statement, the man produced a return ticket that indicated the following day he was booked on the 7pm flight to Tirana.

The officer noted traveller's passport bore previous UKIS entry and exit stamps and with a courteous nod, waved him through.

The man returned the passport to his inner suit pocket and breathing a little easier, made his way to the nearest short stay car park outside the terminal building.

The passport *had* been legitimately issued by the Albanian authorities, however, only he knew that the name and the date of birth belonged to a child who had died in infancy, but in the man's country, these details were never fully checked.

Pushing past the line of travellers waiting at the taxi rank, he made his way to the nearest short stay car park and sought out the vehicle that had earlier left for him.

The three years old black coloured BMW Series 3 saloon was parked where he had been told with the vehicles keys hidden on top of the rear driver's wheel.

He opened the boot and lifted the carpet that covered the spare wheel. As previously arranged, the holdall bag contained the double-barrelled sawn-off shotgun and a box of solid shot cartridges as well as a set of black coloured workman's coveralls, black leather gloves and a black, woollen ski mask.

An envelope containing a wad of British currency lay inside the holdall. He removed some notes and stuffed them into his trouser pocket.

The man slipped off both his suit jacket and tie and carefully folded them on top of the boot's carpet and got into the driver's seat.

Pulling down the sun visor, the parking ticket and a route map fell into his hand.

He smiled at the inclusion of the map and wondered if his London contact had heard of SatNav's.

The engine started at the turn of the key and he drove towards a pay point, got out of the vehicle and after waiting his turn, inserted the parking ticket and one of the British notes into the machine. The change in coin tumbled down the chute and the ticket was stamped for departure from the car park. Returning to the BMW, he drove slowly towards the exit.

As he waited in the line of vehicles to exit the car park, the man checked his watch and switching on the radio, selected the CD player and grinned at the digital display when he saw who was about to play.

With a smile and a nod, he inwardly promised to thank Fevzi for his thoughtfulness for including the wonderful Frank Sinatra's greatest hits.

In the car park outside the large gardening warehouse at Braehead shopping precinct, DC Cat MacDougall's husband Gus loaded the van with the materials he needed for his gardening business and getting into the cab, checked off the items on his list. He glanced at the passport sized photograph of his wife pasted to the dashboard and once again thought of the story she had related, of the bastard that raped the woman.

Drumchapel, he knew, wasn't too far away.

In fact, his eyes narrowed, a quick twenty minutes drive over the Erskine Bridge and he could be there.

He would never tell her, but he often worried himself sick about Cat and the animals she sometimes had to deal with; animals like this guy Thomson she had told him of.

He glanced behind him at the stout wooden posts that he had loaded into the van and once more it crossed his mind that there really was only one way to deal with evil sods like the man Cat had described. With that grim thought in his head, he started the engine.

DI Jamie Dalgleish stood in front of his team in the incident room with DCI Cathy Mulgrew sitting in a wooden chair to one side as she listened to his updated briefing.

"The good news since we last spoke, ladies and gentlemen, is that we now believe the murdered woman Cathy Porteous was soliciting for business when she met her killer. Statements noted earlier this morning from a young bartender who works in a city hotel indicate she was in the company of a white male, tall and well built who the witness is almost certain he will identify again."

He waved a hand to cut out questions and continued, "I know it's not a positive identification, but it's a start in the right direction. I've got two of the team and members of the Stewart Street division trawling through hotel CCTV footage to try and identify our victim and the man she was seen with.

A hand was raised at the rear by a young female detective, who asked, "Is the guy you are referring to our primary suspect, sir?"

Dalgleish quickly glanced at Mulgrew before replying, "As of now and in the absence of any further information to the contrary, I am declaring the man last seen with our victim as our number one suspect."

A phone at the rear of the room rung and was answered by a civilian analyst.

Dalgleish continued, "The woman who accompanied the victim's neighbour when he entered and discovered the body, has been traced. At the minute she is *not* a suspect, but cannot be categorically eliminated either. The tasks for today…"

He could see that the analyst at the back of the room was waving at him with the phone clutched in his hand.

"Can you take a message?" Dalgleish called out.

"Sorry boss, the SOCO woman says it's urgent," replied the red-faced analyst, uncertainly holding up the telephone handset towards Dalgleish.

"I'll get it Jamie, you carry on with your briefing," Cathy Mulgrew stood up from her chair and made her way through the team towards the analyst.

"As I was saying folks," continued Dalgleish, "the teams for today will concentrate on identifying our number one suspect."

"DCI Mulgrew," she said into the handset, "DI Dalgleish is busy. Can I help?"

"The office manager DS Prentice will divide you into pairs…"

"Are you certain?" asked Mulgrew as she scribbled the information onto a scrap of paper.

"…who will concentrate on guests who were booked into the hotel where the victim was last seen on the night before and after the discovery of her body," said Dalgleish.

"Give me that description, please," snapped Mulgrew into the phone.

"I know that it will be painstakingly laborious, but it needs to be done," he said.

"And that's the last address you have?" Mulgrew unconsciously nodded her head at the phone.

"I'm also keen that where possible, you speak with the receptionist who booked the guests into the hotel…"

"Yes, thanks, that's very helpful. I'll ensure you are informed if we get a result," said Mulgrew and replaced the handset.

"…to determine if the receptionist is able to describe the guest concerned."

A hand went up and the detective asked, "What about a photofit from our witness, boss?" but before Dalgleish could respond, Mulgrew raised her own hand and called out, "Apologies for interrupting your briefing, but can I have a word please, Mister Dalgleish?"

"Give us a minute, folks," said Dalgleish and followed Mulgrew into the corridor.

He could see she was agitated and her face was flushed. His stomach knotted, realising that whatever she had been told was important.

"That was the SOCO supervisor who attended the flat. Do you remember the empty packet of bleach wipes discovered in the bathroom bin?"

He nodded and replied, "Aye, she thought they might be of use, maybe a print?"

"Well," grinned Mulgrew, waving the scrap of paper at him, "she wasn't far wrong, Jamie. She did manage to lift a print and she found a match, but it's not evidentially conclusive in that there isn't the full sixteen matching points, only the ten matching points. However, she is convinced that the prints belong to a Michael Thomson who, as of a few months ago, has an address in Drumchapel. What she did though was check his antecedent history and not only is she e-mailing it over to you here, but I had her read it out to me and physically, he fits the description of the man seen with your victim; bald with beard and strong physique. According to his profile, he has a history of violence."

"Yes," he bent his head back and slowly drawled, punching the air with one fist.

"Right boss, here's what I plan to do," he added.

Des Brown rolled onto his back and wondered again at his good fortune.

Grace, lying beside him, her hair spilled out across the pillow and her hand on his chest, quietly sighed in her sleep, the worry and exhaustion of the last twenty-four hours having finally caught up with her.

Well, he happily grinned, that and their frantic lovemaking.

He turned his head slowly to stare at her and his brow creased.

She and Steven couldn't hide forever from Mick Thomson.

No, something would need to be done to sort that bastard out, something permanent.

He imagined himself confronting Thomson, ordering him to stay away from Grace and her son, but then reality kicked in and he realised if he *was* to confront Thomson, he would need to arm himself with something big and solid; something like Paul's wooden baseball bat, he inwardly grinned.

Des did not consider himself to be a violent man, but neither had he ever shirked from a fight.

The digital clock on the bedside table said it was almost one o'clock. As quietly as he dared for fear of waking Grace, he slid from the bed and grabbing his clothes from the floor, made his way into the en-suite to get dressed.

A moment later, he crept back into the bedroom and seeing her still fast asleep, opened the door and gently closed it behind him.

The hurriedly called and very private meeting that took place in the conference room on the fourth floor of Pitt Street comprised of just three officers; Detective Inspector Peter Murray from the Intelligence Department, the Detective Chief Inspector in charge of Covert Human Intelligence Source handling and the Detective Constable who was the police handler for the late and unlamented William 'Billy' Purvis.

The midday sun streamed through the window onto the highly polished table and reflected onto the red face of the DCI.

"How the hell could this happen? It's too *fucking* coincidental that he gets himself murdered just after losing thirty-two grand of drug money," ranted the DCI. "When the shit hits the fan we're all going to have to explain ourselves as to why we didn't take down the money and the courier!"

"Aye, but can I remind you that it was *you* who instructed we didn't take any action on that issue?" Murray glared at him, keen to impress upon the DCI that if any shit was getting thrown, it wasn't going to be *his* career going down the toilet pan.

"But who was it that knocked the money off?" interrupted the DC, fearing that he was going to have to referee the other two. Turning to the DCI he timidly asked, "I mean, boss, are we *absolutely* certain it wasn't a leak from one of us, the polis I mean? Is it possible that this *might* be internal, that it might be a Police Standards Unit issue?"

"Well, as far as my department is concerned…" began Murray, only to be cut short by the DCI who, now on his feet, almost screamed at him, "Don't give me any of that holier than thou shite, Murray. *Your* mob leaks like a fucking sieve! Half the neds in the city are drinking in the pub round the corner so they can earwig what your tossers discuss when they're in there soaking up the bevy!"

"That's not fucking fair!" snarled Murray in response, standing now, his knuckles white and teeth bared.

"You have to remember too, boss," the DC gulped hard as he turned towards the DCI, "it was only us three in the job that knew about the handover."

"Then explain to me that if it wasn't any of the three of *us* who leaked the info, who else knew?" the DCI rounded on the DC.

"Probably some other drug gang or maybe Purvis himself orchestrated it?" mumbled the DC, feeling miserable because as the junior officer present, he knew fine well that if anyone was to be thrown to the wolves or in this case, the rubber heels, it was bound to be him.

The DCI stopped and stared hard at the DC.

Murray stared hard at the DCI.

The DC shrugged and stared miserably at the table.

"If there's only the three of us know that the money was stolen at the handover and that Purvis was involved…" said the DCI thoughtfully.

"And besides Purvis, who is now dead," Murray pointedly remarked, "then there's only the three of us knew about the handover and only us three knew that Purvis was a police tout," added Murray.

"And if the paperwork identifying Purvis as a police tout…"

"…were to get lost," continued the DCI.

"…so then, there would be no questions asked of why we didn't seize the money," the DC completed the sentence. He then added, "And if Purvis is no longer registered as a police informant then of course nobody will connect any of us three with the Purvis murder inquiry."

"Gentlemen," the DCI took a deep breath and almost with relief at a career saved, sat heavily back down, his hands flat on the table in front of him. "I do believe we have reached an agreement."

For the fourth time that day, Mick Thomson checked the laptop for incoming e-mails, but so far there was none from the guy who called himself John.

It didn't take a genius to work out that John, whoever he might be, would be thoroughly pissed at the loss of the money.

What Thomson needed to do now was Inform John that the problem had been taken care of, that he would ensure another courier would be recruited and the deliveries could continue.

Yes, all he had to do was convince John and besides, he reasoned, if John wanted to continue to have his cut of the money delivered to his accounts, then he'd need to sweeten the deal, Thomson grinned to himself.

It suddenly occurred to him that maybe now instead of being the local supplier in the chain, it was time for him to demand that John consider him for a full partnership.

He threw the laptop onto the cushions on the couch and stared around him at the room.

She'd be back tomorrow to clean up and bring in his shopping and maybe he would park the car out of sight and have a little fun with her.

He rubbed at his crotch and closed his eyes tight, imagining what he would do to a naked Grace and then his thoughts turned to the swollen breasts of Casey Lennox.

His eyes opened and he wondered what she would tell the cops when they found her spineless boyfriend dead. Would she grass him up?

One thing was for certain, he began to giggle then laughed outright at his own humour.

Billy Purvis wouldn't be doing any grassing; not anymore.

He had waited for over half an hour in the cold close for the little shit and was confident nobody had seen him enter or leaving the close at the rear. Other than his hands round the little shit's throat, he hadn't left any marks or anything that could identify him in the close and the gloves ensured that he didn't leave any DNA on Billy's skin either.

No, he smiled with confidence at his own ingenuity; the cops had nothing on him. He was free and clear of any involvement in Purvis's murder.

He gave no further thought to the killing of the redheaded prostitute, an issue that was already dismissed from his mind.

He rose from the armchair and went into the kitchen to fetch a celebratory beer from the fridge, but then remembered he was out of drink and that it was on the list of shopping Grace was to bring tomorrow, with his groceries.

Fuck it, he thought, I'll nip down to the Co-op and get a half dozen cans, then fetching his car keys from the worktop, locked the flat door behind him and made his way downstairs to the ground floor. Walking along the path to the pavement his attention was on his pride and joy, his parked gleaming white coloured Nissan Juke and that was unfortunate, for had he glanced across the street, he might have seen the man lurking in the darkened close opposite, who watched his every move.

Buoyed by the news of fingerprint information obtained by the Scene of Crime supervisor, an animated DI Jamie Dalgleish had divided his inquiry officers into an arrest team and a search team; the arrest team to be led by him while the search team would be led by a Detective Sergeant who were tasked to scour the suspect Michael Thomson's flat in Goyle Avenue for anything of evidential value that might link him to their murder victim, Cathy Porteous.

However, for the time being the two teams waited frustratingly at Renfrew Office for the return of Dalgleish and DC Helen Meadows, who were in attendance at the Procurator Fiscal's office in Inchinnan, impatiently waiting for the arrest and search warrant to be typed up. That done, they would then drive need to the Court in Paisley where Dalgleish would swear on oath that the warrant was essential to the inquiry and would, he was confident, be granted by a Sheriff.

Dalgleish finished his call and closed his mobile phone as Meadows returned with two Styrofoam cups of weak tea.

"Sorry, bloody machine stuff, but better than nothing," she gave a sad grin. "So, what's happening, boss? Are we any further forward?" she asked as she sat on the hard wooden bench beside him.

"No, the typist's working as fast as she can…or so she says," he sighed, then added, "I know it's very time consuming, Helen, but we need to get it right or this bastard could walk on a technicality. If we barge in without the proper warrant, a defence Counsel could argue that we railroaded their client."

"I was also wondering, boss. If we have a witness, the young barman Neil Kerr who can identify our suspect, wouldn't it be simpler to show Kerr a photograph? After all, we have Thomson's photo on file."

"That would be too easy," he nodded, "because what it might do is if say we arrest and charge Thomson for the murder and the case later goes to trial, the defence Counsel could allege that we unduly influenced Kerr by showing him a photograph of the accused and that's why he picked Thomson out at the parade. It would therefore negate the best evidence of identification. No, it's best to keep Kerr's identification for the formal parade."

"Okay," she nodded, "I see that," then chewing at her lower lip, asked him, "What if he's not at home, boss?"

"I just got off the phone with DCI Mulgrew and she told me she has contacted Drumchapel CID to request that they make a discreet inquiry to house our suspect, see if he's at home. She says that apparently they've just commenced their own murder inquiry and surprise, surprise; our suspect is known to their victim too. What if any is his involvement, I've no idea. She also told me that the Drumchapel DI is off today, but she spoke with a pal of hers, DI Charlie Miller, who's standing in for the time being and has landed himself the murder inquiry."

"Bet he's pleased about that," she grinned at him.

He smiled in return and replied, "I know Charlie. We were on a cognitive behaviour training course at Tulliallan, a couple of years back. He's a good guy." He turned to stare at her. "You might recall the incident when the car blew up in the east end of Glasgow a few years ago?"

"Aye, was that…?"

"Yeah," he nodded. "Charlie was a DS at the time. He was lucky to be alive after it, by all accounts."

"DI Dalgleish?" said the voice from the doorway.

He turned to see the typist holding a sheaf of papers that she held towards him.

"I believe this is what you're waiting for, Mister Dalgleish."

CHAPTER TWENTY-THREE

The Scene of Crime personnel in their white suits were painstakingly searching the lounge of the flat while on the chilly landing outside, DC Cat MacDougall and her neighbour, Colin Munro, stood with DI Charlie Miller.

"So, what else did you see in there?" he asked her.

"I'm certain it was blood staining on the carpet and there seemed to be a brownish powder residue as well, but it looked like it there had been an attempt to sweep or scoop it up. There was a bottle lying on its side with what looked like the remains of a liquid inside. We didn't touch anything, just got out of there and decided it was better being examined by the SOCO guys."

"Good call," he nodded his approval. He turned and cocked a thumb over his shoulder towards the opposite door. "Any idea who the occupant is in there?"

"We knocked on the door when we first arrived, but it was an old guy that clearly didn't want anything to do with us. We thought…" but she was interrupted by the SOCO supervisor who came through the flat door. Pulling down his face mask, the supervisor addressed Miller and said, "We can confirm it *is* blood staining on the carpet, Mister Miller. The detective here," he nodded to Cat, "says it's likely to match an OD that you guys turned up a couple of days ago, so we'll have the deceased's blood grouping on file back at the office. As for the brown powder," he wheezed, "I can't categorically confirm it here, but my guess is it is heroin and from what I seen of it, it looks as though it's pure and unadulterated."

"What about the bottle that was lying there," Cat asked. "Is that significant?"

"We managed to save a drop of whatever was in the bottle and curiously, the stuff in the bottle is similar in appearance to an adulterant that I saw being tested back at the lab and apparently has been doing the rounds here in Glasgow and also in north Ayrshire. I haven't had any dealings with it myself, but my understanding from my colleagues, who got the info from the Drug Squad, is that the stuff is potently lethal, so much so the Squad are in the process of compiling for issue a public health warning about its use. Of course, I can't confirm that's what is *in* the bottle until the forensic boys do their test, but if you want my humble opinion…"

"Mixed with the heroin, could it cause death?" asked Miller.

"Again, it's *only* my opinion, but from what I hear…undoubtedly," nodded the supervisor and then added, "One other thing. We discovered a couple of floorboards have been taken up in one of the bedrooms. It looks like the space underneath has been used to secrete something, so I'll have it photographed and examined too."

"Right, so as you suspected," Miller turned towards Cat, "there is a real likelihood that this flat is the locus for your dead guy, remind me…"

"Ian Fagin, boss," Munro chipped in.

Miller smiled and repeated, "Aye, Ian Fagin," then turning again to the SOCO supervisor asked, "I take it you guys will conduct a full fingerprint examination of the premises?"

"Not a problem, but I take it you already have suspects who were using the flat?"

"I'll e-mail you the names and details for comparison," interrupted Cat, inwardly pleased that her first gut reaction to the death of Ian Fagin might prove to be correct.

"Right," Miller vigorously rubbed his hands together and turning towards the supervisor, said, "now that's settled I'll have the uniform stand by the flat while you guys are working here. In the meantime," he beckoned Cat and Munro to one side, "I've had a call from DCI Cathy Mulgrew about your suspect Mick Thomson, so here's what I need from you."

Mick Thomson stood behind the elderly woman in the queue at the Co-operative and loudly sighed when with shaking hands, she searched her shopping bag for her purse.

"For fuck's sake, missus, get a move on," he growled at her through gritted teeth.

The teenage female assistant, like everyone else on the shop, knew exactly who Thomson was and though angry at his impatience with the old woman, was too afraid to intercede and fearfully glanced away.

At last, the woman got out her purse and slowly counted out the coins, then lifting her purchases, hurried away from the till.

Thomson banged down the plastic-encased brick of six cans of lager and flicking a five pound note onto the counter, watched as the assistant scanned the cans.

"All right, darling?" he leered at her.

She knew who he was as well as his reputation and ignored him, casting her eyes down while nervously placed his change back onto the counter.

"Want to come up to my flat and help me drink these, hen? Have a wee private party with me, maybe?" he teased.

A faltering voice behind him said, "We don't want any trouble, Mister Thomson, so if you've made your purchase sir, please leave the store."

He turned slowly to stare at the youthful manager, a slightly built man in his early twenties who pale-faced and tight-lipped stared wide-eyed back at him.

The half dozen customers in the queue behind Thomson all suddenly remembered some items they had forgot to place in their baskets and melted away from the queue to stand between the aisles and to watch, but not to witness.

"What did you say?" he turned slowly towards the manager, who took a half step back.

"I said…."

"I heard you the first time, you fucking wee arse," Thomson bent down till his nose was no more than a few inches from the manager's nose, the virulent hate clear on his face.

"Your conduct, Mister Thomson…" his voice breaking and unable to tear his gaze from the bigger mans eyes yet determined to finish, the manager continued, "…is unacceptable and you are barred from this store, sir."

Thomson begun to raise a fist and said, "Why you…"

"If you don't fuck off *now*, the polis is getting called!" hissed the teenage assistant at the till.

He turned to see she had stood back from the counter, out of his reach and with a mobile phone in her hand, the forefinger of her other hand threateningly poised above the number nine on the keyboard.

He smiled menacingly at her insolence and standing upright, stared from one to the other and in a voice oozing menace, pointed his own forefinger at each in turn and threatened, "I'll not forget this. I'll not forget *you two*!"

Grabbing the lager from the counter, he ignored the loose change and strolled slowly from the shop.

His anger knew no bounds.

On any other day he would have battered the shite out of the pair of them and not a soul in the place would have seen a thing, because he was Mick 'Tommo' Thomson, the hardest *bastard* in the Drum.

However today, the last thing he wanted was the cops calling on him, asking questions.

But he wouldn't forget, he snarled; no by fuck.

He would *not* forget at all.

With increasing confidence now that he was in possession of the warrant, DI Dalgleish contacted his two teams and arranged that he and Meadows rendeavous with the teams at Drumchapel police office, where they would stand by till they heard from DI Miller's officer who was being tasked to check if the suspect Michael Thomson was at home.

If he was, they would immediately set off from Drumchapel office and serve the warrant by arresting him and searching his flat.

If Thomson was not at home, they would wait until such time he returned home.

Dalgleish silently prayed that the wait wasn't too long.

Chic Fagin straightened his tie and pulled open the door to the funeral home in Kinfauns Drive.

With a weary sigh, he went in and was greeted by a solemn faced woman wearing a black skirted two piece suit who shocked at his pale appearance immediately led him to an interview room and made him sit down before fetching him a glass of water.

With professional courtesy and personal compassion, the woman took her time in explaining to the distraught old man what the funeral home would offer Chic's grandson Ian.

A short time later, with the arrangements duly made, he left the premises and slowly made his way home.

Cat MacDougall instructed Colin Munro to slowly drive along Goyle Avenue, but to her disappointment, there was no trace of Mick Thomson's white coloured Nissan Juke.

As they passed by Thomson's close, they could not to know of the man who stood in the cold of the close, a few stairs up above the first floor landing and out of sight of Mick Thomson's door as he awaited Thomson's return.

Grace Thomson awoke with a start, first wondering where she was then wriggled in the bed with a sigh of pleasure and, feeling a little embarrassed at her nakedness beneath the quilt, called out, "Des?" She called out again, but this time a little louder, then getting no response, slipped from the bed. She saw his blue coloured cotton dressing gown hanging from the hook behind the door and shrugged into it. Padding on bare feet downstairs, she called out, "Des?" as she descended the stairs.

She discovered the handwritten note on the kitchen worktop propped up against the kettle that informed her he had popped out, that he had something to do and suggested she take a leisurely bath. She read that he had arranged that his father pick the boys up from school and bring them to his parent's house, that he had also arranged he and Grace would join them there later this evening for dinner. She twice read the line that said how keen he was to introduce her to his mother as '...the new woman in my life.'

Her hand unconsciously strayed to her throat and she bit at her lower lip when she saw he had ended the note by telling her that he loved her.

Harry McInnes, feigning a headache, left the office a little earlier than three o'clock and waited nervously for Sally Nelson in the wine bar in Sauchiehall Street.

A few minutes after three, he saw Sally cross the road and watched as she pushed open the door of the bar.

He stood and waved her over, seeing that her blonde hair was brushed and lying loose on her shoulders and that she had applied make-up before coming to meet him.

"Hi," she said, glancing at him then looking away.

He realised almost immediately what was wrong and softly asked, "Sally, are you as nervous as I feel?"

As she sat down, she almost sighed with relief at his admission and replied, "I thought it was just me, Harry. Yes, I'm nervous," then wringing her hands together below the table and a little anxiously told him, "I really like you, Harry. I really do. I just didn't want you to think…well, think that…sorry," she shyly lowered her head. "I don't know what to say. I'm just unsure if I might be doing the right thing, here."

"Then don't say anything. Just listen to what *I've* got to say," he smiled at her and for some reason he couldn't explain, he felt happier than he had for a long, long time.

As the hour passed by, he told her of his unhappiness and his plans to leave his wife, of the arrangement he had made so that she would not suffer financially. He blamed himself for much of the failure of their marriage, but she suspected otherwise, that Harry's wife did not fully appreciate what a good man he was.

She told him of her husband Archie's disability, of his wasted opportunities, his drinking and gambling and the servitude he demanded of her; of the verbal and physical abuse that she would no longer tolerate and her sudden decision to leave and take temporary accommodation with her sister Elsie and her family. She smiled when she related her nephew's comment, that the family were now happy because they worried about her safety while she was living with Archie.

She glanced at her watch and asked, "Goodness, I didn't realise the time. Haven't you got to go home?"

He stared at her for a few seconds and then quietly replied, "Actually, I've an appointment in about twenty minutes with an old friend that I must keep and as for going home? No, there's nothing there for me now Sally and besides," he smiled at her, "Right now I'm exactly where and who I want to be with."

Tom Fraser didn't want to admit that he was worried.

Several times during the day he had phoned Dick Smith on both the mobile and landline, but got no response.

The worst case scenario running through his mind was that somehow or other, the cops had cottoned on to the heist and lifted his old friend.

Nervously, he found himself glancing periodically through his front window, wondering if or when a squad car might be turning up at his door.

Cat MacDougall instructed Colin Munro to park the CID car a couple of streets away from Goyle Avenue and used her mobile phone to update DI Charlie Miller.

"Right, wait another ten minutes or so and give it another drive-by, Cat. Keep that up till you're reasonably sure the suspect is at home, okay?"

"Got that, boss," she replied.

"Oh, one other thing, Cat; DI Dawson from the surveillance unit called looking for you. Said it was a personal matter and can you phone him back?"

"Right boss, I've his number on my mobile here, thanks."

Ending the call, she scrolled down her directory and pressed the number that was answered almost immediately by Andy Dawson.

"How is it going wee pal?" he greeted her.

"Fine, Andy," she replied and teased him by asking him to guess who was currently a suspect for a murder. When at last she told him, he was surprised and a little jealous that Thomson was being arrested for something other than drugs and inwardly wondered how it would impact on his investigation into identifying the main man who was orchestrating the importation of the heroin into the Glasgow area.

"I'm sure you'll get your man in the end, Andy," she smiled at the phone. "Now, what was it that you wanted to tell me?"

"Can you take this call?"

She glanced over at Munro who was busily watching a short skirted, long legged blonde walking on the opposite side of the road.

"Shoot," she replied.

"You'll be aware that your DI is not at work today?"

"Yeah, day off I think," she slowly said, but suspecting that Dawson was about to tell her otherwise.

"Not quite," it was his turn to tease her. "Want to guess what I know?"

She pretended to be annoyed until at last he told her, "I heard on the grapevine that the rubber heels called at his house this morning, early doors. It seems that a number of complaints have been made against your DI by several of our colleagues and the Fiscal is charging Walters under the Moorov doctrine."

Cat's eyes widened as she gasped, "No way!"

Munro turned to stare at her, curious as to what caused his neighbour to be so startled.

"Yeah," continued Dawson, "it seems that there are a number of polis women and before you ask, I don't know how many, who have been subjected to a sexual assault of some form, either physical or inferred, by Mister Walters; so as of this morning he was arrested by the Police Standards Unit and charged. I reckon you *might* not be seeing him any time soon."

Though an experienced detective, Cat had never been involved in a Moorov case, recalling that one witness's testimony alone was insufficient to charge a suspect, however, the evidence of several victims experiencing a similar assault by the same individual was recognised in law as corroborating each other and thereby charges could be brought against that individual.

It suddenly brought to mind the attitude of the young policewoman, Morag Stewart, who at the location of the discovery of Ian Fagin's body, was wary of Walters and Cat wondered; was Morag a victim?

"Right, thanks for that Andy," she replied and promising to let him know if Thomson *was* arrested, ended the call.

Mick Thomson parked the Juke outside his close and grabbing the lager from the front seat, exited the vehicle and locked it. Making his way into the close he still fumed over his treatment at the hands of the two Co-operative staff and turned over in his mind all manner of retribution. For the young manager, he was considering numerous broken bones while for the tart assistant, he had more pleasurable ideas.

On the stairs, hidden from Thomson's door by the close wall, the man took a deep breath and nervously readying himself, raised and rested the wooden stick on his shoulder.

As he climbed the stairs in the close to his flat, the brick of lager encased in its tight plastic wrapping casually carried across his right forearm, Thomson's mind was fully occupied by thoughts of revenge.

Arriving at his door, he fumbled with his free hand in his left pocket for the door key, then realising it was in his right hand pocket, was transferring the lager to his other arm when the first blow struck. Almost as if by instinct, Thomson was turning towards the heavy wooden stick when it came swishing through the air to strike him a glancing blow on the right temple; not enough to knock him down, but sufficiently forceful to split the skin and cause a fine spray of blood as well as causing him to both stumble against the door and drop the brick of lager.

Falling with his back against the door, he tried to turn to face his assailant just as the heavy wooden stick came down a second time. Attempting to deflect the blow, he managed to raise his right forearm only to hear the radius bone snap as another hammering blow struck home.

He shrieked in pain and anger and instinctively drew back his arm to protect it, unwittingly exposing his unprotected head that took the full force of the heavy stick that quickly come down a third time, this time to strike him squarely on his skull.

With a soft murmur, his legs folded beneath him and he collapsed with his back against the door and began to slid down, leaving a trail of blood on the woodwork. Vainly, he tried to force his head upwards to see who was attacking him, but the man wasn't finished yet.

With almost a futile gesture, Thomson began to open his mouth to appeal to his assailant as he tried to raise his uninjured arm to ward off the blows, but to no avail.

Mercilessly, his attacker pummelled at Thomson's head again and again and again until at last, the murmuring had stopped.

The man, now soaked in bright red, arterial blood, stepped back and his body shaking with revulsion, breathlessly stared down at what remained of Thomson's head.

Cat MacDougall was still pondering Andy Dawson's information when Colin Munro turned into Goyle Avenue.

"It's there!" he excitedly exclaimed as they approached the parked Nissan Juke and then unaccountably, he slowed down.

Cat was about to tell him to speed by the vehicle and reaching for her mobile phone glanced at the close entrance. Shocked, she saw a bloodstained man carrying a heavy wooden stick exiting the close.

"Stop!" she screamed at Munro, who slammed on the brakes.

Cat quickly got out of the passenger door and stepping warily onto the pavement, ignored Munro's shouted plea that she wait for him. The man, his face, his hands and clothes and the stick all thickly covered with blood, stumbled on the pathway and with wide eyes, stared at her.

To her horror, as she cautiously approached him, she realised who he was and simply said, "Oh no! Oh dear God, no!"

CHAPTER TWENTY-FOUR

Harry McInnes walked Sally Nelson to her bus stop with the agreement that she would meet with him later that evening in a pub near to where her sister Elsie lived, at which time they would further discuss what, if any future they might have.

Almost with a spring in his step, he began to walk towards the city office of his lawyer friend.

The meeting lasted almost an hour and he was happy with the proposition that the lawyer suggested be set before Rosemary, a proposition that would be formally delivered by courier that evening. Bidding his friend cheerio he was outside the office and beginning to make his way to George Square to catch his bus when his phone rung in his pocket.

"Hi Tom, how's it hanging?" he cheerfully answered the call.

"Harry, we might have a problem," was the curt reply. "Have you heard from Dick at all?"

"No, the last time I saw him I was with you. Why, what's up?"

"I can't raise him," replied Tom. "I'm worried that maybe our former colleagues might be having a chat with him."

Harry was too elated after his meeting with Sally to be spooked and smiling at the phone, said, "Look Tom, its Dick we're talking about here. The daft bugger's probably out on a bender. There's nothing to worry about, old son. We're clear and free." Then knowing what would calm his friend's fears, he added, "I'm in the town anyway, so I'll pop by his flat and let you know if he's at home, okay?"

"You sure that's all right? I mean, you haven't heard anything at your place, have you?"

"No," he dodged round a number of pedestrians waiting for a bus and shook his head, "nothing at all. I'm telling you, Tom, there's *nothing* to worry about. Now go and spend time with that lovely wife of yours, eh?"

Satisfied that for the moment, he had eased Tom Fraser's concern, he decided that Tom was right, it wouldn't take long to check on Dick and started walking towards the nearest underground station that would take him to Kelvinbridge.

Twenty minutes later, Harry got off the busy underground train and climbed the stairs that led out onto Great Western Road. A few short minutes later, he was pressing the button on the outside close security door, but got no response.

"Bugger," he muttered with a shake of his head and stepped over the small fence into the patch of wiry grass that served as the lawn outside Dick's ground flat lounge window.

The curtains were drawn, but Harry was almost certain there were no lights on inside the room.

"Can I help you, mister?" said the voice from the path.

He turned to see a young woman in her late teens, a student he thought if her brightly coloured spiky green hair and biker jacket adorned with peace and anti-war badges was any indication. She stared curiously at him.

"I was looking for Dick…Mister Smith, that lives here," he pointed towards the window.

"Who are you then, his pal?"

He realised the girl was suspicious and nodding, said, "Aye, we were supposed to meet for a pint, but he never turned up."

"Probably out looking for a bird," replied the girl in a surly voice. "Horny old bastard isn't he?" and at that, she used her key to open the security door and disappeared quickly inside.

Harry grinned. He didn't need to be a genius to work out that at some time Dick had likely tried to chat up the girl, who was probably a neighbour in the close.

It was as he stepped back across the fence that it occurred to him it *was* unusual the bugger wasn't at home nor answering calls.

Grace Thomson was nervous about meeting Des's mother that evening and after showering, spent some time trying to find the right outfit from the packed suitcases. At last, she settled on a plain, light grey coloured short sleeved blouse and knee length, black coloured flared skirt. Both needed ironed and it was while she searched the kitchen cupboards for the steam iron she glanced at the clock and wondered where Des had got to?

DI Jamie Dalgleish, hands in his coat pocket, stood with DI Charlie Miller on the landing, both blinking at the bright flash of the cameras in the confined space as they stared down at the bloodied corpse of Michael Thomson. Some ten feet away, the white paper suited Scene of Crime personnel worked their way around the body.

"So," said Miller in a flat voice, "I assume you'll be treating this as a detected crime then, Jamie?"

"Oh indeed I will, Charlie," replied Dalgleish in a chirpier voice. "The bugger might not be going to jail, but he's got his comeuppance and that's what matters, isn't it? You could say that justice has prevailed, even though it wasn't exactly by the rules, eh? Anyway," he sighed, "my understanding from what I hear is that he's no sad loss to either the community or society at large. In fact, I hear he was a thoroughly evil bastard."

"So you're more than happy this is your killer?"

"Oh aye, I'm happy enough he's my man. When I heard about the murder here, I had one of my team immediately contact our eye witness, a young barman who saw this bugger with the deceased on the night she was killed and take with him a police head shot photograph of Thomson. With him lying stiff here, there's no problem regarding corrupting the evidence, so an ID parade is academic now anyway. I'm told the lad picked Thomson out of a group of photos. I'm satisfied he's my man, right enough," Dalgleish sighed and scratched at an itchy nose.

"He's also the suspect for the killing this morning of a young drug dealer called Purvis," said Miller, "but so far we've no direct evidence to link him to the murder other than supposition. I've landed that inquiry, but I don't see it going anywhere now."

"So, it would have been a whodunit, then?"

"Aye and likely would have remained like that because the people around here were apparently shit scared of Thomson, so I don't think I could have dug up any witnesses. For what it's worth though, I'll be suggesting our man Thomson here," he nodded down at the body, "as the main suspect and you can bet your bottom dollar the inquiry will be wound up pretty quickly. Besides, I've a statement from the deceased's girlfriend that Thomson threatened the dead guy just before the murder. You know what management's like. They'll do anything to save a few bob and likely it will be suggested I write off Purvis's murder as solved." He smiled humourlessly and nodded towards the dead Thomson. "Suspect detected and murdered, end of."

"Pity there wasn't more inquiries like that; murdering the suspect I mean," Dalgleish chortled. "It would sure as hell make *our* job that wee bit easier."

Again, both narrowed their eyes against the bright flashes from the SOC officer's camera, then Dalgleish asked, "The man your DC's caught coming out of the close, Charlie. What's the story there, then?"

Miller turned to him and eyes narrowed as he shook his head, exhaled softly and replied, "Well, therein lies a tale."

Sitting at her desk in the Drumchapel CID office, Cat MacDougall lifted her mobile phone and with a happy sigh, said, "Hi Gus. Thanks for getting back to me."

"No problem sweetheart. What's up?"

"Nothing, it's just that I might have to work on a bit later this evening, so if you want to go ahead and have dinner…"

"No," he interrupted her more sharply than he intended, but in a softer voice, continued, "I'm busy unloading the van at the minute and it'll take me a while, so I'd rather wait till you're home and we can eat together, okay?"

"Will that include a bottle of red?"

"Oh," he softly laughed in her ear, "I think I can arrange for that and I'll stick a straw in the top of the bottle for you," he joked. Then he asked her, "You really okay, hen? I'm thinking you sound a bit upset."

"Good and bad day at the office," she slowly replied. "Good news from an old pal of mine and a really shitty thing that I still have to do."

He heard her sigh and wished he was there to hold her, but knew even better than Cat herself did that she had tremendous inner strength and no matter what she had to do, she would finish it. Then he would be waiting for her when she got home.

"Right, text or phone me when you're leaving the office and I'll see you when you get in and have a bath run for you; that and a bottle of red complete with the straw."

"Okay," she smiled and ended the call.

Colin Munro sat a mug of coffee down on her desk in front of her and almost apologetically said, "Thanks for today, Cat. I was a bit lost when I saw him coming out of the close covered in blood like that. I just didn't know what to do."

"Don't think I was any better," she replied, sipping at the coffee.

"When I saw who it was, I was as shocked as anyone. Anyway, once we've finished these statements for the DI, we'll head out and make that visit, eh?"

"Yeah," he nodded, but heard the lack of enthusiasm in her voice and asked, "It will be difficult for you, won't it?"

"Yes," she nodded, "but they tell me that's why I get paid the big bucks."

It was twenty-five minutes later when Colin Munro switched off the CID car's engine and turned towards Cat.

"You ready for this?" he asked and was surprised how pale she looked.

Wordlessly, she nodded and getting out of the passenger door, saw the lounge light was on and someone was definitely home.

Grace finished the cup of tea and put the mug into the dishwasher and glanced at the wall clock. Where the heck had Des got to, she wondered yet again.

The knock on the front door startled her and she hurried to answer it.

Cat could hear the footsteps hurrying along the hallway and prepared herself. When the door was pulled open, she could see that the woman was surprised.

"Hello, Jessie," said Cat, "can we come in?"

"Sorry," apologised Des with a sheepish grin, "hard to believe, but I forgot my bloody door key."

Now dressed in the grey top, black skirt and with her auburn hair freshly shampooed and held back with a black velvet bow, Grace stood aside to let him in. He brushed past her, uncertain what to say.

As he turned towards her she wrapped her arms about his neck and pulled him close to her.

"I missed you when I woke up," she whispered.

He put his arms around her slim waist and breathed in the fresh scented smell of her hair. They stood entwined for a moment and then he released her and said, "Come through to the kitchen. I went out to get something for you."

It was then she saw he held a large brown envelope in his hand.

He sat her down onto a kitchen stool and pulled a half dozen sheets of paper from the envelope and handing them to her, took a deep breath.

"I realised how upset you were after Mister Fagin disclosed the information about your mum and how relieved you were when you found out that Michael Thomson *isn't* your real father," he begun. "Anyway, I had a thought and I went to the local registry office in Glasgow and obtained those forms," he pointed to the papers in her hand. "I thought that if you wanted to, you can change your own name and Steven's name to your mother's name, Meikle. Well, any name that you might like…" he shrugged and his voice trailed off almost to a whisper. He was a little perturbed by her silence as she stared at the forms and for one awful moment thought he might have overstepped the mark, that she would hate the idea.

She raised her head and he could see tears glistening in her eyes.

"You did this for me?" she quietly asked.

"Yes, well, for us Grace. I thought you might like to use your mum's name, for now."

"For now?" she hesitantly repeated.

Again he took a deep breath and continued, "Well, unless you consider changing it again, maybe some time in the not so distant future?"

She threw herself off the stool and once more wrapped her arms about his neck and hugged him so tightly he thought he might choke. Her slim body was wracked with sobs and she smothered his face with wet kisses.

"So, I'm guessing you're okay with it?" he managed to mumble, yet so very, very happily.

They sat together on the couch with Colin Munro in the armchair, facing them; the same armchair that Michael Thomson had occupied on the day he had visited and raped Jessie Cochrane.

"One of the neighbours chapped the door an hour ago," said Cochrane, her voice almost breaking, a half smoked cigarette between the fingers of her right hand. "Told me that she saw you lifting my Gary out of Thomson's close. He's been arrested, then?"

"Aye, Jessie," replied Cat. "He has been charged with the murder of Michael Thomson and will be appearing at two o'clock tomorrow, at the Sheriff Court. I have to ask you, did you know what he intended doing?"

"And if I did does it make me some kind of accessory?"

Cat turned towards Munro and said, "Colin, can you go and put the kettle on, pal?"

His eyes narrowed as he realised that he was being dismissed, that for some reason, Cat didn't want him to be present when whatever was to be discussed, was said.

"Aye, no problem," he replied and leaving the room, closed the door behind him.

"Did you know, Jessie?" Cat persisted.

Cochrane took a deep lungful of tobacco and nodded.

"He was never the same after what Tommo did to me. He even cried and said he felt like he wasn't a man anymore. It was me that was raped, me that was fucking *battered*, but the shame was Gary's. He told me that he couldn't live with the humiliation." She stared at Cat with watery eyes and trembling lips, then continued, "I even lied to you, hen. I told you that I wouldn't report what Thomson did to me to the polis. Well, the truth of the matter is that I *wanted* to tell the polis, see the bastard go to jail, but Gary," she shook her head, "he was worried sick that people would find out and they'd know that he didn't do anything to protect me. Jesus, as if he could, the gimpy wee bastard."

She began to softly weep and Cat laid her arm across her shoulder to comfort her.

She took a deep breath to compose herself and continued. "He started to tell me what he was going to do to Thomson, how he was going to fucking get him, but I sneered at him, called him names and told him he hadn't the guts, that Thomson would laugh at him and then batter him, that he was no match for the big bastard. I just didn't really believe…."

She fell sobbing against Cat's shoulder and lay like that for several minutes until, taking a deep breath, she again composed herself. She turned a tearstained face towards Cat and asked, "How did he…I mean, what did he do?"

"His walking stick, Jessie; he battered Thomson over the head with that heavy walking stick he uses."

"Well," she venomously snarled, "I hope the bastard suffered!"

Cat didn't reply for a moment and then with a glance at the closed door, said in a low voice, "I'm not just here to inform you about Gary's arrest, Jessie, but also to take a statement from you. The thing is, if you tell me that Gary was distressed and out of his mind with anger because of what Thomson did to you, it could be used as a motive, like a defence; like some form of mitigation, do you understand?"

She stared at Cat and asked, "What, you mean like an excuse? That Gary killed him because he raped me and beat me?"

"Aye, something like that."

"No way," Cochrane violently shook her head, the ash from her cigarette falling unattended to the floor as she waved her hands back and forth. "You don't seem to understand, hen. *We* both know why Gary killed Tommo, but nobody else will know and remember," she squeezed Cat's hand tightly, "you promised me you wouldn't tell. As far as anyone will be concerned, Gary murdered him yes, but when he did that he won back his self-respect. If people round here were to find out what Thomson did to me, they will start to wonder why Archie didn't stop him, do you not see that?"

"Yes, I do, but…"

"No hen, I don't think you *do* see. Gary thinks he killed Tommo for me, but he really did it to make himself feel like a man again and I won't take that away from him. As far as Gary is concerned, he *loves* me and he thinks that killing Thomson was getting revenge for *me*, do you not see that?" she said, almost with a hint of pride in her voice.

Cat inhaled and slowly nodded. No matter what she thought, no matter what she said, Gary Cochrane would plead guilty and go to prison for what would be judged as the callous murder of Michael Thomson. He would be hailed locally as a hero, the crippled man who stood against the neighbourhood bully and with his guilty plea the rape and humiliation of his wife Jesse would never be heard in evidence and never, ever publicly disclosed.

CHAPTER TWENTY-FIVE

The Albanian stopped for a toilet break at the M74 northbound service station close to Hamilton and parked the BMW a short distance from the entrance. From his infrequent visits to the United Kingdom, he was familiar with the British roadway system and the service stations that served it, as well as also acutely aware of Britain's love affair with CCTV cameras that he knew were usually located above the entrance doorways at these stations.

Before he entered the service station, he opened the boot and donned his tie and suit jacket and from the inside pocket, fetched a pair of thick black framed spectacles. Passing through the entrance, he remembered to glance down at his watch in the knowledge if the camera was recording it would simply get the top of his head. Confident as he was that nobody would pay him much attention, he believed that human nature being as it is, the appearance of a smart business suited man was less likely to attract attention than a scruffy individual.

A few minutes later, his toilet complete, the man purchased a pack of sandwiches and carton of coffee that he consumed sitting in the car. Ten minutes later, he disposed of the rubbish in a bin and driving from the car park, rejoined the motorway and continued his journey.

As arranged earlier that afternoon, Harry McInnes met Sally Nelson in the quiet lounge of the pub near to where she was staying with her sister Elsie.

He was as nervous as Sally when he saw her enter.

Standing as she approached the table he had the good sense to compliment her on the lovely dress she wore and unaware that it was the sixth dress from her sister's expansive wardrobe that she had tried on that evening.

Still, the compliment made her blush and with a start, she realised it had been a very long time since a man had paid her any such attention.

She noticed that Harry was wearing the same shirt and had a day's full facial growth. With a woman's intuition, she guessed he hadn't returned home since she had seen him last.

"Have you eaten?" she asked him, but was keenly aware that he likely had not.

Harry tried to pretend that he was fine, that he was not hungry, but she wouldn't listen and instructing that he sit where he was, she ordered him a meal from the bar.

Standing at the bar, she turned to stare at him and felt a curious pride that he had permitted her to take charge of him, to make a decision on his behalf.

When the food was delivered by the smiling barman, she watched as he hungrily tucked into the meal and felt a strange feeling in the pit of her stomach. Though she couldn't explain nor find the words, she knew in her heart that she wanted to be with this big, thoughtful and courteous man.

When he had finished eating, he almost shyly took her hand and they, a middle-aged couple, sat together like teenagers on their first date.

Her face clouded over when she told Harry that when arriving back at Elsie's home in the late afternoon, her sister irately informed her that earlier that day Archie had arrived by taxi, ranting and raving and demanding to know where she was. His behaviour, according to Elsie, had been so abusively threatening that she was on the verge of calling the police, but Sally's brother-in-law had taken Archie by the collar and threw him into the back of the black Hackney cab.

However, the driver did not want any trouble and apparently angry at Archie's language and behaviour, promptly hauled him back out of the cab and threatened to punch the cowering Archie if he tried to get back into the taxi.

"The whole thing finished up," she quietly giggled, "with my nephew telling Archie if he didn't bugger off, he was going to take his leg and fling it in the bin and the last Elsie saw of him he was hobbling away down the road. Curiously though," her shoulders seemed to sag and she sighed, "when Elsie told me the story, I didn't feel anything for him, not even sympathy.

A little uncertainly, Harry smiled and saw Sally visibly relax.

"So, you've made your decision," he asked her. "You're not going back to him?"

She didn't reply, but merely shook her head.

It was time he decided and mentally crossing his fingers, told her, "Starting tomorrow, I'm going to be looking for somewhere to live. It won't be anything fancy, probably a small flat. Obviously to begin with I won't have any furniture or a car. I *will* have my polis salary and part of my pension…"

"Yes!" she interrupted him, her eyes wide and bright as she tightly squeezed his hand.

"Eh, yes what?" he asked, eyes narrowing and now mentally crossing his toes as well.

"Yes, I'd like to come and live with you," she grinned at him and moved close against him.

"Bit presumptuous, aren't you missus?" he teased her, but couldn't help himself from grinning widely.

"What, you want to knock me back as well as the *huge* salary that I get as a cleaner?" she continued to grin at him, now as excited as a schoolgirl.

"Well," he sipped at his pint, and pretending indifference, with a gentle smile said, "That seems to be that settled then, doesn't it?"

The intended visit to Des Brown's parent's home had been a short, but nervous trip for Grace. No matter how many times Des assured her, she worried that Missus Brown wouldn't like her, that she would see a younger, unmarried woman with a nine year old son who in such a short time had designs on her own son, Des.

The tightness in her chest and contractions in her stomach didn't help, either.

Sitting in the passenger seat of Des's car as they approached the house, she again nervously smoothed down her skirt and once more sought assurance that she was respectfully dressed and her outfit was suitable for the visit.

"You look gorgeous," he smiled at her and switching off the engine, teased her, "We could always cancel the dinner, just go back to the house and jump into bed."

She pretended a scowl and together, they walked along the path. He insisted she take his hand and couldn't know that for that simple act, she was eternally grateful.

The door was opened by his father Eddie and almost immediately, Des knew that from the look on Eddie's face and his formal greeting, there was something amiss.

"Come in, come in," he ushered them through to the comfortably furnished lounge where Paul and Steven sat watching television with Des's mother, Agnes, who stood up from the armchair, her hands held clenched in front of her and her face pale.

While Steven grinned and rushed to hug his mother, Des could see that Paul too was ill at ease.

"Paul," said his grandfather, "how about you take the wee guy up to the spare room and watch the tele there son, eh?"

With a nod, Paul forced a grin and persuaded Steven to follow him, closing the door behind them.

Standing with his parents, Des glanced from one to the other and knew there was definitely something wrong.

"Okay, mum, this is Grace; Grace, my mother Agnes," he started and then asked, "What's wrong?"

"You'd better sit down, hen," Eddie took Grace's elbow and led her unresistingly to the couch that had just been vacated by the boys, while Agnes used the remote to switch off the television.

The glance between Eddie and his wife didn't go unnoticed by Grace.

"Dad?" prompted a now anxious Des.

"I was down at the shops getting some messages for your mum for the dinner tonight," begun Eddie as he stared at Des, then turning towards Grace said, "The precinct was in an uproar, hen. I don't know what the story is but whatever happened, it's the talk of the place. It seems that there was a killing in a close in Goyle Avenue." He took a deep breath and prepared to impart what he believed to be the worst of news. "I'm sorry to break the news like this Grace, but your father, Mick Thomson. People are saying that he was murdered."

She stared up at Des's father, her face calm and took a deep breath. Agnes moved to sit beside her and placed a comforting arm across her shoulders.

"Dad," began Des, who shook his head and unaccountably relieved, then slowly exhaled and said, "There's something that you both should know."

They sat for the next half hour with Des doing most of the talking. His parents listened in shock as Des related the nightmare that had been Grace's life.

"I'm sorry, hen, we didn't know about any of this," whispered Agnes, her voice breaking as she tearfully hugged the younger woman to her and reaching, took Grace's hand in her own. "Oh my dear, my poor wee lassie. *What* you must have went through."

Grace sat numbly while Des told her story, but his mother's kindness proved too much for her and leaning back against Agnes, she began to softly weep.

At his father's nod, Des followed Eddie through to the kitchen where he saw the table had been set with six places squeezed into the narrow table.

Eddie filled the kettle and set it to boil.

"Might be better to let them have a few minutes, son. You've brought the car, so a cuppa then?"

"Aye, that'll be fine, dad."

"Will she be okay?" asked Eddie, nodding his head towards the closed kitchen door.

Des grimly smiled, but a smile without humour. "Grace is a lot stronger a character than she thinks," he replied. "If anything and I think she will be the first to admit it, having that bastard Thomson done in has been a bit of a blessing in disguise. At least now with him dead, he's not in a position to do her or wee Steven any harm now." His brow furrowed. "Is that as much as you know, dad, what told us in there?"

"I didn't want to say *too* much because I thought it was going to upset Grace, but I did hear that somebody's been arrested. Apparently whoever murdered Thomson was caught there, at the scene, I mean." He shook his head, the disgust evident on his face. "He knew all along that she wasn't his daughter and was trying it on with her, making her believe that what he was doing was…" Eddie struggled for the word.

"Incestuous?"

"Aye," Eddie gave an involuntarily shudder and exhaling, placed both hands on the kitchen worktop as he leaned forward. "Evil bastard that he was and while I don't as a rule speak ill of the dead, I hope he rots in hell!"

He turned to see the kitchen door had opened and Grace standing there with Agnes's hand on her shoulder.

"Sorry, hen…" he stood upright and tried to mumble an apology, but she put her hand up and with her lower lip trembling, gave him a tearstained smile.

"No, Mister Brown, its fine." she said. "In fact, I couldn't agree more."

Des moved towards her and she smiled at him and he knew, just knew that she would be okay.

"Right then," Agnes gently pushed Des back into the kitchen as she ushered Grace through the door and handed the younger woman a freshly ironed apron. "Eddie call the boys down and then you men sit at the table while Grace and I get the dinner served."

It was during the meal that Grace realised that she was accepted as Des's girlfriend when his mother turned towards Steven and in a firm voice told him, "Right, young man, finish your dinner or it's no pudding. You're in your grannies now, son."

Patrick McLaughlin, lounging back in the comfortable armchair in the TV room of his affluent home holding a glass with two fingers of whisky, watched the six o'clock Scottish Television News, but paid scant attention to the third item that reported police investigating the murder of an unnamed man in the Drumchapel area of the city. Muttering under his breath, he shook his head and mumbled, "Bloody thugs."

The curtains in the brightly lit room were open and cast the light onto the expansive garden and tree line beyond.

With his back to the window he was relaxed and a little tipsy and totally unaware of the Albanian who dressed in the black coverall's and ski mask, stood silently watching from the shadows of the trees with the loaded double barrelled shotgun in his gloved hands.

Harry McInnes insisted on walking Sally to the door of her sister's house, though graciously declined a late night coffee, telling her that perhaps it was a little soon to call on her family and that as time passed, he would be pleased to meet them when things had settled down a bit.

"You mean, like when we're really together?" asked Sally, the expectant hope shining in her blue eyes.

"Exactly," he grinned at her as they exchanged a parting kiss. Hailing a taxi, he thought over his evening, of the tentative plans they had made that included each other and the agreement made that as far as anyone at the office was concerned, they would keep their budding affair secret.

"Or maybe let Fiona in on it," she finally had made him agree.

It took just over twenty minutes for him to arrive home at the darkened house.

By now, he was certain Rosemary would have received the hand delivered proposal from Harry's lawyer friend outlining the financial conditions of his departure from her life and prepared himself for her hate-filled argument when he arrived home.

However, his suspicion that the letter had been delivered seemed to be proven when the light come on in the upper front bedroom. The light cast its brilliance across the front garden where he saw all his clothes scattered about the grass lawn.

Suddenly, the window was thrown open and Rosemary, her face a mask of hate, screamed vitriolic abuse towards him.

From behind closed curtains, his neighbours watched and listened to the tirade that was directed against the hapless Harry until one elderly man in his slippered feet and wearing in a heavy overcoat over his pyjamas, hesitantly approached from next door and with sympathetic eyes, handed him a fistful of thick, plastic bags.

"Thanks," Harry weakly nodded and though still being berated from the window and helped by the old man, began to stuff the clothing into the bags. When three bags were full of everything from socks to shoes to suits, he thanked the elderly gentleman and strode down the street, the spiteful screams from Rosemary still echoing in his ears. Curiously and to his own surprise, as he walked away, he was smiling.

One phone call and a few minutes later, Harry caught a passing taxi on Kilmarnock Road. Fifteen minutes after that he was greeted by his old friend Tom Fraser and his wife Sheila, who insisted that no matter how long it would be, Harry was always welcome to stay in her home.

Dumping the bags on the bed in one of the Fraser's spare bedrooms, Harry joined Tom in the lounge as Sheila, first planting a kiss on both men's cheeks, excused herself and went to bed.

He watched as Tom poured three fingers of single malt into two chunky glasses and then handing one to Harry, both men clinked their glasses together and toasted each other with the traditional greeting, "*Sláinte.*"

"So you've done it then, you've left her?"

"Aye," nodded Harry and then added, "And I'm not sorry. Not one little bit. In fact, I feel kind of relieved"

Tom sipped at his drink then said, "To digress a bit. I take it you still haven't heard from Dick?"

"Nothing," he shook his head. "There's been nothing said at work either about any rip-off of drug money, so either it's not yet been disclosed or as I suspect, it's been covered up. No matter, I won't be raising the subject anytime soon," he grinned.

"Tell me," Tom leaned forward and peered at Harry. "Would you be up for another crack at taking some more money, if the opportunity arose, I mean?"

Harry stared at his old friend and slowly shook his head. "We got lucky this time, Tom. To take another chance, that would be too risky and too greedy."

"Aye, you're probably right," Tom sighed. "Ten grand each for a night's work; ten minutes work actually," he grinned.

Finishing his whisky, he placed the glass on the table between them and leaning forward, slapped Harry on the knee and said, "I'm with Sheila on what she told you, Harry. You're here for as long as you need to be," and with that, left his friend to go to his bed.

The Albanian had no doubt that the man he watched was the target. The description fitted him and so, confident that the darkness would hide him, crept up to the brightly lit window and stood to one side, his back against the house wall.

He smiled at his own ingenuity for he knew that curiosity would be the target's undoing and reaching a hand forward, gently tapped with his gloved knuckles at the window glass.

Inside the room, Patrick McLaughlin heard the tapping noise and as the Albanian predicted, stood and walked towards the window, making the common mistake of looking from a brightly lit room into darkness and seeing nothing but the room and himself reflected back by the glass.

The Albanian took two steps back then walked in front of the window as McLaughlin stood in front of it, his hands cupped above his eyes to shade them from the bright light as he tried to peer outside.

Suddenly he startled when as if from nowhere, he saw the dark figure appear outside the window.

From a distance of less than five feet, the Albanian pulled the triggers of both barrels.

The shells of solid shot exploded from the weapon and first shattered the double glazed window before striking McLaughlin in the chest. The first shell pierced his body a millisecond before the second shell which only added to the extensive damage to his chest. The impact lifted him bodily and threw him backwards almost twelve feet, slamming him against the rear wall and creating a crimson sheet of blood that splattered not just him, but the furniture and everything between.

Patrick McLaughlin was dead before he struck the wall, his heart, lungs and other organs physically torn from his torso.

The Albanian had no need to check if the target was deceased, but turned and made his way back towards the darkness of the woods, walking quickly rather than running to reduce the risk of falling and injuring himself in the dark. As he stepped from the manicured lawn into the tree line, he smiled when he heard the high pitched screams behind him.

CHAPTER TWENTY-SIX - Saturday 12 July

Charles 'Chic' Fagin thought it fitting that his grandson Ian be buried on this, the morning of the twelfth of July, the one day in the year when the Orange Order demonstrated their strong support in the West of Scotland and their resolute determination that they would never succumb to the Roman Catholic Pope of Rome.

As the Band Sergeant of the Drum Loyal True Blues, he had coaxed and cajoled the bandsmen throughout the year to prepare for this special day and as usual, had submitted the bands annual application to the Grand Master for permission to participate in the massive Orange walk that paraded through Glasgow city.

However, accompanying Ian's body in the cortege to the Church of Scotland, to his surprise and secret delight he discovered the band had not as he had arranged attended the parade, but instead stood smartly formed up in the church yard in rank in their uniforms. Following the undertakers who bore the coffin, he almost faltered when he entered the foyer of the church, but for the gentle support on his arm from the female undertaker. He was gratified to find the church pews to be almost full with neighbours and friends who were there he realised not only for Ian, but to show their support and respect for him.

With tears in his eyes, he maintained his dignity as head held high he was escorted by the undertaker to the front pew and settling himself into the seat, felt a comforting hand on his shoulder.

Turning, he saw his old friend, Sister Margaret who again was accompanied by the younger nun.

"In with the enemy, Sister?" he smiled tearfully at her.

"There is no enemies in the house of God, my dear Charlie," the venerable old nun returned his smile and giving his shoulder yet another friendly squeeze, sat back in the pew beside the young nun.

The Minister conducting the service had hardly known Ian Fagin, but was acquainted with his grandfather whom he knew as Charles and during his homily, made much of Chic's contribution not only to the Church, but to his community at large.

At the conclusion of the simple service, when Chic slowly followed the plain brown coffin down the aisle towards the great wooden doors, his glance fell upon the blonde haired detective DC MacDougall, who stood with her partner, the young black man in the last pew.

With the faintest of nods in appreciation of their attendance, he stepped into the bright sunlight and was directed towards the black saloon car that would follow the hearse as it conveyed Ian to Dalnotter Cemetery, where he would deliver his grandson to his wife Sara, who was already reposing there.

That same morning, the post-inquiry conference that occurred within the incident room at Renfrew police office was chaired by DCI Cathy Mulgrew. Also present was the Senior Investigating Officer, DI Jamie Dalgleish and a Miss Hamilton who as a Depute Fiscal, represented the Procurator Fiscal's Office.

Upon a tray that sat on the table between the three of them was a pot of coffee, jug of milk, three unused cups and a plate of digestive biscuits.

"So, those are the circumstances," said Mulgrew, pointing to Dalgleish's typed report on the murder of Catherine Porteous, a copy of which lay before each of them.

Hamilton turned towards Dalgleish. "You are one hundred per cent convinced that this Michael Thomson," she flicked a carefully manicured finger towards the photograph that was on the table in front of her, "is responsible for the murder of Miss Porteous?"

"As convinced as I can be with the little circumstantial evidence that we have accrued," he nodded. "The finger print discovered by the Scene of Crime personnel in the bathroom, albeit not the full sixteen points, is sufficient evidence to indicate he was within the murder location and is likely responsible for the cleaning of the locus of any DNA or fingerprint evidence. The young barman, Neil Kerr is unequivocal in his statement when he identifies Thomson by photograph as the man last seen with the deceased. A subsequent examination of the vehicle owned by Thomson," he leaned forward to his written notes, "a Nissan Juke vehicle, indicated almost microscopic traces of blood spillage in the boot, probably from some seepage that penetrated the material of the sheet that was wrapped around the body. Forensics matched the blood staining to the deceased and this seems to suggest that the body was transported in the car, probably when the deceased was dumped into the River Clyde. On that issue, we did not find any other fingerprints or any trace of another individual in the vehicle and that causes us to suspect Thomson was the only user of the vehicle. What we *did* find was that the front passenger seat and inside door of the vehicle had been cleaned with a bleach type liquid that seems to indicate Thomson had erased all trace of a passenger being conveyed. Why he didn't bleach the boot," Dalgleish raised his eyebrows and grimaced, "I can't say, but would speculate he believed the sheet wrapped round the body was sufficient to contain any blood spillage. Added to this forensic evidence, Thomson's own history of violence is a clear indication that he had the propensity for this type of crime and in the absence of any further information or any other suspect, I *am* satisfied that Thomson is the killer of Porteous."

Hamilton audibly sighed and staring at the DCI, said, "To be frank, Miss Mulgrew, I believe that if we *do* accept Thomson is the culprit, we're taking a leap of faith here. There is no clear and hard fast evidence that he committed the murder, though obviously the evidence indicates he was at least art and part. However, to be honest I would be reluctant to send what evidence you have to Crown Office for their consideration, for I am of the considered opinion that Crown Office would not proceed with an indictment *for murder* on this evidence alone. However, in this closed room, the three of us are well aware that the cost of further inquiry and any subsequent trial, if another suspect *should* be discovered, would be prohibitive and in these days when we are constantly being reminded by the Crown Office to take stewardship of our limited resources," she said, unable to keep the sarcasm from her voice, "I am inclined to agree that the deceased Michael Thomson must be considered to be the murderer of Catherine Porteous. Can I presume that you both agree and therefore this murder inquiry is to be concluded as solved?"

Mulgrew turned towards Dalgleish and asked, "Jamie?"

"You know my feelings about it boss. I'm convinced Thomson is the killer," he nodded.

"Then it's unanimous," Mulgrew said and turning towards the Depute, stood up from the table and extending her hand, said, "Thank you for coming out this morning, Miss Hamilton. I only hope the rest of your Saturday is more relaxing."

She smiled a goodbye as Dalgleish held open the door to permit Hamilton to pass through.

Closing the door, Dalgleish resumed his seat and said, "What's the word from Charlie Miller about his murder, boss. The last I heard is that Thomson was being considered for that one too."

"According to Charlie," she replied, "Thomson had both the means and the motive to kill his victim, a young drug dealer called William Purvis. Seems there is evidence from Purvis's girlfriend that a couple of days before the murder, Thomson threatened to kill Purvis so it looks like two in a row for Thomson and two detections for the polis," she added with a soft grin. "Besides that, it seems that Purvis wasn't such an innocent soul himself and was suspected of peddling drugs in the Drum as well and as if they haven't enough going on, Drumchapel CID is also dealing with the drug overdose of a local youth who was discovered in the back courts behind a tenement. A poor attempt had been made to conceal the body, but later circumstances led the CID to a flat that was the locus of the overdose. It seems that Purvis was using the flat as a storage place for drugs because his prints and DNA were found in most of the rooms. Charlie Miller is of the opinion it was Purvis who was with the youth when he overdosed and then tried to hide the body."

"Sounds like Charlie's landed himself some quality detections, then," Dalgleish grinned, then added, "I hear that you have another murder on your plate, some businessman shot to death at home. What's the story there then?"

"Another whodunit," she grimaced as she carefully poured coffee from the steaming pot into two of the cups and offered him the milk, "but I was told late last night there is a wee development there too. At the minute, Jamie it's a need to know," she tapped the side of her nose with a forefinger.

She saw the curiosity in his eyes and sipping at her coffee, continued.

"At the outset it *seemed* the victim, a Patrick McLaughlin, had no previous convictions, no association with any known criminals and was well thought of in the community; a member of a prestigious golf club and a Rotarian. I know that," she sighed, "because shortly after his death was announced in the media I had a phone call from a Superintendent who claimed to be a close personal friend and demanding to know what had happened."

"How did you handle that?" asked Dalgleish.

"Told him to fuck off," she grinned, "and if he called me again to ask about an ongoing murder investigation that didn't concern him, I'd have the rubber heels at his door asking what his involvement is. I haven't heard a peep from him since."

"Aye, well done boss, you really know how to make friends, don't you?" he slowly shook his head, his voice filled with feigned sarcasm. Then he stared at her, curiosity on his face.

"Wait, you said *seemed*. What changed then?"

"That's the interesting bit," she grinned. "You know that the usual routine when a murder or serious inquiry ensues, the forensics' seize phones and computer equipment and record all details that might be significant; called numbers, computer IP addresses and those sort of details?"

He nodded, clearly wondering where this was going.

"Well, there didn't seem to be any motive for McLaughlin's murder so I figured maybe it was a business venture gone wrong. I had McLaughlin's mobile phone, his laptop and desk computer sent for forensic examination and guess what? The call I had late last night informed me that the forensic guys hacked into McLaughlin's e-mails and discovered addresses to where he has been e-mailing information. I don't have the full details yet, but it seems he was in communication with a laptop owned and used by Michael Thomson whose laptop was *already* at the forensics lab awaiting examination."

"What," Dalgleish was stunned, "you mean *my* Michael Thomson?"

"The very same," she nodded. "Obviously, the inquiry is ongoing, but I spoke earlier this morning with DI Andy Dawson from the surveillance unit. He's been hunting a local contact who was the go-between for a heroin supplier that Dawson suspected to be Thomson. The go-between acted as the middleman for Thomson and some drug cartel from down the London area that is importing the heroin that has been flooding Glasgow and the south west of Scotland. Anyway, it now seems increasingly likely that Dawson's go-between, the middleman if you will, was McLaughlin."

"But why was McLaughlin murdered?"

"Who knows," she shrugged. "It could be any number of reasons, but unfortunately what it does is leave me and the inquiry team with a headache. I'm of the opinion that the killer was a professional and with the inference that London gangsters might be involved, I don't see me getting a result any time soon."

"Well, if nothing else, it's maybe stopped the regular importation of the heroin," replied Dalgleish.

"For now, anyway," she thoughtfully nodded as she sipped at her coffee.

From the sidelines, Des Brown watched his team lose yet another easily prevented goal, but wasn't too disheartened; not with Grace warmly wrapped and hanging onto his arm.

"We're taking a hammering, aren't we?" she said.

"Aye, we are," he agreed, his attention momentarily taken with the cortege that was passing by on the nearby main road.

"I think that's the funeral of the young lad who died from the overdose, Mister Fagin's grandson," Grace interrupted his thoughts.

"Did you want to go to the service?"

"No," she shook her head. "It would have been very crowded and there's time enough for me to visit Mister Fagin again, when things have settled down. I've still got questions for him that I'd like answered; questions about my mother. The next time I go, I think I'll take Steven with me," she said, briefly lost in her own thoughts, then turned to stare curiously at him. "Maybe you could come with me," she hesitantly suggested.

"Course I will," he smiled at her and drew her even closer to him.

On the park, the school team conceded their third goal and the young players, their head downcast, turned miserably to stare towards Des, who began to shout encouragement.

As the referee blew his whistle for the game to again commence, Des softly said, "You know that the polis will likely contact you regarding the funeral arrangements for Thomson?"

"I'm surprised they haven't been in touch already," she replied.

"Well, you haven't been back to the flat and they'll not know you and Steven are living with me, now. It might be an idea to give them a heads up, let them know that you want nothing to do with any arrangements."

"Will that affect your job?" she turned to ask him. "I mean, being with me, us as a couple?"

"What, other than all the guys being jealous because you're so beautiful?" he quipped, but then added, "Why should it? After all, you're not related to Thomson," he raised an eyebrow as he reminded her, then groaned when the teams centre-forward missed a sitter. "Besides," he gallantly added, "I really couldn't care less what the polis will think about me, not when I've got you now."

"Oh you," she grinned and hugging him round the waist, replied "you're just a real old sweetie, aren't you?"

By now, Tom Fraser and Harry McInnes were really getting worried. Constant phone calls and two visits by Tom to Dick Smith's address had so far turned up nothing. Satisfied that the police were not at all in involved in Dick's mysterious disappearance, both men then began to discuss with dread the only other option that they feared; that somehow or other, Dick had been identified by the drug dealers they had ripped off and who had exacted their own revenge.

That evening, they decided to once more call at Dick's flat in Cowan Street before driving to collect Sally Nelson and bring her for dinner and to introduce her to Tom's wife, Sheila. However, on this occasion, they agreed they would make knock on some doors in the close and inquire with Dick's neighbours as to his whereabouts. Abandoning his car in a residents' bay, Tom had a quick glance about to ensure no traffic wardens were loitering before following Harry up the narrow path to the close security door. As they expected pressing the call button of Dick's flat produced no response. Fingers crossed, Harry then pressed all the call buttons and a minute later with a click, the security door unlocked.

At Dick's front door, Harry bent down onto one knee and first listened at the letterbox then used the trusty old indicator, his nose. He turned to stare up at Tom and shook his head to indicate almost with relief that he could not smell the familiar odour that he knew was associated with death.

"I'll try next door," said Tom with a nod of his head, "if you want to start upstairs."

While Tom knocked at the ground flat door, Harry made his way up to the next floor. The first door he chapped was opened by the surly, green-haired young woman he had encountered some night previously.

The girl, wearing a black coloured Nirvana tee shirt and faded, holed jeans, stared with an insolent pout and peered suspiciously at him before saying, "Oh, it's you, the old pervert's pal."

Harry was a bit taken aback at being associated with any kind of pervert, but smiled tolerantly and said, "Good evening, I haven't heard from my mate Dick Smith for some time. I was wondering if you had any idea of his whereabouts or can you tell me when you last saw him?"

The girl rudely shook her head and without replying, was closing the door when Harry heard Tom calling his name.

Returning downstairs, he saw Tom standing with a flustered, middle-aged woman wearing a heavy woollen coat who held a set of keys in her hand.

"Harry, this is Missus Cuthbertson, Dick's landlady. I've explained that we haven't heard from him for a while and we are a wee bit concerned."

"I'm sorry you are so worried about him," the woman interjected as she addressed Harry and held a key to the door lock, "but as I told your friend, Mister Smith is some months behind in his rent." She stopped and stared at them in turn. "You're not here to settle his bill, are you?"

"Eh, I regret not," Tom firmly told her and watched as she unlocked then pushed open the door.

Reaching inside, she switched on the hall light and was about to step inside when Harry said, "Perhaps we should go first, just in case…" He didn't finish the sentence, but left the rest to the woman's imagination.

Not surprisingly, she stood silently watching from the front door while Tom and Harry checked the flat's two bedrooms and lounge, but apart from a slight musty smell, the flat was empty.

In the kitchen, Harry pulled open the fridge door, his nose wrinkling at the smell of sour milk.

"Well," Missus Cuthbertson stepped into the lounge and sniffed, "at least he's kept it very clean and tidy."

Following them into the lounge, Harry saw Tom with a pile of mail he had lifted from behind the door. Tom waved the mail towards Harry and said, "Seems he might not have been here for several days."

It was then that Harry saw the plain white envelope propped against a clock on the shelf above the fireplace that was addressed to both him and Tom.

Unsealing the envelope, he withdrew the single sheet of handwritten paper and after reading it, handed it to Tom.

Tom read:

Dear Tom and Harry,

By now you will have realised that I'm not here.

As you both know, I have been struggling with my finances for some time now and am maxed out on my credit cards, three months behind on my rent and I cannot keep up the payments on my bank loan. My half of the police pension goes nowhere covering my bills and cutting a long story short, I'm up shit creek without a paddle. I know I should have told you guys and that you would have offered to help, but I couldn't face admitting how badly off I am, so when the opportunity came along to make some easy money, you will realise now why I was so eager.

You might recall me telling you some time ago that I have a cousin Bobby on my mothers' side who for the last thirty-four years has been running a bar in the Costa Del Sol. Well, last week I received a letter from Bobby to tell me that he has had some health issues, his heart has been giving him some bother and he's decided to retire, but intends maintaining an interest in the bar. According to Bobby, the bar isn't doing too well as it needs some repairs.

He has offered me a share in the bar if I can come up with twenty-five grand. It would also mean me working in the bar and I could live in a flat above the place. As you will have guessed, twenty-five grand means some left over from what we...

Tom saw that the words 'took from' had been scribbled out and replaced with the word 'collected' and guessed Dick was worried someone else might have opened the letter before he and Harry had the opportunity to see it. He read on,

...collected and the extra money will help pay for the repairs and tide me over until I start to make a profit from the bar.

I know what I'm doing is a really shitty thing, taking your share of the money, but my share wouldn't even cover what I owe in rent and to the bank, let alone what I've spent on the credit cards. This way I get to leave the debts I've got behind me and have another chance at starting again.

Running off like this wasn't an easy decision to make guys, because I've always valued your friendship and you both have always stuck by me.

I won't say I'll stay in touch because likely you'll not want to see me again.

All I can do is again say how sorry I am and ask you to forgive me.
Your old pal,
Dick.

"Bastard!" burst out Tom and crumpling the letter in his fist, stared in amazement when Harry began to laugh uproariously.

Missus Cuthbertson stared wide-eyed at both of them in turn and nervously said, "Is there anything in the letter about when Mister Smith is returning home?"

Harry, almost bent double while he laughed and holding onto the back of an armchair for support, wheezed as his laughter turned to a huge smile. Turning to her, he shrugged his shoulders and replied, "I'm sorry to tell you, Missus Cuthbertson, but he's done a runner.

He won't be coming back. He's stiffed you for your three months rent and he's stiffed us for money we…" he hesitated, then smiled at Tom and turning towards Missus Cuthbertson, continued, "Money we loaned him."

"Oh my goodness," she replied and then brow furrowed, added "I really don't see the humour in any of this."

Harry slowly exhaled then glancing about him, said, "Well Missus Cuthbertson, the good news is my new girlfriend and I happen to be looking for a nice, furnished flat at the minute. So," his eyes narrowed, "what monthly rent are you considering for this place?"

****

Needless to say, this story is a work of fiction.
If you have enjoyed the story, you may wish to visit the author's website at:
www.glasgowcrimefiction.co.uk

The author also welcomes feedback and can be contacted at:
george.donald.books@hotmail.co.uk

Printed in Great Britain
by Amazon.co.uk, Ltd.,
Marston Gate.